Sisters of the Lone Star

Frontier Woman

Rip Stewart had always dreamed of having three sons—fine, strong boys he would train to be everything a Texas man should be. And though his wife bore him three daughters, Rip held fast to his dream.

Sloan, his eldest, was his rock, his heir. An auburn beauty whose petite size belied her strength, she hunted, rode, and managed Three Oaks all with the same quiet grace.

Timid, violet-eyed Bayleigh did not take as kindly to Rip's survival lessons, no matter how hard she tried. But her Boston education made her a valuable asset to Three Oaks, and her sweet good nature helped keep peace in the Stewart home.

But Rip's youngest daughter was his pride and joy. Creighton, nicknamed Cricket, was tall and lithe, as quick as Rip himself with rope, rifle, or arrows—and just as stubborn. Even in buckskins, she was an unsurpassed beauty, though both she and Rip refused to see it. This is her story . . .

"The first of three delicious western romances . . ."
—*Romantic Times*

Frontier Woman

Sisters of the Lone Star

Joan Johnston

POCKET BOOKS

New York   London   Toronto   Sydney   Tokyo

Another *Original* publication of POCKET BOOKS

POCKET BOOKS, a division of Simon & Schuster Inc.
1230 Avenue of the Americas, New York, N.Y. 10020

ISBN: 0-671-62898-4

First Pocket Books printing August 1988

10 9 8 7 6 5 4 3 2 1

POCKET and colophon are trademarks of
Simon & Schuster Inc.

Printed in the U.S.A.

For my friends:

*Billie Bailey, who started the
trip with me in Texas;*

*Sally Schoeneweiss, who traveled the
long, hard road with me;*

and

*Susan Elizabeth Phillips, who
brought me home.*

PROLOGUE

In HIS DREAMS, Rip Stewart envisioned three sons sweating shoulder to shoulder with him as his cotton plantation along the Brazos River blossomed in concert with the new Texas frontier. He had his sons' names already picked out before he ever married Amelia, chosen because she was the only daughter in a nearby Scots family of seven healthy children.

His eldest son would be named Sloan. Sloan would be strong and brave, a proud, capable heir to take Rip's place. Bayleigh would be Rip's surety. He would be the educated one, bred to be a loyal and steadfast help to his elder brother. Rip's youngest son would be named Creighton. Creighton would be the child of Rip's heart, the child he played with, and indulged, and lavished with his love. Creighton would be fiery-tempered and bold, demanding everything the Texas frontier had to offer a man, and getting it.

Unfortunately, Amelia gave Rip three daughters. That did not deter Rip Stewart. He named the eldest Sloan, the second Bayleigh, and the youngest Creighton, and set about to make his dreams come true.

CHAPTER 1

The Republic of Texas
1840

AT SEVENTEEN Creighton Stewart didn't need anyone, and she liked it that way. That was why she'd been particularly disturbed by father's heated rejoinder during their argument that morning: "Perhaps a husband can curb your tongue!"

Cricket hadn't meant to holler at Rip, or to call him a noodleheaded lumpkin. But if he thought a husband was going to do any better at controlling her than her own father, well, he was a worse wag-wit than she'd accused him of being. Besides, it was his fault she was the way she was. What man in his right mind would willingly choose to raise his daughters as sons?

Thanks to her father Cricket possessed all the skills necessary to survive on the Texas frontier without the aid of another living soul. That sort of self-reliance was a real advantage in a wilderness where she might meet Comanches or Mexican bandidos or outlaw drifters over the next rise. Actually, Cricket and her nineteen-year-old sister, Sloan, had taken to Rip's survival lessons like a newborn calf to a cow's teat. However, their eighteen-year-old sister, Bayleigh, had never managed to meet Rip's high standards of excellence. The truth was, Cricket admitted, Bay didn't even come close.

Still, she should have known better than to try to convince Rip that it was a waste of time to send Bay out hunting. He just didn't want to hear it. Rip Stewart hadn't become the richest gentleman planter in Texas by giving up. His last words as she'd stormed out of the house had been, "Take Bay with you. Make sure she does the tracking. And don't come home empty-handed!"

Cricket shook her head as she watched Bay draw her bow to take aim on a stag. Bay's arms hadn't the strength to hold the bow cocked for long, and they were trembling so much it was spoiling her aim. That wouldn't have been so bad, except Bay kept taking her eyes off her target. Was it any wonder Cricket had called her father a stubborn oat-eater when he'd insisted that Bay only needed a little more practice?

Cricket opened her mouth to suggest that Bay raise the angle of her arrow upward, but before she could speak Bay yanked the gut bowstring and loosed the shaft. Cricket watched the arrow dart, swift and—totally off the killing mark.

"You've only wounded him, Bay! Another arrow! Quick!"

The deer bolted and was gone from sight before Bay even had another arrow out of her quiver.

Bay toyed with her bowstring distractedly. "I'm sorry, Cricket. His eyes kept pleading with me not to do it, and at the last second—"

"At the last second you jerked the bowstring instead of just releasing it!"

Their prey had disappeared into the heavy growth of sagebrush and gnarled mesquite as completely as if it had never existed, yet the fierce yowling of Cricket's three half-grown wolves in full chase gave raucous witness to Bay's failure.

Tears welled in Bay's eyes, making Cricket instantly contrite for the sharpness of her reprimand. At least Bay didn't flinch with a bow and arrow like she did every time she shot a Kentucky rifle. However, the choice of weapons wasn't really the problem. The truth was Bay simply had too soft a heart for killing. Cricket distinguished between a too soft heart and compassion. She couldn't bear to see the wounded suffer either, and so she'd learned to kill quickly and cleanly.

"What do we do now?" Bay asked, keeping her eyes focused on the whitened knuckles that held her bow.

Cricket encircled her older sister's shoulders with an arm clothed in fringed buckskin, and gently tipped Bay's chin up with the callused fingers of her hand. "My wolves will keep pace with the stag over this rough terrain. I'll catch up and kill him. You follow me as quickly as you can, and . . . keep trying, Bay. You'll learn to do better."

"No, I won't."

Cricket wasn't about to argue, since she agreed whole-heartedly with Bay. She sighed in sympathy with Bay's plight. "You're right. You won't. I guess I'll have to take another stab at convincing Rip this is a bad idea."

Bay shuddered. "Do you really think another shouting match like the one you two had this morning is going to make any difference?"

"All right, so I lost my temper a little. Next time—"

Bay arched a brow in exasperated disbelief. "A little?"

Cricket grinned. "Maybe more than a little. But it was in a good cause. You're right, though. If I just kept a tighter rein on my temper—"

"Nothing you say is going to change his mind."

Cricket possessed more than a little of Rip's bullheaded-ness and wasn't as willing as Bay was to give up the fight. "That doesn't mean it isn't worth another try in this case."

"You'd be wasting your breath. He's got this grand plan for who we are and what we'll become, and he isn't going to let anyone or anything get in the way of his seeing it become a reality . . . not even us. And Cricket, his threat about finding you a husband . . . it was more than an empty threat. He's seriously thinking about it."

"Why? Just because we argued? I've bantered cusses with Rip for years!"

4

"You've never called him a knotheaded lobcock before," Bay said with a grin.

"No, I've called him a lot worse!" Cricket retorted. "So why threaten me with a husband now?"

"You're seventeen now. A grown woman."

Cricket's face contorted into such a wry grimace that Bay laughed. "Think for a minute. If all Rip's dreams are going to survive he's got to have grandchildren. In fact, I wouldn't be surprised if he's planning to pick husbands for all of us."

"Not for me! I'm never getting married."

"Who says?"

Cricket's lips flattened in determination. "I say."

"Then you better speak to Rip before he gets his mind made up."

"He'd never force me to do something I didn't want to do."

Bay shrugged. "He wouldn't have to use force—on any of us. Sloan would do what he asked because he'd take time to explain the good reason for it. I'd do what he asked because I haven't the courage to defy him. And you . . . you'd do what he asked because you love him and want to please him." Bay held up a hand to stop Cricket's interruption and continued, "Not that you wouldn't fight him every step of the way if you didn't like the idea. But in the end, you'd do what he wanted."

"You're wrong, Bay. About this you're wrong. I don't want to get married. And I won't, no matter what Rip says."

"Would it be so bad?"

"For me it would."

"Why, Cricket?"

"I can manage my own life. I don't need some man telling me what to do. Besides, what kind of man would want me, anyway?" Cricket rushed breathlessly on so Bay wouldn't have a chance to answer the question she'd raised. She wasn't sure she wanted to hear Bay's answer. She had a pretty good idea what the gentlemen planters along the Brazos River thought of Rip's youngest brat. She wouldn't set herself up to be rejected as a wife by any one of those pompous male popinjays. "I'm much better off by myself. There'll be no husband for me, and you can believe I'm going to give Rip the sharp edge of my tongue the first chance I get. He'd better not—"

Both girls whirled abruptly toward the agitated howling that rose on the wind like the moans of the bereft survivors of a Comanche massacre. The wolves had cornered their quarry. From the occasional agonized yelps it was apparent their prey was fighting back.

Bay's eyes betrayed her alarm. "The wolves!"

Cricket had already mounted her pinto stallion, Valor, and paused only long enough to yell over her shoulder, "Follow as soon as you can! Don't let Star get the bit in his teeth. That mustang is just waiting for the chance to set you down in some sagebrush!" Then she was gone.

With the confidence of experience, Cricket hugged closely to her mount's neck. She guided him with her knees and the slim leather bridle as he galloped pell-mell across the rugged, rolling country, among the ancient oaks, stark and proud, still awaiting spring's green mantle.

The howls of her animals soon became distinguishable and Cricket could hear Rogue's growl, Rascal's answering savage bark, and Ruffian's distressed yelp that was cut off suddenly in midstream by violent splashing noises. How strange! The wolves had caught their quarry in the water! The beast must be very sorely wounded, Cricket thought, to allow such a thing to happen. Hadn't the arrow merely pierced the shoulder? She must be mistaken. Cricket hurried to put the frenzied creature out of its misery.

She broke from the trees at the edge of a small oval pond almost hidden by the thick brushy undergrowth. She arrived in time to see Rogue, her favorite of the three wolves she'd raised from pups, cracked upon the head by a large branch swung as a club. The wolves hadn't cornered the stag Bay had wounded—they'd caught a man! And he was trying to kill her wolves! In an instant Cricket was off her stallion and standing spread-legged at the edge of the pond.

"You clabberheaded idiot! What the hell do you think you're doing?"

The cacophony ceased, but a heavy tension lay in the air as though a thunderbolt had struck. The man in the pond stared at her, his eyes wide with disbelief. Then the young wolves abandoned him for the new arrival, their excited yowls drowned out by their splashing swim to Cricket's side.

The stranger surged through the water after them with the shouted warning, "Watch out for those wolves!"

"Those wolves are my pets, you beanheaded jackass!"

The man froze in midstride, still wary, but clearly perplexed.

"Those vicious beasts are pets?"

"I raised them myself from pups and they're not vicious."

"Then perhaps you should have taught them better manners," the stranger snapped, eyeing the bloody gashes the wolves' sharp teeth had torn on his forearms.

"My wolves wouldn't have attacked unless—"

Cricket shut her mouth and squinted her eyes to avoid the barrage of flying water that assailed her from shaking pelts. By the time the wolves were done, a rainbow of crystal dew-flecks spattered her golden skin, the soft deerskin shirt that was belted at her slender waist, and the fringed leggings that hugged her lithe figure and disappeared into knee-high moccasins. Cricket leaned down to soothe the hurts of her beasts.

"Poor Ruffian. Oh, Rogue, look at all this blood!" Cricket knelt to check Rogue's wound. "It's not deep, boy. You'll be all right." Cricket smoothed the wolf's wet fur one last time. She swiped the beast's blood from her hand onto her buckskins as she rose to turn her magnificent fury back upon the object of her wrath.

Hip deep in the middle of the shallow pond, lowered club still held in readiness by powerful hands, stood the most proudly handsome man Cricket had ever seen. Water streamed down his face from his wet curls, dripped off his angled cheekbones and jutting chin, and shimmered like a mountain waterfall down his glistening body. His heart-shaped nostrils flared to bring air to the broad, still-heaving chest.

Cricket felt breathless, felt her pulse racing, but told herself it was concern for her wolves that had her so upset. Of course this rugged-looking stranger had nothing at all to do with her pounding heart. She knew better than to let herself think of any man that way. She clenched her trembling fingers into fists and stuck them on her hips.

The man's nakedness had kept her eyes riveted to his body. Her stallion's trumpeting neigh broke the spell and sent her attention to the source of the pinto's interest. Hidden in a brush corral near the pond, five of Rip's mares, which had been stolen a week past, circled in anticipation of the stallion's command.

Cricket's gray eyes narrowed as she brought them back to bear on the stranger. She searched the edges of the pond for the pile of clothing he'd doffed, and finally found it on the far side of the water. A smug smile twitched at the corners of her mouth. Well, well. Her wolves had certainly caught this horse thief with his pants down!

"Who are you and how'd you get here?" she demanded. She flushed as the stranger's topaz eyes boldly assessed her tall, well-curved form.

"I might ask you the same thing," he drawled. "You're a long way from anywhere, little girl."

"I'm plenty big enough to take care of you."

"I'm sure you are. Would you like to join me, or shall I join you?"

The stranger's brazen invitation caught Cricket by surprise, and her belly tightened in pleasure. As though sensing her reaction, the naked man took a step forward.

"You stay right where you are!"

The stranger smiled, his eyes revealing his amusement at her response to his blatant virility.

Cricket frowned as she realized the stranger represented a greater—and very different—threat than she'd first thought. She'd long ago made it plain to the gentlemen from the cotton plantations surrounding Three Oaks that Creighton Stewart wasn't about to give them the only thing they wanted from her. This stranger was about to learn the same lesson—the hard way, if necessary.

8

"I asked you a question, you wet-goose lackwit, and I expect an answer. Who are you and how'd you get here?"

The mysterious man's eyes focused on the bow in her hand and the quiver of arrows slung across her back, as though trying to decide whether she knew how to use them. Cricket smirked. Let him take another step toward her and he'd find out quick enough! Her smoky eyes flashed at him in contemptuous challenge.

Instead of answering her question he asked one of his own. "Who are *you?*"

"That's none of your business." Cricket glanced pointedly at the five horses the stranger had corraled within the bushy barrier. "But I think you'd better tell me where you got those horses."

"Ah, *mi brava,* my fierce, wild one. You answer my question and I'll answer yours."

Cricket calmly pulled an arrow from her quiver and slotted it in the bowstring. She pulled the bowstring taut, the arrow aimed at the thief's heart, and asked again, "Where'd you get those horses?"

The intense, golden eyes that were his best feature in a face full of perfect features, scorned her use of the weapon, even as his jeering laugh filled the air.

Cricket pulled the bowstring tauter. The man's gaze dropped to her hands and the laugh caught in his throat.

"Be careful with that thing, Brava," he cautioned. "I'm not ready to be spitted like a beef at Christmas."

"Tell me what I want to know."

The man swore under his breath. But he still didn't answer her.

Cricket held the shaft firm against the gut bowstring. No tremor showed along the muscles of her wrist, even though she'd held the bow thus for almost a minute. She could stand like this long enough to wait out a deer. She could certainly wait out the man standing so irritatingly close-mouthed before her.

The horse thief looked from her to the wolves and back again. He stood his ground, club in hand, and stared coldly at her.

Cricket found her patience with the mysterious stranger less great than she'd supposed. "Listen, you hardheaded lugloaf," she warned, "those mares over there were stolen from Rip Stewart a week ago. Unless you give me some reasonable explanation how you got hold of my father's mares, I don't have much choice except to see you hanged— that is, if I don't kill you first myself!"

Cricket felt a swell of satisfaction when the man's whole body tensed warily. At least he'd taken what she said seriously for a change.

"Ah, Brava," he said at last. "I guess you've caught me red-handed."

Stunned by the man's admission, Cricket pondered the situation for a moment. What should she do now? It only took a moment to decide she should take him to Rip. After all, they'd lost the stag, and hadn't Rip admonished her not to come home empty-handed? Cricket grinned as she ordered, "Come out of that water."

The stranger took a step, then paused and looked down. The water now barely kept him decent.

Cricket bit her lower lip when she realized why he'd stopped. He probably thought she was going to be embarrassed at the sight of a naked man . . . or fall in a swoon at his feet. Well, she'd never seen a naked man before, but she knew it wasn't going to have any effect on her. Hadn't Rip made sure she was different from other girls?

"Come out of that water," she repeated.

The stranger snorted derisively once before he obeyed.

Cricket felt the pleasurable tightening again in her belly, as inch by inch the man revealed his powerful stalking form. She'd never imagined a body could threaten so much strength, yet be so pleasing to gaze upon. She felt a fullness in her nipples that was totally foreign, and wondered what it was about this man that caused her body to feel at once both unbearably tense and undeniably languid.

She fought to turn away, but couldn't take her eyes off the stranger's body. Beads of water glistened on the ropes of muscle in his chest and shoulders. Goosebumps erupted on her arms as her gaze followed a long, thin scar that ran diagonally from under his left nipple across the bronzed expanse of muscle-ridged abdomen to the jutting hipbone on the opposite side. She detected another scar that curved along his sinewy flank, leading her eyes to the bold proof of his masculinity. She stared in awe at the sight that greeted her. When he cleared his throat, she raised her eyes to his mocking grin.

"See anything you like?"

Before her shocked anger at his effrontery had a chance to explode, the bloodied stag Bay had wounded crashed across the clearing from its hiding place in the underbrush. Without the necessity for thought, as a reflex almost, Cricket loosed the arrow from her bow, piercing the animal in the heart. The wolves rushed away from Cricket's side to the edge of the clearing to savage the fallen stag.

In that split second Cricket was weaponless and her protective wolves were gone from her side. She watched appalled as the tall, intimidating man dropped his makeshift club and surged through the shallow water toward her.

"Stop! Don't come any closer!"

Cricket could've killed the naked man with bow and arrow before he reached the edge of the pond. Likewise her horse was trained to attack a man on foot at her command, and she could call her wolves if all else failed. But she didn't want to take the chance of injuring him before she'd satisfied her curiosity about who he was, where he'd come from, and why he turned her senses upside-down. Too late she realized her hesitation had cost her whatever advantage she'd had. She shrieked in pain as the stranger reached her and wrenched the bow from her hand.

"The game's over, Brava."

"Damn you, *horse thief!* Let me go!" She gripped his wrist, pivoted, and flipped him over her shoulder so that he lay stretched out before her on the ground with his head at her feet.

"What the hell?!"

The stranger shook his head groggily, trying to catch his

breath. The bare flesh of his back and buttocks nestled in a bed of fragrant columbine. His eyes appeared confused and a little bleary. Cricket stood above him with her fists on her hips. She forced her thoughts away from the feel of his hair-roughened skin where she'd touched him. She hadn't intended to engage in a wrestling match, but her lightning-quick reactions came instinctively, a result of the hard lessons Rip had taught.

"I warned you, mister. You'd better give up while you still can. You can't escape. How far do you think a flapdoodle chaw-bacon like you can get naked and unarmed in this land? You'll starve or be killed by some wild—"

The man's jerk on her ankles interrupted Cricket's speech, sending her to the ground on her rear amidst a whorl of dust and sagebrush. She was so astonished by his attack she didn't have a chance to move before he rolled over and lunged at her. Cricket swore a nasty oath when her quiver pressed painfully into her back as the stranger shoved her down and came to rest on top of her. All thoughts of the stranger's attractiveness faded as she grabbed her hunting knife from its sheath. She got a painful taste of his strength when he knocked it away into the undergrowth.

"No more weapons between us, Brava," he snarled.

A shiver of fear ran down Cricket's spine when she realized the stranger was considerably stronger than she, and perhaps even more agile. She lashed out at him with the only weapon she had left, slashing several furrows down his cheek with her fingernails.

"Dammit, that hurt! Settle down!"

He captured her punishing fists and fingernails with his powerful hands as she bucked for freedom beneath him. Frantic, Cricket tried to bring her knee up to the naked man's vulnerably exposed manhood, but he was ready for her. He pressed his sinewy thighs down hard against her own more supple ones.

"Whoa, Brava. I intend to stay the capable stud I am."

"You bragging ass! You lop-eared mule! Let—me—go!"

"Not a chance."

Cricket shoved with all her strength, but she might as well have been an ant trying to lift a watermelon. Slowly, inexorably, the horse thief pushed her wrists into the crushed columbine blossoms on either side of her head.

"You won't escape," Cricket hissed.

A broad smile broke out on the stranger's face. It was clear she was in no position to enforce her threat. Cricket turned her head away from the horse thief's arrogant grin, her breathing as harsh and uncontrolled as her thoughts about him.

"I have no wish to escape at the moment," he said meaningfully as he pressed an impulsive kiss on the racing pulse beneath her ear.

Cricket panicked, frightened by her body's instant response to the stranger's caress. She wasn't about to lay herself down under any man. She never had and she never would. Rip had headed her life in a different direction altogether, one she liked just fine. If she had anything to say about it, this stranger's intended tryst was about to come to a very abrupt and unsatisfying conclusion. She arched her head as far away from the horse thief as she could get it in preparation for the commands that would set the wolves upon him.

"Rogue! Rascal! Ruffian!"

The stranger quickly covered Cricket's mouth with his own to quiet her, straining as he did so to see the reaction of the wolves.

The gray beasts lifted their slavering muzzles from the feast before them, but when Cricket gave no further command, they rejoined their vicious repast.

The thief had used his mouth brutally, as a weapon, and Cricket could taste her own blood. In retaliation she bit down hard upon his lower lip until the taste of his salty blood joined her own.

The thief reared back in shock and pain. "You're a wild one all right!" he muttered, licking at his bloody lip.

To Cricket's dismay, he sounded pleased, rather than angry. She had to get free! She twisted with all her strength, dislodging his hold on her legs. She wrapped one leg around the naked man's body and used the other for leverage to roll him over so he was laid out on his back.

"That was a nice move, Brava," he rasped. "You'll have to teach it to me."

"Rogue, Rascal, Ruffian!"

"Dammit, Brava, stop calling those wolves!"

Hearing the authority in Cricket's voice, the wolves responded immediately, surrounding her where she sat with her knees pressed into the tender shoots of mesquite grass on either side of the naked man, the insides of her thighs resting on either side of his belly. By this time, the horse thief had covered her mouth with a large palm to silence her, while his other hand had circled the back of her neck. When he yanked her down close to his chest, her arms were caught beneath her so she was helpless.

Their faces were so close each breathed the other's breath. His skin was hot, scorching her where they touched, and he smelled fresh like . . . Cricket choked back a hysterical laugh behind the rough hand that covered her mouth when she realized that what she smelled on the thief's newly washed skin was the delicate fragrance of columbine.

"This is cozy," he murmured. "Would you care to call off those wolves so we can enjoy ourselves?"

The man's insolence infuriated Cricket, and the feel of his body against hers was wreaking havoc with her senses, but there was nothing she could do. They were at a standoff. The thief couldn't move without releasing his hold on her and giving her the chance to order the wolves to attack. Yet, although she struggled desperately, Cricket wasn't strong enough to free herself from the thief's grasp.

The wolves whined anxiously as they continuously circled the harshly breathing couple. Now and again one or another of the beasts growled menacingly as they watched the silent struggle of flesh against flesh before them. They awaited only a word from Cricket to close in for the kill. Unfortunately it was a word she was in no position to give.

"Don't struggle, Brava. You're exciting the wolves."

Cricket struggled harder.

The thief's voice was low and husky as he said, "Sooner or later those wolves are going to remember that stag, Brava, and when they do I'll teach you a few lessons of my own."

Cricket's eyes rounded hugely as she sought out the fierce wolves and saw their attention wandering. The horse thief was right. It was only a matter of time before the wolves left her and returned to the fallen stag. Cricket refused to think what would happen to her then. If the horse thief kissed her again would her body betray her? Would she respond as any ordinary woman would to this man's sensual commands? Surely she wouldn't— Surely she couldn't want— Her stomach knotted as she detected the knowing gleam in the thief's golden eyes.

"Take your hands off my sister and don't make any sudden moves."

Cricket's whole body slumped in relief when she heard Bay's quavery voice.

The stranger frowned at Bay, who stood not ten feet away with her bow drawn and her arrow aimed at him. However, instead of releasing Cricket, he tightened his hold and said, "Aren't you afraid you'll hit your sister?"

Cricket's head jerked up in time to see that the words had struck Bay like a very precise dagger thrust. How had he so quickly discerned Bay's lack of confidence? Cricket tried to encourage Bay with her eyes, but all Bay's attention was focused on the thief.

Bay swallowed convulsively, obviously trying to conquer her fear, and finally replied, "No. At this distance I can't miss."

"I suppose you can't," the horse thief ruefully agreed.

Cricket wriggled again, demanding release. Bay's trembling body betrayed her nervousness, and there was no telling how long her courage would last.

Apparently the horse thief feared Bay's nervousness for a different reason. "Steady, now," he soothed. "I'm going to let her go."

The instant she was free, Cricket jumped to her feet,

straddling the man. "Watch!" she commanded the wolves. "I'll have them lame you if you move," she threatened tersely.

The stranger lay motionless, his lips pressed tightly together, his jaw muscles tightened.

Cricket located her hunting knife in the undergrowth, then crossed to retrieve her bow. Her back hurt where the quiver had gouged her and the muscles in her arms ached from her struggle with the stranger. She couldn't repress a shudder at the memory of the horse thief's hard, muscular thighs pressing on her own through her buckskins. She had come too close to capitulation for comfort.

She shied from recollection of her reaction to the thief's possessive lips upon her mouth and throat. She licked her swollen lips, and found the taste of him still upon them. Cricket wiped her mouth with her sleeve. Even those few moments of domination by this man didn't sit well with her. In all her years, this *horse thief* was the first man to treat her like a woman. And she despised him for it. She began to doubt the wisdom of not shooting him when she'd had the chance.

Cricket mounted her stallion, keeping an eye on the stranger so Bay could find Star and join her. Meanwhile, the horse thief lay in the patch of mesquite grass and columbine where he'd fallen, his upper body held up by his elbows. When both sisters were ready, Cricket amended her command to the wolves so they allowed the thief to stand.

Bay couldn't suppress a gasp when she saw the height and breadth of the man. She consciously kept her gaze safely above his waist. "What'll you do with him, Cricket?"

"I'm taking him home."

"He's not a stray puppy, Cricket," Bay argued. "You know what Rip said the last time."

The horse thief raised a questioning brow.

Cricket flashed an irritated glance at the man, then snapped at Bay, "He belongs to me. I found him. He stole Rip's mares, and I'm going to make sure he's punished!"

"But surely Rip—"

It was the condescending grin on the stranger's face that goaded Cricket into snarling at Bay, "I'll handle Rip!"

Bay pictured Rip and Cricket faced off toe to toe, fists on hips, neck hairs hackled. It was the fearsome equivalent of a blustery blue norther meeting a Texas tornado . . . and she intended to be nowhere near when it happened.

"Get moving, horse thief," Cricket ordered.

"You can't mean to make him walk naked the whole way home!" Bay gasped.

"Who's going to stop me?"

Bay's defiance melted away beneath Cricket's wrath. What Cricket proposed to do was wrong and no good could come of it. Bay couldn't repress the shiver of foreboding that tore through her body.

"I'll get the mares." Bay freed the mares from the brush corral, and herded them toward Cricket.

Cricket's jaw jutted antagonistically for a moment before she relented. Bay was right. She was being foolish. Besides, she didn't want to spend the entire trip home watching the muscles ripple in those lean flanks.

"Bay, bring me whatever weapons he has over by those buckskins, and then toss him his pants and his moccasins."

Bay passed a long Kentucky rifle, two Colt Pattersons, and a Bowie knife to Cricket. When the stranger reached out to take his pants from Bay the three wolves growled and bared their fangs.

"Whoa, *lobos,*" he breathed softly. "You going to tell these wolves I can put my pants on?"

At Cricket's quiet command, the three wolves lay down in a circle around the horse thief, who swore vociferously as he jerked on his buckskin trousers and moccasins.

"What about my shirt and hat?"

Bay held up the stranger's shirt to show Cricket there was no weapon concealed in the folds of the beautifully beaded buckskin, and when Cricket shrugged, Bay threw the garment to the man. She examined the round-brimmed black felt hat with a turkey feather stuck in its leather band, and passed it on as well.

The man nodded at Bay, who was unable to meet his eyes. He set the hat rakishly on his head so the turkey feather trailed onto his shoulder, then turned to face Cricket.

Cricket grimaced. He was even more intimidating fully dressed, because she knew what the simple clothing hid. "All right, horse thief. You're dressed. Now, get going."

"What about that stag? That venison won't be any good later unless you take care of it now."

The thief was right, but Cricket was too stubborn to admit it. Besides, the three wolves hadn't left much of the animal to butcher. Rip had warned her when she'd brought the wolves home that someday she'd have to kill them. She'd take them deep into *Comanchería* and leave them, Cricket vowed, before she'd do that. For now, she wasn't going to let the stranger get the better of her.

"The scavengers can have what's left of the stag. Start walking, horse thief. I'm giving the orders now."

"For now, Brava," he conceded, his voice husky again.

Cricket tensed at the implied threat, and the unspoken promise that had unaccountably caused her nipples to peak. Before she could retort that he was unarmed and helpless and totally in her power, the tall, mysterious stranger turned his back on her and sauntered away.

Cricket nudged her horse into a trot, vexed and apprehensive when she belatedly realized how naturally he'd taken the lead—and how naturally she'd followed after him.

CHAPTER 2

WITHIN AN HOUR after they'd left the pond, Cricket acknowledged that the trip back to Three Oaks wasn't going to be as easy as she'd anticipated. A not-altogether-unexpected complication had arisen.

"Of all the days for this to happen!" she muttered.

Her face blanched white with the effort to conquer a fierce abdominal contraction. Tight-lipped, she fought the pain, as she fought all it represented. The woman's curse. The female miseries. The monthly reminder she was not her father's son.

Cricket wanted to curl up somewhere in a tight ball to ease her cramping muscles, but to do so she needed to be home. She increased the pace as much as she dared, forcing the broad-shouldered, lean-hipped horse thief into a steady jog that proved he was in as good shape as he appeared to be. After running for several miles, a fine sheen of sweat had built up on his skin, but Cricket noticed he wasn't even winded. Meanwhile, she was sitting her horse doubled over like some stove-up cripple. How infuriating to be female!

Cricket felt another powerful cramp rise and crest across her abdomen. She wanted to whimper, to sob, to scream, but controlled the air trapped in her lungs by pulling her lips flat and thin, and then exhaling in a controlled sigh. Before the muscles had a chance to clench again, she turned resignedly and pulled a fragile silver flask from her saddle-bag. She stared at the delicately etched container, which had been Bay's present to her on her fourteenth birthday, then opened it and drank long and deep of its contents. Cricket welcomed the burning in her throat, and the blessed relief the whiskey promised from the pain of being a woman.

Bay had been watching Cricket's facial contortions for the past half-hour, but it was the sight of the whiskey flask that spurred her to close the distance between them so they could talk without being overheard by the thief.

"Are you all right, Cricket?"

"I'm fine," she spat.

"Oh, my. It *is* the monthly miseries. Is there anything I can do to help?"

"Hell's bells! Just let me suffer in peace!"

Cricket glared at the thief, who'd turned to see why she'd raised her voice. "What are you staring at? Get moving!"

When the thief resumed his steady jog, Bay whispered, "I only want to help. Surely I—"

"Can you make the miseries go away?" Cricket hissed.

"No."

"Then you can't help!"

"All right, Cricket. But if you think of anything, let me know."

Bay kneed her horse, leaving Cricket by herself again.

Cricket shook her head in disgust at her short temper. Every month she tried to be stoic about the female miseries. And every month she failed. It was her helplessness in the face of nature's inevitable claim on her body for a few days each month that left her so frustrated. Bay only wanted to help. Make that, Bay *always* wanted to help. In fact, it was Bay who'd come to her rescue the first time she'd gotten the female miseries, when she was thirteen. She'd been curled up in bed, buried under a quilt, with a horrible bellyache, when Bay had heard her moaning and come into the room.

"What's wrong, Cricket?" Bay had asked.

"I'm dying," she'd responded. "I'm bleeding . . . there's blood . . ."

"I'll get Sloan."

Cricket could smile now at her ignorance. It hadn't been so funny then. Her mother had died when she was born, and Rip kept no women in the household. Somehow, Sloan had known what was happening. Sloan knew everything. However, Sloan found the pain during her own monthly courses bearable, and believing Cricket's to be the same, she'd merely advised, "It's only a little bellyache once a month. You don't have much choice except to get used to it."

When Cricket had opened her mouth to argue, Sloan had added for good measure, "There's only one way I know to stop it." She had then proceeded to explain in graphic, somewhat-appalling detail how Cricket could avoid the miseries for a while by allowing a man to spill his seed in her, thus making a baby, which would stop the monthly courses. "Of course, Rip may know something I don't. I've never talked to him about this. You're welcome to ask."

Cricket hadn't known quite what to do. Lying down under some man was out of the question as far as she was concerned. And although it was tempting to ask Rip if he knew a way to stop the pain, she'd never remind him she was a girl by confronting him with a female problem. So, she'd wound herself into a fetal curl in bed and endured, whimpering under the covers like some poor, wounded animal.

Unable to bear her sister's distress, Bay had finally suggested Cricket turn to liquid spirits for relief. It was also Bay who'd stolen into Rip's plantation office in the dead of night to procure a bottle of his finest Irish whiskey. A cup had become two cups and the surcease of pain had finally come only with alcoholic oblivion. That was the first time.

Now, once a month, Cricket just got riproaring drunk. The binge lasted one day, or two, depending upon the severity of the cramps, which often started before the bleeding began. When she passed out cold in the barn, or on the great leather chair in Rip's office, or under the spreading, moss-covered branches of the majestic live oak out back, Rip threw her over his shoulder and hauled her upstairs to bed. It had become almost a ritual. If her father recognized the regularity of her alcoholic excesses, he never mentioned it, and Cricket never felt the need to make excuses. She was what she was—and it was the only way she knew to cope with the monthly agony.

Cricket moaned out loud, then bit her lip when the stranger dropped back to run beside her, still surrounded by the three wolves. He eyed her speculatively.

"What do you want?" she snapped.

"Thought I heard you groaning."

"Hasn't been a man yet heard a moan from my lips, horse thief."

"Is that some sort of challenge?"

Before Cricket could hurl a sufficiently sarcastic response, another cramp seized her, and she gasped aloud.

The stranger reached for the reins and stopped her horse. "What's the matter with you?"

Cricket bent over and pressed the heels of both hands against her abdomen as hard as she could to counter the cramping muscles inside. As she juggled her flask, its pungent contents spilled out on her buckskins.

The horse thief stepped closer. He sniffed once, then sniffed again.

When Cricket turned her head, her eyes met the look of utter disbelief and disgust on the face of the thief before he blurted incredulously, "You're drunk!"

The rebuke hit Cricket like a slap in the face. She opened her mouth to make excuses and then snapped it shut again. How dare he condemn something he knew nothing about! And there wasn't a chance in hell she was going to tell some perfect stranger she was dealing with a *female* problem!

"You're an idiot to be drinking in Comanche country. The Comanches aren't known for their tolerance of foolish mistakes."

It took a moment for the stranger's criticism to sink in. When it did, Cricket exploded like an overripe melon.

"Look, you long-nosed, shaggy-haired excuse for crowbait! I don't know what hole you crawled out of, but I've been dealing with the Comanches my whole life—"

"All sixteen years of it," he interrupted patronizingly.

"Seventeen years! And no Tennessee toad—"

"I'm *Texan.*" He said it softly, and there was both pride and menace in the single word. "And no brat in buckskins—"

"Texan?" she sneered. "The noises I've heard out of you are straight from the Tennessee hills or my name isn't Creighton Stewart!"

"That's enough, Cricket." Bay had perceived the flush that always appeared on her sister's face before she really lost her temper. It was frightening to contemplate the possible results of Cricket's growing drunkenness. Bay wasn't looking forward to dealing with their captive by herself. But, as usual, Cricket ignored her warning.

"Don't you worry, *horse thief.* I'll get you to your hanging safe and sound!"

Cricket shouted an order to Rogue, who growled at the stranger and nipped at his heels. The man shot Cricket a condescending glance before he once more paced out in front of her, panting like the wolves who loped beside him, pink tongues lolling from their mouths.

With whiskey-blurred eyes, Cricket scanned the oak-studded plains, but she never saw the changing terrain, never felt the sun beating down upon her, never smelled the wildflowers in bloom nor heard the gentle plodding of her horse. She'd turned all her senses inward. The horse thief had called her a *brat in buckskins.* She'd thought that kind of name-calling couldn't bother her any more. In truth, she hadn't let such insults bother her for a long, long time . . . not since Amber Kuykendall's ninth birthday party.

Even at the tender age of eight, Cricket had known she was different from other girls. She didn't wear dresses, and she always rode astride. She was talkative with adults but tongue-tied around other children. But Amber Kuykendall seemed not to care. She always made Cricket feel at ease on those occasions when Rip visited Sam Kuykendall on business.

So when Cricket received a written invitation to Amber Kuykendall's ninth birthday party that told her to "be sure to wear a dress," she'd hugged the parchment close and made plans to do exactly that. The only problem was, Cricket didn't own a dress.

She'd sought out Rip in the fields, where he sat on a sleek horse and surveyed the furrows planted with the spring crop of cotton.

"Amber Kuykendall invited me to her birthday party," she began.

"Oh? Are you planning to go?"

"Sure. Why not?"

"I wondered what you have in common with a bunch of sissyish girls, is all," Rip said.

Cricket's heart began to thrum a little faster.

"Amber's not a sissy," she defended. "And we're going to have cake and punch and play games and such."

"What kind of games?" Rip challenged. "Things you can play in dresses, I bet."

"Well, yes. Amber asked me to wear a dress and I—"

Rip hooted with laughter.

"What's so funny?"

"The thought of you in a dress," Rip said with a chortle of glee. "Imagine how much material it'd take to cover those legs of yours. Pants're much more practical for a long-legged filly like you."

Cricket's face flushed with embarrassment. But, determined, she continued, "I have to wear a dress. Amber said so, and Bay said she'd make me one if you'd buy the cloth. So will you?" Cricket waited anxiously for Rip's reply.

"I'm surprised at you, Cricket, letting somebody else do your thinking for you. You go to that party, but you go in what you want to wear. Don't let Amber Kuykendall be the one to tell you what to do."

Even at eight years of age, the need for Rip's approval was great—so great that Cricket went to Amber Kuykendall's birthday party in a buckskin shirt and trousers. She got no further than the porch before Amber caught her.

"Hurry up and get your dress out of your saddlebag and change," Amber urged. "You're the last to arrive. Everyone else is here."

"I . . . I didn't bring a dress," Cricket blurted.

"But why not?"

"I . . . I . . ." It was hard for Cricket to answer because the reason she wasn't in a dress was that Rip hadn't wanted her to wear one. Cricket would never have admitted even to herself that her father told her what to do. She made her own decisions.

"She didn't bring a dress because she'd rather wear boys' clothes. In fact, she'd rather *be* a boy," Felicia Myers inserted, trooping out onto the porch followed by the other nine girls who'd been invited to the party. "No boys are allowed at this party. So why don't you go home."

"I'm not a boy," Cricket replied belligerently, noting the hand-hidden smirks of the other femininely dressed girls.

"Could've fooled me," Felicia taunted, spreading the folds of her dainty satin dress. She eyeballed Cricket up and down, and then turned disdainfully and pranced away toward the porch swing.

Cricket had never been cut quite so obviously before, or with such a large audience, and responded impulsively by grabbing Felicia's sleeve to turn her around. Unfortunately, the shoulder seam of the satin dress couldn't withstand the strain, and with an ominous rip it tore free.

Felicia whirled on Cricket with a vengeance, screeching, "Now look what you've done! Why don't you go back home where you belong, you freak!"

Cricket stood stunned for only a moment before she grabbed a hank of Felicia's curly black hair and shouted, "You take that back right now!"

"I won't take it back, 'cause it's true," Felicia screamed. "My ma says you're growin' up a boy in a girl's body. She says you're a freak of nature. Freak! Freak!"

"Stop! Wait! Don't do this!" Amber cried frantically.

"Take it all back or I'll give you a black eye!" Cricket warned in a voice choked with rage and pain.

"Just you try it!" Felicia spat, swinging a fist.

Cricket dodged, and the small, pointed knuckles aimed at her eye landed on her mouth instead, cutting her lip and sending a trickle of blood down her chin. At the same time, her own fist swung round smack dab into Felicia's right eye, knocking Felicia completely off her feet.

Three of the girls rushed to help Felicia get back up, while Cricket looked daggers at the rest, several of whom had started to weep, daring them to say anything.

Amber's hysterical screaming brought her mother on the run.

"You little heathen! Look what you've done," Martha Kuykendall accused, grabbing Cricket by the shoulders and shaking her until her teeth rattled. Realizing at last exactly whom she held, Martha suddenly released Cricket, who stumbled away a step or two.

Cricket was in shock. Dazed. Disbelieving. Defensive. It wasn't her fault. Felicia had only gotten what she had coming to her. Cricket wasn't a freak. She wasn't. Just because she didn't want to wear some old frilly dress was no reason to call her a freak. Felicia wore pants too, sometimes. She couldn't deny it. So why was Cricket a freak because she'd worn buckskins to a birthday party? It was all a big mistake.

Cricket's mouth was dry of spittle, yet she turned and tried to croak an explanation to Amber anyway. "Amber, I—"

Amber burst into tears. "How could you do this, Cricket. I thought you were my friend. You've ruined my birthday party. I'll never forgive you. Never! Get out! Go home! I never want to see you again!"

Cricket pleaded with her eyes, but she wasn't about to beg. She stared at the other girls until there wasn't a one without her gaze focused on the shiny toes of her shoes. Then she spat on the porch at Felicia Myers's feet, and left. She didn't need any of them.

But she missed playing with Amber Kuykendall.

And she never got invited to another birthday party.

After that, she'd built walls to protect herself. She never let what other people said about anything she decided to do bother her. She drew her confidence solely from Rip's approval.

So why had this horse thief's scorn suddenly mattered?

Cricket's eyes gradually focused again on the man in front of her, trying to remember the look on his face when she'd caught him at the pond. Fiery eyes, full of pride, anger, and a little surprise, then taunting, teasing, burning with some unknown emotion. What color were his eyes? When she couldn't remember, Cricket felt a momentary panic, followed by a relaxation of her entire body. With the recess of memory, perhaps the awful implications of the day's events would begin to fade as well. She was determined to forget the warmth of that Tennessee horse thief's lips upon her throat and mouth. Even as she fought to deny the past hours, her fingertips found their way to her swollen lips in wonder. A man had kissed her.

To acknowledge the rightness of that kiss meant a denial of her entire existence. It would turn her world upside-down. And Cricket liked her life exactly the way it was. She knew what was expected from her. Rip had made no pretense about what he wanted from his daughters, and Cricket had tried hard to be everything her father had wished for in a son. She was an expert shot. She could ride like the wind. She could break a wild bronc and track better than an Indian. She always strived to win, and never settled for second best. And even though it was the part of her life she liked the least, she knew when to plant cotton, and when to pick it. In actual fact, she'd never failed at anything she set her mind to do, and she was ready to try anything once. But not kissing. Or touching. Or being female.

She'd played the role Rip had given her for too long and knew it too well to want to give it up now. No one was going to start changing her life around, especially not some too-big-for-his-britches horse thief! Cricket groaned at the thought of Rip ever finding out that, momentarily at least, the horse thief had gotten the better of her. She could have argued the thief was stronger, and bigger, and oh, so clever. But excuses didn't work with Rip. Cricket groaned again. Damn that horse thief!

"Does it hurt bad, Cricket?"

Cricket glanced over and discovered an anxious Bay riding knee to knee with her.

"What?"

"You were groaning again. I thought maybe it's more than . . . more than the miseries hurting you . . . I thought maybe the horse thief had—" Bay stopped and gulped, unwilling to think what the thief might have done. "Are you sure you're all right?"

"Stop trying to mother me and I'll be fine!"

Cricket took one look at Bay's liquid eyes, her lips trembling at the reproof, and her harshness melted. "Oh, hell's bells! I . . ."

Bay waited for Cricket to say more, but she merely stared morosely at the man who raced boldly ahead of them. When a full minute had passed, Bay could stand the waiting no longer. "Cricket?"

Cricket turned and scowled at Bay, all her pentup frustration and anger and confusion contained in that one forceful black expression.

Bay kicked her horse into a gallop, leaving Cricket sputtering in the dust.

"Bay, wait!" Cricket shouted after the disappearing figure. "I'm not mad at you! It's this good-for-nothing horse thief! I can't stand that he—"

The thief turned and Cricket shut her mouth. She defiantly met the look in his golden eyes, daring him to say anything. She was spoiling for a fight, but the hard-muscled horse thief didn't give it to her. He angled his head, as though to question whether she could stay on her horse without falling off, and then headed away again at a trot.

It was only then she noticed they'd reached the double row of facing log cabins at the edge of the cotton fields where Rip's sixty field slaves lived. Each cabin had a garden behind it where even now the trash gang of slave children worked hoeing, thinning, and suckering corn. Nearby, Mammy

Pleasant cared for the smallest of the children, while in the cotton fields, the hoe hands did for the cotton what their children did for the corn. The plantation house, nestled between three giant live oaks, lay hidden a half-mile to the south of them, and the cotton gin and baling screw stood a half-mile to the north.

When they finally arrived at the two-story white frame house, its double gallery porch was awash with the last warm, golden rays of the afternoon sun. A balding Negro man, hands gnarled with age, was seated in one of the two rockers on the lower gallery porch.

"Where's Rip?" Cricket asked.

"Your pa's gone visitin' Señor Juan Carlos Guerrero. He ain't goin' to be back till late this evenin'," the Negro answered.

Cricket turned to the thief and said, "Guess you'll do best tied up in the barn till Rip gets home."

"Aw, hell! Look, kid—"

Cricket swiftly pulled one of the thief's Pattersons from her belt, and the tall man found himself looking down the barrel of his own gun, which was pointed right at his nose.

"Don't say another word," she warned.

"Hey, Brava, I—"

Cricket cocked the gun.

The thief pressed his lips in a flat line. He looked around for some other authority he could appeal to, but there wasn't any. His body was a spring coiled for instant action, but Cricket left him no choice except to head in the direction she gestured with his gun.

They passed the kitchen, the cistern, and the bachelors' quarters on their way to the barn located a short distance north of the house. Cricket herded the mares and the thief's gelding into a corral beside the barn with the help of another Negro, more bald than the first, but no younger.

"See you got them mares back," he said.

"Sure did, Jim. Caught me a thief, too."

"Good-lookin' man-buck, ain't he?"

At Jim's observation, Cricket gave the thief a thorough once-over, focusing on the width of his chest in contrast to the narrowness of his hips, the casual stance that disguised brute strength. Her attempted nonchalance fell somewhat flat because in her mind she also saw him naked, water streaming in rivulets down his brawny chest, the curving scar on his flank disappearing into the shiny waters of the pond. She flushed when the stranger returned her bold perusal, but managed an unconcerned shrug before agreeing, "He's all right. But looks don't matter much when you aren't going to live long enough to make use of them."

She gestured again with the Patterson and the thief moved to the door of the barn. There they encountered a third Negro, his wiry hair frizzed into a gray halo around his coal-black face. His dark eyes were perceptive, and once he got a good look at the stranger, cautious.

"'Lo there, Cricket," he said, taking the reins of Cricket's pinto as she stepped down from the saddle.

"Hello, August." Cricket grabbed her saddlebag and used the gun to head the stranger into the barn. "I'll need your help tying up this horse thief."

"Sure, Cricket, I'll get some rope. Don't let all them wolves in here, now. That ole mare, Bluebonnet, she gonna have Valor's foal soon and I don't want her riled none."

Cricket sent Rascal and Ruffian away, but kept Rogue at her side as she ushered the horse thief into the shadowy barn, redolent with the lingering smell of fresh manure.

"Smells good in here," the thief said.

"Smells like a barn," Cricket retorted.

"That's what I said."

August tied the thief's hands together snugly but not uncomfortably, then forced him down on the clean straw in the stall next to the foaling mare before also securing the rope to one of the low slats in the partition.

"You be fine now, mister, long as you don't try nothin'. Cricket, she usually shoot first and ask questions later," he said with a toothy grin that appeared suspended in the darkness of the barn.

"I have the feeling you're not kidding," the thief muttered.

August chuckled. "I kin watch 'im for you, Cricket, since I gotta be here for Bluebonnet anyway."

"I don't mind watching after Bluebonnet till Rip gets home. Why don't you get some rest," she suggested, setting the thief's Pattersons in the straw at the edge of the stall, well out of his reach.

"Matter of fact, I could use a nap. That ole mare, she liable to keep me up some later tonight," August said.

After August had gone, Cricket wondered whether she should've volunteered to care for Bluebonnet. She felt distinctly woozy. But she wanted to be here to see the pleased look on Rip's face when she presented him with the thief who'd stolen his mares. She also wanted to confront him about that marriage business right away. Rip wouldn't need to find her a husband because she wasn't ever going to get married.

Bluebonnet whickered softly, and Cricket moved into the stall with the heavy-laden mare.

"Hello, pretty lady." Cricket rubbed the mare's nose, and then scratched behind her ears. Her hand slid down the mare's neck and over her greatly distended girth. Then Cricket laid her cheek against the mare's neck and let her hand caress the taut belly that held Valor's foal.

"You'll foal a handsome colt, girl, I know it, a fine son for Valor . . . or maybe a beautiful filly, who'll grow up sleek and strong like you."

All the time she spoke, Cricket handled the mare, recognizing in the tensing flesh the labor contractions that were already underway. It was the mare's first foal, and Cricket wondered whether the animal had any inkling of what was happening to her.

"How long before the foal's born?"

Cricket searched the stranger's face and saw he had somehow discerned the mare's laboring state.

"It's her first, so it may be a while."

"You're in no condition to help."

Cricket scowled. "I'll manage."

At that moment Bluebonnet's legs buckled at the knees

and Cricket made room as the mare lay down. Cricket dropped to her knees in the straw beside the mare, which was breathing heavily.

"Shouldn't you call August?" the thief asked.

"I've done this before. I can handle it."

"I could help."

Startled at the thief's offer, Cricket contemplated the man's solemn face for a moment before she repeated firmly, "I can handle it."

"All right, Brava, but the offer holds."

Over the next few hours, Cricket wished more than once that she'd called August, or even taken up the thief's offer of help. It wasn't a particularly hard labor, but because it was Valor's foal, and the mare's first, Cricket found herself worrying over every little thing that didn't happen exactly as she expected. To complicate matters, her own cramps, dulled by the whiskey she'd drunk on the way home, began to attack with renewed vigor, and she wasn't willing to lessen what ability she had to help the mare by drinking more whiskey. Cricket swiped at the sweat on her forehead and sighed heavily, soothing the tired mare with her hands as best she could.

"You're doing fine."

Cricket's head snapped up at the thief's comforting words, which were the first he'd spoken since he'd made his offer of help.

"I don't need you to tell me that."

She watched the thief frown at her sharp retort. Well, it was true. But why couldn't she have accepted his compliment with more grace? For his approval *had* pleased her. She frowned in confusion at her inexplicable prickliness with the stranger. At that moment the mare grunted loudly, and Cricket saw the foal's nose appear.

"Keep working, girl. He's almost here. Keep on working. Don't give up now," Cricket urged.

Within minutes the foal was born, a fine pinto colt.

"Oh! He's beautiful!"

Cricket slumped back in the straw, leaning against the slats of the stall as she watched the mare lick the colt clean.

Bluebonnet soon rose to her feet, followed by the colt, wavering on its spindly legs. Cricket felt her throat closing at the overwhelming wonder of new life, but managed a choked laugh of delight as the tiny colt nudged at its mother's teat.

At that moment a horrible cramp hit Cricket and the laugh became a gasp. She waited for it to pass and then shoved herself up out of the straw. She headed for the silver flask she'd left in her saddlebag, which was draped over the stall in which the thief was tied.

Cricket grasped the flask in one hand as she slid down into the straw, leaning her back against the stall partition opposite the stranger. Once she was comfortable, the gray wolf, which had been relegated to the far side of the barn during Bluebonnet's labor, stretched out beside her. She pulled her knees up tight to her chest, trying to lessen the pain of the cramps without drinking any more whiskey. God, she felt so awful! And she was so tired! Her eyelids kept drooping closed, so she widened her eyes unnaturally and blinked several times in an attempt to keep them open. She had to stay awake and wait for Rip.

The fingers of one hand threaded into the wolf's fur and worked their way against the grain all the way to his head. Then the slender fingers smoothed down the black-tipped silver fur they'd ruffled, stopping occasionally to scratch at the sources of greatest sensitivity on the animal's hide.

"You should be doing that to a man."

Cricket looked up at the thief and their eyes caught. He was looking at her again like he had at the pond, with that indefinable expression. A frown furrowed her brow. What was he thinking? He looked almost . . .

"Are you hungry?"

The thief laughed harshly.

"What's so funny?"

The stranger smiled enigmatically, but said nothing.

"Well, you can starve for all I care! That is, if you don't hang first, mister . . . mister . . . whoever you are!"

"Jarrett Creed."

"Well, Mister Creed—"

"Creed is fine."

"Creed, I—"

"I like the way you say my name. Say it again."

His voice caressed her. Flustered, Cricket hesitated, only to find herself assailed at that moment by another cramp. Surrendering to the pain, she raised the silver flask to her lips.

"Don't you think you've had enough of that belly-wash?"

Cricket grimaced. She wasn't any more willing to explain the situation now than she had been on the ride home. She settled for saying, "As a matter of fact, I haven't," and scooted down further until her head nestled in Rogue's fur. She lifted her head to take another deep swallow, recapped the flask, laid her head back down on the wolf, and closed her eyes.

"Listen, Brava," Creed began. "You better . . . hey, are you awake?" When the girl's eyes didn't open, Jarrett Creed shook his head in disgust.

She dressed like a Tennessee mountain man.

She drank like a trooper in Sam Houston's army.

She wrestled like an Indian with his honor at stake.

And she swore like a bullwhacker stuck in mud.

In fact, there wasn't one feminine thing about her. So how could he find her so desirable? He took another look at the buckskin-clad figure. The almond-shaped gray eyes that had flashed fire at him were closed now. Her eyelashes were a black fringe on honey skin that was smudged with dirt from their fight, and blood from the delivery of the foal. In sleep she didn't hold her aquiline nose quite so arrogantly, but the high, proud cheekbones remained, exaggerating the almost gaunt thinness of her face. Her smooth brow was crowned with a simple leather band, and a thick braid of rich, auburn hair fell across her shoulder and trailed into the straw.

He was confused by the emotions rushing through him. He simply couldn't believe he was physically attracted to the unfeminine female lying across from him in the straw. Why, he even admired the girl a little! Actually, it had been something of a feat for her to wrestle down a man, even if she did have the element of surprise on her side. And what about that quick draw with his Patterson, despite the fact she was drunk as a fiddler? Then there was the calm, experienced way she'd handled that foaling mare. And how could he forget the sensuous way her hands had moved through that wolf's fur? Oh, there were things he admired about her, all right. But there were things about her that bothered him as well.

On the Texas frontier a woman was often expected to do more than simple tasks like spinning cloth, hoeing a garden, or chopping wood. She might have to help with the plowing and planting, or she might have to take up arms and protect her home from whatever threat came her way. But she remained a woman, bearing her children, obeying her man, and clinging to the petticoat rituals of her sex. The behavior he'd seen from Cricket had gone far beyond those bounds. She didn't fit the feminine mold at all, and Creed wanted to know the reason why.

Creed tensed when the barn door opened, his nerves on edge because he was trussed up like an animal fit for butchering. The muscle in his jaw ached where he had it clamped down. Whoever was at the door was taking his own sweet time coming in, he thought irritably. Slowly, he moved to ready himself for what defense he could make. He hadn't lived as long as he had in this violent land by being careless. Creed pulled his moccasined foot up where he could reach it and fingered the outline of the sharp knife concealed in the lining.

If his late-night visitor wasn't friendly he was going to find himself in for quite a surprise.

CHAPTER 3

Cricket?"

Creed breathed a heartfelt sigh of relief at the sound of the feminine voice that had come out of the darkness. He quickly tucked his knife back into its hiding place as the voice was followed shortly by the gangly girl who'd rescued Cricket earlier in the day.

"Cricket?" she repeated.

Cricket's snuffling snore filled the quiet barn.

"She's asleep," Creed said.

"Oh, my." After a cursory check of her sister, Bay hung the lantern on a hook at the end of the stall. "I really came to see you anyway."

Creed's eyes narrowed suspiciously. "Why?"

"I brought some food for you, and some water to clean your wounds."

Creed had already noticed the basket and towel over her arm, and the tin of water she carried. "Your name's Bay?"

The girl nodded.

"Do you always clean up after your sister, Bay?"

"I help when I can," she replied.

"I suppose I'm at least as deserving of your attention as the last stray pups she carted home."

"You don't seem quite as hungry as the wolves were," she answered with a timid smile.

Creed was tempted to smile back, but didn't.

Bay placed the basket of food on the ground near him, then settled the tin of water in the straw and dampened the towel and wrung it out. She stood before him with the cloth in her hand, and gestured toward the dried blood where Cricket's nails had clawed his face.

"May I?"

"By all means. Help yourself."

The girl carefully cleansed the blood from his cheek and the dust and sweat from his brow. Creed examined her closely as she worked, noting the deep, violet eyes and the bright coppery-red hair that curled naturally around her milky-white skin. She'd changed out of her buckskins and wore a green print muslin dress protected by a sturdy osnaburg apron. The puffy-sleeved dress, which fit snugly through the bodice and waist, showed the promise of the woman she'd become. He should have been attracted to her, but felt no stirring in his loins like that fostered by the smoky-eyed lass in pants, snoring away in the straw across from him.

The girl's hands were cool and competent when she pulled up the buckskin sleeves of his shirt to reach the gashes the wolves had torn in his arms. She clucked her tongue at one particularly deep slash. "That probably won't need stitches if you're careful for a few days."

"Then you don't think I'm going to hang tomorrow morning?"

The girl looked uncomfortable. "Did you steal Rip's mares?"

"It sure looks that way, doesn't it?"

The girl ignored the only conclusion to be drawn from his statement and said instead, "Finding you at the pond was quite a shock."

"I gathered that from some of the language your sister used. I've heard bullwhackers who spoke more delicately to strangers."

"Oh, my. Don't blame Cricket. Half the time she doesn't even realize she's saying those things. The summer she was fourteen she helped a teamster who'd lost his arm in the War for Independence drive his load of cotton to Galveston. She enjoyed it so much she's been helping him out ever since."

"She apparently learned a lot more on those trips than how to drive a team of oxen," Creed said.

Bay ignored his gibe as she unwrapped the basket of food she'd brought. "I'll have to feed you, since your hands are tied."

"I seem to have lost my appetite," he replied. "Just tell your father when he comes home that Jarrett Creed wants to talk to him."

"Was my father expecting you?" Bay asked, startled.

"Just tell him I'm here."

Bay nodded her agreement to the abrupt command.

"Is your sister going to spend the night here in the barn?"

Bay glanced over to where Cricket lay curled in a ball, her cheek resting on Rogue's massive chest. "Rip will come and pick her up when he gets home and bring her into the house. He usually does."

"Usually? You mean she gets drunk like this all the time?"

"Not all the time!" Bay hurried to explain. "Only when she has the . . . only some of the time," she finished lamely.

Bay quickly collected the items she'd brought with her from the house, including the lantern that provided the only light in the barn. She looked worriedly from Creed to Cricket and back. "Good night, Mister Creed."

"Creed."

"Good night, Creed." Bay headed for the barn door, leaving Cricket and Creed alone in the darkness.

Creed hadn't thought he'd be able to sleep with all the turbulent thoughts racing through his head, but a blaze of light from the doorway of the barn woke him from his restless slumber just before he heard bootsteps crackle in the straw.

Creed had never seen Rip Stewart before, yet he felt certain that was who held the lantern that lit Cricket's sleeping form. Creed lay a bit outside the yellow aureole, and decided to remain quiet in the shadows a moment in order to observe the mammoth man before making his presence known. Rip's hair lay in curls over both brow and collar, and his blunt features looked sinister, rather than soft, in the candlelight.

Creed knew all about Rip Stewart. He had a reputation for being a notorious bully, stubborn and opinionated. He also was clever, or maybe cunning was a better word for a man who'd started with nothing and now controlled the flatboat trade on the Brazos River, the only way for the Texas planters to send their cotton to market in Galveston. He was known to be a bit of a scoundrel, albeit a likeable one. And Rip Stewart loved his children.

Creed couldn't say what made him so sure of the last, unless it was the look reflected in Rip's eyes when he beheld his daughter. After hanging the lantern on the hook at the end of the stall, Rip bent down on one knee next to Cricket and reached over to smooth away a piece of straw that clung to her cheek. He spoke a word of reassurance to the wolf, which had raised its head and growled low when he touched Cricket. Then he gently turned Cricket and reached under her shoulders and knees, lifting her into his arms and holding her embraced to his chest. He bent forward as though he might kiss her brow, but paused abruptly before completing the gesture. With a speed fast as hummingbird wings, Cricket was thrown back into the straw and a Colt Patterson appeared in Rip's right hand.

"Step forward where I can see you, or I'll shoot!"

"Whoa! I'm tied up here!"

At the same moment Creed spoke, August came running from the back of the barn with another lantern. "What's goin' on?"

The additional light confirmed Creed's trussed-up condition.

"Where'd he come from?" Rip asked August, pointing at Creed with his Patterson.

"Cricket brung 'im home. She brung home them five mares, too. Said this here fella stole 'em."

"Well, well," Rip said with a chuckle. "Well, young man, what do you have to say for yourself?"

"If you'll untie me I'll explain everything," Creed said. "Your daughter, Cricket—"

"No, no, on second thought, I don't think I'm ready for any long explanations right now. I've had a tiring ride home and it's late. I'm sure your story will keep until tomorrow."

"But I'm—"

"No buts," Rip interrupted, waving his Patterson for emphasis. "August, if he makes too much noise, knock him out. I'll send Cricket out to get him in the morning."

Incredulous, Creed watched the large man reach down and grab the drunken girl by the arms. He pulled her limp form upright and then slung her headfirst over his shoulder. He grabbed the lantern he'd brought in with him and stalked from the barn with Cricket's head bobbing against his huge back, her long auburn braid dangling almost to his knees. The half-wild wolf, whose sharp teeth had raked Creed's arm and nipped his heels, followed them docilely out the door.

"A mouth open wide like that, catch a lotta flies in this here barn," August said. "You jus' get comfortable now, mister. It not be long 'fore mornin'. Cricket, she come get you first light." August headed back to his room in the rear of the barn, leaving only quiet, velvet darkness behind him.

Creed shut his mouth and resignedly closed his eyes. Getting a word in edgewise around a Stewart was quite a chore. He should have suspected the father would be as bad as the daughter. When he finally got a chance to speak in the morning, you could bet he wasn't going to start with any sociable preamble. He sighed disgustedly. He probably should have told the girl who he was in the first place, but he'd figured she was some brat out playing, and the fewer people who knew he was here. . . .

Of course the worst that would result from his error in judgment was that he'd spend the night tied up in the barn. Surely in the morning they'd give him a chance to explain before they strung him up. On the other hand, in light of his recent experience with Cricket and Rip, maybe not. He'd taken enough foolish chances with what had started out as a routine mission. It was time to deal himself a better hand. Creed brought his moccasined foot up to meet his tied hands, and began to work the concealed knife free.

Dawn found Rip drinking coffee at the breakfast table with two of his three daughters. Cricket wasn't one of them. Rip had noted Cricket's absence this morning with a concerned frown. It was true that ordinarily her presence wouldn't have been missed. While Sloan had duties as overseer, and Bay had been bookkeeper for Three Oaks the past year, Cricket had no specific duties on the plantation. Of course, that was easily explained because he was grooming Sloan and Bay to take their rightful places as heir and surety for Three Oaks, while Cricket was simply his pride and joy.

It was only recently he'd decided to provide Cricket with a role in life other than the prodigal son. Naturally, the plan he'd contrived to secure her future was far grander than that for either of his other two daughters. Yet, Cricket's latest drunken episode, together with the discussion he'd had yesterday with Señor Juan Carlos Guerrero, made him think perhaps it was time he began preparing her for what was to come.

"Bay, go get your sister out of bed," Rip ordered.

"I already tried," Sloan interjected. "She was dead to the world and feeling no pain."

"Wake her up anyway!"

"I'm going." Bay grabbed her cup of coffee from the table, planning to pour some down Cricket's throat. Before she got to the stairs she remembered her promise to the horse thief and turned back to Rip. "Cricket brought a man home with her yesterday. He's tied up out in the barn."

"Yes, I know." Rip chuckled. "Caught her a horse thief. By God, we'll have us a hanging today!"

Bay struggled to balance the coffee cup on the saucer, which teetered alarmingly in her hands at Rip's announcement. "He said to tell you his name is Jarrett Creed and—"

"What?"

"His name is Jarrett Creed and—"

"I'll be damned!" Rip burst into uncontrollable guffaws, slapping the cherrywood table so hard the delicate china rattled.

Bay looked to Sloan for an explanation of Rip's jovial humor, but Sloan just shrugged and shook her head.

"This is rich! Well, I promised Jarrett Creed I'd send Cricket out to get him in the morning and send her I will."

Rip rose from the table and passed Bay on his way up the stairs. She turned and followed hurriedly after him. Rip threw open Cricket's door so it slammed against the ivy-papered wall.

The resounding bang brought Cricket, still fully dressed except for her moccasins, bolt upright in her maple four-poster bed. She clapped her hands to either side of her head to try to quiet the hundred Indian drums pounding inside.

"Rise and shine!" Rip ordered.

Cricket moaned loudly and fell back down in a prone position.

"You have a prisoner to free," he said.

Cricket squinted one eye open. "To hang, you mean."

"You heard me right the first time."

Cricket dragged herself back upright. She grabbed her head again. She hated the monthly miseries. Her head and stomach were definitely on the warpath, and she felt god-awful. If Rip wanted to fight over that horse thief, she was in a rotten enough mood to oblige him. "That Tennessee horse thief deserves to hang if ever a man did."

"He's no horse thief," Rip replied with a grin.

"I caught him myself with your mares!"

"The man in the barn is Jarrett Creed," Rip explained.

"I know his name," Cricket retorted.

"Texas Ranger Jarrett Creed."

"What?!"

"I sent a letter to the captain of the Rangers in San Antonio when we started getting raided by the Comanches. Jack Hays promised to send a Ranger lieutenant named Jarrett Creed to see if he could help us out. Guess Creed must have come across the Comanches who stole our horses and taken them back," Rip concluded.

"But he said . . . he never . . . he told me . . ." Cricket sputtered to a stop. A herd of mustangs was galloping through her skull, down her throat, and into her stomach. "Why that lowdown, one-horned billy goat! He must have been laughing up his sleeve at me all day. Nobody laughs at me and gets away with it. I'll fix his wagon, but good!"

"You won't do anything of the kind," Rip countered. "You'll go out to the barn and release him, and *politely* invite him into the house for some breakfast."

"Like *hell* I will," she raged.

"Like hell you *will!*" Rip raged back.

The two strong personalities battled as they had many a time before. Eyeball glared at eyeball. Hackles rose on the backs of two necks in anticipation of taking up the gauntlet and plunging into hostilities. Fists formed. Breathing quickened. Nostrils flared.

Bay shrank back against the open door while Sloan, the smallest of the three sisters at only five feet four inches stepped further into the room.

"This is getting you nowhere fast," Sloan said, her dark, chocolate-brown eyes warm with humor. "I'll go untie him."

As one, the two combatants shifted the focus of their belligerance. Cricket was the first to respond. She hurdled off the bed, pausing only long enough to yank on her moccasins before flying past her father.

"No! I'll get him." She shoved past Sloan and raced out the bedroom door.

Rip pounded down the stairs after her roaring, "You'll be *polite!*"

"In a pig's eye!" she shouted back, already out the front door.

Bay hung back by Cricket's door, still frightened of being caught up in the terrifying clash between her sister and her father. Meanwhile, Sloan came down behind Rip and caught his arm before he could leave the house.

"You've made your point," she said. "It won't hurt to let her vent a little spleen before she unties him. Now that she knows who he is she's not likely to kill him, and anything less than that she does to him, he probably deserves. After all, he could have told her who he is at any time."

Rip hesitated a moment, torn between his desire to observe how Cricket dealt with the Ranger and the knowledge that if he were there he'd probably be tempted to interfere and protect the man from Cricket's wrath. No, it would be infinitely more fun to let the Ranger pay for his foolishness. He could see the sense of Sloan's suggestion and, grunting his assent, turned away from the front door and back to the dining room. He only hoped Cricket would remember to bring the fellow in for breakfast when she was done with him.

Cricket's pride hurt almost as much as her head and her belly. As she stomped toward the barn she planned all the horrible things she was going to do to Jarrett Creed before she untied him. He would learn she couldn't be manipulated like the other females he knew. She was different.

She shoved the barn door open and slipped inside to the stall where Creed was tied, using her foot to hunt through the straw for her silver flask. The top of her head almost came off when she bent over to pick it up. She bolted down a slug of whiskey that burned her throat and did nothing to settle her stomach. There was no hope for her stomach. It was Jarrett Creed's fault she was out of bed when she felt like a squashed cotton worm, and she was going to make him suffer the way she was suffering. No man made a fool of her and got away with it. That Texas Ranger was going to wish he'd never met Creighton Stewart! He was going to wish he'd never been born!

Cricket marched over to the sleeping man and slammed the toe of her moccasin into his ribs as hard as she could.

"Wake up!"

Before she could get in a second kick, the Ranger had scissored his legs around her feet and dumped her in the straw.

"That's enough, Brava! I'm awake!"

Cricket scrambled onto her knees, nose to nose with the Ranger. "Good! Because I want you to hear every word I have to say before I hang you!"

"Look, you little savage," he snarled, his golden eyes flashing, "before you do anything you'll regret, let me tell you I'm a Texas Ranger. I got those mares from the Comanches who stole them from your father. The Rangers sent me here to trail the Comanches that have been raiding—"

"I don't believe you," she said. "You're making that up so I won't hang you, and it won't wash. Try to be a man for a change, and take what's coming to you."

The Ranger's flush at her insulting accusation pleased Cricket hugely.

"Ask your father—"

"My father rode away at dawn," she lied. "He told me to do with you as I see fit. And I see fit to hang you!"

"Aw, hell."

Cricket wanted to laugh, but knew that would give away the game, and Jarrett Creed hadn't suffered nearly enough yet to pay for what he'd done. "Do you have any last requests?"

"Would it be too much to ask for breakfast?"

"Sort of a last meal for the condemned man?"

"*Sí,* Brava."

"My sisters and I were having breakfast when I remembered you were out here. Would you like to join us in the dining room?"

"You want me to join you . . . in the house . . . at your table . . . for breakfast?"

"Yes, since it's your last request. Why not?"

"All right. You'll have to untie me though."

Cricket pondered his request for a moment, and came to the quick conclusion that Creed had offered her the perfect opportunity to pay him back for his deception before she delivered him to her father. She would pretend to have trouble untying the ropes. When she used her knife to cut him free the blade would slip and leave a little nick, a tiny scar which would be there always as a reminder of how a woman had held him in her power, rather than the other way around.

"You won't try to escape, will you?" she said in a syrupy-sweet voice.

"Of course not."

Green as grass, Creed thought.

I've got him now, Cricket thought.

They both moved at the same moment. Creed's hands miraculously came free just as Cricket leaned over to untie him. Stunned, Cricket didn't resist when Creed caught both her wrists in one hand and quickly secured them with the same rope which had once tied him.

"You're going to have to learn to be a little more considerate of your company, Brava."

Cricket stared down at her hands in disbelief for a second, then looked up at Creed. He'd done it again! This was not to be borne! Like a lassoed bronc, she gathered her muscles to explode.

"You birdbrain! You hobclunch!"

"Now, now, Brava. Temper, tem—"

Cricket rammed her head up under Creed's chin, knocking his teeth together and slamming his head back against the wooden stall partition. Creed grunted in pain. He was too dazed to avoid her next attack as she threw her full weight behind her shoulder into his solar plexis. Cricket tried to bring her knee to bear, but Creed rolled to the right, using his legs to knock her onto her side. She could see him getting ready to lunge at her, and knew if he caught her his sheer weight would pin her to the floor. As he dove, she rolled, and he landed on his stomach in the straw next to her.

"You missed!" she taunted.

In the next moment, she slammed her knees down in the middle of his back. She surrounded his head with her arms and brought her tied wrists up under his throat, cutting off his air. Cricket could feel the rough hemp abrading Creed's neck. She knew how raw a rope burn could be, and conscious of Rip's wrath if she did too much damage to the Ranger, she slackened the tension slightly.

Creed was on his knees in an instant, and her arms, which encircled his head, slipped down around his shoulders almost to his waist as he struggled upright. Creed turned to face her and Cricket found herself embracing him with her hands tied behind his back.

"If you want to fight like a man, Brava, then so be it!" the furious man hissed. "But I'm going to prove to you once and for all that you're a woman!"

There was no way Cricket could resist Creed when he put his arms around her. He shoved her against his muscular chest with one broad hand, and at the same moment wrapped a handful of her braid around the other and urged her mouth up to meet his. Cricket could feel his heart pounding. The muscles of his chest were hard, like granite, unrelenting, like the man.

His breath rasped in her ear as he said, "You're a woman, Brava."

How could she deny it? But she'd labored so long and hard not to acknowledge her female nature! She fought against the savage kiss and all it represented, clenching her teeth, pressing her lips together so hard her cheeks bulged from the effort. Creed bit her lips until she opened for him, and then his rough, wet tongue thrust against her teeth, forcing its way into her mouth, plundering virgin territory.

"Don't—" Cricket jerked back so hard she sent them both tumbling into the straw, Creed's full, hard length pressed against her from breast to thigh. She could feel his arousal, at least she supposed that was what it was. She shuddered, and turned her face away from Creed.

She didn't want to be a woman. Why couldn't he understand that and leave her alone?

Creed's strong hand cupped her jaw to turn her face toward him. "Look at me, Brava."

Cricket snapped her head around and glared at him, but his next words confirmed that he'd seen more of her distress than she'd wanted him to see.

"Ah, Brava, we make sparks together. You shouldn't play

with fire if you don't want to get burned," he said in a voice harshened by subdued passion.

"I'll kill you for this!" she spat.

"Then I might as well die a happy man," he crooned, lowering his head toward her mouth.

"Stop! You can't do this!"

"You don't want me to kiss you?" he teased.

Cricket sizzled with mortification. "That's what I just said, isn't it?"

"Give me one good reason why I shouldn't finish what I've started."

"Rip wants to talk with you."

Creed's eyes narrowed. "I thought you said Rip left this morning."

"I lied."

"So why should I believe you now?"

"Rip knows who you are. He made me come out here to get you and invite you in to have some breakfast. Coffee. Eggs. Ham. Sausage. Flapjacks. Grits with butter. Biscuits with jalapeño jelly."

Creed took a deep breath and to Cricket's amazement actually licked his lips. It was true, she thought, what they said about a man and his stomach.

Creed eyed her doubtfully, but said, "I could sure use a good meal, so I'll make a deal with you. You promise not to try to kill me, and I'll release you and we'll go have breakfast."

Cricket brightened. "Okay."

"Lift your arms up over my head," he instructed.

Cricket could feel her breasts rising against Creed's chest as her arms came to rest stretched up over her head in the straw. She relaxed completely beneath him, her body molding to his. As she looked up at him, her lips parted.

His eyes were hooded, his gaze intense.

"You can get up now," she said. When Creed didn't move she added, "Aren't you hungry?"

"I'm hungry," he admitted. "But not for flapjacks."

Cricket could feel the changes in him, the tension that

tightened the muscles in his arms and thighs, the bulge that grew against her belly. His breathing harshened and his heartbeat pounded erratically. She remained still beneath him, waiting. She knew he wanted her as a man wants a woman. So she waited to see whether she would want him as a woman wants a man.

But nothing happened.

Of course she did feel that same scorching heat everywhere they touched that she'd felt when he'd been naked at the pond.

But the day was warm, the barn even warmer . . . and his skin was hot.

And she had the strangest urge to arch her back up into his hard chest.

But the straw was scratchy beneath her.

And her breasts had gotten all swollen and pointy.

Obviously a result of the female miseries.

She felt a little relieved that the Ranger's amorous advances hadn't had any effect on her. What if she'd fallen under his spell?

Feeling safe from the threat that her "female nature" would betray her and subjugate itself to the Ranger, she allowed herself to speculate about what *might* have happened between them. She had to admit she was curious about the things men and women did together. Jarrett Creed had given her an opportunity she'd never thought to have, an opportunity to see what it felt like to lie beneath a man, and to be kissed by that man.

His most recent kiss had been harsh and unforgiving, meant to punish. She'd liked the touch of his lips on her throat yesterday much better. They'd been so soft. As for the rest of his touches, well, aside from the ones that had bruised her, she hadn't had enough of them to decide one way or the other. Perhaps if she lay still long enough, he would try again.

She held herself steady as Creed's knuckles caressed her cheek. "I don't know what game you're playing this time, Brava, but what you're offering is too delicious to resist."

Creed bent his head until his lips closed over her mouth. As he deepened the pressure she closed her eyes to enjoy the sensation of his lips moving ever so softly against hers.

Suddenly, Creed's weight was yanked away and a thunderous voice bellowed, "What the hell's going on here?!"

CHAPTER 4

I WANT AN EXPLANATION, and I want it now!"

Creed wasn't sure from the look on Rip's face whether he was about to be ushered to the altar or hanged after all, and cursed the day he'd ever set eyes on Creighton Stewart. "I know this looks bad, but—"

"This is none of your business!" Rip interrupted. "Well, Cricket?"

Cricket could feel the blood rushing to her face. She ground her teeth in chagrin. It was clear from the fact that her hands were tied that Creed had caught her unprepared and bested her. The worst of it was she'd neither achieved her revenge nor assuaged her curiosity. There was no way she could make this look any better to Rip than it did, but she certainly wasn't going to apologize for what had happened. "I thought his hands were tied. They weren't."

Rip looked with new respect at Creed. "How'd you get free?"

"I carry a knife hidden in my moccasin."

Rip spun back to his daughter. "Didn't you check his clothes for weapons?"

Cricket frowned in recollection. "Yes, I did. Or rather, Bay did."

Rip raised a bushy brow as though that explained everything.

Creed was confused. He didn't understand the purpose of Rip's cross-examination of Cricket. The sharp-tongued man ought to have been flaying Creed's hide for throwing the girl to the ground, and instead he was harassing his daughter for being bested by a man.

"Are you ready for some breakfast, young man?"

Creed shook his head as though to clear it. He must have missed something. Was that all Rip was going to say about the way he'd found the two of them? What kind of father was he? Where was the outrage for what Creed had done to Cricket? Where was the concern for his daughter's honor? "I can explain—"

"There's nothing more to explain," Rip replied. "Cricket wasn't paying attention and you caught her unaware. She usually learns from her mistakes. I don't expect it to happen again. Now, I'm ready for some breakfast. Coming?"

Creed watched dumbfounded as Rip stalked—he seemed to stalk a lot—from the barn.

"Are you going to cut me loose, or just stand there with your mouth gaping open?" Cricket snapped.

"From the way your father talked I'd have thought you could manage to free yourself."

Cricket was in no mood for Creed's wry humor. "Just cut the ropes." She held her bound hands out to Creed, who pulled the concealed knife from his moccasin and cut her loose. While she rubbed her wrists where the hemp had scraped her skin, he reached down into the straw and located his two Pattersons. Cricket winced when she touched a particularly sore spot.

"You all right?" Creed asked as he tucked the guns into the belt at the waist of his buckskin trousers.

"Don't worry about me. I can take care of myself."

"So I noticed."

Cricket's fists clenched at his pointed response. "You caught me off-guard this time. It won't happen again."

"This time? You mean there's going to be a next time?"

Cricket snorted. "Not if I can help it. Frankly, I don't see why men make such a fuss over kissing."

"Have you been kissed often, Brava?"

"You're the first who has—and the last who will. If you hadn't gotten lucky, you wouldn't have kissed me either."

"Luck had nothing to do with it," Creed replied. "I'm simply a better wrestler than you are." Cricket opened her mouth to argue the point but was interrupted when Creed continued placatingly, "Which is only to be expected. You're a woman. I'm a man. Men are stronger than women." Cricket's second attempt at a response was also cut off as Creed added, "But I'd be willing to wrestle you again, if that's the only way I can prove my point and win another kiss from you."

"You won't be kissing me again."

"Why not?"

"Kissing leads to other things."

"Such as."

"Fornicating, for one."

Creed's brows rose.

"I have no intentions of laying myself down under some buck like you, because fornicating leads to marrying."

Creed shifted uncomfortably, but Cricket didn't seem to notice as she finished, "And I want more out of life than being stuck at home as some planter's wife, being told by my husband what to do and when to do it. It's a trap I'm aiming to miss, thank you very much. I'll be no man's other half. I plan to spend my life doing just as I please. So, like I said, you won't be kissing me again."

With that, Cricket stalked—a perfect imitation of Rip, Creed thought—out the barn door ahead of him.

"Ah, my fierce, wild woman," Creed replied softly to Cricket's retreating form. "You're so very wrong about that."

He quickly followed after her, shaking his head at the female logic that had deduced that kissing led to fornicating and fornicating led to marriage. She was at least half-right, Creed thought, chuckling. It might behoove him to expand his acquaintance with a woman who had no intention of marrying, but first he was going to have breakfast. Coffee. Eggs. Sausage. Grits with butter.

Creed followed Cricket to the house. It was built, as were many of the houses in Texas, as two square, separate buildings, with an open dogtrot in the middle connecting them. Only in the case of Three Oaks, each of the two buildings was rectangular and had two floors, the dogtrot had been enclosed to make a spacious hallway in the center of the house, and a double gallery porch graced the front of the entire abode, giving it a feeling of being a single structure. Stairs in the central hallway led to the second floor. Otherwise, the hallway was bare except for an open-sided sleigh-type day bed centered along one wall, and a rocker bench on the other.

"Rip's office is over there," Cricket said, gesturing to the first room on the left, "and the guest bedroom is the next door back."

Creed could see a canopied four-poster bed through the door she'd indicated.

"The dining room is this way. Follow me." She led him into the parlor through the first door on the right off the hallway.

Creed was impressed by the subdued elegance in every facet of the simple furnishings: silk and brocade in the curtains and upholstery, polished cherry and maple in the furniture, porcelain figurines, pink marble surrounding the fireplace, silver candelabra, and Persian carpets on the hardwood floors. He was sure there wasn't anything that could begin to match it anywhere else in Texas.

The graciously appointed home was neat and spotlessly clean, and he couldn't imagine Cricket being comfortable living there. When he thought of her, he pictured the more traditional Texas home of unfinished pine, with its earth floor and stone fireplace. She belonged in a room with cedar tables, simple ladderback chairs with rawhide seats, homespun tablecloths, and linsey-woolsey curtains. He imagined Cricket standing in an open doorway leading to the shaded dogtrot, with the smell of spring wildflowers wafting around her. For his *brava* he envisioned a home where everything was raw and natural, in a land as equally wild and untamed as she was.

Cricket led Creed through the rear parlor door into the dining room. Rip, Sloan, and Bay were already seated at the table eating.

"I see you made it," Rip said.

Sloan stood and reached a firm hand out to Creed. "I'm Sloan."

Creed hesitated, then shook the work-hardened hand offered by the petite woman.

"Help yourself to whatever you want to eat," she said.

Cricket had already taken a Wedgwood china plate from the stack at the end of the sideboard and filled it to overflowing with a healthy sample of each of the dishes provided. She then comfortably straddled the needlepoint seat of an almost-fragile cherrywood chair.

She'd thought she was hungry, but one look at the plate of delicious food in front of her changed her mind. She was going to be sick. There were buffalo stampeding in her stomach, and her belly would have made a nice drum, it was so taut.

"Hell's bells," she muttered. "I give up." She grabbed an unbuttered biscuit and shoved the plate away, pulling her coffee cup over in front of her.

"Is that all you're going to eat?" Creed asked, setting his plate of food down at the place next to Cricket's.

"Mind your own cotton-picking business!"

"Cricket's feeling a little under the weather," Bay excused.

"Cricket's stomach is still full of whiskey," Sloan said with a laugh.

Cricket frowned at her sisters and then turned a sullen eye on Creed. "I'm not hungry," she grated out.

"Whatever you say, Brava," Creed murmured so softly only Cricket could hear him.

The table quieted as everyone concentrated on the business of eating.

The thing that struck Creed, now that he'd met them all,

was how very different the three sisters were from each other. Their choice of clothing, perhaps, told the story better than words. Bay wore the purple chintz long-sleeved day dress of a proper plantation owner's daughter. Sloan wore a plaid gingham shirt with a tan linsey waistcoat and dark-brown fitted osnaburg trousers tucked into knee-high black Wellington boots, a working-man's costume, to be sure. Cricket wore the skin of a wild animal.

As for their personalities, unquestionably, Bay was the most timid of the three. He already knew she was kind-hearted, unsure, and unsatisfied with herself. On the other hand, Sloan exuded self-confidence. You could tell a lot about people from their handshakes, and based strictly on Sloan's grip, Creed thought she possessed a maturity, a sense of who she was and what she wanted from life, that seemed lacking in Cricket. Cricket was arrogant as a man, spoiled and willful as a child, and totally unconscious of her femininity.

Yet they were all three beautiful women. Perhaps Bay was the most distinctive, Creed thought, with those violet eyes, and that hair that, like her father's, was red and brown and bronze all at the same time. She was tall and still growing. A promise of perfection if he'd ever seen one. Sloan should have seemed petite next to her two statuesque sisters, but again, her presence and confidence made her seem taller than she was. Her dark, chocolate-brown eyes offered intelligence and humor, and the waist-length sable hair she'd captured with a black ribbon at the base of her neck was indeed a crowning glory. As for Cricket, her smoky gray eyes promised nothing but trouble, and that lustrous auburn braid—he wanted to unravel it and run his fingers through it, have it drift across his naked body, have it tease him, tittilate him, taunt him. And she wanted nothing to do with him, or any man, so it seemed.

"This is a nice place you've got here," Creed said, finally breaking the silence that had reigned at the table.

"Bay's responsible for the look of the house," Rip replied. "When she got back from Boston a year ago she brought a lot of fancy ideas with her. I let her have a free hand, and what you see is the result."

"I've been wondering," Sloan asked, "how you found those mares so fast."

"I happened across a band of Comanches camped in a cedar brake. They had the mares hobbled nearby."

"How'd you know they belonged to us?"

"I didn't, but they weren't Spanish ponies, and they weren't Indian mounts, either. I figured if I could get them back from the Comanches the owner would turn up sooner or later to claim them."

Sloan shook her head. "You took a pretty big chance. You could've gotten killed."

"I enjoyed the challenge."

"You're lucky you got away with your hair."

"Luck doesn't help much where the Comanches are concerned," Creed said.

Creed had stared at Cricket when he spoke and she knew he was referring to her drunken ride back to Three Oaks. She opened her mouth to retort but never got a chance because Bay asked, "What made you become a Ranger?"

"It's a job," Creed answered. "You provide your own gear and ammunition, but it pays thirty-seven fifty a month, and you get to fight outlaws and Mexicans and Comanches. How could I pass it up?"

"You don't make it sound like such a good deal," Sloan said with a laugh.

"I like to fight," Creed replied quietly. "I'm good at it."

Cricket shivered at the ruthlessness in Creed's eyes. She remembered the scars she'd seen on his body. Oh, yes, he'd fought before. She realized now how careful he must have been of his strength when he'd wrestled with her. Well, she hadn't asked him to be careful!

"It sounds like Jack Hays sent the right man to catch those horse thieves, all right," Rip said. "By the way, was there any news in San Antonio about whether the Mexican government is cooking up another plot to invade Texas?"

"When aren't they plotting?" Creed replied.

Cricket watched as Creed's glance darted quickly from Rip to Sloan before he added, "There's been nothing definite since that letter we intercepted from Manuel Flores last year, but the Rangers are on the lookout for any suspicious activities."

"I'm glad to hear someone's keeping a close eye on those Mexican bastards," Rip said.

"We do what we can," Creed said. "Sometimes I wonder if it will be enough."

There was a silence at the table as they considered Creed's words.

Cricket remembered the cold and hunger they'd all endured four years ago when they'd fled Three Oaks in a panicked escape from Santa Anna's ravaging army. It was generally understood that continued Texas independence from Mexico was a matter of constant vigilance by the Texas Rangers and instant reaction to any threat of invasion.

It had fallen on the Rangers to protect the four-year-old Republic for the simple reason there wasn't anybody else to do the job. Because of a treaty signed with Mexico in 1819, the United States had refused political recognition—and thus military support—to the new Republic of Texas. And although Texas President Mirabeau Buonaparte Lamar had repeatedly asked, no Yankee bankers would loan the bankrupt Texas government money to pay a regular army to protect itself.

Abandoned to its fate by the mighty mother of its emigrants, with no army of its own, and no money in its treasury with which to pay one, the threat of invasion by another pillaging Mexican army was frightening to contemplate. So Texas had printed her own money, enough to pay an army of irregulars—the Texas Rangers. The Rangers had no uniforms and were responsible only unto themselves, but they were known for their ferocity against, and their merciless contempt of, the Mexicans who threatened the new sovereign nation. The small, elite force of Rangers had become the real border between Mexico and the Republic of Texas.

Of course, while they waited for the sleeping threat of

Mexico to wake, the Rangers provided the law and order needed by the new land. Thus planters like Rip Stewart were able to call upon the Rangers to provide the same fierce aggressiveness against Comanches and outlaws that the army of irregulars promised to use on the Mexicans should they ever attempt to cross the Rio Grande again.

"I don't doubt the Rangers have the mettle to handle the Mexicans," Rip said, breaking Cricket's reverie. "What I want to know is how you're planning to stop these horse-thieving Comanche raids on Three Oaks."

"The Indians stealing your stock are probably Comanches, but they might be Apaches or Tonkawas letting the Comanches take the blame. I'll wait for the thieves to come, and then I'll follow and make an example of them. After that, you shouldn't be troubled."

There was no question in Cricket's mind that the tactics he'd employ would add to the reputation the Rangers had earned as *Los Diablos Tejanos,* The Texas Devils.

"I don't really care what methods you use. So long as they work," Rip said. "By the way, you're welcome to stay in the bachelors' quarters out back of the house."

Cricket wasn't sure she wanted Creed staying that close to the house. He'd be able to see every move she made. It was obvious the same thing had occurred to Creed when he smiled at her and said, "I'm much obliged."

"Good. Then you'll be around to join us for the *fandango* celebration next week."

"Who's having a *fandango?*" Creed asked.

"Señor Juan Carlos Guerrero. His vaqueros have finished their roundup and he's celebrating with a barbeque and a *días de toros*—that's the Spanish version of fancy riding and roping contests. He's invited most of the planters hereabouts and their families, and arranged to have a dance in the evening to give the ladies a chance to dress up."

"I didn't think the Texans around here got along with the *tejanos,* the Texas-Mexicans," Creed said.

"Señor Guerrero isn't Mexican," Rip replied. "His ancestors were Castilian Spanish, and his family has lived in Texas for over a hundred years. I understand things went hard for him after the Mexicans ousted the Spaniards and gained control of Texas. When the chance presented itself he decided he was better off siding with us Anglos against the Mexican government. In fact, his son fought for Texas independence with Sam Houston at the Battle of San Jacinto—his elder son, Cruz, that is. Sometimes I think Juan Carlos wonders if he made the right choice. Seems he's had to fight with us Texans as much as he did with the Mexicans to keep what's his," Rip finished with a chuckle.

"I'd enjoy attending Señor Guerrero's *fandango*," Creed said, "If you're sure he won't mind."

"He won't mind at all. You'll be my guest," Rip replied.

"Would you excuse me, please?" Bay asked. "I need to send out that order for oak to repair the gin."

Bay didn't wait for a response, merely rose and left the room, followed almost immediately by Sloan who said, "There's some kind of fever that's been plaguing the hoe hands. I want to see if it looks like something a doctor should treat or whether that African witch woman we bought off Sam Kuykendall last month can handle it."

Cricket slurped the last of her coffee and announced, "I'm going back to bed. Call me for supper." Then she too was gone.

Creed was still staring after her in amazement when Rip asked, "Well, what do you think of my daughters?"

"I don't think I've ever come across girls quite like them before," Creed admitted honestly, if a little cautiously.

"Sloan will own this plantation one day. I've trained her well, and she knows what to do to make it prosper. I've also made sure Bay has all the schooling she needs to be a proper helpmate for her sister."

"And Cricket?" Creed asked.

Rip sat back and smiled. "She marries Cruz Guerrero. On the day Juan Carlos dies, Cruz inherits everything—an empire—thousands of hectares of land, and the largest herd of Spanish longhorn cattle in Texas. Cricket will be the wife of a very rich and powerful man."

"Why would Señor Guerrero agree to let his heir marry

Cricket when you've just told me it's Sloan who'll inherit
Three Oaks?"

Rip smiled. "Gold. He needs gold. He's rich in land and
cattle, but since the War for Independence trade with the
United States has tightened up, and of course there's no
more trade with Mexico. Naturally, we all expect things to
ease off as soon as the United States recognizes Texas as a
sovereign nation, but that could take years. Juan Carlos
doesn't want to wait. I'm more than happy to help him out."

"For a price."

"For a price," Rip agreed.

Everything inside Creed was wound into a knot. Even
though a marriage to join two wealthy families wasn't
unusual, Creed found this one particularly distasteful. Did
Cricket know Rip's plans for her? It hardly seemed likely,
given her confession of this morning. And what did Cruz
Guerrero know of Cricket? Did he know she drank? Did he
know she could wrestle, and ride like an Indian? Did he
know the feel of her soft lips and the silky touch of her
auburn hair? That thought reminded him of Cricket's
aversion to being kissed by a man. How was Cruz Guerrero
going to cope with that? Would he be considerate of her
fears? Would he be gentle with her?

Creed tried to put a stop to the feelings tearing at his gut,
but his concern grew until he couldn't hold his tongue.

"What does Guerrero's son think of having a wife like
Cricket?"

Rip pursed his lips. "He doesn't know yet. Juan Carlos
and I are still working out the details."

"And what does Cricket think of this marriage?"

For a moment Rip seemed uneasy, his eyes shifting away,
but he straightened and brought his steely gaze to bear on
Creed. "Cricket isn't privy to these plans, and I don't intend
she should be until things are settled. Then she'll do as she's
told. I don't intend to let anything interfere with her future
as the wife of a Spanish *hacendado.*"

It was obvious to Creed from Rip's last comment that the
planter hadn't been as blind to what had happened between

his daughter and the Ranger in the barn as he'd appeared at the time. Apparently Rip considered him a threat to be dealt with immediately. And, despite the cries for attention from his churning emotions, Creed knew he would heed Rip's warning, at least for the time being. Because he had reasons for being on Three Oaks that Rip Stewart knew nothing about.

The talk of Mexican plots to invade Texas had become more than just talk. Word had come to Ranger Captain Jack Hays in San Antonio that someone in Rip Stewart's household was working with a band of Texas-Mexican revolutionaries. It was also rumored that someone in the Guerrero family led the band of traitors. Until Creed had determined the truth of those accusations he couldn't afford to make matters any more complicated than they already were by getting involved with Creighton Stewart.

"I'm going to take a ride around Three Oaks," Creed said. "I want to scout the terrain, see from which direction the horse thieves are most likely to attack."

"By all means. Make yourself at home," Rip encouraged.

At the door Creed stopped and turned back to Rip. "I don't expect to be back for supper. Give my regrets to . . . your daughters."

Creed hurried from the elegant dining room. He was late for his appointment with the Ranger spy in San Felipe de Austin who was watching the Guerrero family. And he very much wanted to seek out an old Comanche friend if there was still time before he returned for his first night under a roof at Three Oaks.

CHAPTER 5

R ISE AND SHINE, lazybones!"

Cricket rolled over onto her back, pulling the feather pillow with her, holding it so it covered her face. "Go away."

Sloan bounced down onto Cricket's bed. "You've already missed dinner and you're liable to miss supper too if you don't get up."

"I'm not hungry."

"Don't worry. The Ranger won't be here to see you turning green again. Rip said Creed had business and won't be joining us."

"Best news I've had all day," Cricket muttered.

"You never cared before who joined us at the table."

"Nobody else ever called me a 'brat in buckskins.'"

Sloan grinned. "A *brat* in *buckskins?* Well, what did you call him?"

"Whose side are you on, anyway?" Cricket mumbled from under the pillow.

Sloan laughed. "Come on. What did you call him?"

"It doesn't bear repeating."

"I thought not." Sloan pulled the pillow off Cricket's head so she could see her sister's glowering face. "Are you feeling any better?"

63

"Not a whole lot." Cricket snatched the pillow back and tucked it under her head. She'd been in bed most of the day, but she hadn't been sleeping, she'd been thinking. Never once, the whole time, had her thoughts strayed very far from Jarrett Creed. "He kissed me, you know."

"The Ranger? Kissed you? When? Did you like it?"

Sloan asked questions like a small dog worried a bone. She didn't give up until the bone cracked and gave up its marrow. Since Cricket willingly shared everything with Sloan anyway, she soon found herself recounting the events of the morning.

". . . there I was lying in the straw beneath him waiting for something to happen . . . but nothing did."

"Nothing at all?" Sloan asked.

"Nothing. Except . . . I guess I did get goosebumps all over when his knuckles brushed my cheek. And when he put his lips on mine . . . it was scary . . . like I was on the edge of a cliff and I was about to fall off. . . ."

"So you backed away from the feelings, where you were safe."

"I didn't back away from anything! There was nothing to back away from! Anyway, whatever I would have felt got cut off when Rip showed up in the barn."

"I'll bet that was an interesting moment," Sloan said with a grin.

Cricket grinned back. "It was worth the balling-out I got from Rip to see the Ranger's face. He was so . . . so confused."

"You felt sorry for him?"

"Hardly. He deserved it after that stunt he pulled. Imagine not telling me he was a Texas Ranger!"

"Are you going to let him kiss you again?"

"I don't see any reason why I should."

"You might change your mind about kissing if you gave it another chance. Who knows? This Ranger might be the right man for you and he might not. A man is sort of like a pair of new fur boots. Some fit, and feel right, and some don't."

"That makes no sense to me."

"Think about it. You could make a pair of warm winter boots from a lot of different furs—beaver, rabbit, fox, wolf, bear . . . They'd all feel nice, but you'd probably enjoy the feel of some of those furs more than others. I'd be willing to bet you'd like one of those furs even better than all the rest. Boots from that special fur would make you feel all shivery when you slipped into them and you'd want to wear them all the time if you could. It's the same with a man. Some are more pleasing to touch—and to be touched by—than others. With a man you like a lot, the feeling can be quite pleasurable indeed."

Cricket sat silently for a moment before she said, "I don't need any new boots."

Sloan shook her head. "You're missing the whole point."

"No, I'm not. I'm not missing anything—least of all kissing some man."

"How do you know until you've really given it a fair chance?" Sloan demanded. "You might enjoy it!"

"What makes you such a know-it-all?"

"I . . . I've been . . . on occasion I've—"

"You've been kissed?!"

"Once or twice," Sloan admitted reluctantly.

"How come you never told me about it? Who was it? When did it happen?"

"I'm sorry I said anything! Look, Cricket, let's drop the subject. I guess you're right. This isn't something that's going to make any difference to you anyway—unless you've changed your mind and decided you *do* want to get married some day."

"No chance of that! As a matter of fact, that reminds me of something Bay and I talked about yesterday. She thinks Rip is planning to choose husbands for the three of us— maybe sometime soon."

"He's what?! I've got my own plans for . . ."

"My thoughts exactly," Cricket said, agreeing with her sister's outraged indignation. "I was going to talk to Rip about it last night but I fell asleep, and I missed my chance again this morning to set him straight. I'm like you. I've got my own plans for . . ." Then Cricket realized the significance of the words Sloan had left hanging. "What plans have you got, Sloan?"

"Plans for who I'm going to marry," Sloan admitted.

"This is a little sudden, isn't it?" Cricket couldn't control the sharpness in her tone, which resulted from a combination of fear and resentment. Sloan was the person she was closest to in the whole world. If Sloan married there was no doubt in Cricket's mind that their closeness would give way to her sister's relationship with her husband; and she deeply resented the fact that Sloan could have gotten so far as to make marriage plans without Cricket even knowing that her sister had been kissed. Cricket's jutting jaw spoke wordlessly of her need for an explanation.

"I've been seeing a man, Cricket." Sloan braced for the outburst she suspected was coming and added, "Señor Guerrero's younger son, Antonio."

It wouldn't have mattered what man Sloan named. Cricket was prepared to dislike whoever it was. But Sloan's announcement was like pouring whiskey on a raw wound.

"A Mexican? You're kissing one of those murdering Mexican bastards? Have you forgotten the slaughter at the Alamo? Have you forgotten all those horrible deaths at Goliad?"

"Tonio's not a Mexican! You heard what Rip said at breakfast. The Guerreros are Spaniards, descended from Spanish royalty. They hate the Mexicans as much as we do! They weren't any happier with Mexican sovereignty over Texas than we were. They were asked to pay the same unfair taxes. They were victims of the same tyrannical military rule forced down our throats by the Mexican government. Cruz even fought with Sam Houston's army. The Guerreros are as much Texans as we are! And I'm going to marry Tonio!"

"Rip won't allow it!"

"Rip won't have any say in the matter!"

The two sisters fell silent, hiding their fears behind the stoic facade they'd learned from Rip.

Cricket knew Sloan well enough to believe that if she'd

made up her mind to marry Antonio Guerrero she would do it.

Sloan knew Rip well enough to believe that if he intended to arrange her marriage to someone else, he would do it.

That was why Sloan needed Cricket's help to keep her relationship with Antonio Guerrero a secret. She needed time to convince Rip she should marry Tonio. But from the look on Cricket's face, Sloan was very much afraid that for the first time her youngest sister was going to take Rip's side against her.

"Cricket, I want you to promise not to say anything about this to Rip."

"It isn't going to matter what I say, Sloan. Rip isn't going to let you marry Antonio Guerrero . . . even if he is descended from royalty."

"You don't know that, Cricket. He's already doing some business with Señor Guerrero. Rip and Juan Carlos spent the whole day together yesterday at the Guerrero hacienda."

"Business is one thing. Marriage is another."

"Promise me, Cricket."

Cricket looked away from Sloan's determined gaze. She knew she was going to agree with Sloan's plea because she loved her sister. But Cricket struggled to find comfortable reason in Sloan's request.

"How did you meet him, Sloan?"

"Remember when I had to pick up those supplies in San Antonio earlier this spring?"

"You met him in San Antonio? What was he doing there?"

"He was there on some business for his father. We met in the hotel dining room. There were no more tables and he asked to sit with me. What could I say? He was so . . . so handsome . . . so dashing . . . He smiled at me and I couldn't see anything or anyone else in the room."

"So you've been meeting him since then?"

"Whenever we can. Wherever we can."

Cricket was trying to digest the enormity of what Sloan had admitted about her relationship with Antonio Guerrero. But it was a lot to swallow in such a short time, and she was pretty much choking on it. "I suppose you must care a lot about this man."

"I love him, Cricket. I want to have his children."

Cricket swallowed over the lump in her throat. "Has he asked you to marry him?"

Sloan looked uncertain. "I'm sure he will. He hasn't said anything yet, but that's only because his family isn't going to be any happier about our being together than Rip. I'm afraid they have their own prejudices against Anglos to overcome. And then, they may have heard stories about us . . ."

Cricket knew the kinds of stories that had circulated about "Rip's girls." It would take an open-minded person to look behind those stories to the truth. Sure "Rip's girls" were different, but anybody who looked twice would see they were special. Cricket knew that whatever Sloan strived to be, she could be. And there was no doubt in her mind that Sloan could meet or exceed any standards Señor Guerrero set for his younger son's wife.

"Are you going to see Tonio at the Guerrero's *fandango?*" she asked Sloan.

"I don't know. We have to be very careful not to be seen together until we can figure out a way to get Rip and Juan Carlos's approval. If Tonio sends word where we can meet privately, I'll go to him."

Cricket shook her head in disbelief at Sloan's plans for a clandestine meeting with the man she loved and who supposedly loved her. If he loved her so much, why were they sneaking around behind both fathers' backs?

"Will you introduce me to Tonio?"

Sloan's face was a picture of indecision. "I don't think that would be a good idea, Cricket."

"Why not?"

"He . . . we . . . I promised I wouldn't say anything to anyone about our relationship. If I introduce you to him he'd know I've broken that promise."

"But I'm your sister! You always tell me everything."

Sloan shook her head. "Not everything, Cricket. I haven't always told you everything."

"What? What haven't you told me?"

Sloans lips thinned to a firm line of intransigence.

"Never mind," Cricket snapped. "Keep your secrets. I don't care." Cricket threw the covers off and grabbed her rumpled buckskin trousers from the floor, yanking them on.

Cricket was shaking, seething with hurt. It wasn't only Sloan's deception. Everything seemed so mixed-up lately. First Rip suggesting he'd find her a husband, when she thought he understood why she was never getting married. Then the Ranger showing up, treating her like a woman, arousing her curiosity about kissing and touching and leaving it unsatisfied. Finally, Sloan confessing she was in love and that she'd kept that and other as yet undisclosed secrets from Cricket.

Cricket yanked her shirt down over her head as she stepped through the bedroom door.

"Where are you going, Cricket?"

Cricket turned back to Sloan. "That's none of your business. I don't have to tell you everything, either."

Sloan flinched. "What do you want me to tell Rip?"

"I don't care what you tell him. Make something up. You must have been doing that for a while anyway."

"Cricket—"

Sloan stared at the empty doorway for a moment before she rubbed her callused palm across her sweat-bedaubed forehead. It was all getting so complicated. She would have to talk with Tonio at the *fandango.* She couldn't go on lying to her family. It wasn't what she would have chosen to do in the first place, but Tonio had convinced her of the necessity for it. She loved him so much she would have done anything he asked—lied, stolen, cheated. She smiled bitterly. She, who would have taken a beating from Rip before bending to his will, had been ready to do anything Tonio asked in the name of love. But exactly how far was she willing to go? Sloan slumped back on Cricket's bed and crossed her arms over her eyes. God help her. She just didn't know.

Miles away that same question was being pondered, because it appeared from all the available evidence that

Sloan Stewart was helping Antonio Guerrero plot the overthrow of the Republic of Texas.

"I don't know, Luke," Creed said. "It's hard to believe Sloan Stewart is the courier for Antonio's letters to the Mexican government. Are you sure it was her?"

"I'm not the only one who saw her carry the messages," the youthful Texas Ranger replied.

"But why? Why would she do it? Her father's the richest planter in the Republic. He's told me she'll inherit Three Oaks when he dies. What does she have to gain if the Mexicans regain control of Texas? It doesn't make sense."

"For that matter, it doesn't make sense for Antonio, either," Luke said. "Unless his father is involved as well. There's a lot of money to be made selling land in Texas—and collecting taxes, too, for that matter. And Juan Carlos has the manpower to back him up. He's probably got more vaqueros working that cattle empire of his than we've got Texas Rangers to patrol the border."

Creed rubbed the back of his neck to ease the tension there. "You may be closer to the truth than you know. Rip suggested this morning that Juan Carlos may not be happy with his decision to side with the Texans against the Mexicans in thirty-six. Seems he's had some problems with Anglos grabbing at what's his. At least it looks like the information Captain Hays got from that informant was on the mark. There's something going on here, and I intend to get to the bottom of it. I just can't picture Sloan Stewart working with Antonio Guerrero."

"Heaven help Sloan if she is a part of that band of traitors," Luke said. "The planters around here aren't likely to be sympathetic just because she's a woman. Too many of them lost friends and relatives to Mexican musketballs and bloody bayonets during the war."

Creed knew Luke spoke the truth. Last year, when the Rangers had discovered the Mexican government's plan to invade Texas from the south with a large army while the Cherokee Indians kept the Texans busy with brush fights to the north, the citizens of Texas had demanded and gotten swift and sure retaliation against the Cherokees. But President Mirabeau Lamar was taking no more chances. Ranger Captain Jack Hays had orders to investigate any suspicious activities that might be connected to another Mexican plan to invade Texas. And so Jarrett Creed had been assigned to follow Sloan Stewart and discover the truth of the accusations against her.

Creed didn't want to think Sloan was guilty, but the evidence against her was damning. Captain Hays trusted him to find out the truth, and Creed hadn't failed on a mission yet. It was all the more reason he had no business getting involved with Creighton Stewart. What would she think of him when he arrested her sister for treason?

"Thinking about the girl again?" Luke asked.

"Hmmm?"

"That frown on your face . . . I thought maybe you were thinking about the girl again."

Creed snorted. *Still* thinking about the girl would be more accurate, but he didn't care to admit that to the young man who sat on the ground across from him. Luke had a way of knowing exactly what you were thinking. While that perception was part of what made the young man such a good Texas Ranger, it was disconcerting for Creed to be on the receiving end of it.

"She got under your skin, huh?"

"I never said that," Creed protested.

"You didn't have to. It shows."

Creed swore under his breath. "I suppose you could have handled the situation better."

"Not better. Different."

"How different?"

"I'd have bedded her when I had the chance. Then I wouldn't have had to wonder."

"Wonder what?"

"What I was missing," Luke said with a grin.

Creed chuckled despite his irritation. "According to my sources you haven't missed anything wearing a skirt in San Antonio."

Luke shrugged. It was the gesture of a much older, almost world-weary man. "I like women. They like me. Why not please each other?"

Creed started to argue, but shut his mouth. In all the time they'd spent together over the past year Creed had learned little more about Luke Summers than the information Captain Hays had given him the day he'd assigned Luke to Creed's command.

"He looks too young to be a Ranger," Creed had protested that first morning when he'd seen Luke up close through the window of Hays's office.

"He's lived his share of life," Hays had responded. "He's a dead shot with a Patterson. He can ride any horse you stand under him. And he uses a rope like a third arm. Never saw a woman he didn't love or a woman who didn't love him. Never heard of him gettin' riled either, 'cept for once, oh, 'bout a year ago."

"What happened?"

"Man called him a bastard. Called his ma a two-bit whore."

"Was it true?"

"Don't know. He shot the sonofabitch dead."

Luke had proved the truth of every kind word Jack Hays had said about him that day. Creed had never seen Luke riled. But then, he'd never heard the dead man's accusations repeated, either. The young man had proved his merit as a Ranger, and Creed had been willing to let Luke keep his secrets to himself. Creed brought his attention back to the business at hand.

"Who's our contact in the rebel camp?" he asked the young Ranger.

"Teddy Perkins made friends with some of Antonio's vaqueros. Haven't seen him for two days, so I guess he's gone with them to their hideaway. I'm sure once he can get some word to us where they are, he'll let us know. Are you going to the Guerreros' *fandango?*"

"I've been invited. Guess I will."

"Maybe you can catch Sloan Stewart and Antonio Guerrero together. I'd give a lot to know whether the whole Guerrero family's involved," Luke said.

"Teddy should be some help finding that out. You hang around at the rendezvous and wait for him to show up. I've got someone else I'm going to talk with who may be able to give us some information."

"You planning to meet with that half-breed?"

Creed tensed at the harshness in Luke's voice. Luke hadn't even pretended to understand how Creed could swear a Ranger oath to protect the citizens of the Republic from the threat of Comanche attacks and still have one of the fierce savages for a friend.

"Whatever else he is, Long Quiet is my friend," he said, to make his position plain to Luke. "Remember that when you pin a label on him."

"He lives as a Comanche, doesn't he," Luke persisted. "He makes his home amongst those Red Devils, doesn't he?"

"Yes, he does."

"And you trust him not to lift your hair?"

"I'd trust him with my life. He'll be working with us some, so I suggest if you have any problems with that you air them now."

Luke raked his hand through his shoulder-length hair. "The Comanches killed my ma."

Creed frowned. "I'm sorry, Luke."

"No need to be sorry. After I thought about it a while I figured they did me a favor."

"What?"

"If they hadn't killed her I'd have had to do it myself."

"You want to explain that?"

"No. I sure as hell don't. Go on and see your Comanche friend, Creed. If you trust Long Quiet, I'll work with him. Don't worry about me."

Creed didn't press the young Ranger. He knew too many men like Luke, with problems that wore on them like hair shirts. As he mounted his horse and rode away from the troubled young man, Creed was reminded of his own painful past. The Texas frontier wasn't kind. It wasn't even merciful. If you survived it was because you didn't make mistakes. You kept your gun handy. You never rode far from water. You treated your horse like family. And you didn't trust strangers.

Luke was right to be careful of Long Quiet. The "half-breed" was a dangerous man. Creed ought to know. He and Long Quiet had taken enough scalps together to decorate two Comanche war shields.

CHAPTER 6

CREED ARRIVED AT the spot where he'd agreed to meet Long Quiet at dusk. He searched the faces of the Comanche warriors huddled around the campfire at the edge of the slow-moving stream, but didn't find the one he sought.

"Your friend is not here, Wolf."

The venomous voice sliced through the dusky light, piercing Creed's consciousness.

"We meet again, Tall Bear. It's been a long time." The Comanche words flowed easily from Creed. He waited to see whether Tall Bear still bore the animosity that had characterized their relationship. Their rivalry had begun long ago when he was a boy of eight and he and his mother had first arrived among the Penateka band of Comanches as captives.

From the beginning, Creed's adoptive father, Crooked Trail, had left him to the mercy of the other Indian youths. Only one boy, Long Quiet, who understood what it meant to be preyed upon, had befriended him. Together, he and Long Quiet had stood against the others and defeated them.

Long Quiet wasn't here tonight, but several of those they'd defeated were. Over the years Creed had spent among them, his peers had come to respect his prowess as a fierce warrior and a cunning horse thief, and no longer challenged him. Only Tall Bear had never let his hatred of the white boy die. But Creed conceded there was good reason for that.

Tall Bear remained squatted where he was, and did not rise to greet the man who had been husband to Summer Wind, thinking *I will do him no honor who stole from me the woman I loved, and then abandoned her.*

"Hihites. Sit, Wolf. Tell us why you have come among us," one of the other Comanches said, attempting to allay the insult to Creed.

Creed returned the Comanche greeting and dropped cross-legged to the ground. The familiar, pungent odor of bear grease and buffalo wool embraced him, though the Indians did not. "I came seeking my friend, Long Quiet."

"He has not returned from hunting," Two Foxes said.

"Have the buffalo strayed that you must hunt so many suns from the land of the Penateka?" Creed asked.

"This land is best for what we're hunting," Tall Bear replied.

"And what is that?"

"The scalp of the White-eyes."

Creed hid his surprise at Tall Bear's response.

"All Comanches must greet the treachery of the white man with lances and arrows," Tall Bear continued as he rose.

"What treachery?" Creed demanded, leaping up to confront him.

Two Foxes felt the bristling tension between the two men and intervened to prevent one from attacking the other. "Muk-war-rah, the Spirit Talker, traveled to San Antonio de Béxar, to talk with the White-eyes, to bargain for the release of white captives in exchange for blankets and food. He went into the Council House of the White-eyes, along with twelve chiefs of the Comanche nation, but they were ambushed, and all were killed. Then the White-eyes attacked the Comanche women and children camped nearby. Many are dead."

Creed's chest constricted until he could hardly breathe.

He wondered who could've been so stupid as to order such an attack. "How many were killed all together?"

"Maybe thirty. Maybe forty."

Creed never blinked an eye, but inwardly he cursed whatever idiot was responsible for the massacre. That number of dead Indians was more than enough to start a war between the white man and the Comanches, and certainly enough for the Comanches to seek white scalps for revenge. It was hard to believe a slaughter of that magnitude could occur right in the middle of San Antonio. "Has there been any reason given for the white man's actions?"

"All within the Council House were killed. We have heard nothing."

"Would it not be better to wait until an explanation can be made before attacking innocent white men?" Creed questioned.

Another of the Indians rose from beside the campfire and demanded, "What excuse will serve when the Comanche came to the White-eyes under a flag of truce?"

"What?"

Two more Comanches joined the first, so Creed was surrounded by a semicircle of angry Indians crying, *"Pei-da tabeboh!"*—"Death to the white man!"—a promise of the bloody justice they intended to extract from the deceitful White-eyes.

Tall Bear crossed his arms, his shoulder muscles rippling beneath buckskin as he did so. "I expected you to ask pardon for the soldiers who killed The People. Your white blood speaks loudly and drowns out the Comanche in you. But then, that has long been true. You made your choice when you left . . . us."

Tall Bear couldn't name Summer Wind aloud, but Creed knew it was their rivalry over the Indian maiden that had caused the greatest conflict between them. Creed had known Tall Bear loved Summer Wind and wanted her for his wife, so when he'd stolen enough ponies he'd presented them to Summer Wind's father and requested the maiden simply to thwart Tall Bear. He'd taken Summer Wind as his wife without loving her, but he'd discovered, to his surprise, that Summer Wind loved him, and in a very short time he'd returned that love.

Tall Bear had never forgiven Wolf for buying Summer Wind from under his nose. But no one else had condemned him. Among the Comanches only the strongest survived and took mates. Wolf had been the stealthier horse thief. He had earned the right to have Summer Wind.

The boy, Jarrett Creed, had thrived among the savage Comanches, all right. But the young man, Wolf, had never been truly happy living among The People, The True Human Beings, until he'd fallen in love with Summer Wind. She was the reason he'd stayed when he was free to go. It was only a quirk of fate, *and fatherly love,* he thought cynically, that had taken him away from Summer Wind, and turned his life back to the path of the *tabeboh,* the white man.

He'd been among the Comanches for nine years, from his eighth to his seventeenth birthday, before Simon Creed found his son one day, quite by accident. Creed had made a habit of going off by himself to hunt, and Summer Wind sometimes accompanied him to dress the kill. Simon Creed had come upon them unexpectedly, and it was a miracle that neither killed the other before they recognized themselves as father and son.

"Jarrett! Son!"

Creed hadn't said anything for a moment, just stared dispassionately. Then he'd responded, "I am Wolf, of the Penateka. My *ap'* is Crooked Trail. I am not your *tua."*

"The hell you say! The Comanches stole you from me, boy. You're my son, all right! Where's your mother?"

"The woman who bore me is *paraibo,* chief wife, to Buffalo Man, a war chief of the Quohadi."

He'd watched Simon Creed's face blanch white, and then flush red with rage. "I suppose every one of those goddamned Red Devils raped her first!"

"It is the way of The People to rape women captives," he'd replied matter-of-factly.

"Who is that with you?" Simon asked, finally acknowledging the young woman who rode beside Creed.

He'd smiled proudly. "This is my wife, Summer Wind, soon to be mother of my child."

"Your wife!" Simon Creed observed the very pregnant woman with disgust and disbelief. "No son of mine is going to sire a bastard half-breed brat." Then, Simon had raised his musket to shoot Summer Wind.

Creed had responded instantly, an arrow nocked in his bow in the time it had taken Simon to aim. "You will be dead before the sound of your bullet echoes in the wind," he'd promised.

His father had believed him, but Creed had inadvertently given Simon a weapon against him much better than a gun. "I don't care whether you shoot me or not," Simon had said. "But if you want your squaw and her brat to live, you'll come along home with me."

"I will kill you and come back here again," Creed had replied.

It was then that Creed's older brother had spoken for the first time. "You'll have to kill me, too."

"Tom?"

"Why don't you come back with us, Jarrett? I've missed you."

Creed had missed Tom, too. As a child he'd shared his thoughts with Tom, who'd been a buffer between him and his father. Creed could have killed the *taceboh,* Simon Creed, and never looked back, but he could never have killed Tom.

So, he'd turned to Summer Wind and said in Comanche, "Go back to The People. Tell them I have gone to live among the White-eyes for a while. But I will return." Then he'd added, "Take good care of our child."

He'd ridden away with his white brother and his father, thinking he'd be gone for a few days, or a few weeks at most. They would see that he was no longer a *taceboh,* and they wouldn't wish for him to stay among them.

Simon and Tom took him to a cotton plantation on the Brazos River called Lion's Dare, which Simon had won from its owner as a wager on a horse race. It was Tom, though, who worked the land.

Creed had thought surely his father would feel the urge to roam and forget about his erstwhile Comanche-raised son. He hadn't counted on the old trapper's orneriness. Simon didn't like having Creed around, but he couldn't let him go, either. Simon had lost his wife, Mary, but the grizzled old man had his son back. At the same time, Simon couldn't help punishing Creed for what the Comanches had done to Mary.

"Your mother was soiled by those Comanches, boy. I could never let that woman back in my bed after she laid herself down beneath those filthy Comanche animals. That woman should've killed herself and spared me the knowledge of what she'd become."

"I am one of those filthy Comanche animals," Creed had said. And he'd seen in his father's eyes that, yes, he was. "I am not welcome here. I will leave."

"You try leavin', boy, and I'll hunt you down and kill that squaw of yours when I find you," Simon had threatened.

There were many things he was not, but Simon was an excellent hunter. So Creed had stayed a little longer. He allowed Tom to dress him in trousers and a shirt, but he wouldn't cut his hair, and he slept inside the house, even though he eschewed the feather bed for the floor.

Tom was a solace to him in those days when he thought he would go mad with the waiting.

"I must leave," he'd railed to Tom.

"He means what he says," Tom had cautioned. "Stay a little longer, Jarrett. I enjoy having you here. It's like old times. I know you're satisfied working the land, I can see it when you walk the fields. I understand how you're missing Summer Wind, because I've been in love myself. But if you love your wife you have to stay here to keep her safe."

The brotherly bond was strong, and Simon was an old man given to gasping spells. Creed convinced himself that Simon would surely die soon.

Creed had been gone five long months when Long Quiet finally tracked him down. It was a fervent reunion, albeit a quiet one, since Long Quiet had sneaked in through Creed's second story window.

"Hihites, Wolf. You have a son."

"And Summer Wind?"

"She is well."

Creed's joy had bordered on euphoria. He wanted to go home. And home was with Summer Wind, not at Lion's Dare. Long Quiet stayed secreted in the woods nearby, coming at night to keep Creed company, and making plans what to do about Simon so Creed could travel back to *Comancheri*a.

Then, one night, Simon caught the two youths together in the barn. Even though his black curls had been straightened with bear grease, Long Quiet's gray eyes proclaimed him white. Simon wasn't one to leave a white boy in the clutches of the goddamned Comanches. Simon had closed off the only escape and called his burly Negroes to subdue the two boys. The fight that followed was savage and bloody. Simon resorted to putting a bullethole in Long Quiet, and even at that, it took more than a few Negroes to hold the two boys down so Simon could chain them hand and foot like recalcitrant slaves.

"There's only one way to get the Comanche outta you boys, and that's to send you where there aren't any goddamned Red Devils for thousands of miles. If either of you causes any trouble, whatsoever, I'm going to round up every planter from one end of the Brazos to the other and wipe out every one of your 'People' I can find, starting with Jarrett's wife and bastard brat!"

Wolf and Long Quiet had looked at each other with wild eyes. Simon Creed made no idle threats. And while the *taboeh* were no match for a band of Comanche warriors on horseback, what would happen to the old men and women and the children if the *taboeh* raided a village while the warriors were gone? And so the two of them spent four long years in faraway Boston, being transformed into what the White-eyes thought were civilized men.

When they were finally graduated from school, Simon Creed granted them permission to return to Texas. Creed had spent four years hating his father. Simon had stolen his life as an Indian, and given him one as a White. He felt no pity when he returned to Lion's Dare and found Simon dying, a withered old man confined to his sickbed. The shell of humanity in the canopied four-poster was no threat to anyone.

"I did it for you, boy," Simon explained. "You wouldn't have been happy as a goddamned Indian. You're blood of my blood, good Tennessee stock. In a few years there won't be any more Comanches. They're savages, and savages can't survive when there's no more wilderness. One day you'll thank me for what I did." Simon coughed, and the Negress with him wiped the bloody phlegm from his lips.

Creed looked down upon his father and felt grief, but not for Simon. Never for Simon. The grief was for the years he'd lost and could never have back. He might have thanked his father, would have thanked him, because Creed had been as greedy for the knowledge he'd soaked up as the dry land for a spring rain. But what he'd gained wasn't worth the price he'd been forced to pay. The pain of four years away from his wife and child was more than he could forgive. He and Long Quiet slipped away from Lion's Dare and disappeared into *Comanchería*.

He was going home.

Why had he thought he would find things as he had left them? The rivers and winds were constantly shifting. The moon grew and diminished in its monthly orbit. Even the rolling prairies developed seams and cracks of age. Creed knew it was so. Why had he expected to find Summer Wind and a four-year-old son waiting for him? Because he did not think he could live the rest of his life without them. So he kept his hope tied tightly to his breast and went searching for them. What he found broke his heart. They had died of cholera the third year he'd been gone.

The white man's disease had taken many in the tribe, who had no natural immunity, but not his enemy, Tall Bear. "She hated you," Tall Bear had hissed at him. "Once, when the loneliness was too great, she gave herself to me. I took her willingly, and would have kept her for my own. But she said you would come back. She waited for you. She buried your son alone. In the end, as she lay dying, she wished you dead too, White-eyes."

The Comanche, Wolf, knew Tall Bear must be lying, but the white man, Jarrett Creed, feared he told the truth. He didn't belong here anymore. There was nothing left to keep him among the Comanches. He said goodbye to his friend, Long Quiet, and fled *Comanchería*. He would find a place in the white man's world. But not near Simon Creed. Nowhere near Simon Creed. He had no father. He was no man's son.

The sound of the Indians' angry voices brought Creed from his reverie.

These were no longer his people. He was a Texas Ranger, and they were his enemies. He'd chosen sides, and if a war came he knew where he'd have to fight. But because he knew a little of both worlds he could understand what made each one hate the other. If there was anything he could do to slow down this headlong rush to war, he was going to do it. He steeled himself to do battle, if necessary, with the man who'd been his lifelong foe.

Cricket couldn't believe her eyes. Jarrett Creed, the consummate Texas Ranger, was surrounded by Comanches brandishing lances. When she'd left Sloan an hour ago, Cricket had saddled Valor and gone riding so she could be alone to think. Little had she dreamed she'd discover a band of Comanches on Three Oaks—or that she'd find Jarrett Creed in such grave danger. Her stomach still didn't feel any too good from the whiskey she'd drunk the night before, and Creed's predicament set her insides churning again. How had the Ranger managed to get himself captured by Comanches?

If there had been more Indians she might have gone for help. If there had been fewer, she might have left the Ranger to fend for himself. But there were too many for Creed to fight alone, and few enough that together she and Creed might be able to make a fight of it.

Cricket reined her horse into the brush and angled him around behind Creed, closer to the Indian camp. She'd done some quiet tracking in the past, but it had never mattered quite so much before if she were discovered. This time the consequences of a mistake could be deadly. Cricket's palms were sweaty by the time she was close enough to dismount. Once on the ground, she planted each foot carefully as she moved through the undergrowth near the stream.

When she tried, Cricket could be very, very quiet. So it stopped her cold when her foot overturned a stone that rattled noisily. Her eyes shot to the Comanche camp. She thought she saw Creed turn toward the sound, but then the Indians distracted him again. She'd been fortunate that none of the Comanches had heard her. She moved more slowly. Her muscles ached from the tension by the time she got to a place where she thought she could do the most damage in the fastest time. She pulled her Pattersons from her belt and took a deep breath to shout a warning to Creed before she started shooting.

"Creeeeed, run!"

"No, Brava!"

As Cricket started to fire, Creed ran directly in front of her. Her first shot went wild as she raised her aim to avoid hitting him.

"Are you crazy? Get out of my way!"

Creed was upon her before she had the chance to fire again, as were a dozen or so furious Indians. Creed yanked her guns out of her hands and threw them away. Frightened by Creed's strange behavior, Cricket whistled shrilly for help.

The wolf and the stallion appeared from nowhere. Rogue attacked a shrieking Comanche, while Valor's hooves grazed another. Pandemonium ensued. The superstitious Indians hardly noticed the berserk stallion when it became clear the woman had summoned a golden-eyed gray wolf, the talisman of that fierce warrior whom they'd been threatening. Who knew what powerful magic he'd conjured?

Creed had Cricket by the shoulders and was shaking her. "Call off your animals!"

"We'll be killed!"

"Call them off!"

Why was he so angry? She'd saved his life. She noticed for the first time that the Comanches had fanned out in an awed circle around them, while Valor screamed his fury, rearing and pawing the air on one side of her and Rogue growled menacingly, sharp teeth bared, on the other. Creed looked deadly. She decided to obey him.

"It's okay," she said quietly. Valor snorted, and shook his head, but came down on all four hooves. Rogue covered his bared teeth, but his furred hackles remained upright and his yellow eyes watchful. Cricket reached out a hand on either side of her to soothe the agitated beasts.

Creed left her to check on the Indians who'd been attacked by the animals.

"They're more frightened than hurt," Creed said, returning to her side. "It's a good thing no one was seriously injured."

Cricket's indignation made her voice sharp. "What the hell's the matter with you? I saw you surrounded by Comanches brandishing lances and assumed you needed some help. Now you tell me it's a good thing no one was hurt!"

Creed lifted his hat and brushed a weary hand through his hair. Then he pulled the hat down firmly again and said, "I know these Comanches."

Cricket's jaw dropped and she jerked it shut again. Her lips pursed thoughtfully. *A Texas Ranger who was friends with the Comanches?* She met Creed's open look with suspicious eyes. He was supposedly here to keep the Comanches from stealing her father's horses. Wasn't this a little like letting the fox guard the chicken coop?

"Who is this woman?"

Creed was so totally absorbed in gauging Cricket's reaction he'd forgotten about the Comanches. Tall Bear's demand caught him unprepared, and he answered without thinking, "She's the daughter of the white man who owns this land."

Cricket's eyes rounded when she heard Creed answer in the Comanche tongue. Where had he learned their language?

A murderous look came into Tall Bear's eyes. Wolf had made fools of them all. He had used trickery to frighten them. But it would not work. He would see to that. "These are no spirit tokens of the Wolf!" he called to the other Comanches.

"But she commanded the beasts," one of the others protested.

Tall Bear sneered at their fear, making them ashamed. "She is merely a woman. There is no magic here. She will be the first to pay for the deaths of The People." He started toward Cricket, pulling his knife from its sheath at his waist. Creed's voice stopped him.

"No. She belongs to me."

Tall Bear turned and a malevolent grin lit his features. "That is good. We will even an old debt. You once took my woman from me. Now I will take yours from you."

Cricket could tell from the tension in Creed's shoulders that all was not right, and she worried about the wicked gleam in the cold eyes of the Comanche who'd started toward her with his knife drawn. She drew her own knife.

"I ought to let you try your luck," Creed muttered under his breath when he saw what she'd done. "You might just win at that." Instead he ordered, "Get on Valor, call your wolf, and get out of here while you still can."

"What about you?"

"I'm not in any danger here. Do as I say, and do it now."

"I can help," Cricket argued.

"Dammit, Brava, do as I say!"

At that moment Tall Bear lunged for Cricket. Creed caught Tall Bear's wrist in an iron grip just before the Comanche's knife blade reached Cricket's heart. The two men turned to face each other and the hatred of one for the other that had seethed for years beneath the surface finally bubbled through, as foul and fetid as a sun-rotted corpse.

The Indian was quick, and Creed had at least three bloody slashes in his flesh before Cricket had time to assimilate what had happened. The other Indians formed a circle around the combatants that excluded her, their guttural shouts inciting the two men to a killing frenzy. Creed had forgotten her. His eyes lit with a barbaric violence that made her shudder. Cricket could do nothing but stand and watch as Creed drew his knife to fight the Comanche.

She should have made good her escape then. No one would have stopped her. But she couldn't take her eyes off the life-and-death struggle taking place before her. The fight was noisy, riotous in fact. But it wasn't the whoops and cries of the circled Comanches that Cricket heard, it was the grunt from Creed as a knife blade seared his skin, his ragged breathing, the ominous moment of quiet when he tripped and fell and life-giving air was knocked from his lungs. Cricket couldn't tell whether he was winning or losing. In fact, the two men appeared surprisingly well matched.

Creed had discovered the same thing. Once he admitted the fight with Tall Bear was inevitable, Creed had settled down to enjoy it. His corded muscles responded when he called upon them, his quick reflexes saved him more than once. He had to find Tall Bear's weakness. And so he feinted and dodged, and even tripped once and fell, lying apparently helpless for several seconds. But Tall Bear didn't lunge in carelessly for the kill. He'd waited, somehow sensing the trap Creed had set.

Tall Bear's cunning increased Creed's cautiousness. It pleased him to find his enemy his equal. It was the Comanche way to admire the courage and resourcefulness of an adversary. He needed an edge to defeat his enemy, and he knew where to find it. Somewhere, deep within Creed, lurked a part of him he normally kept hidden, a part of him kept under control, a part of him as savage, as cruel, as barbaric as any Comanche. Creed set it free.

Cricket sensed the change in Creed immediately, but didn't know what had caused it. Her animals sensed it, too. Valor pawed the ground and shook his head. Rogue growled and bared his teeth.

More importantly, Tall Bear noticed the difference in his foe. He didn't know how the balance had shifted—he only knew it had. There was a confidence, a certainty of success that emanated from Wolf. Tall Bear responded to it by checking surreptitiously for his avenues of escape. He was surrounded by his friends, whom he led as war chief, urging him to victory. In retreat lay humiliation. He turned back to Wolf, his muscles tensed for action. He had fought the white boy, Jarrett Creed, and scarred him with his knife, but that was long ago. No frightened boy faced him now. He looked into the heartless eyes of a feral animal. He was trapped.

Creed's nostrils flared when he caught the scent of fear, and like a predator he began to stalk his prey. But a trapped animal fights more viciously than one who can flee, and the same was true of Tall Bear.

"I think I will give you another cut across your belly to match the other," Tall Bear taunted, "before I kill you."

"Come and try. I am waiting for you."

Creed's words sent a chill down Tall Bear's spine. If he hadn't been so unnerved he might have begun his death chant then. But fear kept him fighting.

Creed's lightning-quick strike caught Tall Bear by surprise, and two of the Comanche's fingers were cut off as the knife fell from his hand. When he reached down to retrieve his knife Creed tripped him and he fell heavily, the short fringes of grass crushed beneath his weight. Creed pressed his advantage and brought the sharpened tip of his knife to the hollow of Tall Bear's throat. When Tall Bear swallowed a trickle of blood flowed from the spot.

"Finish it," the Indian rasped.

The braves around them had fallen silent. Cricket held her breath for the moment the plunging knife would end the Comanche's life.

Creed savored his victory, the feral glint in his eyes shining brightly. He had vanquished his foe. The lifelong enmity that had existed between them would end now. He waited, rejoicing in Tall Bear's defeat, prolonging the anticipation of his enemy's death like a mountain lion toying with its prey before the kill. But he waited too long. The civilized man he'd become sent the savage back to its hiding place. The blood lust was gone. He could not kill a defenseless man.

"If you attack the white man," he warned Tall Bear, "I have sworn an oath to kill you. It cannot be wrong to wait until the truth about the Council House deaths is known. I give you your life in order to take this message back to The People." Creed rose and sheathed his knife. The hate in Tall Bear's eyes spoke volumes. The Indian owed Wolf his life, but did not thank him for it. Tall Bear would return to The People and deliver the message, but Creed knew he hadn't seen the last of him. Tall Bear confirmed his thoughts.

"I am bound to this task," he said. "But I will return. Enjoy your woman now, for the day will soon come when she will be mine."

Cricket watched in astonishment as the Comanches gathered their few belongings, mounted their ponies, and rode away.

"Why didn't you kill him? He would have killed you if he'd had the chance."

Creed barked a harsh laugh. "Because I'm not a savage. Haven't you noticed?"

Cricket glanced into his eyes and shivered. He was not a savage, but he wasn't far from it. That knowledge excited rather than frightened her. She liked wild things. She dared to defy them, challenged and confronted them. She had even, in some cases, tamed them to her hand. It was the thrill of constant danger, the unpredictability of the brutes that lured her to them, and she felt that same attraction drawing her to Creed.

"What are you doing here?" he asked. "I thought you planned to spend the day in bed."

"What are you doing here?" she countered. "How come you can speak the Comanche tongue?"

"As a boy I was captured by the Comanches and spent a part of my youth among them," he said. "I grew up with several of the braves you saw here today, and I came here to see one of them."

"The one you fought?"

"No, my friend wasn't here."

It was doubtful whether Creed could have told her less and still answered her questions. She pressed for a little more information. "Did these Indians steal my father's horses?"

"No, they were here for another reason, which I need to discuss with Rip. Let's get back to the house. I don't want you riding off anymore by yourself. As you can see, it's too dangerous."

Cricket made no attempt to hide her irritation. "You don't tell me what to do! I manage fine on my own."

"You almost managed to get yourself killed!" Creed ignored Cricket's rising anger and continued, "I told Tall Bear you're my woman. That makes you a target for his revenge. If he has his way, you'll find yourself a Comanche squaw lying down under every buck who has the price and a yearning for a white woman with flashy red hair."

"Saying something doesn't make it true. I'm not anybody's woman. I'll do what I please!"

"No more, Brava. I'll be giving the orders from now on."

"Like *hell* you will!"

Cricket waited for the response her father always gave, but it wasn't forthcoming. Creed simply ignored her and went to retrieve his chestnut gelding.

"Mount up," he ordered.

Cricket bristled. "I'll walk back before I'll obey you."

Creed reached over and took Valor's reins. "Fine, enjoy your walk." He kicked his chestnut into a trot and headed for the plantation house.

"What do you think you're doing?" Cricket yelled after him.

Creed didn't answer.

Cricket whistled shrilly, and a satisfied smile settled on her lips when Valor reared and plunged, yanking on the reins. She heard Creed speak to the horse in a guttural voice, the words Comanche. Valor quieted. Cricket narrowed her eyes. That wasn't supposed to happen. She whistled again, and again Valor reared, this time almost escaping Creed's grasp. But Creed quieted the stallion with his Comanche incantation and kept on riding.

Cricket watched Creed's retreating figure, her horse trotting docilely beside him. She looked down at Rogue, who waited patiently, tongue lolling. "How the hell do you suppose he did that?" Then she realized that if she didn't catch up to him she was going to have to walk all the way home.

"Creed," she shouted. "Wait for me. I changed my mind."

Creed stopped the horses. She was a lot smarter than he'd thought, and she wasn't as stubborn as he'd feared. But he could already see it was going to be hell protecting her from the Comanches. What on earth had possessed him to claim her as his woman?

CHAPTER 7

THE COUNCIL HOUSE massacre created a stir among the Texas colonists, but it didn't send them scurrying into their homes in fear of Comanche retribution. Instead they armed themselves for defense. They donned bandoleers of ammunition, stuck two Pattersons in a double holster thrown across the saddle horn, laid a Kentucky rifle across their knees, and fingered a knife in boot or sheath while they rode. But travel they did, as less than a week later, planters from along the Brazos congregated for Señor Juan Carlos Guerrero's *fandango* celebration.

Creed had spent nearly the entire trip riding beside Rip, but as they neared their destination he spurred his horse up next to the shiny black one-horse carriage in which Cricket rode with Sloan. He smiled at Cricket, who merely stared balefully back at him from beneath the fringed canopy of the carriage before turning her eyes to gaze out over the rutted road that led to Señor Guerrero's hacienda. Creed kept pace with the carriage, content to simply look at her, amused by her fidgeting, amazed when she managed once to sit stock still for a full minute and a half.

Cricket could feel Creed's eyes on her, as she'd felt them on her the past week while the Ranger moved freely about

Three Oaks scouting for horse thieves. She'd felt imposed upon, invaded, uncomfortable when he stared at her with that heavy-lidded gaze. And he was doing it again today. Cricket resisted the urge to stare back at Creed. When she could stand his perusal no longer she asked, "What do you want?"

"You look awful pretty today."

"Buffalo piss," she muttered under her breath.

"I didn't catch that."

"I wasn't speaking to you."

"You should wear a dress more often."

"I prefer pants. I wouldn't be rigged up like this now if Rip hadn't insisted on it. Every other girl attending Señor Guerrero's *fandango* will probably come on horseback with a pair of her father's knickers under her skirt and her ballgown in her saddlebag. They'll get a good laugh when they see me show up in a fancy shay wearing this outfit."

"Why would they laugh at you? You look fine in a dress."

The wounds from Amber Kuykendall's birthday party had never healed cleanly, and Cricket blanched before she retorted, "I feel about as comfortable as a pig in a parlor. Besides, this dress doesn't fit."

She retied the green ribbon on her straw bonnet, but still felt choked, so she stuck a finger into the white butterfly collar of her dress and yanked it forward. Then she tugged at the white lace trim that trailed the V-shaped bodice down to the constricting waist. There simply wasn't any room to be had within the confines of the bright yellow linen material. She'd been reduced to shallow panting because it was physically impossible to take a deep breath.

Cricket could count on four knuckles and a toe the number of times she'd worn a dress, and couldn't understand why Rip had insisted she wear one today. Granted, she would be formally introduced to Señor and Señora Guerrero and their sons for the first time at the *fandango*. But she knew the fact she was wearing a dress wasn't going to make any difference in her reception by the Spaniards. She was certain her reputation—or rather the reputation of

"Rip's girls"—had preceded her. Bay had known what was coming, and so she'd stayed home, which was a shame, Cricket thought, because of them all, Bay was the one most comfortable in this kind of social situation.

"Bay said she'd alter this dress to fit a little better," Cricket said finally, "but I told her not to bother."

Creed eyed the snug bodice, which provided an intriguing outline of Cricket's full breasts. "It doesn't sound to me like it was such an unreasonable suggestion."

"It would have been a waste of time, because I'm planning to shuck this outfit as soon as I can and put on buckskins for the *días de toros*."

"Can't you watch those Spanish riding and roping contests in a dress?" Creed asked.

Cricket didn't bother to answer because they'd reached the first of the *jacals*, the homes of Juan Carlos's vaqueros. The dwellings consisted of mesquite posts stuck upright in vertical walls which were chinked with mud and topped by a thatched roof. There were also adobe homes constructed of thick mud and straw bricks, their cool, dim interiors a welcome refuge during the searing Texas summer. Near the dwellings were gardens with small patches of spring corn and other vegetables.

The entire pueblo, comprised of numerous *jacals* and the few adobe homes, an adobe cantina, and a Texan-style cedar frame mercantile store, had grown up around an old, war-torn Spanish mission at the outskirts of the Guerrero hacienda. The priestless mission, with its octagonal belltower housing two bells to call the parishioners to a mass that was no longer held, endured as a stark memorial to the Spanish Texas that was no more. Its adobe grandeur, which had once risen majestically into the sky, now stood eroded by age and scarred by circumstance.

Sloan drove the shiny black carriage past the ancient mission and on toward the Guerrero hacienda. The ranch house, its thick adobe walls plastered white, stood on a rise, with its broad veranda overlooking the Brazos River. Rip brought his mount even with the carriage as they pulled to a stop inside the heavy wooden gates of the high, fortlike adobe wall surrounding the hacienda. "Sloan, Cricket, I expect you both to stay with me long enough to greet Señor and Señora Guerrero and their sons."

"I don't want to meet anyone," Cricket protested.

"I didn't ask you what you wanted," Rip replied brusquely. "And Cricket," he warned, "behave yourself."

Creed frowned at the admonition. It was a warning better given to a seven-year-old brat than a seventeen-year-old young lady. But then, from what he'd seen so far, Cricket could hardly be described as the typical young lady. Creed had a feeling Cricket's dress wasn't going to fool anyone.

Cricket glanced anxiously at the elegantly dressed men and women aligned around a splashing tile fountain at the center of the patio in front of the Guerrero hacienda. Amber Kuykendall was here with her mother. Cricket breathed a sigh of relief when she didn't see Felicia Myers. Cricket looked down at her ill-fitting linen dress and then at the fashionable satin gowns of the other women. It wasn't that she cared what they thought, but she dreaded the looks she knew were coming and hated having to make small talk when she had nothing to say to them.

A mestizo servant attended to the carriage and another took care of the horses as they were gestured into the line. Cricket stepped in line behind Rip and Sloan with Creed following her. She turned around and frowned at him once when he seemed a little too close, and he cocked his head as though he didn't know what he'd done.

Cricket tried to stand still in line, but was too nervous not to fidget. She brushed back the few wisps of hair which had escaped her thick auburn braid to tease her face, then fussed with the decorative buttons up the front of her dress, wondering if the tiny green squares looked too childish. She flattened the curling tip of the white butterfly collar, and yanked on the lace-trimmed sleeves which, she now realized, were about an inch too short. She tried hunching her shoulders, but that didn't help. Oh, well. She brushed the dust off her skirt and industriously wiped the toes of her black shoes off on the backs of her white stockings. There. She'd done the best she could. She pulled her shoulders back into a stiff T and waited patiently to do her devoirs.

"Welcome to my home, Señor Stewart," Juan Carlos said, shaking Rip's hand.

"I'm honored to be here, Señor Guerrero. I'd like to introduce my daughters, Sloan and Creighton."

Cricket was busy yanking on her sleeve when Creed nudged her from behind. She looked up into the bronzed face of the tall, lean Spaniard, and gratefully returned his pleasant smile. She stuck out her hand for him to shake, and stiffened when he turned it slightly and lifted it to hold it in both of his. Cricket felt a little like a mare at auction, as he examined her face and form. He couldn't help but note all the flaws in her attire. However, no hint of condemnation showed in his dark brown eyes.

Then it was over, and Rip was introducing Creed.

"This is Jarrett Creed. He's visiting with us."

"My pleasure, Señor Creed. Please make yourself at home with us. Any friend of Señor Stewart's is welcome here. These are my sons, Cruz and Antonio, and my wife, Lucia."

Cruz Guerrero greeted Cricket with indifferent formality. From Antonio, Cricket received the haughty disdain she'd expected from Juan Carlos. She wondered how Sloan could have come to love the young Spaniard, and resisted the urge to say something to him that would reveal she knew his secret. But he quickly passed her on to his mother and the chance was gone.

As lush in figure as Juan Carlos was lean, Lucia Esmeralda Sandoval de Guerrero was strikingly beautiful in a layered, wine-colored silk gown that gave an impression of royalty. An ivory comb, set in the raven tresses gathered at the crown of her head, held a delicate black lace mantilla in place. She held her chin tipped upward, so the lace edged her patrician profile.

There was no question in Cricket's mind from the look on the woman's face that Señora Guerrero hated her, loathed her, didn't want to touch her sweaty palm. So Cricket made a point of speaking to her.

"Buenos días, señora. Thank you for inviting me."

"De nada, Señorita Stewart."

"Oh, I'm sure I'm welcome as worms in cotton," Cricket shot back with a grin. "But I don't mind." She turned and walked away before the incensed woman could respond. It felt good to salve her wounded pride, but she could hardly blame the woman. She knew her behavior wasn't condoned by even the most liberal of her Texan neighbors, and she hadn't expected the Spanish Guerreros, with their belief in daughters protected by *dueñas,* to enfold such an unseemly virgin as she to their bosoms.

The real test was yet to come. Cricket tried to decide which of the circles of conversation it would be safest to join. There really wasn't much choice. She headed toward the one that contained Amber Kuykendall and her mother.

Creed had been angry at the way the Spanish woman had snubbed Cricket, but soon saw she was well able to take care of herself. He reminded himself he was here on business. He planned to judge for himself the relationship between Sloan Stewart and Juan Carlos's younger son, Antonio, and so he'd closely watched their greeting to one another.

If he'd been expecting some sign of recognition, he was disappointed, because the young man seemed singularly disinterested in Sloan. It was the older brother, Cruz, who couldn't seem to keep his hawklike gaze off Rip's eldest daughter, although he'd dismissed Cricket without a second glance. Creed found that state of affairs intriguing, considering the fact that Rip intended Cruz to be Cricket's husband.

Still, Creed couldn't help tensing when he took Cruz's hand. The Spaniard was too attractive, too proud, too vital, for Creed not to feel a spiral of jealousy toward him. However, Cruz greeted him with such gracious friendliness that Creed found himself responding favorably to the slightly older man, despite his initial reservations.

On the other hand, Creed had no trouble at all disliking Antonio Guerrero, especially since the feeling was mutual. Antonio was more handsome than his brother, with large hazel eyes and soft, boyish black curls that fell over his brow. His mouth was full and sensual above a smaller version of the cleft that rent his older brother's strong chin. He was as tall as Creed, but still two inches shorter than his brother. Creed measured the slender man's disdain in his handshake, which barely clasped Creed's hand before it was released.

It wasn't hard to imagine the fiery-eyed young man plotting the overthrow of the Texas government. However, it was not his job to jump to conclusions. Creed set his personal antipathy for Antonio Guerrero aside. He needed proof of treason, and his best chance of finding that proof at the *fandango* was to stay near Sloan Stewart.

Creed followed Rip as he trailed his daughters to the gathering of elite plantation folk. The circle of men widened naturally to include Rip, but the nearby cluster of women appeared decidedly annoyed by the prospect of entertaining Cricket and Sloan. Creed stood where he could hear the women's conversation.

"Hello, Amber. How are you," Cricket said.

"Fine, thank you."

Cricket looked for something else to say to Amber, but she had nothing in common with the beautiful, perfectly dressed young woman standing across from her. Sometimes she wished . . .

"What have you been up to lately?" Amber's mother, Martha, asked Sloan, her voice barely civil. "Has that African witch woman been giving you any trouble?"

"Not since her back healed from the beating your husband gave her," Sloan returned coldly.

"Don't look at me like that, Sloan Stewart. Sam had to whip that Nigress," the gray-haired woman replied. "She was practicing magic and inciting the Nigras to talk back!"

"She's a human being, not an animal."

"I should have expected to hear that sort of heresy from you, being raised like you have in the bosom of those Nigra men, without a mother to shield you from their wickedness. It's no wonder no decent man will have anything to do with you!"

"Does that mean you want me to turn down your son's request for a dance this evening, Mrs. Kuykendall?" Sloan asked, with a bitter smile. "Phillip seemed most pleased by the prospect of escorting me when he stopped by Three Oaks yesterday."

Martha Kuykendall turned a bright crimson before she sputtered, "Phillip is a man. I can hardly blame him for seeking out what's offered for free, can I?"

"Mrs. Kuykendall?"

Martha Kuykendall looked over her shoulder to find Cricket, who'd stepped up close behind her.

"Yes, Creighton?"

"Your skirt is on fire."

The elderly woman let out a howl and hopped around in a mindless circle like a beheaded chicken. She tore at the voluminous folds of her layered satin skirt to determine the danger, which, as it turned out after she'd made an utter fool of herself in front of her two closest neighbors, was nonexistent.

"My mistake," Cricket calmly admitted to the furious woman. "What I saw must have been the smoke from that cigar." Cricket pointed righteously to the stub of a cigar smoldering in the grass near where Mrs. Kuykendall had been standing.

Martha Kuykendall's outraged dignity demanded retribution, but when she turned to insist that her husband, Sam, do something, even if it was only to retire from the scene of her disgrace, she found him deep in conversation with Rip Stewart. Her vengeance thwarted in that direction, she turned back to Cricket.

"You . . . you . . ." Martha searched for a word she could say in front of her neighbors, and finally settled on hissing, "You hussy! You don't belong in polite company. Your father ought to take a switch to your backside until you can't sit down."

"Shame, shame, Mrs. Kuykendall," Sloan said, coming to Cricket's side. "I should think that you, of all people, would have learned by now that violence only leads to greater rebellion. Come on, Cricket. I think I'd like to take a closer look at that silver inlaid saddle we saw on display in the mercantile window."

The two women casually took their leave.

"Thanks, Cricket," Sloan said when they were out of hearing of the other women.

Cricket grinned. "It was definitely my pleasure. Do you really want to see that saddle?"

"No, I . . . I'm meeting Tonio."

"Can I come along?" Cricket asked.

Sloan put her hand on Cricket's shoulder. "I hope you'll understand if I say no."

Cricket shrugged, hiding a twinge of apprehension and a trace of irritation. "Sure, if you want to be alone—"

"I need to speak with Tonio. Please try to understand, Cricket."

"Sure, I understand," Cricket said as a lump grew in her throat.

Sloan reached out to grasp Cricket's shoulder, but dropped her hand when Cricket stiffened. "I'll see you later."

Creed had hastily excused himself and followed the two sisters at a safe distance. Before they left the hacienda walls, they separated. Cricket headed toward the carriage in which she'd come. Sloan, meanwhile, looked around once as though searching for someone, and then stepped beyond the adobe fortress and moved hurriedly toward the Mexican village. Creed followed her, making sure to stay back in the crowd, out of her sight.

A voice stopped him as he reached the fortress gates.

"Señor Creed. I'd like a word with you."

Creed cursed under his breath as he watched Sloan disappear into an alley between the adobe cantina and the frame mercantile store next to it. He hid his irritation in a pleasant smile before he turned, only to have his smile fade when he saw who'd accosted him.

"What can I do for you, Señor Guerrero?"

"Please, call me Cruz."

"What can I do for you?" Creed repeated, stubbornly refusing to call his unacknowledged rival by name. The Spaniard's English was only slightly accented, which made him sound as aristocratic as he looked in the tight black pants, black boots, white frilled shirt, and matching waist-length black jacket he wore.

"I hoped you might answer some questions for me. Would you mind joining me inside?" Cruz gestured toward the impressive hacienda, and with a nod Creed followed him.

The interior of the hacienda bespoke the Spanish heritage of the Guerreros, and was a mix of the old world and the new. In what would have been the parlor of a Texan home, elaborately inlaid Moorish tables brought from Spain were interspersed among heavy, purely functional Mediterranean chairs with rawhide seats. The delicately spooled legs of the tables which had been crafted by Spanish artisans con-trasted greatly with the wooden pegs and wrought-iron hinges made by the Mexicans to survive the rigors of the new world.

Creed noted the recessed arches decorated with various religious symbols, including a carved wooden statue of San Miguel and a painted crucifix. A touchably smooth blue Talavera jar stood in the arch by the front door. The thick adobe walls kept the room cool and the small, high windows made it seem dark. Even now, sweetly scented candles burned to allay the dimness of the room.

The Spaniard offered Creed a crystal glass of very old brandy, which he accepted. However, he refused Cruz's offer to sit, moving instead to stand near the stone fireplace that took up the entire wall at one end of the room. Both men sipped in silence until Creed asked, "What can I do for you?"

"I understand you're staying at Señor Stewart's place." Cruz paused before adding, "And that you're a Texas Ranger."

"You're very well informed."

"I have friends in San Antonio," the Spaniard replied.

"So?"

"I need a favor from you."

Creed hid his surprise well. He looked down at the priceless crystal in his hand, pondering the possibility that his investigation of the Guerreros was not so secret as he'd thought. He took another sip of the fine brandy. "I'm listening."

Clear blue eyes met tawny gold as Cruz said, "Because of our stand with the Texans during the war, both my family and the pueblo of our vaqueros have been subjected to continuous reprisals instigated by those unhappy *tejanos,* Texas-Mexicans, in Texas who would rather the Mexican government had remained supreme. Several attacks have resulted in loss of life and livestock. I want to see these attacks stopped, but so far I haven't been able to discover who's behind them. I thought as long as you're going to help Señor Stewart recover his livestock you might be willing to go a step further and help me find out who's been arranging for the attacks on my people."

Creed fought to keep a frown from his face. Cruz had painted a picture of his family as victims, not traitors. Could it be that Antonio Guerrero wasn't working with the Mexican government after all? Or did Cruz intend to use this ploy to keep an eye on Creed?

"I work alone," Creed said at last.

"But you'll help," Cruz urged.

It would be better to accede to Cruz's request, Creed rationalized. That way he could keep an eye on the Spaniard while the Spaniard was keeping an eye on him.

"Yes, I'll help."

"Thank you. Now, shall we go observe the *días de toros?* I can point out the vaqueros whose activities I've found suspect, and you'll have a chance to see why the Spanish are known as the best horsemen in Texas."

By the time they arrived at the corral together, Creed found himself almost comfortable in Cruz's company. He was looking forward to a fruitful, pleasant afternoon—until he saw Cricket. She was dressed in her buckskins as she'd promised, but she wasn't sitting in the stands which had been erected for observers. She was perched on the edge of the corral near the stockpen along with the vaqueros competing in the *días de toros.*

"Excuse me," Creed said, "I see someone I need to talk to."

"But of course. Join me when you can."

Creed left Cruz and made a beeline for Cricket. He had to look up to where she sat on the top rail of the corral to speak to her. "What's going on? Where are your father and Sloan?"

"They should both be here soon," Cricket reassured him. "I see you're sitting with Cruz Guerrero. I hope that means he's not competing today. I'll have a better chance of winning first prize."

"First prize in what?"

"The bronc riding, of course."

Cricket was startled when Creed's hand shot out and grabbed her arm, yanking her off the top rail of the corral.

"Let go of me, you lamebrained jackass!"

She was still struggling for balance when he grabbed her other arm and dragged her up close to his chest, hissing in her face, "Did I hear you right? You're planning to *compete* in the *bronc riding?*"

"Of course!" she hissed back, unnerved by how uncanny it was that every time she had one of these encounters with the Ranger her pulse raced as crazily as a rabbit chased by a hawk. "Why do you think I bothered to come today? There are money purses for the three best riders, and I expect to win."

"You're going to break your neck! What does Rip have to say about this idiotic idea?"

"I expect her to win, too," Rip said.

Creed dropped Cricket's arms as though he'd discovered himself holding a scorpion and whirled to confront Rip. "She'll be killed! How can you allow her to do this?"

"It's better than having her compete in the *coleada,*" he replied with a shrug.

Creed turned incredulous eyes toward Cricket. In the *coleada* the mounted vaquero had to catch up with a running bull, grasp its tail, and by an expert maneuver throw the beast off-balance. "You're crazy!"

"This is none of your business, Ranger. I know what I'm doing."

"Yes, she does," Rip agreed, putting a reassuring hand on Creed's shoulder.

Creed shook it off and pivoted back to Cricket. "I thought we'd settled the matter of your supposed strength, woman."

"We settled nothing except that your brains are in the seat of your buckskins!" Cricket turned her back on Creed and climbed back up on top of the corral to join the other contestants.

Rip chuckled, then tried to cajole the furious Ranger into joining their host and his elder son in the stands. Antonio wasn't present, Creed noticed abstractedly. Nor could he find Sloan in the crowd.

"I think I'll watch from here," Creed announced to Rip. "Please tell Cruz I'll meet him later to discuss our business."

Rip cocked a questioning brow at Creed's message, but nodded his agreement to deliver it.

Creed found a spot at the edge of the corral, near where the mustangs would enter the arena, and leaned against the barrier. "Somebody has to be close enough to pick up the pieces," he muttered under his breath.

Cricket glared at the Ranger's stiff back, while she stewed at his accusations. It wasn't going to take great strength for her to win this competition. She knew how to let her supple body flow with the action of the bronc, so balance and timing did as much to keep her atop the animal as brute muscle. Jarrett Creed would see for himself how good she was. Not that she cared one whit about what the Ranger thought, of course, but when the contest was over, and she'd won first prize, he'd have to eat his words!

Cricket's eyes glowed with excitement as the Spanish cowboys demonstrated their skill on horseback. Each vaquero rode a different horse in the contest, all rawboned Spanish mustangs, wiry and full of fight. As her turn came closer her heart began to pound. She was nervous in ways she never would have been if Jarrett Creed weren't watching. Nothing so gentle as butterflies fluttered in her stomach. The stampeding buffalo were back.

She'd drawn a Roman-nosed dun, its eyes white with fear and hate. It was bound to be a great ride if she could hang on. When she slid down from the corral fence her knees almost buckled because she'd been sitting so long. She shook her hands trying to relax, and caught Creed's eye. He shook his head, his lips pressed in a flat line. She searched futilely for Rip in the crowd. His was the only opinion that mattered to her. She didn't give a tinker's damn whether this lardheaded Ranger approved. She turned her nose up at him and walked to where the vaqueros struggled to saddle the blindfolded mustang.

Suddenly they were done, and she stuck her foot into the stirrup and settled herself in the saddle leather. She took a deep breath and moved her tongue out of the way of her teeth before she nodded to the handlers to uncover the animal's eyes.

Creed's heart rose to his throat as the bronc erupted in a bone-jarring leap, raced headlong for the fence, and then stopped dead in front of it. Cricket had leaned forward for the horse's run and only barely managed to avoid coming off in a heap when the mustang stopped. Then the dun's nose went down and he sprang into the air, alternately landing stiff-legged on his front hooves and throwing his rear hooves into the air. He began to twist in a circle, then arched around in the opposite direction. Creed swore out loud when he saw a trickle of blood on Cricket's lip where she'd bit herself as her head whipped painfully to accommodate the mustang's violent gyrations.

Cricket had shut out the rest of the world. She clenched the rope reins with one fist, while the other hand swung wildly in the air to help her maintain her balance. The dust in the arena filled her nostrils and slid down her throat, choking her. She knew the crowd must be shouting comments because she occasionally saw an open mouth as the mustang bucked by an observer, but she heard nothing except a dull roar of background noise in her ears.

At long last, the mean-eyed mustang, exhausted by its efforts, came to a dead stop. Cricket felt equally exhausted. It had been a harder fight than she'd have wished for. But, oh, how sweet that made the victory! She managed a triumphant smile for Creed, but felt a stab of disappointment deep inside when he scowled back at her in obvious displeasure.

Cricket wiped the blood from her chin with her sleeve, and searched again for Rip in the stands. This time she found him. He smiled and gave her a thumbs-up sign. She returned a forced smile of her own, but was disturbed that she didn't feel more elated by his satisfaction with her performance. She turned back to the arena, feeling vaguely unsettled.

She only had to wait out the performances of three more vaqueros and a half-breed Comanche to see whether she had won. Two of the vaqueros were quickly dumped by their mustangs. The third stayed aboard, but barely, leaving only the half-breed Comanche as any competition. Cricket tensed as she awaited this last ride. She was sure that so far she was winning. Creed would soon see she was not a competitor to be sneered at. She chanced a glance at the Ranger and he smiled sardonically. She quickly looked back at the arena, appalled to be caught looking at him.

The vaqueros hadn't welcomed the breed's company, so he'd stood at the edge of the corral, near Creed. When his turn came, the half-breed glided out to the center of the arena and spoke into the horse's ear before throwing himself onto the animal's back in a single fluid move.

Cricket had never seen a more graceful man. Once on the bronc, the half-breed seemed molded to the animal. His sinewy strength was evident in the easy curve of his body as the animal plunged and pitched in an effort to rid itself of its burden. Cricket watched in horror as the mustang reared over backward, attempting to crush the Indian. But when the mustang clambered to its feet, the half-breed slipped onto its back, and stayed there through sunfish and crow-hop. When the beast tried to scrape the Comanche off by skimming the edge of the corral, the Comanche simply lifted his leg over the horse's withers, then righted his balance for the stiff-legged leap that followed that vicious move.

When the death-dealing animal tried for the third time to savagely unseat its rider, Cricket realized the vaqueros had put the half-breed on an outlaw, fully expecting the Indian to be maimed or killed. But the half-breed Comanche was not to be denied. He rode the wild-eyed bronc to a standstill. When the brutish animal stood head down, defeated, at the end of the ride, the Comanche slipped off its back and waited patiently for the decision from the three Mexican judges.

Cricket knew the half-breed had beaten her. It was crushing to think she'd come so close, and then lost. She glanced at Creed, who watched the half-breed with the hint of a smile on his face. She hated Creed for gloating. Her ride had been damn good! She couldn't help it if the half-breed had been better. Cricket turned bitterly toward the judges, waiting for the winners to be announced. They announced the third-prize winner first, and Cricket's head snapped around in surprise as the half-breed Comanche strolled forward to receive his purse. Second prize went to Juan Carlos's head vaquero.

Cricket should have been glad when she heard her name announced as winner of the first-prize purse, because she had wanted to win today more than ever before. But although she'd been given the prize, she knew she hadn't been the best. So she accepted the winner's purse and stalked right past Creed, not stopping until she stood before the half-breed Comanche.

"What's your name?" she asked.

"Long Quiet."

She handed the purse to the half-breed. "This belongs to you."

The corners of his mouth tipped in a smile, but quickly straightened again. "Judges not say I win."

"The judges were wrong. Your ride was the best and you should have won."

The Indian gave her back the purse. "Not take prize from woman. Keep money. Give to your man." The Indian pointed behind Cricket and she turned to find Creed standing there.

"Not take it from a . . . ? *My man!*" Cricket sputtered. "Of all the ungrateful—"

"That's enough, Cricket. A man has his pride," Creed said.

Cricket turned the heat of her pentup anger and confusion on Creed. "All I'm trying to do is make things right. I wasn't the best, he was. He should take the prize." She turned back around only to find the half-breed had disappeared.

"He's gone! At least I proved to you that I could ride," she muttered.

"Now I suppose you'll prove you can drink up your winnings like the other vaqueros."

Cricket's head snapped up at Creed's taunt. "I would if I felt like it."

"Over my dead body," he dared.

Cricket never could resist a dare.

"Watch me!" She shoved him aside and marched toward the cantina.

"I think I can find better things to do with my time," he called after her. Creed watched her go in mounting frustration. He couldn't believe he'd just spent the length of her ride on the mustang worrying about her. She was as unpredictable, as mulish, as infuriating as the day he'd met her, and he didn't see any hope that she was going to change anytime soon. But, God, he had to admire the way she'd broken that Roman-nosed dun! He pursed his lips thoughtfully. If he wasn't careful his admiration for her was going to get out of hand. No brat in buckskins was going to get under his skin. He approached the sloe-eyed Mexican girl who'd been sending unspoken invitations all afternoon, and when she smiled coyly at him he pulled her into the shelter of his arm. Then he followed Cricket to the cantina.

Cricket heard the woman giggle behind her but refused to look. However, before she reached the cantina, Creed passed her with a full-bosomed *chica*, dressed in a ruffled peasant blouse and skirt, tucked under his arm. He whispered something in the girl's ear that made her giggle again. They disappeared beyond the swinging cantina door ahead of Cricket, who'd stopped outside trying to sort through the jumbled emotions running riot through her.

How had she let herself get talked into drinking at the cantina? She only drank for one reason, at one time during the month, and that time was thankfully over for a while. Still, she didn't want Creed to think he'd won his point. And she certainly wasn't going to turn tail and run just because he was inside with some sloe-eyed Mexican girl. She was made of sterner stuff. Jarrett Creed could flatten his lips in disapproval all he wanted. It wasn't going to bother her. And he sure as shooting wasn't going to tell her what to do. Cricket straightened her shoulders and shoved her way through the cantina door.

CHAPTER 8

THE TWO BROTHERS stood in the shadows of the moonlit veranda, their heads bent toward one another as though to share quiet words. In the distance, a lone guitarist strummed a melancholy melody, a halting refrain unlike the crisp, lively tunes of the strolling violinists who'd entertained at the *fandango* earlier in the day. Cruz reached out to place a hand on Tonio's shoulder, but it was jerked out of his reach. The physical hostility evidenced by that withdrawal was echoed in the harsh words that followed.

"I'll see the girl if I like. It's none of your business!"

"Tonio, you know there's no hope of a marriage between you and Sloan Stewart. Even if Señor Stewart would allow it, she's totally unacceptable to Mamá. It can only lead to hurt for both you and the girl if you continue to meet with her," Cruz warned.

"She loves me, you know."

"How can she love you when you hate her family?"

"We don't talk about her family." Tonio smirked as he added, "We're too busy doing other things with our mouths."

Cruz breathed deeply to curb the curt response on his tongue.

"She'll do anything for me," Tonio boasted, "and I've asked for quite a lot. She's learned much about how to please me. . . ."

Cruz felt a growing irritation at his brother's remarks. The young man defamed a beautiful woman who loved him. He treated her love casually, and derided her willingness to please him in all things. Cruz wondered at his desire to protect the young lady he'd met for the first time today. He slowly but surely gathered in his protective feelings like a struggling calf at the end of a *reata*. Obviously Sloan Stewart knew what she was doing. Rip's daughters were notorious even in the Spanish community for their cold-blooded self-sufficiency. Oh, yes. His concern was definitely wasted on the sable-haired woman with the huge brown eyes.

"If she's accommodating, that's all the more reason not to cause trouble for her," Cruz said, venting his irritation. "Be careful who you antagonize. Rip Stewart would be a formidable enemy. And be discreet. There'll be other eyes watching than mine. Today I asked the Texas Ranger, Jarrett Creed, to help us find out who's inciting these raids."

Tonio spat his distaste on the ground. "Why did you do that? We don't need that *Diablo Tejano* to fight our battles for us!"

"Does that mean your own search has borne fruit at last? Have you discovered the source of our troubles?" Cruz demanded. "Tell me the raids will stop and I'll call off the Ranger."

Even though his pride stung at Cruz's censure, Tonio held his tongue. There were more necks than his own to be hung in a noose if the wrong ears heard what he could tell. He reminded himself that Cruz would thank him when it was all over and the Guerrero family held positions of power in Texas. Soon they would no longer need to bow their heads to the Anglo-Texans who ruled them now. Still, he chafed under his brother's criticism.

"I don't understand why you're so upset about those raids," Tonio replied petulantly.

"Those bandidos are killing people and stealing stock."

"We've lost only a few horses. Otherwise, they haven't bothered us, only a few mixed-breed mestizos and some of those two-faced Mexican jackals who fought on the side of the Texans at San Jacinto."

Cruz shook his head in disbelief. His younger brother's narrow vision distressed him. When would Tonio learn that whatever hurt the growing Texas community hurt them as well? He saw the delicate hand of his mamá in Tonio's warped view of what the future promised. Lucia Guerrero wasn't willing to admit that the hope for a return to the royal Spanish reign in Texas was over and done.

Cruz had spent too much time fighting alongside Texans against General Santa Anna to still hold any illusions about their possessive attitude toward Texas. He was all too painfully aware he faced a new world with new masters. The Spanish who owned land in Texas would either have to learn to live beside the Texans, or be trodden down by the Rip Stewarts who would gladly march over them, waving the Texas flag in their muddy faces.

"You will cooperate with the Ranger," Cruz said. "And if you know what's good for you, you'll stay away from the Stewart girl."

"I hear you, *mi hermano mayor*. I even understand you," Tonio added. "But I am afraid, big brother, I cannot obey you."

"Why not?"

"I would not piss on a *Diablo Tejano* to save him if he were on fire." Tonio paused and smiled. "And I want the girl. To take such a woman makes me feel . . . powerful."

Tonio sauntered away toward the front door of the hacienda, leaving Cruz alone to finish smoking his cheroot, the red tip glowing in the darkness.

Jarrett Creed slipped away unnoticed from the dark shadows at the side of the house. Attending Juan Carlos's *fandango* had proved to be most informative, despite the fact he hadn't caught Sloan Stewart and Antonio Guerrero alone together. In fact, the only time Creed actually saw them in the same place at the same time, other than in the receiving line, was when Antonio helped Sloan into her carriage and sent her on her way home.

Creed had construed Antonio's gesture merely as the courtesy of a host, but after the conversation he'd just overheard, he knew it probably had been far more than that. The intimate relationship between Sloan and Antonio gave Creed the missing piece of the puzzle as to *why* Rip Stewart's daughter might be involved with the rebels. Antonio's comment—"She'll do anything for me"—bothered Creed. Had Sloan even been willing to betray her country?

Creed headed for the cantina, wondering if Cricket would still be there. She'd toasted him with a smile on her face when he'd left earlier with the sloe-eyed Mexican girl. She was probably drunk as a skunk by now, and heaven only knew what trouble she'd caused at the cantina. He'd hoped Rip might take her home, but had seen him leave without Cricket shortly after the dancing had begun in earnest. Sloan's departure had come several hours later, but Cricket hadn't been with her, either. Creed had his answer when he reached the end of the street where the cantina was located. Cricket's pinto stallion, which had been tied to the back of the black carriage on the trip to the Guerrero hacienda, stood tied now to the hitching rail in front of the drinking establishment. As he stood watching, Cricket staggered from the cantina. She was apparently so drunk that the two Mexicans with her had to hold her upright.

"Damn it, Brava! That's the most stubborn woman I ever met. Where does she think she's going now?"

Creed set out for the cantina as fast as his legs could carry him.

Cricket hadn't spent the evening thinking much at all. She'd passed far beyond that rational state, and was very close to a drunken stupor. In the past, the only times she'd ever been drunk, she'd also been in pain. Right now she felt different. Almost . . . euphoric. She'd enjoyed playing monte, which the vaqueros preferred to poker. In the past hour she'd won about half of the second-prize purse from Juan

Carlos's head vaquero, whose name, she'd discovered, was Enrique Vasquez. "But call me Riqui," he'd said. She'd won even more from the other three players at the table.

"Aiiii, señorita, you win again!" Riqui cried, his mouth turned downward as Cricket revealed her cards.

Cricket gave the leather-faced vaquero a cheery smile. She'd compared him to the only men she knew well—her father's slaves. His dark, kind eyes and polite deference throughout the evening had reminded her of Jim, while his bushy brows and constant smile were very like those on August. But his narrow black mustache was unique. It made him look like a bandido, and maybe that hint of danger was what appealed so much to her. He probably wasn't much older than Jarrett Creed, but the Texas wilderness had suffered his presence less kindly. Cricket thought him a very nice person, and would have liked to get to know him better.

She had no such pleasant associations for the other three men at the table. Paco worked for the Guerreros, but his face and his behavior both reflected the hard life he'd lived. His visage was seamed in lines of fatigue, and he was curt and unfriendly almost to the point of surliness. Oscar and Clemencio worked together, but Cricket didn't know exactly what kind of work they did. If she hadn't been so drunk she might have wondered more about the anomaly of their fine clothes and fresh young faces in this poor, hard-working village. They'd gotten progressively less friendly as they lost to her at monte, but they didn't cheat, so she had little cause for complaint.

Suddenly, the room began to spin and Cricket placed her elbows firmly on the table to keep her balance. She waited for the dizziness to pass, but it persisted. Cricket gave in gracefully to the alcoholic oblivion that threatened. This she understood. It dawned on her, abruptly, that she wasn't at Three Oaks. She couldn't give in to the weariness that pulled at her. She had to get herself home first. Bother!

"Are you going to deal, señorita, or sit and look at the cards?"

Clemencio's irritated voice pierced Cricket's veil of insensibility. "I'm passing the deal to Riqui. I'm going home."

"You can't leave now. You've got a pile of my money in front of you," Clemencio protested.

"I'm done for tonight. Maybe next time."

Cricket rose unsteadily, missing the look that passed between Oscar and Clemencio. She made it all the way to the door of the cantina before she felt a presence behind her. She stiffened. It wasn't fear, exactly, but a premonition of danger that made her pause. She glanced over her shoulder, then smiled with delighted surprise.

"Oh, it's you."

Riqui Vasquez returned Cricket's bright smile, his crooked teeth suddenly appearing below the bushy mustache.

"*Sí*, señorita. I thought perhaps you needed an escort home."

Cricket let her relief out in a small chuckle. How silly for her to think there was any danger for her in this tiny Mexican village. After all, she was Rip Stewart's daughter and that title alone guaranteed her safety. Not that she needed it.

"Thank you, señor, but my horse knows the way home. I'll be fine."

By now, they had exited the cantina and stood in the moonlight near the hitching rail. Cricket tucked her winnings into her saddlebag, but the vaquero put a hand on her arm before she could untie Valor. Cricket stared for a moment in disbelief at the dark brown hand with its blunt, dirty nails. The touch was a breach of etiquette the vaquero would never have considered were she a proper plantation owner's daughter. Of course, she admitted, no lady she knew would spend the evening playing monte in a cantina.

The hand tightened until Riqui had a firm hold on her arm. When he began to pull her toward the alley next to the cantina, Cricket was too surprised to resist, and too disappointed. She'd liked Riqui so well. He'd seemed like such a nice man, and might have made a good friend. Well, she shouldn't have any problem putting him in his place. Thanks to Jarrett Creed, she'd had some recent practice curbing the unwanted advances of an aggressive male.

What Cricket hadn't anticipated was the total lack of coordination she possessed as a result of the whiskey she'd drunk. Whenever she'd imbibed in the past, she'd been safe at home. So, when she reached for her knife to end her evening with Riqui, he was there ahead of her. When she attacked with her knee, he turned aside and she hit only the hard muscles of his thigh. It never occurred to Cricket to scream. She took care of herself. She didn't need help from anybody.

By now, the vaquero held her shoulders in both hands, and had pressed her back against the adobe wall of the cantina, using his body weight to hold her still. She could smell the liquor on his breath, and realized he must be more drunk than he'd appeared to be.

"Don't fight me, *chiquita,*" he purred. "I'll make you feel good."

But it wasn't in Cricket's nature to give up. She lifted her moccasined foot and came down hard on the vaquero's little toe.

Riqui's yelp was followed quickly by an angry curse. *"Puta!* You'll pay for that!" He slammed Cricket hard against the adobe wall, knocking the breath from her, and very nearly making her lose consciousness.

Riqui's once-kind eyes glittered with malicious intent. The facade had disappeared, and what she faced was a hard man who looked every bit as mean as his bandido mustache. Deep in her drunken depths, Cricket shuddered with something very like fear. She wished Jarrett Creed were here to help her.

In the next instant, it appeared her prayer had been answered, for Riqui Vasquez sank like a stone before her, as though he'd been clubbed. As indeed, he had, but not by Jarrett Creed.

"We meet again, señorita."

Cricket blinked twice, but Oscar and Clemencio were still there. She hadn't imagined them.

"Th . . . thank you for rescuing me," she stuttered.

"Our pleasure," Oscar said. "And now, señorita, we'll

take the money you won tonight, and whatever else you might have to give."

The greater meaning of Oscar's speech was not lost on Cricket. She had, it appeared, been ushered out of the frying pan and into the fire. Two against one was not her idea of fair play, and she was ready to accept reinforcements, but there were none to be had in the dark alley. "I put the money in my saddlebag. My horse is tied up in front of the cantina."

"Then you'll come with us to get it," Oscar said, grabbing her by the arm, leaving her little choice but to follow after the two men. As soon as they reached the end of the alley, Cricket made her break for freedom. She wrenched her arm from Oscar's grasp and raced for the cantina door. She never made it. The same club which had rescued her, now made her captive, and Cricket sank senseless to the ground.

"Why did you do that?" Oscar hissed.

"She would have raised the pueblo against us. I had no choice."

"What do we do now?"

"We take her with us, of course. We'll take our pleasure when she awakens."

At that moment, there was a commotion at the cantina door. Oscar and Clemencio each grasped one of Cricket's arms and hauled her unconscious body upright, holding her in the darker shadows next to the wall. They waited until the reeling patron had wandered farther down the otherwise-abandoned street before they put their plan into action. Oscar held Cricket while Clemencio retrieved their horses and Cricket's pinto.

"Once I get mounted, hand the girl up to me," Clemencio said.

"Why can't I carry the girl?"

"When we get out of the village you can have her as much as you please. Right now, we'd better get out of here."

Clemencio's warning didn't come a moment too soon. For as Oscar put the girl in his arms he heard a commanding, "Hey! What are you doing there?"

Creed could hardly believe his eyes. The two Mexicans weren't helping Cricket, they were kidnapping her! And she appeared to be hurt. Creed cursed himself up one side and down the other. He should've known better than to leave Cricket alone in the cantina. Sure she was headstrong and spoiled, but she was still just a girl—and an attractive one at that. That thought set his heart to pounding. The two men could have no good in mind, and Cricket was helpless to defend herself. Damn Rip Stewart and his ridiculous ideas for raising his daughters!

Creed didn't think to raise an alarm. There wasn't time. He needed to follow and follow quickly. He grabbed the nearest horse at the hitching rail and mounted up. He was on the heels of the kidnappers in moments.

Oscar and Clemencio exchanged heated words of accusation against one another for the fix in which they found themselves, but they kept their horses galloping on over the moonlit plains.

"Let the girl go! Otherwise you're dead men!"

In Creed's howled warning, Clemencio recognized a way to escape the irate man's pursuit. He merely obeyed Creed's order, and literally let Cricket go. She fell from the galloping horse in a tangled heap, and Creed barely managed to stop his mount before he trampled over her. He was off his horse in seconds and kneeling next to Cricket. His hands ran over her body in a flurry of anxiety, trying to determine whether anything was broken. At Cricket's groan he snapped, "Lie still till I see if your neck is broken!"

"They stole my money and they took Valor," she mumbled.

"They almost stole *you*, you idiot! To hell with the money and the horse!"

"I'm not an idiot."

Creed had never thought he'd be grateful that Cricket drank, but he knew no other reason than her loose-jointed drunkenness that she hadn't broken every bone in her body in the fall.

"My head hurts."

Creed lifted her into his arms. "You must have hit it when they dumped you."

"No, one of those bandidos clubbed me."

Creed was feeling distinctly murderous toward the two Mexicans, and he looked up with thoughts of what he'd do when he caught them. First he had to get Cricket safely back to Three Oaks.

Nausea churned in Cricket's belly. "I think I'm going to be sick."

Creed laid her on the ground again and held her head while she emptied her stomach. He gave her his bandanna to wipe her mouth, then lifted her in his arms.

"Come, Brava," he said softly. "It's time to take you home."

Cricket felt awful. And she felt wonderful. Creed's strong arms surrounded her shoulders and knees, and held her close to his body. Next to her ear she could hear the powerful beat of his heart. He shifted her in his arms as he mounted his horse, then shifted her again when he was in the saddle until her buttocks rested across his thigh. He'd come to help her . . . and he didn't even like her very much. She knew that because of the way he acted with her . . . always yelling . . . always criticizing . . . always telling her what to do. Cricket drifted off to sleep imagining that Creed was kissing her brow. How silly! He didn't even like her.

Creed nuzzled Cricket's forehead with his nose and chin. He let his lips chase across her brow. He clutched her tightly to his chest, thinking how close he'd come to losing *his woman*—and not even to the Comanches. He enjoyed the pleasure of holding her for half the distance back to Three Oaks. Then he forced his thoughts to consideration of the immediate problem at hand. What was he going to do with Cricket when he got her home?

He could picture himself knocking on the front door of the Stewart house in the middle of the night, and when Rip answered, saying, "Here's your daughter. I rescued her from kidnappers. She's all right except for a bump on the head and a few bruises." He wouldn't do it! If Rip Stewart had cared what happened to Cricket, he wouldn't have left her alone in the cantina all evening. Creed knew Bay would take care of Cricket, but he couldn't think of a way to reach her without going through Rip. By the time he reached the bachelors' quarters at Three Oaks he'd convinced himself he should be the one to take care of her. Creed purposely refused to consider what Cricket would think about his solicitous concern for her well-being. She was too young to know what was good for her.

And you do? a voice inside him asked.

Yes! he answered. At least he wouldn't manipulate her the way Rip did, the way his father had manipulated him. He knew how you did things to please, to be loved, to be wanted. He also knew that no matter how much you did, it was never enough. They always wanted more. If he could help Cricket learn that lesson before he left Three Oaks, he was doing her a favor. She'd be able to escape the bonds of parental love and duty by which Rip held her in such an unnatural role.

Bay hadn't treated the bachelors' quarters to the same elegant makeover as the main house. Creed carried Cricket to the bedroom on the left at the end of the main hall. The door stood open, and the feather bed had been turned down invitingly by one of the Negroes who were ever ready to serve on the plantation. A candle on the functional dresser beside the bed warmed the room with its cheery glow. Creed started to lay Cricket on the clean sheets, then changed his mind. She was wearing the same dusty, sweaty buckskins she'd worn to compete in the *días de toros*. He laid her on the quilt folded at the foot of the bed and unlaced her moccasins.

Cricket became vaguely aware she was in a bed and that someone was untying her clothing.

"Hurry up, Bay, I'm tired," she grumbled. Then she wiggled around until she'd pulled off her buckskin shirt. She shoved Creed's hands out of the way and pulled off her breeches as well.

Creed smiled in amusement when he saw the dainty chemise with its pink bow tied between her breasts and the lacy white pantalettes which Cricket wore under the hardy buckskins. The amused smile became more strained the longer Creed looked, for he could also see the dark outline of her nipples through the chemise, and the darker triangle at the apex of her long legs. Creed clenched his teeth as tightly as he clenched his fists. Unfortunately, there were also other things tightening over which he had no control.

Creed knew he had to get Cricket covered more decently, and fast. So, although Cricket seemed perfectly satisfied to lie where she was, Creed shifted her so her head lay on a pillow, and slipped her delectable body under the sheets. Then the full force of what he'd done hit him. He'd just tucked Creighton Stewart into his own bed.

"Sleep tight, Brava," Creed whispered in her ear.

Cricket swatted at the noise, as though batting at a fly and caught Creed square on the nose.

He grabbed his nose and stood in the same motion. So much for romance! She was drunk. She was hurt. She was asleep.

But he was no gentleman, and he wanted her.

Creed strode to the simple ladderback chair in the corner and flung himself into the rawhide seat, staring morosely at the four-poster that was centered in the room. What was the matter with him? He'd had no business bringing the girl here. He should have given her back to her father. Rip had created this ambivalent creature. Let him cope with her. Creed merely felt sorry for the girl, that was all.

So how did he explain the urgent messages from his body that spoke of so much more? He couldn't, and he didn't want to try, at least not tonight. He was tired and it was a big bed, so he needn't even get near the girl. Besides, it wasn't as though anyone was going to fight him tomorrow over Cricket's honor. Rip had made that issue quite clear in the barn. No, the one person who cared at all about Cricket's honor was the person who was as likely to take it as he was to keep it safe.

Creed rose, pantherlike, and reached for the rawhide tie on his beaded buckskin shirt. He'd lie down next to her, but he wouldn't touch her, he'd just sleep. Tomorrow he'd begin educating her about the feminine wants and needs of which she was so ignorant . . . and the demands of manipulating fathers like Rip Stewart with which she was entirely too familiar.

During the night, Cricket woke feeling strangled by her underclothes. And so she tore them off.

During the night, Creed woke feeling the need to hold Cricket. And so he pulled her into his arms.

In the morning, all hell broke loose.

CHAPTER 9

Wʜᴇɴ Cʀɪᴄᴋᴇᴛ ꜰɪʀꜱᴛ ᴡᴏᴋᴇ she was disoriented, but thought it the result of the whiskey she'd drunk the night before. The ceiling wavered and the four corners looked cockeyed. Nor did the bed feel right. It was softer. Or was it harder? The pillow was softer, the bed was harder, she determined. The objects outlined by the gray-black haze that comes before dawn were unfamiliar. For instance, what was making the sheets bunch up like that? Cricket stared at the shapeless lump across from her in stunned shock as the truth hit home. Not only was she not in her own room, but someone else was in the bed with her!

At that moment Creed shifted so he was lying flat on his back, his profile etched against the predawn light. It took mere seconds for Cricket to identify her companion.

"What the hell are you doing here?!"

Creed squinted one eyelid open and stared sleepily at Cricket. "What does it look like I'm doing?"

Cricket bolted from the bed, then realized her state of undress and scooted back under the covers.

"I'm naked!" she shrieked.

"So am I, but you don't hear me squawking like a turkey

at Thanksgiving. You're going to wake up everyone on Three Oaks if you don't quiet down."

Cricket tried to calm a racing heart, tried to steady a trembling hand, tried to swallow over a throat thick with unshed tears. She pulled her knees up to her chest and pressed her balled fists into her eyes, breathing deeply. She was in control. She *never* cried.

The last thing she remembered clearly was walking toward Valor with Oscar and Clemencio. Then everything was pretty much blank. She didn't really want to know what had gone on after that because it was too easy to conclude that "you know what" had happened here last night. And she didn't think she could face Creed knowing he'd done "it" to her. She railed at the fates that had made her female. It was so awful to know a man could do "that" to her, and do "it" without her even knowing!

Cricket's emotions ranged quickly from dismay to disgust to high dudgeon. She'd make sure Creed paid the consequences for the past evening, all right! But how did one avenge oneself for such a wrong? It was clear she was going to have to think seriously on the matter. She couldn't help voicing her very first thoughts.

"Rip will *kill* me," she gritted out. "After he kills you, of course."

Creed laughed and rolled onto his stomach, resting his chin on his palm. "Ah, Brava, you are such a delight."

He thought she looked wonderful, flushed and wide-eyed, with portions of her braid falling loose around her face and the sheet pulled primly up to her neck.

"I hope you enjoyed yourself," she said, her voice now steady, despite the tornado whirling inside, waiting to spin free. "When Rip finds out what you forced me to do, your life won't be worth an old hat."

"What I forced you to do?"

"I assume you've had your way with me. At least, I feel bruised enough to believe more went on in this bed last night than sleeping." Cricket examined several large bruises on her arms and held the sheet out, wincing as she investigated a sore spot on her ribs.

Creed fought another laugh. "You've been reading too many lurid novels. Those aren't passion bruises. In case you've forgotten, you were dropped like a sack of potatoes off a galloping horse last night."

"I was?" One of the Mexicans had hit her on the head, she remembered. The sensation of falling, the memory of being sick, of Creed offering her his bandanna, flashed behind her eyes. Cricket began to feel hopeful inside. Maybe "it" hadn't happened after all. "How did I end up here?"

"I saw you being kidnapped and came after you. When I shouted out for the two riders to stop, they dropped you. I didn't want to wake up the household so I brought you here to the bachelors' quarters."

"And undressed me."

"Yes. I undressed you."

Cricket found herself caught by Creed's gaze. His eyes stroked her lazily, making her skin tingle beneath the thin covering of sheet so she almost forgot her train of thought.

She swallowed and said, "And then you did . . . 'it.' "

Creed sat up in bed facing Cricket. The sheet dropped so it lay at the base of his hips. "It?"

"You know . . . 'it,' " Cricket said, irritated with him for being obtuse and with herself for ogling his navel and the line of hair leading down from it to what she knew lay under the sheet.

Creed didn't know whether to laugh or cry. Cricket's attitude toward making love shouldn't have bothered him, but it did. He wondered what she'd do if she believed she'd really done "it." Shoot him? Go into hiding? How would she react when forced to face the fact she was a woman?

His curiosity was so great he replied, "I never had to use force on you last night. You were very cooperative." He spoke nothing less than the truth. Let her make of it what she would.

Cricket remained silent for a moment. She had a headache and an upset stomach. There was a knot the size of a rock on her head and the rest of her body boasted bruises. There existed a faint memory of Creed's mouth feathering over her brow, but nothing else. Oh, dear God. She'd become a woman last night, but she couldn't remember a damned thing about it!

Creed watched Cricket's mobile features run through a dozen different emotions, but he was unprepared for the terse question she voiced.

"Did I enjoy myself?"

"You mean you don't remember?"

Cricket was in no mood for Creed's teasing. "Just answer my question!"

In for a penny, in for a pound, he thought.

"Immensely," he replied.

Cricket squeezed her eyes shut and breathed deeply. The first and only time she'd ever been with a man and she'd missed it all! She hadn't been forced. She'd been willing. She'd even enjoyed herself—*immensely!* She couldn't blame Creed for what he'd done under the circumstances. It wouldn't be fair. And above all things, Cricket prided herself on being fair. She shoved the covers away and swung her feet onto the floor.

"I suppose if I enjoyed myself *immensely* there isn't much of me you haven't seen, so modesty between us is ridiculous."

Creed sucked in his breath when Cricket straightened up after leaving the bed. The shadowy glimpse he'd had of her when she'd first awakened was tempting, but dawn had become daylight, and Cricket without a stitch of clothes was a feast for the senses. High, full breasts with rosy nipples; a hand-span waist; curved hipbones separated by the taut belly he'd held under his splayed hand last night; the triangle of dark, curly hair, her nest of femininity. And everywhere, all over, red raw scrapes and purple and black bruises. She was beautiful.

He was torn between a multitude of feelings: guilt that he'd left her with the impression she'd lost her virginity; disbelief that she was apparently going to ignore making love to him last night as though it had never happened; sympathy for the obvious pain of her aches and bruises; and passion. . . .

Creed waged a futile war with his body as Cricket matter-of-factly donned her clothing. She pursed her lips ruefully at the torn chemise and pantalettes, muttering, "You must have been in one hell of a hurry."

Creed had the grace to blush. He couldn't let her go on thinking he'd made love with her, when the most he'd done was hold her in his arms. The memory of how he'd woken during the night, with one hand on Cricket's taut belly and the other cupping a breast, her buttocks spooned into his groin, made him so hard he brought his knees up under the covers to protect what little innocence she supposedly had left.

"I don't know how your underclothes got torn," he protested. "I didn't do it."

"And I did?" She shook her head and clucked her tongue disgustedly. "Just because this happened once, you better not try doing 'it' again! Or else!"

"Or else what?" Creed challenged.

Cricket hesitated. Or else what? What could she do? You hung a man for stealing horses. And rape, well, you could hang a man for that, too. But what could you do if the woman was willing, and enjoyed herself *immensely?*

"Just don't try anything, or you'll find out!" she threatened finally.

Creed had to swallow before he could speak again, since Cricket leaned over to step into her buckskins and her full breasts pressed lovingly into the cotton sheets. He managed, "It's your own fault, you know. All I did was rescue you from those two Mexican kidnappers. I couldn't very well knock on your father's door in the middle of the night with his unconscious daughter in my arms, could I?"

"Couldn't you?" Cricket speared Creed with her gaze. What she saw was that same hunger she'd seen in the barn. Didn't the man ever think of anything except his stomach? "We'd better get going or breakfast will be gone before we get there. I want to get an early start after those two bandidos."

Creed was so busy watching Cricket lace her breasts into

her buckskin shirt that what she'd said didn't sink in for a moment. When it did he still wasn't sure he'd heard her right.

"You're planning to go after the two fellows who stole your money?"

"When Rip hears what happened, I won't have any choice. I got robbed. My horse got stolen. I even spent the night in a man's bed. A pretty rotten evening, if you ask me. Of course, if I can get out of your bedroom before Rip finds out I'm here, maybe we can save your skin. But I'm in for a whipping unless I can get back what was taken from me."

"Rip would *whip* you?"

Cricket's lips screwed into a disarming grin. "It usually hurts him more than it does me. You should see his face when . . . Anyway, his leather lessons are so memorable they don't usually need to be repeated."

"He *beats* you?" Creed repeated, aghast. "You're a girl!"

"I guess after last night, there can't be much mistake about that," she admitted ruefully. "Are you coming?"

She was fully dressed, ready to leave, and Creed was still sitting naked in the bed with the sheet pulled up to his waist.

"Wait," he said. "I want to explain what happened last night."

"Don't bother. I'm not interested."

"Look, Brava—"

"I said it doesn't matter," she interrupted. "I've got more important things to do today than listen to you recite the lurid details of an evening—"

"But there aren't any—"

"NO! Don't explain *anything*. Just keep your mouth shut about last night, do you hear? And maybe, if I'm lucky, I'll be able to forget it ever happened." Of course that was going to be no problem, Cricket thought. She'd have to remember it first in order to forget it.

Creed bubbled inside with anger. He didn't know when he'd ever been so furious with another human being. If she would only let him finish a sentence she wouldn't have to worry about forgetting something that had never happened!

But she kept interrupting! So be it. If she was determined not to let him tell the truth, then she could learn to live with the lie!

"Creed?" The sound of Bay's voice startled them both.

"Hell's bells! I knew this would happen. We're in here, Bay," Cricket called out.

Bay approached the bedroom door apprehensively, afraid of what she'd find. When she entered the room she discovered Creed sitting in the large bed with the sheets pulled up to his waist. He was obviously unclothed beneath the covers. Cricket stood next to the bed. She wore her buckskins, but Bay saw her underthings in a heap on the floor beside her. She blushed and stammered, "I was worried when you didn't show up last night. I thought Creed . . ."

"Your instincts were right, as usual," Cricket said. "Creed took very good care of me. In fact, he even shared his bed with me last night."

"I'm sure Creed did nothing—"

Cricket's harsh laugh stopped Bay. "What you see is—" She paused dramatically, "What you see, Bay, is exactly what it looks like."

"Oh, my."

"And now, if nobody minds, I'm going to get some breakfast."

Cricket turned on her heel and, Creed noted with a shaking head, *stalked* from the bedroom. If her walk was any indication, the events of the evening hadn't been at all devastating to her self-confidence.

"I . . . I . . ." Bay couldn't get out anything that sounded vaguely like the apology she felt she owed for butting in where she wasn't wanted or needed, but she'd been so worried about Cricket and . . . She should have known Cricket would land on her feet. She always did, no matter what the situation. However, this was certainly a unique set of circumstances—especially for Cricket. "I'm sorry," she finally blurted out.

"No need to be. I'll admit the evidence is pretty damning, but nothing happened here last night."

"It didn't?"

"Not that Cricket would let me get a word in edgewise to explain that to her."

Bay grinned. It was the first time Creed had seen her face light up like that, and he found himself grinning back at her.

"So Cricket thinks—"

"The worst," Creed finished ruefully.

"Sometimes Cricket can be a real pain in the—" Bay put her hand over her mouth, aghast at what she'd been about to say in front of the Ranger. Five years in Boston had gone a long way toward improving her speech, but there were times when the first twelve years of her life came back to her with a vengeance. "Very stubborn," she finished primly.

"Yes she can," Creed agreed.

They laughed together, and Creed realized how much he genuinely liked Cricket's sister.

Cricket had forgotten about Bay and Creed as she strode toward the house, planning the best way to explain to Rip what had happened last night. It would be easy to place the blame for everything on Jarrett Creed. After all, if he hadn't taunted her she would never have entered the cantina in the first place. Weak, Cricket. Very weak excuse. She had no one to blame but herself. She should have gone home when Rip asked her to join him. She'd assured him she'd be along shortly, and then she'd played monte for another three hours—waiting for Creed to come back to the cantina, she admitted.

Cricket was surprised to discover Rip sitting in one of the two huge rockers that graced the lower gallery porch. She almost hadn't noticed him, he sat so still. He rose as she approached, and she checked surreptitiously to see if it was apparent she'd come from the bachelors' quarters. No, she could just as easily have been coming from the barn.

"Where have you been? I looked everywhere for you last night."

Cricket hadn't expected her father to know she hadn't come home last night, or to meet her at the front door and question her about where she'd slept. "I was out," she mumbled, moving past him into the large open hallway just inside the door.

Rip followed, towering over her shoulder and lumbering after her like a grizzly reared up on its hind legs.

"Where were you?"

How was she going to answer that?

"None of your business," she tried.

Rip slammed the door behind him, then pulled his leather belt from around his waist and folded it in half.

"Where did you spend the night?" he roared.

Rip's tirade brought Sloan down the stairs. She quickly appraised the situation and said from the bottom step, "Does it really matter? She's home safe now."

"Stay out of this, Sloan," Rip warned. "I asked you a question," he repeated to Cricket. "I want an answer. Now."

At that moment Bay opened the front door. She saw the belt in Rip's hand and almost went back out again. She looked quickly over her shoulder and saw, to her relief, that Jarrett Creed was right behind her.

"Creed's here for breakfast," she said, throwing the front door wide.

Even though Cricket had warned him, Creed was still appalled to see the belt in Rip's hand. The mammoth man seemed not to mind at all that Creed would witness him disciplining his daughter.

"Some problem?" Creed asked, a note of warning in his voice. The space was large, but with the five of them crowded in, Rip was going to hit more than Cricket if he raised the belt. Not one of them moved, however, to get out of his way.

"Don't interfere, Creed. This doesn't concern you."

"You're going to whip your daughter because she was robbed?"

"What? Say that again?"

"Cricket was kidnapped by two Mexicans who were after a little more than the prize money she won yesterday. I saw what was happening and managed to rescue her, but the bandidos got away with her *días de toros* purse and her horse. Surely you can't blame her for that."

Rip listened to Creed's explanation with narrowed eyes. "So you brought Cricket home."

"Yes, I did," Creed confirmed, his eyes steady on Rip's.

Rip turned back to Cricket, suspicion simmering under his demand, "Where did you sleep?"

"I found her in the loft of the barn," Bay supplied.

Rip wheeled on Bay, and she seemed to shrink before Creed's eyes. "I looked in the loft," Rip said. "She wasn't there."

"She was," Bay argued back, her words coming in breathy spurts. "Under the hay. In the corner. Really."

Rip grabbed Cricket's chin in his hand and pulled her face up to look at him. "Next time you say you're coming right home, I'll expect to see your backside in bed the next morning. Do you understand?"

"Yes."

"Yes, what?"

"Yes, *sir*." Cricket replied belligerantly.

"Now let's get some breakfast. I'm hungry as a she-bear in spring."

Rip strapped his belt back around his waist as he headed for the dining room. Creed could feel the tension ease in each of the three girls as they followed their father, exchanging glances that spoke volumes of questions and answers, rebukes and explanations.

"I looked for you last night," Sloan whispered to Cricket. "Where were you?"

"You wouldn't believe me if I told you," she whispered back.

"We have to talk," Sloan said. "I have something important I need to discuss with you."

At that moment they arrived at the dining room and Cricket hissed, "Same here. After breakfast?"

"Sure."

It amazed Creed that Rip had accepted Bay's flimsy, madeup story, and that he hadn't asked Cricket to confirm or deny it. Surely, from what Creed had said, Rip could deduce where Cricket must have spent the night. But Cricket's father hadn't pressed the issue, and before Creed even asked "Why not?" he knew the answer to his question. Rip didn't want to confront the most logical answer—that Cricket had spent the night with Creed. Creed didn't wonder any longer where Cricket had acquired her ability to simply ignore unpleasant realities.

Still, it was plain Rip had been worried about his daughter. He wasn't the uncaring father Creed had accused him of being. He'd threatened Cricket with punishment, but out of concern, and by accepting Bay's excuse he'd given himself a valid reason to forego whipping Cricket.

Creed followed the unusual family into the dining room, and filled a plate with the sumptuous fare provided. He sat at the table and ate in silence, but he was doing some fast thinking. Someone had to forestall Cricket's attempt to go after the Mexicans. He didn't trust Rip to do it, so he broached the issue himself.

"I think I'll take some time off from my work here and go after the two Mexicans who robbed Cricket," he announced.

"That sounds reasonable," Rip agreed.

"I'll go with you," Cricket said.

"I work alone."

Cricket wasn't about to be deterred by Creed's rejection. "Then I'll go by myself."

She watched Creed's fist clench around his fork.

"You'll only get in my way. I'd rather you stayed home."

She stopped chewing when he looked to Rip for support. Surely her father wasn't going to side with Creed!

The big man's chin slipped to his chest and his lips pursed in thought. He turned his fork around and around in his hand. The last thing he wanted was Cricket in Jarrett Creed's company. It was a safe bet she'd spent the night with him last night, but he'd looked into Cricket's eyes and found no feminine awareness there. He'd swear she was still untouched as a woman.

He'd never worried before that Cricket might give herself to a man before she was safely married to Guerrero's son. But something special happened between Cricket and the Ranger every time they got together, and now was not the time to be taking unnecessary chances. Rip lifted his chin.

He stabbed a forkful of fried eggs and stuffed it in his mouth as he announced through the food, "You stay home, Cricket. I've got things for you to do."

Creed's relieved sigh was interrupted by Cricket's sharp retort.

"It was *my* stallion and *my* money that got stolen. I was the one who got knocked on the head and thrown off a galloping horse. I'm not going to sit home while this blade-nosed Ranger takes care of *my* business."

"You'll do as you're told," Rip ordered.

"Like *hell* I will!"

"Like hell you *will!*"

It was the same argument they'd had a hundred times. By the time they got to this point Cricket knew she was but a hair's breadth from having her way. Only this time, the Ranger interfered.

"You're staying with your father."

The quietly spoken words struck like a thunderbolt, interrupting the oft-rehearsed scene. Neither of the two characters were prepared for Creed's cold certainty.

"I won't!" Cricket cried.

"Will you excuse us, please?" Creed said. "Cricket and I need to talk."

Cricket was so disconcerted by Creed's suggestion that she didn't think to object. At Rip's hesitant nod, Creed came around the table. Cricket eyed him like a coiled rattler as he waited for her to stand.

"Is there a place we can speak privately?" he asked.

"You can use my office," Rip volunteered.

"Follow me," Cricket said. Her anger at this point greatly overrode any other emotion. She wondered why Creed wanted to speak privately with her, but she was sure it boded no good.

They stepped into a room as raw and rugged as the frontier. It was clear Bay's gentle influence had not trespassed here. The distinctive smell of leather emanated from the heavy tomes in the bookcase on one wall. Cricket immediately dropped into the smooth rawhide seat of the largest of three cedar chairs near the fireplace. She hoped to give herself a measure of authority by taking Rip's tradition-al place, since it was positioned for power. However, Creed never sat down in one of the two opposing chairs.

He walked over and stood looking down at her from his over-six-foot height, his feet spread wide and his fists perched on his narrow hips, his shoulders back and his chin jutted forward. It was an altogether intimidating posture, and Cricket swallowed hard and reminded herself that she'd never allowed a mere man to intimidate her.

"I don't want you with me when I go after the Mexican bandits. I don't want you to follow me. In fact, I don't want you to leave Three Oaks at all while I'm gone."

Cricket laughed, but it came out as a harsh bark. "What makes you think I'd do anything you asked me to do?"

"I'm not asking. I'm telling. Don't leave Three Oaks while I'm gone."

Cricket had to look up so far to see Creed she had trouble swallowing. There was an easy solution to that problem. She stood up, mimicking his aggressive stance. It helped because she didn't have to look up so far, but now she stood less than a foot away and could feel the tension of coiled muscles, the threatening strength of a man who would not be denied. Except Cricket didn't know the meaning of the word no.

"You're way out of line, Ranger," she purred. "No man tells me what to do."

"I'm not just any man," Creed said, reaching out to caress Cricket's cheek with the knuckles of his hand. "I'm your lover."

Cricket flinched, but held her ground. "I fail to see how that changes anything I've said so far."

"I have an interest in seeing that nothing happens to you, Brava."

"Why is that?"

"My babe may be growing in your belly."

Cricket gasped as her hands flew to her abdomen. Of course! She'd forgotten all about that. She struggled to remember everything Sloan had told her four years ago. Was that all it took? One time? Was she going to have a baby now?

Creed had taken desperate measures to solve what he considered a desperate problem. He was making choices for Cricket again, but he didn't think that could be helped. There wasn't any way he was going to have her tagging along with him or even behind him. She belonged home, safe with her family. He'd get back her money and her horse a lot quicker if he didn't have to worry about her well-being the whole time he was doing his job.

"You need to take care of yourself until you find out for sure one way or the other," he said.

Cricket thought about it for a second and flushed when she realized how she would know "one way or the other."

"I don't want to have a baby," she said, her lower lip thrust forward mulishly.

Creed's large hands came up to cover Cricket's, which were still on her belly.

"Don't be upset, Brava," he soothed, "that's why God made women."

Cricket stepped back from Creed and looked him straight in the eye before she spat, "Well, God can just think again! I've got plans of my own!"

She was gone from the room before he could think of a suitable response to that.

CHAPTER 10

CRICKET LEFT THREE OAKS within minutes after stomping out of the study. She stopped only long enough to tell Sloan their talk would have to wait, to grab necessary supplies and weapons, and to saddle a horse before she was on her way with Rogue at her side. Cricket figured the two bandits had gone south along the Atascosito Road, which ran through Victoria to Goliad, both of them towns populated by *tejanos*. She followed the blaze-marked trail, so confident she would come across some sign of the two Mexicans that she spent the time planning exactly how she would retrieve her stolen possessions.

Several hours later, Cricket's hunch was rewarded when she found the campfire where the two men had spent the past night. They'd camped in a stand of cypress near a stream. There were butts from several cigarettes smoked down to just one inch, exactly as Clemencio had smoked his in the cantina, and remnants of some personal items from her saddlebags, which had been used and discarded.

"See anything you recognize?"

Cricket whirled, drawing her Colt Patterson at the same time, but didn't fire because the mellow Tennessee voice

137

registered in the few seconds it took her to complete her turn.

"You always walk up behind strangers like that?" Cricket demanded, surprised and irritated to find Creed barely a foot away from her. His Comanche upbringing had made him stealthy, she conceded, but she wasn't going to admire him for a trait which made it possible for him to sneak up and frighten her like that.

"You're hardly a stranger." Creed closed the distance between them until the bore of her gun rested against his iron-hard abdomen. He seized her chin with one hand, while the other snaked around her nape so his thumb rested on the pulse at her throat.

"This is no place for a woman, Brava," he said, his face inches from her own, his breath fanning her mouth. "Not even a woman like you."

Cricket could feel her blood pounding as his thumb began to move in slow circles on her neck. She tried to jerk her head from his grasp, even grabbed the wrist holding her chin with her free hand, but it was like struggling against granite. His hold tightened inexorably, then gentled the instant she stopped resisting it. The gun was the only thing that kept them apart, and Cricket could feel the muscles in Creed's belly fighting back against the pressure she applied.

"I could blow a hole in you so big a horse could walk through it," she hissed.

"Why waste a bullet? Why not let your wolf rip out my throat?"

Although she couldn't move her head, Cricket's eyes quickly searched left and right for Rogue. Where was he, anyway?

The Ranger whistled shrilly and the wolf came bounding into sight. He loped over to Creed and Cricket and sat down expectantly between them, his tongue lolling from his mouth.

"Little trick I taught my first pup," Creed said with a mischievous grin. "Works on wolves too, I discovered."

Cricket's face flushed with chagrin. How dare he steal her wolf's allegiance! She closed her eyes, since Creed's grip wouldn't allow her to turn her head away and she didn't want to give him the satisfaction of seeing that she appreciated the almost impossible feat he'd accomplished. Rogue had been tolerant of others, but he'd obeyed no one but Cricket. That is, until Jarrett Creed had stuck his arrogant nose in where it didn't belong.

When she recovered her composure Cricket opened her eyes. "I'm not going home," she said between clenched teeth, "until I get back what was stolen from me."

"I thought not." He sighed heavily.

She felt him assessing the madly racing pulse under her ear for another moment before he abruptly released her and stepped back.

"All right. We'll go together."

Cricket stood for a moment with the gun aimed at Creed before it dawned on her what he'd said. Her eyes narrowed suspiciously. "If this is some kind of trick . . ."

"No tricks, Brava." He held his hands up to show they were empty. "Let's get this over with so we can go home. I'll fetch the horses." He turned from her and disappeared into the stand of cypress.

Cricket stuck her Patterson back in her belt, her brain searching madly for the reason Creed had agreed to let her go with him. Of course there was no way he could make her go home, and he must know that if he took her back she'd only steal away again. But why bother to ask her to join him. Why not just go on by himself?

Creed reappeared momentarily with both their horses. "Ready?"

"I thought you worked alone," Cricket said as she mounted, still not trusting his easy capitulation.

"Who would want to work alone when he could work with a lovely creature like you?" he replied, smiling as he settled into the saddle leather. Creed kicked his chestnut and headed south, leaving Cricket to follow him or not, as she pleased.

Cricket wondered why she followed him, even as she did. She wasn't sure what it meant to be a *lovely creature*. It didn't sound like a compliment, but because it wasn't exactly an insult, either, she decided not to make an issue of it. She could understand the Ranger's need to be alone. Normally she would rather be alone, too. She could also understand why he didn't want them to ride together, since they always seemed to end up arguing. Still, you never knew what would happen when you dealt with bandits. And two guns were better against two bandits than one.

They rode for several hours in silence, and surprised each other with how well they got along. They both kept an eye on the trail, and it took no spoken word to change their course, only a meeting of their eyes, or a nod or a simple gesture.

Cricket fought against the growing thread of admiration for Jarrett Creed which spun itself like a web around her. So what if he could track like a Comanche? So what if he rode as easy in the saddle as a Mexican vaquero? So what if he could spend the entire afternoon beside her, yet leave her free to enjoy the vast solitude that was untamed Texas? He was still a man who'd treated her like a woman. For that alone, he was to be despised. So why didn't she despise him? It was a mystery she thought might unravel if she could only find a place in the skein to start.

In the end, it was Creed who finally broke the silence between them.

"Did Rip always treat you the way he does now?"

At Cricket's confused expression he explained, "I mean, did he always treat you like a boy, let you wear pants and ride mustangs and shoot a gun?"

"I don't ever remember things being any other way," Cricket said tentatively. "My mother died when I was born. I don't remember her at all. If I ever needed anything I went to Sloan, and if she couldn't help, then to Rip."

"So what do you think about the life you lead?"

"It satisfies me."

"Does it?"

"Why wouldn't it?" Cricket demanded.

"I don't know. You tell me."

"I have Rip's approval, and that's what matters to me. The rest of the world can go hang for all I care."

She bristled at Creed's disapproving snort.

"Why do you call him Rip? Why not pa or father?" he asked.

Cricket shrugged. "I don't know. I just always have." She could see from his frown that Creed didn't like that answer, either, but she didn't have a better one. "What do you call your father?"

"Which one?"

Creed's retort brought Cricket's head around with a snap. "Which one? Do you have more than one?"

She could see Creed struggling to find an answer before he spoke.

"I called the man who sired me Pa when I was a small boy," he began. "Then I was captured by the Comanches and adopted by a mean sonofabitch named Crooked Trail. I called him *ap'*—that's Comanche for father—to his face. Behind his back, I called him . . . other things. When I was seventeen and my natural father found me, he was only another White-eyes. Now they're both dead and the problem doesn't arise anymore."

"Did you hate them both so much?"

"Let's just say I don't have much use for fathers."

Cricket heard the bitterness bared by the harsh edge in his voice. "I love Rip," she said quietly. "I love him and I respect him. He's the most important person in my life."

"And he plans to sell you to the highest bidder," Creed shot back.

"What are you talking about?"

"Nothing. Just mouthing off when I shouldn't be."

"Hold on a minute! You can't make a statement like that and pretend you didn't. Rip would never do such a thing!"

"What does your father have planned for your future, Cricket? Sloan gets Three Oaks. Bay gets to be Sloan's right-hand *man*. What about you, Cricket? What do you get? Has Rip told you what he's got in mind for his youngest daughter? Are you ready to be a wife?"

"I already told you I'm never getting married."

Creed barked a laugh. "Guess again. Rip's busy arranging a marriage for you right now!"

"You're lying!"

"I never . . . not about this! Rip is making arrangements right now for your marriage to Señor Guerrero's elder son."

"That doesn't make sense. Marriage is the last thing Rip would suggest for me. He never said anything . . . we never talked about . . . about marriage. He'd never make me do something I truly didn't want to do." Cricket recognized the desperation in her voice, but added, "He wouldn't."

"Rip can and will do anything he pleases. Look at you! You're manipulated by your father like a puppet. He pulls the right strings and you respond. But he's got the strings all tangled, Cricket, and he's pulling in directions you just can't go. You can never satisfy Rip, because no matter how hard you try you can't be his son . . . only his daughter. And daughters get married, Cricket, to rich *hacendados* who—"

"No! No! No!"

Cricket held her hands over her ears because what Creed said was too frightening to hear. She'd discounted Bay's warning about Rip choosing husbands for his daughters because she'd been sure it wouldn't apply to her. Her father was pleased with her. He loved her. She was his favorite, and he'd do anything for her. And she'd do anything for him except . . . He'd never ask her to marry some rich man he'd picked out for her, because he knew she'd never make a good wife. The whole idea of marriage was so . . . so wrong.

She wouldn't let Creed's bald-faced lie shatter her sense of well-being. She didn't believe Jarrett Creed. She wouldn't believe Jarrett Creed. She couldn't believe Jarrett Creed.

But deep, deep down, she did believe him. How often had she cursed being female, because it robbed her of the ability to be the one thing she knew her father wanted most in life—a son. But hadn't she done everything, *everything* Rip had asked her to do? Wasn't she the next best thing to a son? How could Rip even think she would be willing to accept the role of wife to some man? Why, she didn't know a thing about being a wife. Cricket's chin quivered, and she swallowed hard over the lump that had risen in her throat. When Rip made up his mind, the deed was as good as done.

But to be Cruz Guerrero's wife? How could she ever . . . ? How would she know . . . ? She couldn't do . . . !

Why hadn't she talked to Rip sooner? Why hadn't she confronted him the moment Bay had mentioned he planned to choose a husband for her? The answers to those questions told more about her relationship to Rip than Cricket cared to admit. She'd found excuses to avoid the confrontation with her father because she'd been so afraid he'd do what he'd threatened despite her feelings on the matter. Now her worst fears were coming true.

Cricket choked on a sob. She *never* cried. She used her rage to cover her fear, attacking Creed. "Just because you hated your father don't expect me to hate mine! Because I won't. No matter how black you try to paint him I won't hate Rip. I won't! I won't! I won't! I won't!"

Each primal cry came closer to a sob of defeat, and Cricket wouldn't allow Jarrett Creed that satisfaction. She whipped her horse into a gallop, leaving Creed standing in the choking dust raised by her precipitous escape.

Creed resisted the urge to chase after her. He would give her some room, keep his distance from her, until they'd each regained a measure of the peace the quiet wilderness could bring to the soul. In a while, Creed nudged the chestnut into a trot. Why had he bothered to argue with her? What business was it of his how Rip Stewart raised his kids? So what if Cricket adored the man? So what if she refused to admit she couldn't be her father's son? So what if Rip was going to marry her to some Spaniard who wouldn't understand her? He didn't care about her one way or the other. He squinted up at the ruthless Texas sun, then out over the plains, shimmering with the relentless heat. He and Cricket might each find peace in the wilderness, he thought, but there was no comfort there.

For she was hiding from the truth.

And so was he.

Cricket rode hell-for-leather away from Creed, her thoughts racing as wildly as the powerful gelding beneath her. She'd never looked too deeply at her relationship with Rip because she'd always known he loved her best. Was there only one piece of candy left? She got it. Was there a special mustang among those recently captured? She got it.

Was there anything new, special, the best? She got it. She'd never questioned the price she paid for that favoritism. She'd never had any reason to question it.

Creed's arguments had raised terrifying doubts in her mind. Was she really a puppet on a string, dancing to Rip's bidding? Was she being manipulated, reaching out for Rip's approval, like a recalcitrant mule following a carrot held out before it on a long stick?

She'd always considered herself the soul of independence, blithely doing what she wanted to do.

But wasn't everything she wanted to do also something Rip wanted her to do?

So what if it was? Was that so bad? Had he ever forced her to do anything that made her feel uncomfortable or unhappy?

What about Amber Kuykendall's ninth birthday party?

Oh, God! No! Rip would never have let her become a . . .

The tiny seed planted on Amber Kuykendall's birthday had grown over the years, watered by snide comments and sly glances. Despite that one insidious weed, she'd flowered into a happy, contented person because she was exactly what her father wanted her to be. She'd learned her lessons well, and she'd truly been her father's son. Now, after seventeen years, he'd changed his mind. He wanted a daughter he could marry off to a rich *hacendado*. Cricket knew if she became Cruz Guerrero's wife now, Felicia's prophecy would very likely come true.

She would be a freak.

The gelding stumbled from fatigue and almost fell. Cricket reined the exhausted animal to a stop. The beast's head hung low, his billowing nostrils causing tiny dust storms in the red dirt. His muscles trembled so he seemed almost to be shivering. A foamy lather lay in ridges along his neck and shoulders. The barrel chest heaved to bring air to tortured lungs.

Cricket's own chest heaved just as mightily, as though she'd been the one running, and not the horse. The sharp aroma of hot sweat and leather rose almost like steam, so Cricket couldn't help but breathe it. She slipped from the saddle and her legs buckled under her, sending her crumpling to her knees on the ground. Her face fell forward into her hands. How many times had she pleased Rip and denied herself, only to discover it wasn't enough? It was never going to be enough. Now Rip planned to change all the rules, and force her back into a role she'd rejected her whole life at his insistence.

She began to tremble all over. The trembling became a shiver, the shiver a tremor, until her whole body was like an earthquake, shifting and grating and tearing asunder all the beliefs she'd held in her heart. And from the yawning abyss the howling of furies threatened to erupt. She tried to strangle the sound, tried to keep it contained within flesh and bone, but the pain and pressure built and built until finally a keening wail tore loose from somewhere deep inside her and rose pitiably on the clear, clean air.

Agonized groans began deep in her belly and wrenched their way through her chest and out her contorted mouth. No cleansing tears came to blur reality and wash it away. Dry-eyed, she faced the past and feared the future. She thrust her fist in her mouth, biting down hard to stem the wails, damning her weakness, her inability to keep the truth at bay. She fought against the hysterical pressure in her chest, unable to choke back the sobs which exploded each time in gut-wrenching groans of pain. At last, tears began dripping in hot hellpaths down her cheeks.

She couldn't stop the cries of anguish. Couldn't stop the trembling of her body. Couldn't stop the pain. She began to rock back and forth, back and forth, gripping herself across the belly with her arms as though her insides might fly out if she didn't hold them tight.

A cold nose poked against her wet cheek, and she grabbed at the comfort Rogue offered, digging her hands deep into the wolf's fur and smothering her sobs against his warm body.

The wolf lay down before her and raised his head to the big, blue Texas sky, wailing mournfully, unsure of the cause of Cricket's distress but fully sharing it.

Creed heard the lone wolf's ululating cry, a prairie song of grief, and wondered at its ability to move him. It was uncanny how the howl captured all the isolation a man felt in this land. The wolf's lament spoke not of birth and hope, but of death and the inevitable end to dreams. He didn't put much faith in dreams coming true, and it had saved him a load of heartache. Not Cricket, though. She'd let Rip's dream become her own . . . and it was a dream doomed to failure.

Had there ever been a time in his life when he'd trusted his father with the same unequivocal certainty as Cricket trusted Rip? Maybe, once, a long time ago he had. Nobody should put his life that fully in another's hands, Creed thought. It was too much of a temptation, too much of a burden for a mere mortal. And despite the way he acted, Rip was only human. Cricket was headed for a fall, all right. He wished to God there were some way he could save her all that pain. But he knew that wasn't possible. Growing hurt. Nothing was ever going to change that.

The howl came again, a sad, solitary sound. And then its echo, equally lonesome.

Creed gave in to the feeling and mourned with the wolf.

CHAPTER 11

CRICKET SHOULD HAVE known better than to start walking in her dazed state, with no thought to where she was or where she was going. And if she was going to wander around like that on foot, leading the exhausted gelding, she should have at least kept Rogue by her side. Of course, she thought as she registered the identity of the two men who'd suddenly appeared before her, it was useless to worry about should-haves now. But she hoped her blunder didn't turn out to be a deadly mistake.

"We meet again, *chiquita.*"

"I get her first."

Cricket looked from Clemencio to Oscar and back to Clemencio again, noting the equally lascivious grins on both faces. Seeing them on their Spanish ponies before her was a shock, but it was the sight of the dozen other grizzle-faced bandidos arrayed around them that stood her neck hairs on end. Still, there was nothing like a crisis to bring out the best in Cricket.

"The first person to touch me gets a bullet in the gut," she said, a Patterson appearing miraculously in her hand. "So, come to me," she taunted Oscar. "I'm waiting for you."

A rumble of surprised expletives traveled through the

motley group when her challenge was translated, but no one moved. After all, a *puta* and a *pistola* were a dangerous combination.

Cricket knew it was only a matter of time before they figured out there were fourteen of them and one of her, even if she did have a gun in her hand. They wouldn't expect her to be an accurate shot, even though she was. From the looks of them, they'd run if she started shooting. But if they didn't run . . .

"Alejandro, talk some sense into the bitch!" Oscar demanded.

Oscar recognized his mistake as soon as he'd made it. Though the band of outlaws had no formal leader, there was a pecking order, and a banty rooster had presumed upon the cock-o'-the-walk. Oscar willed himself to disappear when the man he'd addressed turned his imperious stare down on him. However, once Oscar's submission was clear, the Mexican cock directed his attention to the tall young woman before him.

"Hey, *puta,* put away the gun and we'll talk," his gravel-rough voice cajoled.

Cricket slowly shifted her focus from Oscar and Clemencio to the man called Alejandro. He sat tall in the saddle, and gave an impression of insolent superiority. He was dressed like a vaquero in a wool shirt, overlaid by a vibrantly striped poncho, and leather *calzoneras* covering buckskin breeches. As he gestured, a wide silver bracelet flashed in the sunlight. His huge sombrero put his entire face in shadow, making his eyes two dark, fiery hellholes. A bushy mustache covered his upper lip, while the lower lip curved downward disdainfully. He held his broad shoulders ramrod straight, unyielding, and Cricket thought, *This man will show no mercy.*

"We have nothing to say to each other," she said.

"If you put down the gun my man won't have to hurt you. He's right behind you."

It was an old trick, Rip had warned, to threaten another enemy behind you. When you turned around, the enemy in front made his move. Cricket mentally thanked Rip for the lesson, and fearlessly faced the merciless Mexican.

"I'll take my chances," she said.

The Mexican shrugged, then nodded.

A tingle of fear raced up Cricket's spine. She dropped and rolled to the left as the Mexican behind her whipped his gun barrel down where her head had been. She came to her feet running, dodging between the cactus and the sagebrush.

The bandidos came racing after her, like hounds after a hare, their howls of glee ringing through the air.

Cricket cursed Rip as she ran. Another lesson gone awry! It seemed this was a day full of disillusionment. She would be overrun if she stopped to aim her gun, so she didn't waste the time trying. She was fast, but her endurance was no match for the Spanish ponies.

Cricket had no doubt of her fate once she was caught, so while she ran, she considered whether she should save the last bullet in her Patterson for herself. The thought that Jarrett Creed couldn't be far behind her decided the matter. This was a time to be reckless.

She spent all five bullets, wounding three Mexicans, before the man called Alejandro lassoed her arms and shoulders with his horsehair *reata* and dragged her to the ground. The man's cruelty was confirmed when, rather than loosening the rope when he reached her, he yanked her upright and wound several more tight loops around her body. When her arms were pinned to her sides from shoulder to waist, he forced her up behind him on his pony.

"The *puta's* shots will have revealed our whereabouts to the Rangers chasing us. Ride!" he commanded.

The two wounded Mexicans who could manage by themselves mounted their horses. The third was pulled up behind a friend. The mood of the bandits was vicious, and Cricket was thankful their revenge had to be postponed. All too soon, she thought, the time would come when they would vent their rage on her body. Unless she could escape. Or someone rescued her.

At first Cricket believed Alejandro was referring to Creed

when he mentioned the Mexicans were being chased by Rangers. Then she realized he'd referred to more than one Ranger. She couldn't help the surge of hope that bounced from edge to edge inside her, despite the fact she was now clearly a prisoner of the bandits. Having wounded three of them, she was in serious trouble if the Rangers didn't ride to the rescue. But it was not for nothing the Mexicans had labeled the Rangers *Los Diablos Tejanos*. She was counting on the Texas Devils to arrive in the nick of time.

As late afternoon wore on into evening, Cricket refused to allow despair to overwhelm her. If the band of Rangers chasing the bandits wasn't right behind them, surely Jarrett Creed was. And one Ranger could whip at least a dozen bandidos. Couldn't he?

They rode without stopping until they couldn't see to ride anymore. Cricket's whole body ached. She wasn't sure which bruises were the result of the bronc riding at the *días de toros*, which were compliments of Oscar and Clemencio, and which she owed to Alejandro, but she vowed that if she got out of this alive, she would try to take things a little easier for a while.

Cricket's heart lost a beat when she realized the Mexicans were stopping. Alejandro helped her to dismount and released her from the coils of his *reata*, while the other Mexicans tethered their horses and then dropped exhausted to the ground nearby. By the time she stood unfettered before their glittering gazes her racing heart threatened to force its way out her throat which, fortunately, was far too constricted to allow it such an easy escape.

Clemencio rose and took a step toward her, but was brought up short when Alejandro announced, "We stop only until the moon is up. Meanwhile, the *puta* stays with me."

Cricket might have been relieved, except as Alejandro spoke his hand punishingly gripped her neck and his callused fingertips probed the quicksilver pulse at her throat. Cricket turned her head away from Alejandro's wool poncho, which smelled of horse and rancid male sweat, but couldn't dodge the sexual heat which emanated from a body coiled in readiness for wild animal thrusting. Cricket shud-

dered. Even the hope of a respite from rape died when
Alejandro brought his mouth to her ear and murmured too
low for the others to hear, "You want me, eh, *puta?* Every bit
of me, *sí?*"

Both Cricket and Alejandro had been oblivious to the rest
of the Mexicans, but their muted grumbling found voice
when one of them demanded, "You must share the *puta!* She
belongs to all of us!" His cry was joined by several others as
the Mexicans left their horses and surrounded the couple. It
appeared Alejandro might have to relinquish his prize when
a series of gunshots erupted in the darkness. An equal
number of Mexicans at the edge of the circle fell where they
stood.

"Los Diablos Tejanos!"

The shouted warning that the Rangers had found them
sent the bandits scurrying for their horses. In the melee that
ensued, Cricket tore from Alejandro's grasp and raced
toward where Valor was hobbled.

"Cricket!"

There was no mistaking that commanding Tennessee
voice, yet Cricket ignored it and kept on running. She was
not leaving without her money and her horse!

"Dammit, Brava, get over here!" Creed shouted.

Cricket ignored him, but several of the Mexicans did not.
Creed found himself the focus of heavy gunfire, and had to
concentrate on sliding away on his belly to a safer spot.

Meanwhile, Cricket reached Valor at about the same time
as Clemencio, who blocked her avenue of escape. The
Mexican grinned before he reached out confidently for her
with his right arm. Cricket was in no mood for games. She
curved her foot deftly behind his ankle as she ducked under
his arm and then shoved as hard as she could at his chest
with both hands.

Clemencio gave a howl as he lost his balance and toppled
over backwards. She grabbed her gun from his hand as he
fell and pointed it at him.

"Don't bother getting up," she warned, "or I'll put a
bullethole right between your eyes."

She quickly checked her saddlebag, and from the chink of

coins inside, determined that her *días de toros* purse was where she'd left it. Then, giving the Mexican one last warning to, "Stay right where you are if you want to live," she mounted Valor and headed back toward where she'd last heard Creed.

"I'll see you at Three Oaks!" she yelled as she galloped past him at a speed horrifyingly dangerous in the darkness.

The Mexicans were in full rout, too fearful of *Los Diablos Tejanos* to stop long enough to ascertain there was only one Ranger shooting at them. However, both Alejandro and Clemencio noted the direction of Cricket's escape and soon were on the trail behind her.

Creed slipped away to his chestnut and was after them in moments. He was furious with Cricket, and at the same time frightened for her. What if her horse stumbled and fell? What if the Mexicans decided to stop her with a bullet? He kicked his chestnut into a faster gallop, praying the animal could see better in the dark than he could. Soon he perceived one of the Mexicans in front of him. He feared to shoot in the dark, not knowing how close Cricket might be.

Cricket could hear the pounding hooves of the horses that followed. She could feel Valor tiring and knew that unless she could come up with a plan, the bandidos would recapture her and she'd have to endure the embarrassment of being rescued by Creed all over again. She remembered they'd passed a deep arroyo not long before they'd stopped, and she strained her eyes to find it again in the dark. There it was! She brought Valor to a sliding stop, threw the reins around his neck, grabbed her saddlebag and canteen, and then slapped him on the haunch, ordering, "Go home, boy!"

The stallion snorted once and then flipped his tail and broke into a gallop heading north. Cricket slipped into the arroyo near the trail and waited with bated breath for the enemies who followed. She saw Alejandro fly by, followed closely by Clemencio and then Creed. She started to shout to Creed, but realized she would likely be heard by Clemencio and Alejandro as well. Cricket settled down to wait. When Creed had disposed of Clemencio and Alejandro he would head for Three Oaks, expecting to find her there ahead of him. She smiled, thinking of his consternation when he discovered she'd sent the stallion home alone. She sighed and closed her eyes to rest for a moment before she began the long walk home.

Cricket awoke disoriented. The moon had risen fully in the sky, providing a blue-white light that revealed the world in shapes, rather than colors. She was surprised by the quiet. She told herself she had nothing to be frightened of. The bandidos were long gone and there was nothing she needed to fear in the dark. But she'd never been more aware of being alone. Absolutely alone.

She fought her creeping uneasiness by standing up and stretching the stiffness out of her arms and legs. Her right hand had that awful dead feeling because she'd lain on it, and it tingled unpleasantly as the blood flooded back through its leaden weight.

The warm water in her canteen quenched her thirst, but it wasn't very refreshing. She poured some out and dabbed it on her eyes, and that felt a little better. She pulled the canteen strap over her head and arranged it on one shoulder while she settled the saddlebag on the other. There was nothing to fear in the dark, she told herself as she began walking. Nothing at all. In fact, she was probably safer traveling in the dark. She only wished it wasn't quite so far to Three Oaks.

Cricket had been traveling for some time when she saw the campfire in the distance. At this point, she would've welcomed any form of company, and she sought out the warmth and light of that faraway fire the way a rattler sought out a sun-baked rock in autumn. She had no doubt the travelers would share their campfire. How good a cup of coffee would taste! It was only as she got closer and made out the three figures hunched around the flickering light that Rip's lessons on using caution with strangers came back to her.

So, instead of approaching the camp directly she dropped to her hands and knees to slither through the brush and grass toward the beacon of light. She was still too far away to clearly see the faces of the men by the fire when she heard the murmur of voices. She inched closer and listened.

"You're the only Ranger I've got available. Can you do it, Luke?"

Cricket tensed. She'd recognize that voice anywhere. She started to stand up, but ducked back down when she heard the response of the man Creed had addressed as Luke.

"I don't see why not. Do you think Sloan suspects we're watching her?"

Sloan was being watched by the Rangers? What for?

"No, I don't think she knows we're on to her. On the other hand, she disappeared for a while during the Guerreros' *fandango,* and was damned careful nobody followed her," Creed said.

Sloan had said she was going to meet Tonio. . . .

"How deeply is she involved with Antonio Guerrero?" a third voice asked.

"If you're asking if she's a part of his efforts to help the Mexican government work out plans to invade Texas again," Creed said, "I'm not convinced she's involved at all. But they are lovers."

They knew Sloan and Antonio were lovers?

Cricket couldn't believe what she was hearing. Sloan, a traitor? Sloan, involved in a Mexican plot to invade Texas? Impossible! Yet hadn't Sloan wanted to talk with her only this morning about something very important? And Sloan had met secretly with Tonio at the Guerreros' *fandango.* Cricket wished she'd taken a minute before she left Three Oaks to hear what Sloan had to say. Well, there was no help for that now. She'd have to listen closely without letting on she was here. When she'd found out all she could about the Rangers' plans she'd confront Sloan and get this mess straightened out.

Ever so quietly she moved close enough to make out the faces of the three men by the fire. She pursed her lips in disgust when she saw Rogue lying on the ground beside Creed, who scratched the wolf's chin unconcernedly. Her eyes widened in consternation when she recognized one of the other two men as the half-breed Comanche, Long Quiet. She'd heard three distinct voices, but one of them hadn't been the broken English the half-breed had used at the corral.

"How soon do you want me to take over for you at Three Oaks?" the man called Luke asked.

"Right away. I'm supposed to be in Galveston in a few weeks. The navy's sloop-of-war *Austin* should be rigged out and ready by then to take me on to New Orleans. I'd as soon leave now as later," Creed said.

Creed was leaving Three Oaks. Why did she find that such a desolate thought?

"This is awful sudden, isn't it?" Luke asked.

"President Lamar wants to get his version of the Council House massacre to the highest-ranking American diplomat he can as soon as he can."

"And who's that?"

"There's no ambassador to Texas since the United States hasn't officially recognized our government. The best they'd give us was a chargé d'affaires, a sort of one-man diplomatic liaison. The man Andrew Jackson appointed as chargé, Beaufort LeFevre, lives in New Orleans, which is where I'm headed."

Luke shook his head. "So why the big hurry?"

"President Lamar's afraid the chargé will read about the Council House massacre in the papers and use it as an excuse to curtail discussions on trade agreements between the United States and Texas. We need those trade concessions, especially for cotton exports."

"How'd you get picked for this job, anyway?" Luke asked.

"I know the chargé."

"Really? How'd you meet him?"

Creed grinned. "Through his daughter."

The other two men laughed.

"I'd forgotten about Angelique," Long Quiet said. "I'm sure you'll enjoy seeing her again. But what can you say to Beaufort LeFevre to make the Council House massacre sound like less than the travesty it was?"

The half-breed Comanche was speaking perfect English!

"Not a thing," Creed admitted cynically. "I'm just supposed to talk him into coming here to see the situation in Texas for himself. That's why Lamar wants this business with Guerrero tied up in a hurry. He doesn't want a Mexican invasion materializing in the middle of the American chargé's visit."

"I'll do my part at Three Oaks," Luke said. "Do you suppose Cricket's done gallivanting around by now? I'd hate to get there and have Rip Stewart ask me where his daughter is."

Creed snorted. "Don't get me started, Luke. I'd like to wring that she-wolf's neck. She flew out of that bandit camp on her horse and lit a shuck for Three Oaks, leaving me in her dust. By the time I made sure those two Mexicans following her weren't going to be any threat she was long gone. She's probably been home in bed—or wherever it is she's sleeping these days—for hours."

Cricket ground her teeth. So Jarrett Creed would like to wring her neck, would he! The feeling was definitely mutual!

"Be grateful, my friend, that your coltish filly isn't around to tempt you into bed with her again," Long Quiet said with a chuckle. "You were lucky to escape with your honor the last time."

Cricket gasped. Creed couldn't have told Long Quiet about that! She quickly covered her mouth with her hand to prevent the escape of any further sound, but it was too late to avoid discovery. The three men at the fire fanned out instantly, and in moments she found herself imprisoned in Jarrett Creed's iron grasp.

"What are you doing here?"

There was no mistaking the fury in his voice, but Cricket snarled back, "I could ask the same thing. Who are you to accuse Sloan of plotting with the Mexicans? What does Antonio Guerrero have to do with all this? And how come that half-breed can suddenly speak perfect English?"

Creed cursed.

"Now the fat's in the fire. What are we going to do with her?" Luke asked.

"Send her home to Rip! Let him handle her!" Creed snapped.

"We can't send her home," Long Quiet said. "She knows too much."

Creed dropped his chin to his chest, as though to ease the tension in the back of his neck, and sighed as he raised his head again. "I know that," he said wearily. "She'd warn her sister in a—"

"You bet I'll warn Sloan! Try and stop me!" Cricket cried. "Wait till Rip hears what you—"

Cricket's tirade was shut off when Creed clamped his hand over her mouth and tucked her bodily under his arm so she couldn't move. "Shut up, Brava, and let us think."

Cricket struggled futilely against Creed's strength, all the while glaring at Rogue, who sat complacently at Creed's feet while the Ranger held her helpless in his arms. How different from their very first confrontation! Well, she wasn't done fighting by a long shot! She jerked in Creed's arms as he suggested to Long Quiet, "Why don't you keep her with you."

"You know I'm headed back into *Comanchería.*"

Long Quiet stared at Creed until he admitted, "All right, that was a stupid idea. But what are we going to do with her?"

"Why not take her to San Antonio?" Luke suggested.

"That's fine for a while," Creed replied. "What do I do with her when I have to meet Commodore Moore in Galveston?"

"You could take her with you," Luke said.

Creed snickered. "I don't think Cricket's going anywhere with me peaceably. How am I supposed to explain the struggling woman under my arm to the commodore?"

The suggestions Cricket was hearing were alarming, to say the least. Surely Creed couldn't seriously be contemplating kidnapping her. She kicked and jerked vigorously in his arms, doing her best to make sure the three men understood that Creed was right—she had no intentions of cooperating with them.

"How about if I grab her by the hair and haul her after me like some fur trapper with his squaw," Creed demanded, suiting deed to word and wrapping Cricket's braid in his fist. "That would surely pacify the commodore and go a long way toward proving to the American chargé we're not savages in Texas! And what do you propose I do with this—this brat in buckskins—while I'm trying to conduct my business? She's going to stick out like a cactus in a patch of bluebonnets."

At that, Cricket lay still in Creed's arms, panting. She told herself she was waiting for her second wind. Creed's words hadn't meant a thing to her. He wasn't saying anything she didn't already know. She'd always been a little different. And she wasn't ever going to change.

Her scalp hurt where Creed had yanked her hair. She told herself it was that pain that choked her throat and caused the burning threat of tears at the corners of her eyes. It had nothing to do with caring about what some wag-wit Texas Ranger thought of her. After all, she had Rip's approval and . . . and . . . *oh, God! What good was Rip's approval going to do her if he married her off to Cruz Guerrero?*

Cricket listened, but the three men only had half her attention. She knew they'd eventually decide they had no choice except to let her go. Right now she had to start figuring out some way to convince Rip when she got home that he'd made a big mistake even thinking about wedding her to the Spanish *hacendado*.

"You could take Cricket along as your sister," Luke suggested.

Creed smiled wryly. "And keep her in the same room with me?"

"You could keep her in the same room if she were your wife," Long Quiet said.

"My wife?"

Creed's exclamation startled Cricket so much she shouted the same thing into his hand, but it came out "Myffe!" The three men suddenly had her full attention again.

"Why not?"

"It's ridiculous, that's why," Creed said.

Cricket agreed with him wholeheartedly. She bobbed her head up and down behind his hand.

"No, it's not," Long Quiet said. "It solves another problem as well, which is how to keep Rip from hunting for Cricket when she suddenly disappears."

"It'd work," Luke said. "You could write a letter to Rip saying you'd eloped with Cricket, and—"

"And by the time you get back from New Orleans with the American chargé we'll have this whole business with Sloan Stewart settled one way or the other," Long Quiet finished.

"It won't work."

"Then make another suggestion," Long Quiet said.

Cricket wrenched her head up so she could see Creed's face. He didn't look happy. Good. Because she wasn't the least bit thrilled by this latest suggestion, either.

"You could spend some time with your brother and his wife before you leave for Galveston, maybe smooth some of the rough edges off the girl," Long Quiet added, to sweeten the sour pill he and Luke had offered Creed.

Creed frowned. A sham marriage was a terrible solution to the problem of what to do with Cricket, but he couldn't think of anything better. On the other hand, it would be a marvelous opportunity to show her a life beyond the unnatural role Rip had preordained for her. They'd never actually consummate the marriage, so they could each go their separate ways with no harm done once the need to keep Cricket away from Three Oaks ended.

He assiduously avoided thinking about all those nights Cricket would be in his bed—but not really his wife. However, with Cricket's attitude toward intimacy he was certain she'd make sure nothing happened between them, even if his willpower wavered.

"I'll do it," Creed said at last.

Creed released his hold on Cricket's mouth so she could speak, but held onto her arms, lest she flee.

"Well I won't!" she snapped. "The sun will freeze cotton before I'll marry you! I'm never going to be a wife to any man!"

Creed smiled sardonically. His theory on the chastity of their marriage bed was proving correct.

"As far as the law's concerned in Texas, Brava, once we announce our marriage and start living together as man and wife, the deed's done."

"I'll never let you—"

"You already have," Creed interrupted Cricket. "Last night." He wasn't about to let her use the consummation of the marriage as an excuse to foil the only plan they had to deal with her.

Cricket blanched.

"I'd certainly be willing to make sure we don't repeat the mistake," Creed added. "Not only that, but when we get back from New Orleans, I'd be willing to divorce you."

Cricket winced. So, she'd enjoyed herself *immensely* but "it" hadn't been so good for Jarrett Creed. That troubled her, but she didn't know why.

"Perhaps you need a little more incentive," Creed said. "Unless you go with me to New Orleans we'll arrest Sloan now. We know enough to connect her with Antonio Guerrero, who's the leader of a small band of Mexican revolutionaries. Even Rip Stewart won't be able to keep a threat to the Republic—like your sister—out of jail. On the other hand, if you cooperate, we'll do everything we can to exonerate Sloan if she's not a traitor and you'll get a short holiday in New Orleans."

Cricket remained stubbornly silent, thinking. She sought for a way she could help Sloan without succumbing to Creed's ultimatum, but nothing came to mind. Furthermore, so long as she stayed with Creed, her father couldn't marry her off to Cruz Guerrero. She was pretty sure even Rip wouldn't be able to pawn off his *divorced* daughter on the Spanish *hacendado*. Maybe Creed was about to do her a big favor after all.

"What do you say, Brava? Will you come along with me and behave yourself?"

"I don't seem to have much choice," she snapped. "Do I?"

Creed dismissed the nagging feeling that besieged him when Cricket acceded without more of a fight. But he couldn't afford to look a gift horse in the mouth. "Good, then it's settled. We'll start for my brother's plantation, Lion's Dare, tonight."

Creed released Cricket as he turned to Luke. "I'd like you to come with us. I'll give you a letter when we reach Lion's Dare that you can take to Rip."

As soon as Creed turned away, Cricket realized there was still a chance she could escape before this bizarre plan was set into action. "Rogue!" she commanded. "Watch!"

The wolf was immediately all fangs and fur as he crouched before the three men. Cricket raced for the horses. She was congratulating herself on her success when a heavy weight came down on her shoulders, then curled around her, twisting to break her fall.

"Dammit, Brava, stop siccing that wolf on me!" a furious Creed hissed, his arms tight around her.

Cricket couldn't breathe, but she wasn't sure her breathlessness had anything to do with her fall. She was lying full length along Creed's body, her back to his chest, her head resting on his shoulder, his nose next to her ear. Their legs were tangled together, and his forearms cinched her breasts. One large male hand grasped her hip and the other clutched the space between her thighs, which had suddenly flooded with heat.

Cricket's fury kept her from examining the strange sensations in all the places where Creed was touching her. Instead she focused on the fact that the stubborn-headed jackass holding her had foiled her attempt to escape! "Why don't you let me go!"

"I can't." The way Creed said it, so calmly, so certainly, infuriated Cricket even more.

"Rip will come after you when he finds out what you've done!" she raged.

"That's my problem, isn't it?" Creed shoved Cricket off, then lurched to his feet and yanked her up after him. "Now call off your wolf."

Cricket started to argue again, but reconsidered when she saw the savage look on Creed's face. "Rogue," she called, "it's okay."

The wolf trotted over to be petted by Creed.

"Traitor," Cricket muttered.

Creed kept a trembling hand on the wolf's head, waiting for the tension to ease. God, how he wanted to touch that wild, fierce woman! He wanted to hold her and kiss her and feel her all around him. Now she was going to be his wife—in name only. It was going to be torture! He'd rather be sent unarmed to face a dozen Comanches.

"One more try like that and the deal's off," Creed threatened tersely. "Sloan will be in jail before you can say 'traitor to Texas.' Settle down and resign yourself to the situation, do you hear?"

Mulishly, Cricket remained silent.

Creed grasped her shoulders and shook her hard. "Do you hear?"

Cricket nodded slightly, clenching her teeth to restrain the the retort on the tip of her tongue.

Creed released her so abruptly she almost fell. He sought out Long Quiet to discuss the half-breed's efforts to assuage the Comanches' anger over the Council House massacre.

Luke approached Cricket as she massaged her aching arms. "You trained your wolf pretty well," he said in a soothing tone of voice. "He seems to like Creed, though, doesn't he?"

Cricket looked for the first time at the youth who'd been talking with Creed and Long Quiet. She felt an affinity to the young man she couldn't explain. She searched his features for an answer as to why she felt so at ease with him. He had dark brown hair and hazel eyes, and he was very tall and thin, with sharp, high cheekbones and a narrow nose over a wide, full mouth. He couldn't be much older than she was, but she could feel bitterness emanating from him like waves against the sandy Texas gulf coast.

"I'm Luke Summers," he said.

"You're a Ranger?"

"Yeah."

Luke seemed too somber to Cricket, and his eyes were sad. Perhaps that was what made her uncharacteristically reach out to him.

"I'm pleased to meet you, Luke," she said, extending her hand. The young man hesitated before he clasped her palm. The feeling of empathy with Luke was even stronger when they touched. She looked up quickly to see if the young man felt the same thing she did. His mouth had tightened grimly and his eyes had gone totally blank. Cricket shivered at the desolation she saw on his face. He didn't speak, merely nodded and released her hand as quickly as he could. Cricket couldn't take her eyes off him, and held him prisoner with her gaze.

Creed gritted his teeth against the jealousy that flared within him when he saw Luke holding Cricket's hand. He thought of Luke's reputation with the ladies in San Antonio. The kid must have some sort of magic in his touch, Creed fumed, because here was his *brava* acting funny and staring at Luke with glazed eyes. Enough was enough.

"We'd better get started," he said, interrupting them.

"Sure," Luke replied, tearing his gaze from Cricket's. "I'll get the horses."

Cricket stared after Luke until Creed took her by the arm. "Where's your horse?" he asked.

She woke from her trance. "I sent him home."

"You'll have to ride with me then." His irritation increased at her obvious preoccupation with the young man.

"I'll be heading back into *Comanchería* now," Long Quiet said. "I'll do what I can to keep tempers calm. But you should expect some reprisals for the Council House massacre and take the best care you can to guard against them. Warn your brother and his wife to be careful. I'd hate for anything to happen to them or their son."

"We'll be careful," Creed said. "Don't worry about us, just take care of yourself." Creed stretched his arm out to the half-breed who clasped it elbow to wrist.

"Goodbye, *haints*," Long Quiet said. He glanced at Cricket and smiled. "And good luck."

163

Long Quiet had disappeared into the darkness by the time the other three had mounted up, with Cricket behind Creed.

"Where's your brother's plantation?" Cricket asked as they rode north on the Atascosito Road.

"Lion's Dare is near the settlement where the Texas declaration of independence was signed, our own Washington, on the Brazos River," Creed replied. "If we ride hard we should be there to meet Tom and Amy sometime late tomorrow."

"What if they don't like me? What if they don't want me there?"

"You're my wife, Cricket. For that reason alone, they'll love you."

Cricket snorted. That was a laugh. She'd met lots of people like Tom and Amy Creed. They'd treat her no differently than all the others, their looks condescending and pitying, even if they bit back their criticism in deference to Creed. But did it have to be that way? For the first time in her life she'd be making decisions based on what *she* wanted, and not on what she thought Rip would approve . . . because Rip wasn't going to approve of this at all. So maybe . . . maybe things would be different.

Of course she had no intention of changing any of her habits. Creed was welcome to chip away at her rough edges, but he wasn't going to find any diamond. She tightened her grasp around Creed's waist, conscious of the ridged muscles she could feel through his shirt with her fingertips. There was a strange sensation in her chest, where the tips of her breasts rubbed against his back. She held him tighter, hoping the feeling would go away, but instead, it got worse.

It was too bad she couldn't remember more about the night she'd spent in Jarrett Creed's arms. Although she and Creed would be man and wife, she'd insisted on giving up an important part of that relationship. It was probably better that way, though. When Creed finally divorced her, there would be no intimate memories to hold them together.

No, it was definitely wiser to avoid being Jarrett Creed's wife in that one particular way.

CHAPTER 12

$\mathbf{D}$ESPITE THE FACT that Lion's Dare appeared exactly as Cricket had pictured it, she was proved startlingly wrong about her reception by Tom and Amy. From the instant Creed introduced her as his wife, she was literally taken to the bosom of the young couple, who greeted them both effusively at the front door of their white frame plantation house.

"My dear," Amy said, hugging Cricket and drawing her inside the central hallway, "you are precisely the kind of woman I'd have chosen for Jarrett."

"I am?" Cricket blurted.

"Why, of course," Amy said, laughing. She released Cricket and gently ruffled the fringe on her buckskin shirt. "Jarrett deserves a bride as much in love with the wilderness as he is."

"Congratulations, Jarrett," Tom said, shaking his brother's hand with both of his. "I must say I'm surprised, but pleased. Two visits in four years and you suddenly show up with a bride at your side. I hope you're planning to stay a while this time."

"We can't stay long. I have to travel to New Orleans in a few weeks and Cricket's coming along with me, but I hoped you and Amy would be willing to put up with us till then."

Cricket tensed when Creed's arm encircled her waist, but didn't jerk away. He'd explained to her on the long ride to Lion's Dare that she'd need to endure certain signs of affection from him for the sake of appearances. No one was to know the true, temporary nature of their relationship. However, she couldn't keep from flinching when his lips brushed her cheek in a swift caress.

Amy smiled approvingly at the tender gesture.

"It's our pleasure to have you here, Jarrett," Amy said with a dazzling smile. "We're so glad you thought to come to us."

Cricket watched Amy move into Tom's arms, saw how naturally his hands encircled her hips, how she leaned her head back against his shoulder, how his lips caressed her temple in much the same manner as Creed's had caressed her cheek. Tom and Amy were obviously very much in love. How were she and Creed ever going to fool them?

"When did you two get married?" Tom asked.

"We eloped yesterday," Creed announced, his grasp on Cricket's waist tightening as he felt her pulling away. "We didn't want to wait any longer to be together. I'm sending a letter to Cricket's father to let him know she's fine and we'll be in touch. I'd rather he didn't know where we are so we can have a little time alone before we greet Cricket's family as man and wife."

Tom winked at his brother. "Can't say as I blame you."

Cricket felt a flush rising as the two brothers exchanged crooked grins.

"You must be tired," Amy said to Cricket.

The two brothers exchanged a second set of leering grins—of which Amy appeared oblivious, but which caused Cricket's flush to worsen.

"Come upstairs with me, Cricket, and I'll show you to your room," Amy said, moving from Tom's arms. "You can rest for a while and change your clothes before supper."

Cricket turned within Creed's arms and looked up at him beseechingly. She wasn't the least bit tired, and she had no other clothes with her besides the buckskins on her back.

She realized Amy thought she'd worn the buckskins to travel in, much as another woman might wear knickers under her skirt. It bothered her to think that after this friendly greeting she'd have to bear the other woman's censure. But she steeled herself against feeling anything. When did Creighton Stewart ever let what other people thought bother her? Not for a long, long time, and she certainly wasn't about to start now. Rip's betrayal made no difference at all in her attitude towards other people's opinions. No difference at all.

"You go on up with Amy," Creed urged. "I'll be in the parlor long enough to write a letter for Luke to deliver to your father."

The letter to Rip would say they'd fallen in love and eloped, and were on their way to Galveston for an extended honeymoon. Cricket had tried to convince Creed that Rip would never believe such an outlandish story, but had to agree that even if he did try to find them after he received the message, he'd never think to look for them at Lion's Dare.

"I'll be up to join you soon, darling," he added, giving Cricket a gentle shove in Amy's direction.

Darling? Cricket fought a grimace at the endearment. Wasn't that carrying things a bit too far? She'd agreed to this charade without knowing how fully Creed had planned to play the game. She glared back at the tender expression in Creed's eyes. For the moment he had the upper hand, and she had no choice but to go along. But she'd find a way to turn the tables, and then Jarrett Creed would pay for every kiss, every caress, every endearment she was forced to endure!

"This was Jarrett's room when he lived at Lion's Dare," Amy said as they entered a room dominated by a large bed with a heavy oak headboard and footboard. "We've kept it ready for him exactly as he left it."

Cricket noticed the bed frame held two feather mattresses so high off the ground she was going to need steps to reach them. She tried to imagine herself sinking down into that bed with Creed, but couldn't. The thought was too appalling to even consider. What if he tried to do "it" to her again? Of course he'd said he wouldn't, but what would she do if he did? She didn't dare make a scene, or he might call off the bargain. Then Sloan would go to jail and she'd be sent home to marry Cruz Guerrero. How had she ever gotten herself trapped like this?

Cricket tore her eyes from the bed and perused the rest of the room. A table on one side of the bed held a small candle and a well-worn book. Cricket picked up the book and discovered it was a collection of Shakespeare's *Sonnets*.

"Creed reads poetry?"

Cricket didn't realize she'd spoken aloud until Amy responded, "Beautifully. He read a short verse for our wedding." A dreamy look came across Amy's face as she recited:

> *"So are you to my thoughts as food to life,*
> *Or as sweet-season'd showers are to the ground."*

Cricket gulped and dropped the book back on the table. She didn't want to think about Creed's Tennessee voice reading love poems. She tested the feather mattress with her hand. It was soft, all right. She and Creed were going to end up sleeping together in the middle of that bed if it sank down like she thought it might. She looked around the room for some other place to sleep, but there wasn't any. The furnishings were spartan. A wardrobe stood along one wall, and a dry sink along the other, with a pitcher and bowl sitting atop it. A simple ladderback chair with a rawhide seat had been placed in the corner. Unless she slept on the floor, she was going to know Jarrett Creed a whole lot better before they left Lion's Dare.

"I had Belle put water to wash with in the pitcher, and there are some towels inside the dry sink. I'll have Belle press one of your dresses and bring it up to you."

The time had come, Cricket thought, to reveal at least a part of the truth. She dreaded seeing the scorn with which she was so familiar replace the friendliness in Amy's blue eyes.

"I don't have a dress to wear."

"Oh, you poor dear! Jarrett dragged you away without even giving you a chance to pack? But then . . ." Amy hesitated, then finished with a shy smile, "the Creeds are lusty men, are they not?"

Cricket watched Amy's blush rise, astounded at the woman's admission and unsure how to reply. Amy's incorrect assumption gave her a plausible excuse as to why she was without proper female clothing. Why deny it?

"What a thing to say to a new bride," Amy apologized, when Cricket made no response. "Excuse my forwardness, please, Cricket. I only thought . . . Tom is . . ." Amy's fingers came up to pinch the growing frown of distress between her eyes.

Cricket felt her heart go out to the young woman. It wasn't Amy's fault she and Creed weren't really sharing a marriage bed. She supposed Amy was probably right. After all, she'd spent a night with Creed and supposedly enjoyed it *immensely*. Cricket only wished she could remember more about what had happened in Creed's bed.

"You're right, of course," Cricket reassured Amy. "It's . . . I just . . ."

"I know, dear," Amy said, a tremulous smile brightening her features, "they *are* rather overwhelming, aren't they."

Cricket didn't know what else to do, so she grinned gamely back at Amy.

"At any rate," Amy said, all efficiency again, "I'll have Belle let down the hem on one of my dresses for you. Except for our heights, I do believe we're very much of a size. If you need anything else, come to the door and give a call." Amy approached Cricket, and Cricket knew she was going to embrace her again. As awkward as she found it, she wrapped her arms around Amy. When she began to feel a warm glow inside, she stepped back abruptly, tearing herself from Amy's grasp.

"I'm so glad you're a part of the family, Cricket," Amy said, smiling again. "I'm looking forward to getting to know you better."

With those words, Amy left Cricket alone in the room.

Cricket pursed her lips in dismay. She didn't know when she'd spent so much time grinning back at someone like an idiot. She fumed and sputtered, but there was nothing she could do about it. She liked Amy Creed. And when Belle showed up with Amy's dress, Cricket knew she'd put it on and pretend she liked wearing it . . . because she wanted Amy to continue liking her.

The insidious pretense had begun.

Cricket crossed to the dry sink and poured some of the water into the bowl. The water was cool and she did feel fresher, she admitted, after she'd rinsed her face and hands. She groped for a towel and as she dried her face she wandered over to the open window and looked down into the front yard where Creed and Luke stood under a budding oak.

She watched Creed hand a letter to the young Ranger with the admonition, "Make sure if Rip comes looking for us you head him in the wrong direction, and keep a close eye on Sloan. I want to know the truth, Luke."

"Sure, Creed," the youth answered. "You can count on me."

"I know I can. Good luck."

"You, too." Luke paused and grasped Creed's arm before he added in a quiet voice, "Take care of her."

"I will."

"You'd better. Because if you don't, you'll have me to answer to."

When Luke was gone, Creed turned and looked up at his bedroom window. Cricket stared back down at him, not bothering to hide her puzzlement at the exchange between the two men. She hardly knew Luke, and the time on the trail with him hadn't been particularly enlightening. He was a loner, polite but distant. Why was he ready to fight with Creed over his treatment of her?

Creed swore under his breath before turning and marching into the house. In moments the bedroom door opened and he stood before Cricket.

"Do you always listen in on other people's conversations?

That's how you got yourself into this mess in the first place, if I'm not mistaken."

Cricket had spent too much time under Rip's tutelage not to recognize a distracting feint when she saw one. Undeterred, she asked, "Why is Luke so willing to defend me? We just met."

Creed shot back, "Luke's always fighting for the underdog. He can't help the way he is. But I can certainly cure you of eavesdropping before we head for New Orleans. In fact, that's only one of a long list of bad habits I'm planning to break."

Cricket didn't bother to hide her irritation with Creed's announcement.

"You know, this isn't going to work. Your brother and his wife are going to figure out we're not the loving couple we're supposed to be."

"How are they going to do that?"

She took a deep breath and said, "Because I'm not going to let you put your hands on me like you did when we arrived . . . and I'm not going to sleep in that bed with you, either."

Cricket waited warily while Creed took the few steps that brought him close to her. She could feel the heat of him. His breath touched her face. He was . . . *overwhelming*. But Cricket was determined not to be overwhelmed. She stood her ground even when Creed closed the distance between them until they stood breast to breast, actually touching each time one or the other breathed. Cricket was forced to look up to meet his gaze. What she saw there made her gasp. She wanted to back away from the fire in his golden eyes, to escape from the heat, but Cricket never retreated unless it was tactically necessary. She wasn't about to start now.

She stood her ground as Creed slowly wound his strong arms around her body and pulled her close. She managed to get her palms up on his rock-hard chest, to keep a small distance between them, but he lowered one hand to cup her buttocks and lifted her until her femininity cradled his blatant masculinity. Cricket stared at Creed, refusing to acknowledge their closeness. However, without her being able to control them, her sooty black lashes slowly, ever so slowly, lowered over her smoky gray eyes.

The spiraling sensation deep inside her intrigued Cricket. She waited to see whether it would change with time, or stay the same. Creed rocked his hips once, sliding his hard body across her soft one. Cricket's fingertips curled on Creed's shirt, and her lips parted in an unvoiced exclamation, but she kept her eyes closed as she willed him to move.

Again.

As though he'd heard her plea Creed repeated the rocking motion, cupping her with both hands to give him better leverage for his thrust.

There it was, that same spiraling sensation, only stronger this time. When Creed thrust the third time, Cricket countered with her own hips, and the feeling was so powerful she felt her knees weaken in response. She grabbed Creed's shirt in both fists and leaned her cheek against her hand, aware suddenly that her breathing had become uneven, and that Creed was in no better shape.

"Ready to cry uncle?" Creed whispered in her ear.

Cricket raised her head off his chest and looked up into eyes that blazed like topaz jewels. She met his challenge with the rasped warning, "I never give up."

"So be it."

Cricket waited, almost detached, as Creed lowered his head toward her. She saw his tongue come out to moisten his lips, which parted as his mouth opened slightly. *He was going to kiss her!* As Cricket saw it, she had two choices. She could let Creed kiss her, or she could back away. Either way, Creed won the battle between them. He was too clever by half! Cricket had only moments to make her decision. She admitted reluctantly that the time had come to make a tactical retreat. As Creed's lips touched hers she wrenched herself from his grasp. He hadn't been expecting her to move, so she was free before he realized she was gone.

Creed stood spread-legged, breathing harshly, his fists bunched and his face a mask of desire.

"So, Brava," he taunted, "you never retreat?"

"That wasn't a retreat," Cricket replied. Why couldn't she catch her breath? Her body quivered with nervous energy, and she had the craziest urge to seek out that spiraling sensation again.

"Not a retreat? What was it then?"

Cricket stuck her hands behind her back to hide their trembling. "A temporary disengagement," she managed with a shaky grin, "while I plan my counterattack."

"So," Creed murmured, his voice soft and husky, "you can't wait to come back for more."

Cricket couldn't drag her eyes away from his mouth. He'd taken a step toward her when a loud knock resounded, breaking the spell. Cricket recognized reinforcements when she heard them and started for the door.

A tiny Negro woman stood at the portal. She pushed her way past Cricket into the room. "I'm Belle. Missus Creed wants you to try this dress on so's I kin stitch it up to fit you."

Creed's glance skipped from Cricket to Belle and back before he shook his head in frustration and headed for the door. "I'll be with Tom," he said as he left. "We'll continue this later."

Creed found his brother in the parlor, sitting at the desk from which he conducted all his plantation business. Creed poured himself a brandy and sat down in the large leather chair next to Tom. He took a gulp of the brandy, then leaned his head back against the chair and closed his eyes.

He felt a tremendous sense of well-being in Tom's presence. Tom was six years older, which had always given him the advantage of age and experience. Tom was wise and all-knowing. Tom could solve any problem. It was Tom who'd kept him sane when he'd returned to Lion's Dare after he'd discovered his Comanche wife and his son dead of cholera.

Even now Creed tensed at the memory. He'd wanted to murder his father; in fact, had come back to Lion's Dare precisely for that purpose.

"I'll kill the sonofabitch!" he'd raged. "I'll flay him alive. I want him to know what it means to suffer!"

Tom was not physically larger than his brother, but when he'd enclosed Creed in his broad, loving arms at the steps leading up to Simon's room, Creed had hesitated to fight him. And then Tom had said, "You're too late, Jarrett. He died a week ago."

He'd howled in pain as he yanked himself from his brother's arms and pounded his fists against the wall. He'd cursed Simon in Comanche. He'd cursed him in English, and even in the French he'd learned at the school where his father had sent him so far away from his wife and child. When his rage was spent he'd sagged to the steps, his bruised knuckles pressed into his aching eyes. Tom had sat down beside him, not touching, just a comforting presence.

"It's okay, Jarrett," Tom had said. "It's okay for you to cry."

Creed had fought the tears harder, then, to prove he didn't need to cry. But when Tom had laid his hand on Creed's head and smoothed the hair back from his brow as their mother had when he was a child, he had turned into his brother's arms, and the tears had scoured their way down his cheeks.

Tom had held him until the pain was gone, and he'd been dry and hollow inside.

"Why did he do it, Tom? Why didn't he let me go back?"

"He thought he was doing what was best."

"And Ma? Did he do what was best for her, too?"

"You know how he felt. Would you have wanted Ma here knowing that?"

"You would have brought her back though, wouldn't you, Tom?"

"I . . . it wasn't my decision to make."

"But you don't think less of Ma for what happened to her, do you?"

"Does it really matter what I think? What's done is done. Now you have to go on with your life."

Go on with his life. Creed had done that. He'd left Lion's

Dare and become a Texas Ranger. But what goes around, comes around. He was back at Lion's Dare with Tom, and supposedly married for the second time. And once again he needed Tom's understanding and wisdom.

Tom crossed his hands on his stomach, stretched his long legs out in front of him, and leaned back in his chair, watching his younger brother speculatively. Creed looked almost asleep. But Tom knew better. He'd seen the coiled tension in his younger brother's body. When Creed opened his eyes at last Tom said, "You look tired. Long night?"

"Yes, but not for the reasons you're thinking."

The two brothers shared a companionable chuckle.

Creed took another swallow of brandy and said, "I need your help, Tom."

"Name it and it's yours."

"It's not that simple, I'm afraid," Creed said. "It's about Cricket."

Tom's face remained blank. "What about her?" he asked cautiously.

"It's hard to explain. What do you know about Rip Stewart?"

"He controls the flatboat trade up and down the river and he's got several of the cotton agents in Galveston in his pocket. Rich as Croesus, I understand."

"Cricket is his daughter."

Tom whistled appreciatively. "He doesn't approve of the marriage?"

"No. But that's not the problem."

"So, what is it?" Tom asked, his curiosity piqued.

"It's Cricket." Creed paused, unsure exactly how to explain what he wished of his brother and sister-in-law.

"She's pregnant," Tom guessed.

"Hell, no!" Creed blustered. He figured he'd better say what was on his mind before Tom started making other guesses about Cricket which might prove even more embarrassing. "It's the way she was raised by her father. Cricket has some habits that . . . that aren't acceptable in polite company. I'd like your help, and Amy's, of course, in teaching her some things that'd help her get along better in New Orleans."

"You know we'll help however we can, but I don't understand how the daughter of someone as rich as Rip Stewart wouldn't know how to manage the kind of company you're going to be seeing in New Orleans."

Creed heaved a gusty sigh. "It's a long story. I hardly believe it myself."

"I've got plenty of time," Tom said, "but maybe I ought to get Amy and you can tell us both what you want from us."

"That's fine with me. The sooner I get this off my chest the better I'm going to feel."

Tom sought out Amy and brought her back to the parlor.

"Is something wrong with Cricket?" she asked concernedly when she saw Creed's distress. "She seemed fine when I left her upstairs."

"She's fine, Amy," Creed reassured her. "I need you and Tom to help me with a small problem."

Amy perched on the settee with Tom beside her while Creed recounted what he knew of Cricket's upbringing. He skimmed over their relationship, leaving the impression that he and Cricket had fallen in love at first sight, and married despite Rip's disapproval.

"I want to take Cricket with me to New Orleans, but the way she's been raised, she's going to end up butting heads with the New Orleans ladies. That's where you come in, Amy. I was hoping you'd be willing to give Cricket some lessons in feminine deportment that would help her get by, along with a few hints about whatever it is ladies do to keep themselves busy when there are no men around."

Amy's eyes teared with sympathy for Cricket's plight. "Why, Jarrett Creed, of course I'll be willing to help in any way I can! That poor, dear girl. Imagine being raised without a mother."

"Where will you be staying in New Orleans?" Tom asked.

"With the American chargé, Beaufort LeFevre."

"Angelique's father?" Tom asked.

"Yes."

Tom whistled, long and low. "What's Angelique going to

say when she finds out you're married? Isn't that going to be a little awkward?"

"I never made any promises to Angelique. In fact, quite the opposite is true."

"Still, the woman was in love with you."

"It's important I stay with LeFevre. I'll have to deal with Angelique the best I can."

"Good luck," Tom said, shaking his head.

"I'll get started tomorrow teaching Cricket a few things that should make her more comfortable when she gets to New Orleans," Amy promised.

"Thanks, Amy. I'd appreciate that," Creed said. "And Tom, I'll need you to keep an eye on your whiskey."

"Why's that?"

"Cricket doesn't know that ladies aren't supposed to drink that hell-broth. I want to make sure she gets out of the habit before we get to New Orleans."

Creed watched Tom struggle to hide his shock before he replied as though it were the kind of request he got every day, "Sure. No problem."

Creed clasped his hands in front of him. "It means a lot to me to know you're willing to help," he admitted to the couple.

"What's family for?" Tom said. "Don't worry about it. Cricket will do you proud. It's plain to see from the way she looks at you that she loves you."

"Yes, well, I love her, too," Creed said, uncomfortable with lying and finding himself doing it again. "Guess I'll turn in now. Thanks again."

Creed took the stairs back up to his bedroom, where he found Cricket restlessly pacing the room from wall to wall in nothing but her chemise and pantalettes.

"Where have you been?" she hissed. "Belle took my buckskins when I wasn't looking and didn't leave me anything else to wear."

As angry as Cricket was, her breasts heaved in agitation under the chemise, and her long-legged stride stretched the pantalettes over her buttocks with each step she took.

Creed's tongue stuck to the roof of his mouth. Lord, his

body was on fire for her! On her next pass by him he reached out and grabbed her by the arm, stopping her in front of him.

Cricket folded her arms across her chest, pushing her breasts up and out of the chemise. "Well? Now what?"

Creed kept his eyes on her face, reminding himself she was still a virgin, knowing he was lost if he let his gaze wander as it wished. "I spoke with Tom and Amy. I told them you needed their help learning how to act like a lady and—"

"You what!" Cricket had never been so humiliated. Her face flushed with anger as her hands bunched into white-knuckled fists which whipped down to balance on her hips. "How could you?"

"Look, Brava," Creed reasoned, "what choice did I have? In a few weeks we'll be heading for New Orleans. I'm going there to argue to the American chargé that Texas is full of civilized folk who form a civilized sovereign nation worthy of receiving trade considerations from the United States. How convincing am I going to be if I show up with a wife in buckskins with barnyard manners?"

"Barnyard manners?"

"Well, maybe that is an exaggeration," Creed conceded in response to Cricket's scowling features. "But you have to admit you haven't shown much inclination to the feminine role since I've known you."

"It's not who I am," Cricket railed.

"No, not yet. But it's what you'll have to become."

"I can't."

"You can, and you will. You don't have any choice. It can't be any more difficult than wrestling or bronc riding or any of the other skills you've mastered. If you can learn to do those things, you can learn to be a woman."

Cricket hugged herself with her arms in an attempt to curb the shivers of fury wracking her body.

"I hate you for this, Creed. I hate you so bad I can taste it."

Before she could stop him, Creed enfolded her in his arms. His head swooped down and his lips touched hers for the first time in gentleness. His tongue teased the edge of her lips, urging them to open. Shocked by his boldness, Cricket jerked her head aside and struggled to be free.

Creed released her immediately and stepped back, his heart pounding, his breathing unsteady. In a voice husky with emotion he rasped, "I only wanted to see what your hate tastes like, Brava."

She could feel the intensity of his gaze, and snapped hers up to meet his, daring him to try touching her again.

"Hate me if you will," he said. "But make no mistake. *You are my wife.* I'll kiss you and touch you as I please, and you'll do nothing to stop me."

"I agreed to be your *wife* for one purpose only—and it had nothing to do with kissing or touching! Lay one hand on me and you'll find it chopped off!"

"Come here to me, Brava."

"When pigs fly!"

"Then stay where you are. I'll come to you."

How could she have fallen for the same trick twice? If she moved she'd be admitting she was afraid of him; if she stayed he'd have her in his arms in an instant. And where could she run in her chemise and pantalettes?

"Go ahead and touch me!" she dared at last, her lip curling in disdain. "Little good it will do you."

Cricket remained rigid as a corpse when Creed enfolded her in his arms. She ground her teeth to avoid flinching when he gently stroked her cheek with the knuckles of his hand. She wasn't going to let him get away with this again. Jarrett Creed had cornered her for the very last time.

Creed could feel Cricket trembling in his arms like a wild thing caught in a trap. His *brava* would never make a docile wife. But she could learn to control her unbridled impulses, and to more closely fit the feminine mold. He was counting on it.

CHAPTER 13

With Cricket and Creed at loggerheads, the evening might have become a disaster had it not been for Seth. When Cricket arrived downstairs for supper clothed in Amy's rose-bordered muslin dress, she found her arms filled immediately with the wriggling two-year-old boy.

"I don't know how to hold a baby!" Cricket protested.

"There's nothing to it," Amy replied. "Just hang on to whatever's convenient."

At first Cricket felt awkward, and the more Seth wiggled the more fearful she became that she'd drop him. Finally, she managed to wrap one arm around Seth's waist and slip the other under his bottom. She pulled him snug against her, as she had her wolf pups, so he wouldn't fall. To her surprise, as soon as Seth was close enough his legs gripped her around the waist and he settled his rump comfortably on her hip. He leaned his head on her shoulder and gazed up trustingly at her from under long, golden lashes with eyes the clear blue of a summer sky. His thumb found its way to his mouth and he sucked contentedly, unaware of the impact he was having on the young woman who held him. Cricket looked down at Seth and promptly lost her heart.

"Men can't do that, you know," Amy confided.

"Do what?"

"Set a child on their hips. They don't *have* hips," Amy continued with a friendly laugh as she crossed to Tom. "Whenever Tom tries it Seth just slides on down." She let her hands skim from Tom's ribs to his hips, to make her point.

"Goes to show why women have charge of the kids." Tom grabbed Amy and pulled her close, linking his arms around her waist. Amy put her hands on either side of Tom's face and held him still while she kissed him quickly on the lips.

Cricket was distracted from the playful scene between Tom and Amy by the softness of the child settled against her. She admired the perfect little being she held in her arms. She took Seth's hefty weight in her left arm while the right came up to brush his blond hair away from his brow.

Seth had Amy's blue eyes and blond hair, but his chin jutted like Tom's and he'd inherited the Creed men's high, angled cheekbones, although his were well camouflaged in baby fat. His nose and mouth were fairly well hidden by his fist and thumb, but she imagined a blade of nose like Tom's, and a lush, full mouth like Amy's. For the first time in her life Cricket wondered what it would be like to have a child of her own. It was not so farfetched an idea. She'd dismissed Creed's suggestion she might be carrying his babe, but she wouldn't know for sure for at least two more weeks. What if she were pregnant with Creed's child right now?

Startled by the thought, Cricket's eyes sought out Creed, only to find him staring back at her. What would a baby of theirs look like? It would have black hair, of course, but would it have gold eyes, or gray? Would the Creed family nose and angled cheekbones breed true? How would those features look on a daughter rather than a son?

"Seth's a beautiful child," she said to Amy and Tom. "And so . . . cuddly."

"Just like his mother," Tom said as he turned Amy in his arms. His hands slipped down to cover his wife's abdomen and Amy put her hands over his. They looked comfortable and happy standing together like that. Cricket remembered the morning in Rip's office when Creed's hands had been on her the same way and felt a fluttering in her belly.

"Seth's been a wonderful child," Amy agreed, "and now he's going to have a brother or sister in the fall."

Creed grinned and crossed the parlor to his brother and sister-in-law. "That's great!" He gave Amy a quick kiss on the cheek, and slapped Tom on the back. "I'm going to be an uncle again."

"Maybe you'll have one of your own, soon," Amy said.

"Maybe," Creed replied as his eyes met Cricket's.

Cricket was surprised when the same spiraling sensation occurred which she'd felt in Creed's arms, only this time he was nowhere near her. She didn't realize until Amy spoke that she was staring at Creed.

"Let me take Seth to Belle, and we can go in to dinner."

Creed crooked an elbow and offered his arm to Cricket. Uncomfortable, uncertain of how she should act, Cricket walked over and rested her hand on his sleeve. As awkward as that moment was for her, it merely provided a hint of the barrage of etiquette that would assail her in the days that followed.

Amy set numerous pieces of silverware at each place so Cricket spent most of each meal trying to find the right one to use. Then there was the custom of seating ladies—and helping them from their chairs when the meal was finished. It did no good to protest she wasn't a cripple. She had to stay seated until Creed came to stand behind her and help her rise.

When Cricket had reached between her legs at that first dinner and grabbed the back of her skirt, pulling it up and tucking it in at the ribboned waist in front, effectively making trousers out of it, she'd thought Amy was going to faint. But how else was she supposed to straddle her chair? Otherwise the blamed skirt scattered everywhere when she tried to sit down.

Amy had been appalled to learn Cricket could neither cook nor sew and hadn't been impressed by her argument that she'd done very well without either of those skills and "never starved or gone naked as a result." Amy had begun her campaign to teach Cricket to cook by rousting her one morning to help make the biscuits for breakfast. Cricket and the kitchen got dusted with flour, but her biscuits weren't fluffy and soft like Amy's. They had a decidedly more chewy texture. The recipe had called for "a dop of lard" and, not knowing the proper measure, Cricket had dopped in a little more lard than she needed. She'd bristled when Creed laughed, but had to admit they were bad. Even Rogue wouldn't eat them.

Then Amy taught her how to salt butter using salt and loaf sugar so it would last for ten years and taste as good as butter newly made. Of course she'd proudly served some to Creed for supper, not realizing the mixture took a full month to cure before it was edible.

The only reason Cricket agreed to try making soap was because Amy's recipe was so simple there was no way she could make a mistake. But after she'd boiled the concoction for a while, it began to thicken much more than Amy said was usual. That was when Cricket realized she'd added *ten* pounds of pulverized resin and *two* pounds of potash dissolved in twenty-eight gallons of water, to the twenty-five pounds of grease, instead of the other way around!

Cricket was decidedly leery when Amy suggested she learn to make a Linament for Sprains and Spavins, and the only reason she gave in was because she thought she might be able to use it on Valor some day. After they'd added the concoction of oil of oraganum, oil of savis, oil of cloves, and tincture of opium to a quart of alcohol, and Amy assured her it was made correctly, nothing would do but Cricket had to try it on herself. She rubbed it on her arms. She rubbed it on her legs. She rubbed it on her stomach. She even had Amy rub some on her back. And it worked! Cricket spent the rest of the day in bed, too relaxed to move.

Cricket balked when Amy suggested she try sewing. But Amy was persistent, and Cricket felt guilty because Amy was taking so much time to teach her things she couldn't seem to master, and *surely* she could learn how to do such a simple thing as running a needle back and forth through a piece of cloth. She was wrong. Because of the calluses on her fingertips, she couldn't feel the needle until it stuck her. By the time Cricket had finished trying to embroider a quilt square, she'd gotten it so bloody from the needle pricks in her finger that it had to be thrown away. Amy discreetly gave up on sewing.

Amy wasn't content teaching Cricket cooking and soapmaking and household remedies. She also included the rules of etiquette on her daily agenda. Every time Cricket made a faux pas, Amy gently pointed it out to her and patiently showed her the correct behavior. What frustrated Cricket was the fact she couldn't seem to recognize when her actions were inappropriate. For instance, how was she supposed to know a lady never accepted a cigar with her brandy after dinner?

As the days flew by, Cricket failed at one feminine occupation after another. Creed's gentle laughter when Amy lovingly recounted the day's disastrous events sent her temper flaring. It was awful to fail and fail and fail, when her whole life had been a series of one success after another. Creed had said he was sure she could learn to do anything, but after two weeks of trying, Cricket was discouraged by her consistent inability to master even the most simple of wifely tasks.

It never occurred to Cricket that her disinterest caused her attention to stray when Amy was explaining the proper way to do things. She only knew that whatever she attempted invariably ended in ruin and calamity.

The only wifely chore she did with any confidence was holding Seth, playing with him, and dressing him, and she had to fight Belle for those opportunities.

However, Creed was not so easily discouraged. He could see positive changes in Cricket after only two weeks spent in the feminine role. She'd learned to consider her skirt when sitting and walking, no mean feat when he considered how she'd hiked it up to sit down to dinner that first evening. She'd almost mastered the intricacies of the silverware at the table, although her manners hadn't been as godawful to start with as he'd feared they might be. And though her biscuits still weren't as tasty as Amy's, they were edible now.

It was seeing Cricket with Seth that convinced him there were more facets to her than she was willing to let anyone see.

Cricket had proved with Seth that she was capable of giving as much love and doting adoration as any man could ever want. She was gentle. She was enchanting. She was funny. Creed found himself wishing she'd give him some of the same attention she gave Seth. But coax as he might, Cricket couldn't—or wouldn't—transfer that openness with the boy to openness with him. He told himself he had to be patient, he had to be understanding, but he was only human. So, when he came home from a particularly tiring day spent with Tom at the gin to find Cricket playing with Seth and ignoring him again, it set his teeth on edge.

"Isn't it time for Seth to go upstairs now?" he asked.

Amy, who was more cognizant of Creed's frustration than Cricket, quickly agreed, "Yes, it is. I'll call Belle."

Cricket relinquished her hold on Seth reluctantly when Belle came to take the small boy upstairs with her.

Creed wanted Cricket to touch him with the same freedom with which she touched the boy. But she never came near him unless she had to for appearance's sake. And although she'd performed every task set for her by Amy over the past two weeks, she'd stubbornly slept on the floor, eschewing the comforts of the feather bed—and contact with him. He knew the floor wasn't comfortable because each morning she awoke crankier than the last. He was fast running out of patience. So, when he crooked his arm and offered to escort Cricket to supper, and she rejected his help, his temper exploded.

"Take my arm, Cricket. That's the way a gentleman escorts a lady to the table."

"I'm no lady!" she snapped, and swished her skirt past him as she entered the dining room alone.

Cricket was also at the end of her patience. She was used to being capable and doing things right. She'd spent two weeks doing her best and being wrong. It had been an exercise in perseverance to take all Amy's helpful hints in stride. The skirt was a hindrance. She hated the sight of biscuits. She'd pick cactus barehanded before she'd try sewing again. And if she had to spend another night on the floor she wouldn't be responsible for her actions. She was stewing for a fight, and it looked like Creed was going to give her one.

Tom and Amy were sensitive to the tensions at the table. So Tom was especially tactful when Cricket picked up the wrong spoon for the soup. He held up the proper implement and remarked, "I've never understood how they expect a lady to eat soup from a spoon as large as this."

Cricket remedied her mistake, but simmered under his censure.

"Tom and I have decided we'd like to have a party for you and Jarrett," Amy said, introducing a topic which she hoped would clear the air and improve temperaments. "A sort of reception to introduce you to our friends and neighbors. What do you think?"

"I don't know," Cricket replied. "I'm not very comfortable at parties." Which probably had something to do with the fact she hadn't been to one since she was eight years old.

"It'll be fun. And it'll give you a chance to practice all that you've learned," Amy said with an encouraging smile.

Cricket turned to Creed, who merely shrugged and said, "It sounds like it would be a fine idea."

"Oh, that's wonderful!" Amy said enthusiastically. "Would you be willing to help me plan it, Cricket?"

Just then Cricket reached for a bowl of peas halfway across the table, and Amy gently rebuffed, "Tom will get those for you, Cricket, dear. You don't have to bother yourself."

Cricket watched the bowl make its ponderous way around the table to her. It would have been quicker to get it herself. The simmer became a boil. As the meal progressed, she was constantly corrected on subtle points. The more careful Tom and Amy and Creed were to be solicitous of her feelings, the angrier Cricket got. The angrier she got, the fewer attempts she made to observe what table etiquette she knew.

When the peach pie was served, she made sure Creed was

watching, then deliberately scooped it up in her hands and took a bite that consumed half the slice, smacking her lips as she relished it. She caught a piece of peach with her thumb as it started to dribble onto her chin and shoved it back into her mouth.

"All right, Brava, that's enough," Creed replied quietly. "You've made your point."

"And what point is that?" Cricket snarled. "That I have barnyard manners? I do, don't I? You've all made that perfectly clear these past two weeks."

Amy's face mirrored her dismay, and Tom's eyes slid to his hands in his lap. Creed simply glared.

"Do this, Cricket! Don't do that, Cricket! This is the way we do it, Cricket! I've managed fine on my own for seventeen years. I don't see why I have to change everything now."

Before she had a chance to say more Creed was out of his chair and had her by a sticky hand.

"Excuse us," he muttered in the direction of Tom and Amy. "Cricket and I want to have a talk in private."

"I don't have anything more to say to you!" she ranted. "I don't want to play this game anymore."

Creed picked Cricket up and threw her over his shoulder.

"Put me down!" Cricket screeched. She pounded on Creed's back as hard as she could with her fists, but she might as well have been a pea left on his plate for all the attention he gave her. The last thing she saw as they left the dining room was Tom and Amy's horrified faces.

Creed marched through the house and out the front door, carrying her only as far as the giant pin oak that grew in the side yard before he let go. Cricket thrashed once more, not realizing he'd released her, and her momentum threw her off Creed's shoulder so she landed in a heap on the grass before him.

"On your feet!"

Cricket was already on her feet and swinging her fisted right hand as hard as she could at Creed's chin. But her knuckles only grazed him as he instinctively feinted sideways when his eyes caught her movement.

"That does it!"

Before Cricket knew what had happened, Creed had grabbed her by the waist, dropped to one knee, and thrown her face down across his other thigh, yanking her skirt up so it impeded the swing of her fists. Her face was mashed against Creed's pant leg, and Cricket just naturally opened her mouth and sank her teeth down deep into his thigh.

Creed's outraged yelp coincided with the first stinging slap of his hand on her buttocks.

"Let go, Brava!"

She bit harder.

"I said"—*smack*—"let go!"

Cricket groaned through the teeth she had clamped in a death-grip on Creed's leg.

It became a contest of wills to see who would first succumb to the pain inflicted by the other. Cricket finally howled in anguish, admitting her defeat . . . and her self-disgust and humiliation at her defeat.

It wasn't until Creed heard Rogue that he came to his senses. The wolf sat next to Cricket's head, his nose turned to the sky as his howls blended with the cacophony created by Cricket. Creed looked at the stinging redness of his hand in some awe, surprised at the violence Cricket had elicited in him.

"Dammit, Brava," he muttered under his breath. "What am I going to do with you?"

Cricket tried to compose her features when she felt Creed pulling her skirt down from over her head. Her body felt hot, flushed, quivery, achey. She didn't think she could move. He turned her gently so she lay nestled helplessly in his arms. She couldn't hide the tears that threatened to spill, but she fought to control her quivering chin in the face of Creed's intense perusal.

"If you wanted to back out of our agreement, Brava, all you had to do was say so. There was no need to embarrass Tom and Amy."

Cricket wanted to argue back, but feared if she spoke she wouldn't be able to control her voice, and she simply couldn't endure any further disgrace. To be spanked like a child! And then to cry like a baby! It was unbearable!

Creed's thumb came up to intercept the tear that spilled down her cheek. She closed her eyes and turned her head away, ashamed of her weakness.

"Don't," he pleaded. Creed's large hand cupped her cheek and turned her face back to him. She felt his lips kiss away the next tear that fell, and then softly caress her cheek, her feathery eyelashes, and finally her lips, which were swollen as a result of her attack on him.

Cricket knew she should flee Creed's dominating presence while she still could, but was captivated by the strange feelings evoked when Creed's tongue slipped past her lips and barely into her mouth, coaxing again, until she opened her mouth fully to him. Creed teased the inside of her mouth with his tongue, claiming gentle possession of her. Cricket lost track of where she was as she absorbed the taste and feel of him. His mouth was soft and warm on hers, and he tasted . . . of peach pie.

Creed kissed her thoroughly, demanding a response that she gave . . . and gave . . . while her muscles clenched and tightened all over. She could feel her whole body trembling. When Creed raised his lips from hers, she turned her face toward his chest, while her hands clutched his shirt. Her breath came in raspy heaves echoed by Creed's.

At last, she shoved herself away from Creed and staggered to her feet. Between her sore buttocks and her rubbery legs she nearly fell before she at last stood, swaying, across from Creed, who had risen as well. "You shouldn't have done that," she rasped.

Creed faced Cricket squarely, trembling himself, aware of the boundary she'd crossed when she'd opened her mouth to him. "No, I shouldn't have," he agreed. "I don't know what it is about you, Brava, but it seems every time you goad me I rise to the bait. At this rate neither of us is going to survive this 'marriage.'"

"Then why don't you let me go home?" she cried. "I can't stand this anymore. I'll talk to Sloan. I know there must be some misunderstanding." Cricket was appalled at the desperation she heard in her voice. What was happening to her? This wasn't like her at all. Was it the kissing that made her act like this? She had to get control of herself. She took a deep breath and said firmly, "I want to go home."

Creed hesitated before he replied, "I wish it were that easy, Brava, but I'm afraid I can't let you go." When Cricket's chin jutted forward mulishly, Creed added, "So I guess we'll have to make the best of this situation. That means both of us giving a little. For my part, I'll talk to Tom and Amy and tell them you've learned enough. How about you? Do you think you can get along with my brother and sister-in-law for two more weeks until we're supposed to meet Commodore Moore in Galveston?"

"No more trying to change me?"

"I think there are a few things you could learn from Amy—"

"Creed, I won't—"

Creed held up a conciliatory hand. "No more lessons."

Cricket sighed in relief. "In that case I think we should all get along fine for the time we have left here."

"All right, Brava. Shall we go back inside and say good night to Tom and Amy?"

"After you," Cricket said, gesturing toward the front door.

"Ladies first," Creed countered.

"Of course." Cricket nodded her head in acquiescence and preceded Creed back to the house.

From the corner of her eye Cricket saw Creed struggling not to limp. He was going to have a whopping big bruise on his leg, she thought, and smiled. Then she considered the condition of her rear end and the smile faded. He'd given as good as he'd got.

They found Tom and Amy in the parlor, where Amy was having a sherry and Tom a brandy.

"Did you work everything out?" Tom asked straight-faced, all the while eyeing Creed's limp and Cricket's reddened eyes and stiff-legged walk.

"Yes, we did." Creed took Cricket's hand in his. "Cricket

and I have decided the New Orleans ladies will have to accept her as she is. There'll be no need for you to trouble yourselves any further."

"It was no trouble," Amy said. "Really, it was our pleasure." Amy's eyes admonished Creed, while they questioned Cricket whether she was all right.

"Thanks anyway," Creed said, his arm going around Cricket's shoulder to show they'd reached an amicable settlement of differences, "but we won't be needing any more help."

Cricket cringed inside at the look exchanged between Tom and Amy. It was apparent a great deal of what had happened under the pin oak had been heard inside. But she didn't want or need their sympathy. Her chin came up another notch. She would manage on her own for the next two weeks. She didn't need anybody's help.

"Cricket and I are going on up to bed now," Creed said.

"Won't you have a brandy?" Tom asked.

"No thanks," Creed replied. "It's been a long day."

"And you're still on your honeymoon, aren't you," Tom said sardonically. "Well, good night, then. Sleep tight."

Cricket suddenly realized she should have bargained harder under the pin oak. She'd gotten Creed to agree to end the lessons from Tom and Amy, but she'd done nothing to negotiate separate places to sleep. And she was awfully tired of sleeping on the floor.

"Do you by any chance have an extra be—"

"Come on, Cricket," Creed interrupted, taking Cricket's elbow to usher her toward the stairs. "It's time for bed."

"But—"

"Keep talking and I'm going to kiss your mouth shut," Creed murmured in her ear.

Cricket hurried ahead of Creed up the stairs, only belatedly remembering to call good night to Tom and Amy.

"Good night," they chorused back.

Once Cricket and Creed were in the bedroom with the door closed behind them and the candle lit, Cricket decided it was worth a try to bargain with Creed over their sleeping arrangements.

"I'm tired of sleeping on the floor," she began.

"So sleep in the bed."

"With you?"

Creed unbuttoned his shirt and pulled it off before answering, "Why not?"

Cricket perused the braided rug on the hardwood floor, and then let her gaze stray to the ladderback chair in the corner, with its rawhide seat. She shuddered. Neither one was a comfortable alternative to the feather bed. She ought to know since she'd tried them both. Well, she wasn't going to be a martyr any longer.

"All right, I will," she announced. She wasn't going to let the need to avoid Creed's touch force her onto the floor again tonight. She glanced back to Creed, and her breath caught at what she saw.

When she'd slept on the floor, Creed had found excuses not to come to bed until she was settled. It was dark each night by the time he came to the room and undressed. But not tonight. Cricket was mesmerized by the expanse of bronzed chest before her. Once again, her eyes found the scar that began at Creed's left nipple and angled down into his trousers. Thus her eyes were focused on Creed's trousers when he unbuttoned them and began to pull them down. Quickly, Cricket's eyes snapped up to Creed's face.

"What do you think you're doing?"

"Getting undressed to go to bed."

"You can't take your clothes off in front of me!"

"Why not? You're my wife. Besides, there's nothing under these trousers you haven't seen before."

"Seeing you at the pond wasn't the same thing as seeing you now."

"Oh, no? How was it different? I assure you I haven't changed."

But I have, Cricket thought. She was aware of him as a man now, in a way that she hadn't been then. The secret to dealing with this situation had to be to pretend a nonchalance about Creed's sex that she didn't feel. She took a deep breath and began to unbutton her dress.

"You're right," she said. "I'm being silly, aren't I? We'll

probably be stuck in closer quarters than this before we're through."

They turned their backs on one another and continued to undress, each pretending to be unaware of the other. When Creed felt the beads of sweat rise on his brow, he knew he didn't have to see Cricket to know she was there. For Cricket, the trembling in her legs revealed her nervous agitation. Cricket had stripped down to her chemise and pantalettes when Creed blew out the candle without warning and slipped into bed. The lack of moonlight made it necessary for Cricket to feel her way in the dark.

"If you're going to get into the bed, Brava, get in," Creed said when Cricket didn't join him immediately.

"I will if I can find it," she bit out. "You could have given me some warning you were going to blow out the candle."

"I thought you saw me."

"Well, I didn't."

Cricket yelped when she stubbed her toe on the bedstead.

"Are you all right?"

"I can't see a blamed thing."

"Here, let me help you." Creed crawled across the bed on his knees until he reached Cricket's side, then reached out blindly until his hand came in contact with her cotton chemise. It took only a second for him to recognize the shape of Cricket's breast.

"Aw, hell," Creed muttered.

Cricket jerked sideways at the touch and started to climb onto the bed past Creed, but he moved at the same time. She crashed into him and the two of them fell into a jumbled heap on the feather bed. The mattress gave with their weight, and when they stopped rolling, Cricket lay sprawled underneath Creed at the center of the bed. Both were intensely aware of bare flesh meeting soft cotton . . . or more bare flesh.

His hair-roughened legs pressed against her thighs.

Her rounded breasts rose and fell under his chest.

His arms captured her shoulders.

Her cheek lay smooth against his neck.

His fingers caught in her hair.

Her moist breath warmed his throat.

His manhood grew hard and hot against her thigh.

"Get—off—me," Cricket said through gritted teeth. She waited, not breathing until Creed finally shifted away to lie on his back on his side of the bed, staring at the ceiling. They lay in silence on opposite sides of the bed for several minutes before Creed spoke into the darkness.

"You're a desirable woman, Brava. No matter how much you try to hide it, or deny it, nothing will ever change that."

Cricket waited for him to say more but all she heard was his steady breathing. How could he say something like that and then go to sleep? She lay awake, restless and antsy to be doing something, irritated that Creed could so easily dismiss everything that had passed between them this evening. She could hardly believe she'd allowed Creed to kiss her. Not only that, but she'd enjoyed it! Since the Ranger had shown up, her life had been turned upside-down. What was she doing in bed with Jarrett Creed? Where was her gumption? Why was she letting this *man* tell her what to do?

Cricket climbed down from the bed, taking the light quilt that had covered both of them with her. She grabbed a pillow and threw it down on the braided rug at her feet and then wrapped the quilt around her several times before she dropped to the floor. She settled her head on the pillow and wriggled around until she got the lumps out of the quilt. There. That was better. No man was going to start ordering her around, husband or not. And if Jarrett Creed thought he could kiss her willy-nilly like that, he could just think again. This marriage wasn't her idea. She didn't need Jarrett Creed. She didn't need anybody.

"I don't believe it."

Cricket hadn't realized she'd said her last thought aloud. "What?"

"You said you don't need anybody," Creed repeated quietly. "That sounds more like Rip talking. I don't think it's true of you. I think you need other people more than you think you do."

"Rip may have suggested the idea to me, but it applies all right. I don't need anybody."

"I don't agree. Oh, you're independent, I'll grant you that. But, there are ways, and ways of needing people, Brava. I don't think you'd last a day all by yourself."

"It doesn't matter what you think," she snapped back. "I don't have to prove anything to you."

"Of course you don't."

Cricket bristled at his patronizing response. "You don't think I can do it, do you?"

"It doesn't matter what I think," he replied. "You said so yourself."

"I can do anything I set my mind to. You want to bet I can't last a day in this room by myself?"

"No, Brava, I don't."

"You just don't want to lose," she snapped cantankerously.

"All right, I give up. You want to stay cooped up in this room all by yourself to prove your point, be my guest."

"Fine! I will!"

Before Cricket had a chance to think about what she'd agreed to, Creed had grabbed his pants and shirt and left the room, slamming the door behind him. The bed was all hers now, and the room, too, for that matter.

Cricket fell back on her pillow and grabbed her head in her hands. What had she gotten herself into this time? How was she going to last a whole day within these four walls? She *hated* staying indoors. Her whole life had been based on the assumption she didn't need anyone. Wasn't it a little late to be worrying about proving it to anybody now?

Oh, well, she'd made her bed, and now she'd have to lie in it. But she'd prove to Jarrett Creed that he was wrong. She could stand the solitude and the confining space for one measly day. She was counting on it.

CHAPTER 14

B<small>Y THE TIME</small> Belle slipped Cricket's breakfast inside her bedroom door she was up and pacing the room like a caged animal. She spent the entire day staring out the window at the sunlit fields of cotton and wondering how Creed had managed to back her into this corner. The truth was, she admitted disgustedly, she'd caught herself in a trap of her own making. It was no less frustrating to know she only needed to walk through the door to be free.

She'd expected to hear Amy and Seth puttering about the house, or at least the sounds of the servants working, but it was quiet as a fox-hunted fawn all day. She wondered where everyone was, but refused to leave the room to find out. She'd said she could spend the entire day in this room alone and she'd meant it. At least, when she'd said it, it had sounded good.

By the time she finally heard Tom and Creed come in to share the day's events with Amy, she was nearly frantic for company. She opened the door to race downstairs and then realized what she was doing. Her hand tightened on the doorknob before she slowly closed the door again, pressing her forehead against the cool lacquered surface. Creed or

Amy would come hunting for her soon, so all she needed to do was wait.

It was a long wait. At dinnertime Belle slipped a plate of food inside the room, but no one came to see her. No one even knocked at the door to ask how she was doing. She wondered what Creed had told Amy to keep her away. Even if a person was sick you came to visit them . . . unless they had something very contagious.

If Cricket was anything, she was stubborn. She gritted her teeth as she crossed to sit in the ladderback chair in the corner. Creed had to come to bed sometime. Only it got later and later and he didn't come. Cricket fought her drowsiness, but the day of boredom finally caught up with her. She eyed the feather mattresses with longing, but she wasn't about to give Creed the chance to join her in bed. She rearranged the quilt on the floor, blew out the candle she'd lit to fight the darkness, and dropped to the rug, covering herself lightly.

Perhaps she'd been too hasty, Cricket admitted as she drifted off to sleep. Perhaps Creed was right, and she needed the company of others more than she'd thought. In the past she'd always avoided strangers because being around them meant subjecting herself to censure, and so she'd spent much of her time off riding or hunting by herself. Still, she hadn't expected the day to chafe quite so much as it had.

When she thought about it, she realized how many times she'd come back from a day alone on horseback to share her adventures with Rip, Sloan, or Bay. At least she'd managed to get through the whole day alone, so there was no reason to admit defeat to Creed. She was glad she hadn't been so impulsively foolish as to promise more than a day of being so absolutely, totally, unbelievably, incredibly alone.

Creed leaned against an ancient oak watching the bedroom window and waiting for the candle to be extinguished. When it finally was, he forced himself to remain outside until he was sure Cricket was asleep. As he climbed the stairs, he wondered how well she'd gotten through the day. It had been hard not to come upstairs to find out, for he'd discovered something unexpected as a result of his argument with Cricket. He'd missed her.

It had come as something of a shock to find himself thinking about Cricket as he worked with Tom on the foundation for the new cotton gin, and he'd wanted nothing so much when he'd arrived home as to pull Cricket into his arms and hold her, as Tom had held Amy this evening. Considering this was a sham marriage and he was eventually going to send Cricket home to Rip, Creed thought maybe leaving her alone for a day or two wasn't such a bad idea.

However, when he saw Cricket sleeping he couldn't resist kneeling down to kiss her good night. Just as her consciousness surfaced he murmured, "Good night, Brava." Then he stripped in the darkness and got into bed.

As soon as Creed was settled Cricket's eyes popped open. She was wide awake. Listening to his steady breathing, she knew it wouldn't be long before he'd be sound asleep. He hadn't spoken a word to her. Or had he said good night? Was that all he was going to say after she'd spent the whole day alone?

"I did it," she said.

For a moment she wasn't sure he was going to answer her. Then he drawled, "One day. What does that prove?"

"It proves I could do what I said I could."

"All right, Brava."

He turned over and pulled the covers up over his shoulder.

She wasn't going to let him goad her into extending that miserable bet. She just wasn't going to let him do that to her. . . .

He turned back around and sat up in bed. "Oh, by the way. Amy and Belle will be away for a day or so. One of Amy's good friends delivered a baby daughter yesterday and they've gone over to cook and keep an eye on the other four kids."

"Then I'll come with you and Tom to the gin tomorrow," Cricket said. She wasn't about to spend another day cooped up alone in this house.

"Amy said if you were feeling better she'd appreciate your help polishing the silverware while she's gone."

"Oh. I can do that when—"

"She said she wouldn't ask, but she isn't going to have much time before the party to get it done herself after she gets home," Creed finished. He lay back down and turned away again, pulling the sheet up over his shoulder.

Cricket's lips were pressed flat as a flapjack with no leavening. If it hadn't been for the baby, she'd have sworn Creed had arranged this set of circumstances to prove his point about her needing other people. At least she'd be able to visit with Creed morning and evening, she thought. She needed to talk to someone.

"I thought we could talk—"

"Not tonight, Brava. I've got to get some sleep. I've got a long day tomorrow. Can it wait?"

"Sure."

"Then good night."

"Good night, Creed," Cricket muttered. "I'll talk to you tomorrow."

But things didn't turn out quite as Cricket had expected. The next morning Creed kissed her awake in time to tell her he was leaving with Tom for the gin, and that evening he woke her up only to kiss her good night. By the time Creed left on the morning of her third day of confinement to an empty house, Cricket was talking out loud to herself. She did not find that a laughing matter. In fact, she was going to go crazy if she didn't have a real conversation with someone soon.

Cricket had heard Amy and Belle returning at first light, and was only waiting until she was sure Tom was gone from the bedroom before she sought out Amy. She donned the hand-me-down dress Amy had provided and made her way down the hall, only to discover Amy was gone. A quick search of the upstairs revealed that Seth was gone, too. She began calling Creed every name she knew, fearing that he'd somehow arranged to spirit everyone away again. By the time she found Belle polishing the last of the silver in the dining room she was getting frantic.

"Where's Amy?"

"Missus is out back workin'," Belle said. "Best you get a hat 'fore you goes out there, missy. Sun mighty hot this mornin'."

"I'll be fine," Cricket said as she headed out the back door of the dining room. An arbored path led to the kitchen in one direction, and branched off toward the back yard in another. Cricket took the path to the back, unconsciously hurrying. She needn't have worried that Amy would escape her, for it was apparent as soon as she saw her that Amy wasn't going anywhere for a while.

"What are you doing!"

Amy turned, and smiled delightedly when she saw Cricket. "I'm so glad you're feeling better," she said. "Jarrett said you needed absolute rest and quiet and he wouldn't let me see you, and I was so worried that—"

"What are you doing?" Cricket repeated, dropping to the ground next to Amy, who was on her knees in the rich, black soil of what was to all appearances a garden. The dirt covered Amy's hands up to her elbows and smudged across her nose and brow. Beside her, Seth sat digging in the earth with a wooden spoon.

"Why, weeding my vegetable garden, of course," Amy replied. "I've got sweet and Irish potatoes, corn, beans, peas and—"

"You're weeding the garden?"

Amy laughed. "Who did you expect to do it? We haven't enough hoe hands as it is, and Belle doesn't have the knack for it."

"Tom makes you do this?"

"Tom can't stop me. I enjoy doing it," Amy explained to an incredulous Cricket. "I love planting things and helping them grow."

"But—"

At that moment, Seth flipped a spoonful of dirt into Cricket's face, catching her full in the mouth.

"Dir'," he said.

Cricket sputtered, spitting dirt and wiping it from her face with her sleeve, leaving streaks of mud across her cheeks and chin.

"Oh, Seth!" Amy chastised. "You mustn't throw dirt." Amy grabbed the hem of her apron to help clean up Cricket. "I can't believe he did that. He—"

At that moment Seth flipped a spoon of dirt into Amy's face. Startled, Amy blinked quickly to clear her eyes, then turned to Seth who was giggling at the two women across from him.

"Dir'," he said, pointing at his mother with the spoon.

"I'll give you 'dir', you little imp," Amy threatened. "Come on, Cricket, let's get him." She put her hands down and began crawling on her knees toward Seth, growling as she came. Seth turned onto all fours and scuttled madly away from them. With a lunge that sent her full-length into the dirt on her stomach, Amy caught Seth's ankle and held on. He curled into a ball with his arms surrounding his head and waited for doom to descend.

"Get him, Cricket," Amy urged.

Cricket wasn't sure how she was supposed to "get him," and her confusion must have registered because Amy added, "I'll keep him pinned down while you tickle him!"

The instant Cricket put her fingers on Seth's ribs he shrieked with laughter and rolled over onto his back, pulling free of Amy's loose grasp. Cricket warmed to her task as Seth rolled into a ball, trying to escape her. His bubbling laughter was contagious, and when Amy joined the fray, the three of them scuffled around in the dirt giggling and shrieking with delight.

When Cricket looked up Creed was standing there watching them. Caught in the mood of the moment she grinned happily up at him, and was surprised but very pleased when he grinned right back.

Amy interrupted their mutual admiration when she said, "This little mischief-maker attacked us and we had to defend ourselves."

Seth stood up and held out a handful of dirt to Creed.

"Dir'," he said.

"Right," Creed agreed, coming down on one knee before the small boy.

Cricket swallowed hard. Nearly three days by herself in the confines of the house had made her extraordinarily aware of sights and scents and sounds. Creed wasn't wearing a shirt, and his chest shimmered with sweat. She couldn't avoid inhaling the healthy odor of hard-working man which emanated from him. It was a scent distinctly Creed's, one Cricket found decidedly and inexplicably appealing.

"I'm glad to see you managed to get outside today, Brava."

There was no taunting satisfaction in Creed's voice, merely pleasure, so Cricket let the mellow Tennessee rumble come inside and fill all the gaping hollows that three days of solitude had left on her soul.

Creed couldn't have explained why he needed so desperately to touch Cricket—he only knew he did. He reached over to smooth away a smudge on her face, letting his thumb caress her soft skin. His thumb lingered, trailing down to the edge of her mouth, testing the fullness of her lower lip.

Cricket held herself from flinching in response to Creed's delicate stroking. After all, he was merely doing her a service he would have done for anyone, and preserving appearances in front of Amy. There was no other reason for him to be touching her so gently. She let her gaze meet Creed's.

It was a mistake. What she was seeing in Creed's eyes was a mistake. For desire burgeoned there. And hope. And promise. Cricket brought her hand up to stop Creed, her fingers wrapping firmly around his thumb. The rest of his fingers captured her hand and brought it toward his lips.

"Don't."

When Creed looked questioningly at Cricket, who was trying to pull her hand from his grasp, she added quickly, "I'm all dirty."

Creed opened her hand and brought her palm slowly, but surely, up to his mouth.

Cricket closed her eyes at the sensation of Creed's tongue

on the center of her palm. It was . . . delicious. "Creed, please stop," she whispered.

Creed wanted to scoop her into his arms and carry her down to the grassy banks of the river, to strip her bare and then bare himself and wash them both clean. He wanted her tall, sleek body pressing next to his own, her long hair unbraided and floating behind her. He wanted her arms around him and her belly joined to his. He wanted to be deep inside her, giving her pleasure and being pleasured in return.

Cricket's eyes widened as she received Creed's unspoken message. She opened her mouth to reply, but never got the chance, for at that instant Seth slung a handful of dirt at Creed.

"What?!"

"Oh, Seth, no!" Amy said, grabbing her son into her arms a second too late.

"Dir'," Seth announced proudly, holding out his empty hand to his uncle.

Creed gave the small boy a rueful smile, then reached up to wipe away the dirt.

Cricket stopped him. "Let me," she said.

It was the first time Cricket had willingly touched Creed, and he wondered what had given her the impetus to do so now, when he felt himself at the farthest edge of his self-control.

Cricket lifted the hem of her skirt and found a clean spot, then cupped Creed's chin in her hand and turned his face away so she could see to work. The dirt had landed on Creed's neck below his ear and left a muddy trail in the sweat along his throat to his shoulder and part of his arm and chest. Cricket looked forward to the coming task with an eagerness that was new for her. Amy and Seth might have disappeared for all the notice she took of her audience while she worked on Creed.

In fact, Amy saw the turn events were taking and gathered up her son, discreetly leaving the entranced couple alone.

Cricket's thin muslin skirt was not enough barrier to

contain Creed's body heat, nor the suppleness of his skin, nor the tautness of the muscles beneath it, but she was nonetheless frustrated because she didn't want anything between her skin and his. Touching Creed became a need that must be satisfied. And so, when she had wiped away the sweat and grime, her fingertips reached for the ridge of bone along his shoulder and traced the hollow above it and the rippling muscle below.

Creed held his breath, afraid that if he moved he'd break the spell. He didn't question the miracle that was occurring, he simply enjoyed it. It took all his willpower to remain still when Cricket's fingertip found the scar that began below his left nipple and traced it across his chest.

The skin was still slick with sweat where Cricket touched now, and she noticed that Creed's nipple had peaked when she touched him. The tiny bud drew her attention and her fingertip followed the scar back up again until she caressed him there. Cricket heard Creed's sharp intake of breath and wondered at the power she had to make him tremble. It was a power that both shocked and delighted her.

Cricket brought both hands flat against Creed's chest and, sure enough, the muscles tightened beneath her fingertips. She slid her hands down to his belly and he gasped again. A smile rose on Cricket's lips. This was . . . fun. She wondered what his skin tasted like, and indulged her curiosity. The tip of her tongue reached tentatively for the sweaty flesh of his shoulder. He was definitely salty. Cricket felt Creed shudder, and smiled again. Would that tiny bud on his chest be equally salty? Cricket lowered her head and took Creed's nipple between her teeth, letting her tongue run across its pebbled surface.

"Brava—"

Creed's raspy plea brought bubbling laughter from Cricket's chest and she released her hold to look up into Creed's face. What she saw there excited her beyond measure. His narrowed eyes smoldered with avidity, his nostrils flared to bring him the scent of her, his mouth had parted to ease his uneven breathing. His head was tipped down to her, his entire body strung tightly as a bowstring with suppressed desire.

She had unleashed the savage in Creed, and greeted his primeval need with joy and exultation. The knowledge rose in her that she was capable of matching his passion. She held herself in readiness, waiting for the panther to end its stillness, to commence its hunt. It was the tension of waiting that made her nervous, not the fear of what was to come. A frisson of the first real sexual need she'd ever known raced through her like a wildfire when Creed slowly lifted her up in his strong arms and headed toward the river.

"Where are we going?" Cricket asked breathlessly.

"Somewhere we can be alone."

"But Amy—"

"Amy's gone to the house with Seth."

Cricket's pulse quickened with anticipation. She could only imagine what Creed intended to do at the river. Would he undress her? Would he undress himself and do with her what husbands did to wives? She only knew she wanted something, needed something, and that only Creed could give it to her.

Cricket was watching Creed's face closely, so she noticed right away when the burning desire she'd seen in his eyes gave way to a gamut of other emotions—confusion, disgust, frustration—until now his golden gaze reflected something very like . . . was that *regret* she saw?

Suddenly Creed stopped dead in his tracks, and let go of his hold on her thighs, standing her upright and placing his hands on her shoulders so she stood facing him on wobbly legs.

"What's the matter?"

"I changed my mind," Creed said.

"You what?!!"

"I changed my mind. Doesn't happen often, but occasionally it does. This is one of those times."

Cricket's body quivered with need. The knowledge that her need wasn't going to be assuaged channeled all that energy into anger. "We're not going to the river?"

"You're going back to the house to tell Amy that Tom will be late getting home for supper tonight. His work at the gin is taking longer than he thought it would."

"Where are you going?"

Cricket watched Creed take several deep breaths, but the sexual sparks that flew between them singed them both, smoldering, burning, threatening to become a raging inferno. Then he drew himself upright and blew a breath of air from his mouth as though to put out the fire . . . but it only fanned the flames.

"I'm going down to the river and cool off," he bit out at last. "Then I'm going to go help Tom finish up. Will you relay Tom's message to Amy for me?"

"I'll be glad to give her the message."

Creed sighed gustily again before he said, "Thanks, Brava, I—"

"As soon as I take a swim in the river. Why should you be the only one who gets to cool off?" Cricket sauntered away from Creed, unbuttoning her dress as she went.

"You stop that, Brava! Do you hear me? Stop what you're doing right now!"

Cricket ignored Creed's panicked shouts and kept walking. He caught up to her seconds later and grabbed her arm, spinning her around. "What do you think you're doing?"

Cricket wasn't sure of that herself. It had only been an enjoyable game tempting Creed, making him tremble, making him gasp and shudder. But the desperate need she felt now wasn't amusing. She couldn't let Creed stop playing, because she wanted to know how the game ended. She smiled at Creed, a provocative smile that invited and promised more than she could possibly know she was inviting or promising.

Creed's lips flattened in an angry line and his entire body tensed as he sought to gather control of his wayward senses.

Cricket felt a sense of the inevitable when he scooped her up in his arms once more and headed for the river as fast as he could go. She didn't have time to say anything before they reached the steep banks shaded by several giant cypress trees. Her heart galloped with excitement as she imagined what would happen next.

"You sure you want to do this?" Creed barked.

"Yes."

"Then enjoy your swim." With that, Creed threw her out into the deepest part of the river.

Cricket came up sputtering, furious and humiliated. "You . . . you . . ." Her entire bullwhacking vocabulary deserted her in the face of his rejection.

Creed fought the urge to go in after her. "I'm going to rinse off at the house and join Tom. I'll see you at supper." With that, he turned and walked away.

She slapped her palms on the surface of the cool water in frustration. Of course, once he'd gone she recalled several quite colorful names to call him, but she was quickly forced to abandon her tantrum to concentrate on staying afloat. Her skirt puffed up around her like a balloon, and her shoes felt like anchors. With the extra effort required by her waterlogged shoes and the long dress, Cricket was hot and tired by the time she finally swam to the edge of the river and dragged herself up its steep, muddy bank.

Cricket squished her way back to the garden where she found Amy working by herself.

"My goodness! What happened to you?" Amy asked as she rose to greet the bedraggled Cricket.

Cricket wrung out the skirt of her soggy dress, making a mud puddle on the ground in front of Amy. "I decided to take a swim."

"With all your clothes on?"

"Creed threw me in!" she snapped back. "I thought he was going to—" Cricket stopped, realizing what she'd been about to admit.

"Let's get you changed, and we can talk," Amy said, urging Cricket toward the house.

"I don't have anything else to wear!"

"We'll find something, don't worry."

What Amy found was one of her calico short gowns and a pair of Creed's osnaburg trousers. Cricket was delighted to be back in pants. Creed was going to be upset she wasn't in a dress, and it served him right for throwing her in the river. While she was dressing, Cricket remembered to tell Amy that Tom would be late for supper.

"That'll work out fine," Amy said, "because I still have a lot of work to do myself. Would you mind if we walked outside while we talk? I need to check on my fruit trees."

Cricket didn't question why Amy was responsible for the trees; she simply followed her out the back door of the house and down toward the river where peach, quince, fig, and plum trees grew. Then Amy led Cricket to another garden where grapes, watermelon, and strawberries had been planted.

"The watermelon and strawberries will be ripe in July. I have the most delicious recipe for watermelon preserves. You cut the rind in chunks and put it in brine until . . ." Amy stopped her enthusiastic recitation when she saw Cricket's eyebrows had nearly reached the top of her forehead. "Don't worry. You won't have to remember any of this, but with the cloves and ginger and . . ." Amy smiled and stopped herself. "You simply must come back again to visit when all this fruit is ripe."

"I'd like that. I have a passion for strawberries," Cricket admitted. Which, she thought to herself, she'd eat fresh! Preserves sounded entirely too complicated!

"You tell Jarrett to bring you, then. I'm sure you can get him to do anything you'd like, he's so much in love with you."

Cricket snickered in disbelief. "From what I've seen it's the husbands who do the ordering around."

"How can you say that?"

"Because it's true. Wives are just servants who do what they're told. Look at you, grubbing away on your knees like some slave—"

"Oh, Cricket, no! It's not like that at all! I work because I like to work, because life would be empty of meaning for me if I weren't helping Tom in every way I can. He works so hard to make a home for us that's everything we want and need. And he loves me, Cricket. He cares for me and makes me feel needed like Jarrett needs you and—"

"Creed married me because he had to," Cricket said flatly, "and for no other reason."

The admission was so unexpected that Amy stood with her mouth open, unable to continue. At last she asked, "Are you expecting Creed's child, Cricket?"

Cricket blushed. She didn't know if she was pregnant or not.

Amy drew her own conclusions from Cricket's silence and enfolded Cricket in her arms. "Oh, you poor dear. I'm so sorry. So sorry. What can that man be thinking to throw you into the river like that," she muttered under her breath. "And with you in your condition."

Cricket pulled herself from Amy's embrace, aware Amy had put the wrong construction on the fact Creed had been forced to marry her. The temptation was there to explain to Amy the strange events that had made her a wife, despite her deep reservations about becoming one. But Cricket had held her own counsel for too many years, and the longstanding barriers didn't fall.

"I know Jarrett cares for you," Amy said, "but I think the more important question right now is how you feel about him."

"What?"

"How do you feel about Jarrett? Do you love him?"

"Of course not!"

"Why 'of course not'?"

Cricket struggled to explain. "I'm not like other girls. Before Creed came along I . . . I never felt anything like the things I feel now."

"And now?"

They'd wandered back to the orchard and Cricket sat down and leaned her head against the bark of a peach tree. Amy sat down across from her in the shade.

Cricket needed to talk to someone about the strange things she'd been feeling, and Sloan wasn't available. She let down the walls a little and admitted reluctantly to Amy,

"It's confusing. Sometimes I want Creed to touch me . . . and sometimes I want to touch him."

"What you're feeling is what any woman feels with a man she loves," Amy explained.

"I told you I don't love Creed."

"Then how do you explain these feelings that never happened before?"

"I don't," Cricket replied stubbornly. "They don't mean anything."

"Have it your way," Amy said. "Only remember the next time you're having those special feelings that they have to come from somewhere, and usually they arise from loving and caring. It's about time we start back to the house, so we'll both have time to clean up before supper."

Cricket followed Amy back to the house in silence, her forehead wrinkled in a pensive frown. Was it possible she loved Jarrett Creed? The thought was so unbelievable as to be laughable. Yet how could she explain the feelings that he elicited in her? How could she explain why she let him touch her and kiss her when she found the prospect of kissing any other man intolerable? How could she explain why she found such pleasure in the feel of his flesh under her fingertips?

"Tomorrow I want to spend some time working on my ornamental gardens. Would you like to join me?"

Cricket was startled from her reverie. "What?"

"I asked if you'd like to work in my flower gardens with me tomorrow?"

"Yes. Yes, I would," Cricket said. "I'd like that very much."

Amy looped her arm through Cricket's as they walked back to the house together. Cricket was surprised by how easy it was to talk with Amy, almost as easy as talking with Sloan.

"Amy?"

"What, Cricket?"

"How do you know when you're in love?"

Amy smiled. "You'll know."

Cricket grimaced. "That's no help."

"It's all the help I can give. After supper would you help me write the invitations for the reception?"

"Are you sure you want to have this party?"

"Absolutely," Amy said with a smile.

"Will I have to dance?"

Amy laughed. "Only once, Cricket. It's traditional for the bride and groom to have a first dance together."

After supper, Amy and Cricket sat down in the parlor with pen and paper to invite the surrounding planters and their wives to the party. "We should have plenty of time this week to get ready," Amy said.

And that gives me one week to learn how to dance, Cricket thought. She shifted her gaze to Creed, who sat on the other side of the room, talking with Tom.

Creed was restless. He wanted to go to bed, and he wanted Cricket to come with him. But how was he going to ask? Since he'd thrown her in the river, she wasn't talking to him. Things might have turned out so differently if he'd had a little more self-control—or a little less, he thought irritably. He rubbed the back of his neck to ease the tension. She'd caught him off-guard with all that touching. If he wasn't careful, Cricket was going to incite him to consummate this marriage, and he didn't want *that* to happen. Did he?

For their own reasons, both Creed and Cricket wanted to be alone to talk. So when Creed's restlessness finally drove him from his chair Cricket asked, "Is it bedtime?"

"Yes, yes it is." Creed extended his hand to her.

Cricket rose and crossed to him, putting her hand in his, as it seemed natural to do. The touch was electric, jolting both of them.

Cricket's new awareness of him transmitted itself to Creed. He tried to ignore the need that spread through him like a brush fire.

Cricket pretended there was nothing different, but her stomach was doing somersaults. Great! Now he was making her sick.

Tom and Amy exchanged a conspiratorial smile. The two lovers might have had a brief spat, but it was obviously mended now.

"Good night, Jarrett, Cricket," Tom said.

His words broke the trance, but not the spell. Cricket and Creed never took their eyes off one another as they ascended the staircase to privacy.

He wanted nothing from her.

She wanted nothing from him.

At least, that's what they told themselves as they headed for the bedroom.

CHAPTER 15

"LOOK AT YOUR LEG!"

Creed had been dressing and undressing in the dark for the past three days, so this was the first time Cricket had seen the spot where she'd bitten him. It looked awful. She reached out to touch the horrible black-and-blue discoloration, which was surrounded by a perfect set of teeth marks. His naked thigh felt hot under her fingertips.

At Creed's sharp intake of air Cricket looked up at him and asked, "Does it still hurt?"

Creed grabbed her wrist and removed her hand. "No, it's fine." Creed's trousers were halfway down, but he pulled them up again.

"Cricket, we have to—"

"Creed, we need to—"

"Talk."

They both smiled, but it did little to relieve the tension. Creed gestured for her to sit on the edge of the bed, and when she was settled, he sat down next to her. Cricket forced her eyes to stay on Creed's face, despite their desire to drift downward to his naked chest.

"Ladies first," he said.

213

As anxious as she was, Cricket would have agreed to anything. "All right." She took a deep breath.

Creed waited patiently, saying nothing until she finally blurted, "I need you to teach me how to dance."

When Creed's brows rose Cricket glared and said defensively, "Amy says you and I have to dance at the party she's giving. And I . . ." Cricket paused.

". . . don't know how," Creed finished for her.

"There wasn't any reason to know how. Who was I ever going to dance with?" she snapped. "Well?"

"I see your problem. Of course, I'll be glad to teach you." Creed wondered if Cricket knew how unusual it was for her to be concerned about doing the conventional thing.

Cricket's relief was tangible. "You will? You'll teach me to dance?"

"Yes, Brava, I will." Creed smiled at her, wondering how she'd managed to make him feel giddy and young and caught up in an adventure. This had to stop.

"I'll teach you to dance, but I have something to ask in return."

The sparkle wavered in Cricket's eyes and the tension slipped back into her body. "What do you want?"

Creed wasn't really sure of the answer to that question. He wanted Cricket warm and supple in his arms. He wanted to bury himself deep inside her and stay there. He'd begun to feel a husbandly possessiveness that was entirely inappropriate under the circumstances. He was also very much afraid that if he ever made Cricket his wife in fact, it wouldn't be so easy to give her up once the business with Sloan and Antonio was resolved. There was no room in a Ranger's life for a woman, especially a woman who promised to be as much pure hell-raising trouble as Creighton Stewart.

So what he wanted had very little relationship to what he planned to ask of Cricket. Quite simply, she had to keep her hands off him. Creed felt a flush rising on his neck. The mere thought of her fingertips on his skin made him hard. He tried to summon anger at his predicament, hoping that would take his mind off his urgent need. The worst of it was, he knew Cricket's desire to touch him was merely the result of her insatiable curiosity. What had happened between them today could have happened with any man. She was learning for the first time what it meant to have a woman's feelings and, ironically, acted very much like a child with a new toy.

However, if she continued teasing him the way she had this afternoon he wouldn't be responsible for the consequences. He'd created his own *diablito*, and he wasn't sure of the best way to control her. Knowing Cricket, if he demanded she leave him alone she was likely to do the exact opposite. Suddenly, Creed chuckled to himself. So if he wanted her to stop touching him, maybe the solution was to demand that she continue her affections.

"After the incident at the river today, I think it's clear we have to establish some new rules," he said.

"New rules?"

Cricket had suspected this conversation was coming. Rather, she'd anticipated it. Still, she wasn't sure whether she was ready to do "it" with Creed, because she wasn't yet sure of her feelings. Amy had said she'd know when she was in love. She'd expected to feel something momentous, something extraordinary. The most she could say was that she didn't find the idea of spending time with Creed distasteful at all. Was that what it meant to be in love?

"A man has certain needs, Cricket, that have to be satisfied when he's aroused by a woman. If you intend to continue teasing me as you did today, then I intend to see that you satisfy those needs."

Cricket bristled automatically at Creed's demanding tone of voice, but forced herself to curb her antagonism while she took time to evaluate his speech. She'd encountered a lot of new feelings lately. Maybe the same thing had happened to Creed. Unfortunately, even based on her limited knowledge, what he'd said didn't sound like the words a man used to a woman he loved. But then, what did she really know about love?

Creed enfolded her in his embrace and gently lowered her so they were both stretched out face to face on the feather bed. He emblazoned her face and neck with kisses that tingled, but he kept their bodies separated, murmuring to her across the distance that separated them.

Cricket felt her bones melting until she was as limp as a day-old starched shirt, pliant and malleable beneath Creed's persuasive kissing. She let her fingertips roam across his bare chest, caressing the smooth skin over hard muscle, while she tried to listen to what he was saying . . . something about satisfying needs. . . . Maybe her woman's intuition had been mistaken. He was certainly acting as though he cared. Would he show her what it meant to be a woman in a man's arms? Would he make her feel those incredible spiraling sensations again?

"It pleases me to be touched by you, Brava."

That sounded encouraging.

"But I'm like any other man when a beautiful woman touches him . . ."

That was even better—he thought her a beautiful woman.

". . . I have animal urges that have to be satisfied—or it becomes very painful."

Animal urges?

"At times like that, any woman will do."

Any woman?

"So I'll be counting on you to take care of that little chore for me, okay, Brava?"

Chore?!

Cricket grabbed a hank of Creed's thick black hair and yanked his head away from where he was nuzzling her neck so fast he yelped in pain. His eyes were lambent with desire and his lips were parted in readiness for another kiss.

"Listen, you shaggy-haired ravager of women, I stopped doing *chores* when I turned ten," she raged. "If my touch is so distressful to you then I think I can manage to control myself. I trust you'll do the same!" She yanked his hair once more for good measure before she shoved herself away from him to the other side of the bed.

"Does this mean we won't be sleeping together tonight?"

Cricket looked down at the hard floor and compared it to

the feathered comfort beneath her. "Now that we've settled this matter of touching one another once and for all, I don't see any reason why we can't share the bed."

Cricket turned to arrange the sheet at that moment or she would have seen the agonized expression that crossed Creed's face. She continued, "And you can expect to lose your hand—or any other part of you—if it so much as slips an inch over on my side! Furthermore, in the future I'll expect you to keep your hands to yourself!"

"That's going to make teaching you how to dance rather difficult."

Cricket's tirade sputtered to a stop. She'd forgotten all about the dancing lessons. She steamed and stewed for a moment before she said, "I'll tell you where and when to touch, Creed, not the other way around."

"Fine, Brava. Now that we have that all settled, how about let's get some sleep."

Instead of answering, Cricket pulled the sheet down and slipped underneath. Even lying stiff as a board, the feather bed was pure heaven. She wasn't sorry she'd given up the floor, even if it meant she had to lie beside Creed without touching all night. She held tightly to her anger because she very much feared the alternative was a deep and abiding despair. Was that all she was to Creed—just another woman? She'd been ignorant of relations between husbands and wives, but she was learning fast, and some of the lessons weren't at all pleasant.

Cricket waited while he blew out the candle, discarded his trousers, and joined her in bed. Then she drew a line down the center of the bed, right through Creed's naked thigh.

"Move it!" she commanded.

Creed grunted, but obeyed. If he wanted to wake up in one piece, he thought, he'd be smart to sleep on the floor himself. But he wasn't about to let her talk him out of his own bed. At least now he wouldn't have to worry about her throwing herself at him. He wondered why that made him feel as though he'd lost something very important.

It had begun to matter less and less that Cricket couldn't

make biscuits or find the right spoon at the table, and she should never hide those firm buttocks and long legs under the current fashions. He'd thought her less than a whole human being because she didn't act like other girls, but how mistaken he'd been!

Despite outward appearances, she cared deeply what others thought about her. He now knew she'd kept all those feelings hidden because she'd been hurt by the painful criticisms, like his own. But he wasn't sorry he'd forced her to acknowledge she was a woman. It had been like glimpsing a cactus unfolding its vivid blossoms to observe Cricket as she accepted her femininity. And like that desert flower she had proven to be surprisingly soft, incredibly fragile, much more vulnerable than the thick-skinned, prickly surface that protected what was deep inside. When he held her in his arms, and her body naturally molded itself to him; when her mouth opened under his, she was all the woman a man could want. Oh, he wanted her, all right. But he wasn't going to have her. Once he dealt with Sloan Stewart and got the information he needed to put Antonio Guerrero out of business, he'd send Cricket back to her father. And that was the end of that.

It was Cricket who woke first the next morning. Creed's arm was curled around her, and she could feel his iron grip on her ribs through her chemise. The flat of his hand splayed possessively across her belly. It amazed her how secure she felt. He held her possessively, his hairy thigh imprisoning her under its weight. The uneasy feeling crept over her that she was caught like a rabbit in a snare. Escape became imperative. She slipped from Creed's grasp and dressed quickly, determined to spend the day under the Texas sun. Perhaps it was only the three days cooped up inside which had caused that uncomfortable trapped sensation. She went to the dining room hunting for something to eat and discovered Tom there ahead of her.

"I didn't think you'd be up so early," he said. "Where's Jarrett?"

"Still sleeping."

Cricket turned away from Tom's speculative look, helping herself to a cup of coffee before she joined him at the table.

Tom perused the young woman who sat across from him. She wasn't what he'd expected. Since the death of his Indian wife, Jarrett had always preferred small, feminine blondes like the American chargé's daughter, Angelique LeFevre. This auburn-haired Amazon in osnaburg trousers hardly fit the bill. It was a shame how she'd been raised, but Amy liked her and seemed to think she was perfect for Jarrett. From the flush on Cricket's face, his wife was probably right. His next thought found its way out of his mouth without conscious thought. "I never thought Jarrett would marry again after the way he mourned when his Comanche wife died."

Cricket's head whipped around to face Tom. "He had a Comanche wife?"

"You didn't know?"

"Jarrett told me he'd lived among the Comanches, but he didn't tell me much else."

"I guess that's not surprising. None of us talk much about what happened."

"What happened?"

"I don't suppose Jarrett would mind me telling you. He and our mother were both captured by the Comanches when he was eight. He spent nine years with those Red Devils before we managed to get him back."

"Did you ever meet his Comanche wife?"

"Summer Wind? I saw her once, the day we got Jarrett back from the Comanches."

When Tom offered no more, Cricket's curiosity prodded her to ask, "Was she pretty?"

"She was a squaw like any other. I thought Jarrett was going to kill Pa, though, when he separated him from her. Jarrett didn't want anything to do with white men. He was Comanche through and through, and he must have loved that squaw, because all Pa had to do was threaten to kill her and Jarrett came with us after that."

"What happened to your mother? Was your father able to rescue her, too?"

"Oh, he found her all right. But she was some Comanche chief's *paraibo* by then. Pa didn't have any use for a squaw, so he left her there."

"But what happened to her wasn't her fault. She had no choice in the matter," Cricket protested. "Couldn't *you* have helped her?"

"Wasn't my place. The decision was Pa's."

"But if it had been up to you—"

"It wasn't up to me. But my pa said she'd lain down under too many Comanche bucks and that kind of dirt wasn't ever going to wash off."

Cricket's eyes rounded incredulously. "Do you feel the same way?"

"Never had to think about it. Wouldn't have done any good. Pa's mind was made up."

"That seems so unfair. You don't treat Creed any different and he was with the Comanches as long as your mother. You're as close as any two brothers I've ever seen."

Tom pursed his lips in irritation. He'd respected his father, and when Simon Creed had said an unpure woman was an unfit mother and an abomination as a wife, he hadn't questioned him. "A brother's one thing," he said at last. "A man's wife is something else entirely."

"But she was your mother and—"

"I don't even know if she's alive anymore, so there's no sense talking about it. What's done is done." Tom shoved himself away from the table. "Tell Creed I'll be at the gin again today." Without waiting for Cricket's acknowledgment he left the room.

Cricket sat at the table only long enough to finish her coffee before she rose and left as well. She didn't want to get caught by Amy and end up having to make biscuits, or pie dough, or bread. She headed for the stable, saddled Valor, called Rogue, and galloped off across the fields before the sun was even well up.

Cricket turned her face to the sky and bathed in the sunshine. Its warmth brought a cleansing perspiration to her skin. When the Texas wind had dried those dewdrops she felt refreshed and renewed. She rode the boundaries of

Lion's Dare, watching the hoe hands at work in the cotton fields, the Negroes mending fences, planting new fruit trees, working on their own gardens.

Lion's Dare presented an almost idyllic picture of what life could be on the Texas frontier. There was peace and prosperity. There was love in abundance: the love of a man for the land; the love of a man and woman for each other; and the love of parents for their child. Cricket wondered what it would be like to have a home and a husband and a child of her own. But the vision eluded her because she couldn't imagine a home that wasn't Three Oaks, or a husband who wasn't Creed, and the child always turned into blue-eyed, blond-haired Seth.

Cricket finally ended up sitting under an oak at the farthest edge of Lion's Dare, working on a chain of dandelions, while Valor grazed nearby and Rogue slept next to her. She was daydreaming again when she was interrupted by a sarcastic voice.

"Seen any Indians?"

Cricket refused to let Creed's fierce expression intimidate her. "Not a one," she replied as she went back to work on her dandelion chain.

Creed dismounted and crossed to stand spread-legged in front of her, his shadow blocking out the sunshine that threaded through the bare branches above them. "You know how dangerous it is to be out here alone. A Comanche would as soon hang a woman's hair from his shield as a man's. Or maybe you'd like to become Tall Bear's squaw. Is that it?"

Cricket looked up lazily from the flowers in her lap. "You don't need to worry about me. I can take care of myself." With that announcement, she pulled her Patterson from the belt at her waist and proceeded to shoot five prickly pears off a cactus that was an astounding distance away. When she'd finished, she calmly reloaded, stuck the gun into her belt, and turned her attention back to the dandelions. "That could just as easily have been five Comanches, sent to the Happy Hunting Grounds."

Cricket's fearlessness irked Creed. He didn't know why he should care so much, but he did. The thought of some

Comanche buck touching Cricket tied his gut up in knots. Yet he couldn't say her self-confidence was entirely misplaced. She was an excellent rider, an excellent shot, and quick to react to danger. One on one she might even stand a chance against a Comanche warrior—if she rode like the very devil while she emptied her Patterson. Against even a small band of Comanches, however, Cricket was going to be in trouble. But how was he going to rid her of her false sense of security?

"Being a good shot isn't going to help you much if you're caught by surprise."

"No one's going to surprise me."

"Oh, no?"

"Between Valor and Rogue I have two exceptional sentinels." Cricket ignored the fact that neither animal had given the slightest hint of Creed's approach. He'd spoiled them both for that purpose. "Of course, I'm not too bad at watching out for myself, either."

Before Creed could guess what she had in mind Cricket hooked a toe behind his boot and lunged at him. Her shoulder hit him at the knees, throwing him totally off-balance. He would've fallen had he not reached up and caught a dead limb of the pin oak above him. However, the rotten branch held him for only a moment before it broke with an ear-shattering crack and sent him tumbling.

Cricket had been so certain of the success of her surprise attack that she'd surged past the point where Creed should have landed. That left her directly under him when he fell.

"Uummph!"

"Oommmph!"

Both Cricket and Creed had the wind knocked out of them, but since Creed landed on top of Cricket, she somewhat cushioned his fall. They lay there in the tall grass catching their breaths, their bodies a tangle of arms and legs.

"Get off!" Cricket grunted at last.

"I don't think I can."

"What?"

"I think maybe something is broken," Creed said.

"Are you sure?"

"No, but I landed on my elbow. Let me lie here a minute and see if any feeling comes back into my arm."

"I'll check it. Which arm?"

"The right one."

Cricket reached around and found the fingers of Creed's right hand. They closed around her own, and like lightning Creed bounded to his feet, jerking Cricket up behind him. He whirled and caught her as she flew into his embrace. As he cinched their bodies together, Creed caught the flare of fury in Cricket's eyes.

Cricket opened her mouth to call Rogue to her aid, and then remembered he'd defected to Creed's camp. Valor was nearby, but how could the stallion attack Creed without also harming her?

"Tell me again how you can take care of yourself!" Creed taunted in her ear.

Angry, frustrated, Cricket threw caution to the winds and whistled for Valor. Let the stallion figure out how to help her without harming her!

Valor's trumpeting neigh sent shivers down Creed's spine. He'd seen the stallion attack the Comanches, but had never expected to see the animal's sharp hooves aimed in his direction. Valor reared and then charged toward them, teeth bared. Creed had no idea whether the stallion would trample both of them or not, but he couldn't take the chance.

"Damn it, Brava!"

He threw Cricket aside and stepped away so Valor would have a clear target that didn't include her. He balanced on the balls of his feet, his muscles tensed, ready to jump out of the stallion's path at the last instant. He'd played this game before, as a Comanche boy, only there'd been a rider, Tall Bear, on the back of the charging animal. He'd survived that incident with no more than the curving scar on his hip to show for it. But after that he'd never underestimated the danger of a frenzied beast.

Creed was ready to pit the quickness of his reflexes against those of the stallion, but if push came to shove he might have to kill the beautiful animal, and he didn't want to do that.

"Call him off, Brava. This has gone far enough."

When the shrill whistle pierced the air Valor changed course immediately. The stallion angled off away from Creed, who remained tense a few more moments until he ascertained that the animal no longer constituted a danger to him. He turned to thank Cricket for her wise decision, only to discover she was no longer behind him.

Then he saw her. The stallion never lost stride as he raced toward the girl waiting for him, Rogue by her side. He watched as Cricket caught a handful of Valor's mane and vaulted onto the stallion's back while he moved at a full gallop. She turned to grin and wave at Creed before she turned Valor back toward the plantation house.

. How had she managed to move from behind him without his knowing it? She was good. He had to admire her for what she'd just accomplished. At the same time he feared for her. The danger from the Comanches was real. If Cricket ignored that danger—or treated it too lightly—it could spell disaster. So what did he care? If she wanted to get herself killed was that any of his business? He'd be rid of Rip Stewart's brat—and good riddance!

Creed stared at the cloud of dust in the air that was all that remained to remind him Cricket had been there. His stomach felt queasy. He rubbed his sweaty palms off on his trousers. Then he picked his hat up off the ground, smoothed the turkey feather, and put it on, pulling it down low on his forehead. He crossed to his chestnut, grabbed the reins, stuck his foot in the stirrup, and pulled himself into the saddle. He kept his mind a blank as long as he could, because he didn't like the thoughts that kept creeping in. Cricket being beaten and raped. Cricket lying dead, scalped, a lance through her heart. He experienced the most unusual sensation, a sort of tightening of his insides, around the region of his heart.

Then he started to laugh. He laughed so loud he scared a

jackrabbit out of hiding. He laughed so loud an eagle swooped down to check out the noise. He laughed so hard his stomach hurt and tears squeezed from the corners of his eyes. And this was *so funny* he didn't think he was going to be able to stop laughing.

He was in love with Creighton Stewart.

CHAPTER 16

CRICKET FELT THE first cramp about an hour after she arrived back at the plantation house. She shrugged off the feeling of disappointment that rippled through her. She wasn't going to have Creed's baby. Blue blazes! What was the matter with her? She wouldn't have known what to do with a baby, anyway. Besides, a baby would have tied her to Creed as tight as a cinched saddle. No, she had reasons to be grateful the female miseries were upon her. Except, of course, there was this one little problem. . . .

Creed had forbidden her to drink and obtained Tom and Amy's cooperation in assuring his order was obeyed. Little had he known his command would cause no hardship for her except at one time during the month. Unfortunately, that time had arrived. The only way she was going to survive the next day or so was with the help of a little whiskey. Make that a *lot* of whiskey, Cricket thought with a wry smile.

Well, she'd stolen whiskey from Rip often enough to know how it was done. The question was whether she could hide her discomfort until everyone went to bed tonight. A hard spasm doubled Cricket over where she stood. White-faced, she grasped a nearby door jamb and slowly straightened up.

She could do it. Unless she wanted to confess her dilemma to Jarrett Creed, she had no other choice.

Creed noticed how quiet Cricket was during supper, but attributed it to their morning confrontation. However, her eyes were unnaturally bright, almost feverish, and her face flushed and glowing. He'd have said she was planning some mischief, but the taut line of her lips wasn't the least bit playful. Something was going on, though, and he intended to find out what it was.

At the first opportunity Creed said, "Cricket and I had a long day. I think we'll go up to bed early tonight." Was that relief he saw on Cricket's face?

"Oh, but you promised we could play cards tonight. Did you forget?" Amy's disappointment almost made Creed change his mind, except from the corner of his eye he noticed that Cricket's face had blanched white.

"I'm sorry, Amy. Not tonight. I'm just too tired." Yes, that was definitely relief on Cricket's face. What was bothering her? Creed's concern brought him around the table to pull back Cricket's chair and take her elbow to help her to her feet. Surprisingly, she didn't resist his assistance, but she stopped for a moment where she was and he felt her whole body unaccountably stiffen. Seconds later she relaxed again.

"Brava?" he murmured.

"Creed, can we go upstairs, please? Now."

Creed reached out and lifted Cricket into his arms. He knew something was terribly wrong when, instead of arguing with him over the presumptuous move, Cricket merely turned her face into his shirt and clung to his shoulders.

"Is something the matter with Cricket?" Amy asked as she rose from her chair. Tom rose also, his concern unvoiced but present nevertheless.

Cricket stiffened in Creed's arms, and he recognized her unspoken plea not to disclose that anything was amiss. "Can't a husband carry his wife up to bed?" he asked with a lascivious grin.

Amy blushed.

"That's not a bad idea." Amy laughed as Tom whisked her up into his arms. "Let's go, Jarrett."

Creed preceded his older brother up the stairs, sharing a wink as they each disappeared into their separate bedrooms. As soon as he was inside the door, however, Creed crossed quickly to the bed and laid Cricket upon it with anything but romantic intentions. She allowed him to help unbutton her dress and strip it off, another first between them that passed uncommented-upon, almost as though it were an everyday occurrence.

However, Creed had little time to be pleased by Cricket's wifely behavior. She turned from him as soon as he was done, her lower lip clasped tight in her teeth, and closed her eyes, effectively shutting him out. He sat down next to her and anxiously examined her, his hands whisking over her, checking for some sign of injury. Again, she endured without complaint or, in fact, any acknowledgment that he was even in the same room with her.

"Did you hurt yourself somehow today?"

"No."

"Are you sure?"

"Yes."

"What's wrong, then?"

"What makes you think something is—" Cricket gasped and bit into her lower lip until she tasted blood. Her whole body tensed, and she grabbed the quilt in her fists and held on tight. *Come on, Cricket, you can do it. Just a little bit longer.* But the litany she'd repeated all afternoon and into the evening didn't seem to be working anymore. Cricket moaned.

Creed gently brushed a strand of auburn hair from Cricket's agonized brow. "Let me help, Brava," he pleaded. "What's wrong?"

Cricket moaned again.

"Tell me what I can do to help."

Cricket's feverish gaze caught the look of desperation in Creed's topaz eyes. She would have to tell him.

"I need some whiskey."

She'd said it so softly that at first Creed didn't think he'd heard her right.

"What?"

228

"Whiskey. I need some whiskey," she repeated, agitated that she had to admit her weakness. While Cricket watched, Creed's eyes turned stone cold. She shivered as she saw the sympathetic concern disappear, the anger grow.

"Is that what this is all about? You want some goddamned *belly-wash?!*

"Keep your voice down!" she warned. "You said you'd help! *I need whiskey.*"

Creed scowled at her, eyes flashing dangerously. "I told you no more drinking and I meant it! That's one bad habit you'll get over if I have to sit on you to keep you away from the bottle." Creed was appalled by the glittering brightness of Cricket's eyes as she glared back at him. There was something else there. Pain? But she'd said she wasn't hurt. How was that possible? A ruse, perhaps, to trick him? She was cunning. In fact, he'd constantly underestimated her cleverness.

Cricket moaned again.

Her act wouldn't fool him this time. "Moan all you want," he said. "You'll get your rotgut firewater over my dead body."

Cricket turned her back to Creed and curled into a fetal ball, tucking her chin down and hugging her knees to her chest. He thought she was a lush! Well, she had a problem with the belly-vengeance, all right, but not the kind he thought. She could never tell him the truth now. After all her talk about being able to take care of herself how could she admit there was, of course, this small exception, when she endured her female miseries. It was too humiliating.

Creed's chest ached. He'd known of men tied to that snake-poison, but how had it happened to his *brava*? His *brava*—a drunk! Dear God, he thought, where had she been getting the whiskey to feed this habit over the past two weeks? He'd taken her flask away, but she must have had some whiskey stashed somewhere else that she'd guzzled. It mattered little now. The damage was done—and he'd never even suspected. He'd heard that withdrawal from whiskey could be awful, and he determined that the least he could do was comfort her through it. But when he touched Cricket on the shoulder she jerked away from him. It was as though he'd tried to free a wild animal caught in a trap. He saw only fear in her eyes.

"Don't you come near me! I'll take care of myself."

"All right, Brava, have it your way. If you want to fight the effects of that hell-broth alone, be my guest. But you're not going to be doing any more drinking, because I'll be here, and I'll be watching."

Cricket never moved. Creed readied himself for bed, blew out the candle, and crawled onto the feather mattress next to her. It was warm, so he didn't trouble her to turn down the covers. He knew there was no way he could sleep with Cricket moaning and groaning on the other side of the bed, anyway. Why wouldn't she let him help?

He reached over again in the darkness, but she stiffened as soon as he touched her shoulder and snapped, "Leave me alone!" He removed his hand and turned onto his back, staring at the ceiling. He lay that way until Cricket's moans stopped. He closed his eyes for an instant and the hard labor he'd done with Tom sent him into a sound sleep.

Cricket had been praying for at least the past hour, and it seemed finally her prayers had been answered. Creed was breathing steadily, a sure sign he was asleep. She need only sneak down to Tom's cache of liquor and steal a bottle, and disappear into the barn until morning. By the time Creed found her she'd have made it through her crisis.

As it turned out, her simple plan was easier said than done. In the first place, she couldn't light a candle without awakening Creed, and it was as dark as the back end of a bear's den. In the second place, she was decidedly unsteady on her feet. She'd eaten very little since morning, and fighting the cramps had taken a toll on her strength. Finally, the cramps attacked her at the most unpredictable times and she had to stop and wait for them to pass.

When she reached her goal, the cabinet that held Tom's liquor, she found out why Creed had felt so safe falling asleep. It was locked! She hadn't the vaguest idea where to look for the key, but she knew where she could find a knife to jimmy the lock. She headed for the silverware drawer in the dining room. There was a slight clatter of silver as she jerked the drawer open, and she waited motionless to see if anyone might have been disturbed. When it remained quiet, she stuck her hand in the drawer and ran her fingers from piece to piece until she located the pointed silver knives. She removed one and headed back to the parlor.

Cricket pried the lock open in minutes, then tried to determine in the dark which of the bottles was whiskey. She resorted to tasting them, and ended up with a mouthful of sweet sherry, a disgusting sip of something bitter that she couldn't identify, and a gulp of elderberry wine before she finally found what she was looking for. It was a good whiskey, very smooth and very welcome. Cricket had tipped the bottle up and leaned her head back to drink again when Creed lit a candle across from her. The shadows made his expression seem even more grim than it was.

"Hand it over, Brava."

Instead, Cricket tried to swallow, only to have the bottle jerked away, whisky spilling on her underclothes and the carpeted floor.

"I need that!"

"No one *needs* whiskey. It's a crutch you can do very well without."

"You don't understand! I have to have it! Otherwise I can't stand the pain!"

Even through Creed's fury, Cricket's words registered. What pain couldn't she stand? She'd said she wasn't hurt. He narrowed his eyes and pursed his lips. If this was a trick . . .

"All right, Brava, you can't stand the pain without whiskey. What pain?"

Cricket's hands came up to cover her face and she mumbled through them. "The female miseries."

Creed was stunned, and then furious that he'd worried himself half to death over a natural female bodily function. "You created all this ruckus over *that!* Of all the mooncalf, nickninny—"

Cricket's groan cut him off. She really was in pain, he could see that. From what little he knew, she wouldn't be the first woman who needed to retire to her bed for a few days each month. But, naturally, Cricket hadn't resorted to typical female behavior. She never did anything the normal way.

"Why don't you take some laudanum and go to bed like everybody else?" he asked with frustrated helplessness.

Cricket peeked through her fingers at him. "Laudanum?"

Creed looked at her in astonishment. "You mean Rip never suggested you take laudanum for the pain?"

Cricket looked down at the balled fists in her lap and whispered, "I never told Rip about the pain."

Creed shook his head. Surely the man had known. After all, he'd carried her up to her bedroom drunk often enough. Why hadn't her father offered to help? *Because that would have been acknowledging Cricket wasn't a son.* So instead Rip had let her hurt all these years. Creed's lips flattened in determination. She didn't belong to Rip Stewart anymore. She belonged to him. And he wasn't going to let her hurt one more double-damn minute!

Creed kneeled down beside Cricket. "Would you try some laudanum, Brava, if I can find some? It'll ease the pain."

Cricket nodded her head glumly. What choice did she have if he wasn't going to let her drink whiskey? She was surprised when Creed picked her up in his arms, and held her close to his chest.

"Come on, Brava, let's get you back in bed where you belong."

Cricket could hear Creed's steady heartbeat in her ear, could feel the smooth skin of his chest against her cheek. She turned her face to him and pressed her nose against his skin like a child at the window of a mercantile store. She inhaled the special, delicious scent that was his, and which she'd recognize anywhere.

She'd found a lot to admire about Creed over the past couple of weeks. Now, as he had the night of the *fandango*, he was taking care of her again. It was so nice to relax and let someone else take control for a little while. He was an exceptional man, and if things had been different she might even have liked being married to him. And, she admitted in a moment of honesty, she was very sorry she wasn't going to have his baby.

All too soon Creed reached the bedroom. Cricket resumed her fetal position as soon as he laid her down. He left again to rummage as quietly as a thief through the dining room cabinets, where he found Amy's store of medicinals, including her supply of laudanum. When he returned, he spooned some down Cricket's throat, setting the bottle on the table next to the bed in case she needed more.

"Where does it hurt?" he asked.

"All over."

Creed chuckled at Cricket's emphatic complaint and shook his head. "Be more specific."

"My belly . . . and my back."

Cricket was in so much pain she didn't realize at first what Creed intended as he sat down beside her and placed his hands on her back at the curve below her waist.

"Here?" he asked, his thumbs finding the clenched muscles with great accuracy.

"Yesssss."

She tensed when Creed began gently but firmly massaging the tight muscles of her lower back under his fingertips.

"Don't fight it, Brava," he whispered. "Relax."

Cricket could feel the tension easing as he moved his strong hands lower, just above the swell of her buttocks. His thumbs caressed in ever-widening circles. Slowly, the combination of Creed's massage and the laudanum began to work. Her legs unfolded and she was able to stretch out flat on her stomach. As soon as she did, Creed let his hands roam. He soothed the muscles in her shoulders. He discovered the curve of her spine. He measured the span of her waist. He enjoyed the shapely firmness of her buttocks.

Cricket felt like she was floating. The pain had become no more than a memory, and it seemed entirely natural to enjoy the feel of Creed's hands on her through her underclothes. She felt better than she'd imagined possible during the female miseries.

"Creed?"

"Hmmm?"

"Thank you."

"Don't mention it, Brava. It was my pleasure."

Tomorrow, when the mellow mood induced by the laudanum wore off, she was probably going to be furious at the way he'd touched her. But Creed couldn't deny himself that joy tonight. He slipped into bed and pulled her into his arms, so they fit together like two spoons in Amy's silverware drawer.

"Creed?"

"Hmmm?"

"Shouldn't you be on your own side?"

"Not tonight, Brava. Tonight touching is the only way I can help you. And I do want to help."

He splayed his hand on her belly and gently caressed her taut skin, working to ease the constricted muscle beneath it. Cricket snuggled her rump deeper into the pocket created by Creed's groin and thighs, and gave him sway to do with her as he pleased. She didn't think about their closeness, she just enjoyed it. She felt peaceful, languorous, sheltered . . . and before she knew it, she was asleep.

When she woke in the morning, she was alone. From the look of the sun it was nearly noon. She sat up, and was surprised at how well she felt, although things were still a little muzzy. She seemed to remember Creed dosing her again with medicine in the middle of the night like he would a sick horse. He'd stayed close to her, his hands constantly moving, soothing, taking away the pain. Cricket flushed. It wasn't as though she'd voluntarily slept in Creed's embrace. It had taken the female miseries to put her there. But—and she was having far too many moments of this God's-truth kind of honesty lately—it had been wonderful.

When the door opened to reveal Creed with a tray of food, Cricket felt a sudden shyness. After all, he'd been treating her for a delicate female condition.

However, there was nothing timid about Creed's greeting. "Good morning! How's the girl with the female miseries feeling today?"

Cricket blushed scarlet as she sank back down into the feather bed and pulled the covers up over her face. Husbands didn't talk about things like that with their wives, did they?

Creed laughed heartily. He brought the tray over and set it down on the table next to the bed.

"Come on, Brava. Sit up and eat something."

"I'm not hungry," Cricket muttered from under the sheet.

"Sure you are. As a matter of fact, if you'll think about it, you're probably starved."

Right on cue, Cricket's stomach growled.

"See what I mean?"

He obviously wasn't going to leave anytime soon, and she *was* hungry. . . . Cricket slowly sat up, keeping the sheet modestly in front of her. "What do you have there?"

"It's soup," Creed said. "A broth, actually. I wasn't sure how you'd be feeling." He searched her face for a clue as to how well she'd survived the night, and their eyes caught and held. Something passed between them that hadn't been there before.

Creed tried to ignore it, but couldn't.

Cricket tried to identify it, but couldn't.

Creed cleared his throat.

Cricket cleared hers, too.

She blinked once.

So did he.

But it didn't go away.

Whatever it was crackled between them like lightning in a thunderstorm and Cricket could feel her neck hairs standing on end. She searched Creed's eyes for some clue to the mystery, and lost herself in their depths.

Creed reached out a hand to touch Cricket's face, to make sure he wasn't dreaming. There was a tingling awareness between them, an imperceptible lure, like pollen to a honeybee. The tugging attraction drew Creed's attention to little things he'd never noticed before, like the way Cricket's eyelashes curled on the ends, and the way her brows arched so symmetrically over her dove-gray eyes. And like a honeybee, he wanted to taste the flower before him. He suited deed to thought, leaning slowly but surely closer to Cricket until he'd closed the distance between them.

Cricket saw what was happening, but was powerless to prevent it. As Creed's lips settled gently on her own she realized she didn't want to stop him.

Creed sucked slightly on Cricket's lower lip, then teased it with his teeth. His tongue traced the edge of her upper lip, and Cricket opened her mouth to give him freer access. It was an invitation Creed didn't ignore. His mouth settled firmly over hers and his tongue came to plunder the treasures within.

"Cricket, I . . . excuse me, I . . ." Amy wished she could take back her words and disappear, because it was obvious she'd interrupted something pretty important.

Cricket was mortified to realize how close she'd come to succumbing to . . . whatever it was husbands and wives did together. What on earth had come over her? She was still quivering from Creed's kiss. She was glad she didn't have to stand because she was sure her legs wouldn't have supported her.

Creed sighed and brushed a hand through his hair. "Come on in, Amy. I know Cricket would like a chance to talk with you. I've got to go help Tom at the gin anyway. I only stayed to make sure she was feeling better."

"So you *were* sick!" Amy accused.

Creed and Cricket exchanged a look, Cricket begging him not to say anything, and while he didn't understand her reluctance to share her problem with Amy, he was willing to abide by her decision.

"A little upset stomach," Creed said. "She's fine now, I think."

"You'll stay in bed, today, though," Amy announced, "and make sure you're all right."

"I'm fine, Amy," Cricket protested.

"I won't hear differently," Amy said in her sternest voice.

Cricket looked to Creed for help, but he shrugged his shoulders as if to say, "You wanted to keep secrets from her, so now you're paying the consequences."

"I'll see you tonight," Creed said as he left.

"I hope you're going to feel better in time for the party on

Saturday," Amy said, worrying her lower lip with her teeth. "Oh, dear, that would be unfortunate, if you were too sick to come to your own party."

Not as far as Cricket was concerned, but she had the good sense not to say so to Amy. Which reminded her that she still had to learn how to dance. Now, however, the thought of spending an entire afternoon being held in Creed's arms was decidedly appealing. Cricket refused to contemplate the changes in her attitude toward the Ranger. Their whole relationship was temporary, anyway, so what did it matter if she let herself enjoy his company. It wasn't as though they were going to keep up this farce once Sloan was cleared of any wrongdoing.

"I'm sure I'll be fine," Cricket said. "I know you have a lot of things to do, Amy, so don't worry about me."

"Are you sure you won't get bored all alone?"

Cricket smiled. "I'll be fine."

"I'll come check on you when I put Seth down for his nap," Amy said.

"You don't have to, really."

"I want to."

Cricket knew arguing was useless, so she gave in gracefully. "All right, I'll see you later."

Amy leaned over to give Cricket a hug. "You get well now, hear?"

"Don't worry. I'm sure I'll be fine," Cricket called after Amy. Actually, she already was fine. But if she stayed in bed she'd have time to think, and Cricket wanted, above all things, to think about what had happened this morning between her and Creed.

For a start, she relived every moment of Creed's kiss: the tightening in her breasts that streaked like an arrow right to her belly, the shortness of breath, that shivery feeling that took away her will to move and kept her quivering in anticipation of his next touch. Then there was the softness of his tongue as it traced the edges of her mouth, and its hardness as he thrust inside, dominating her senses. And there was the taste of Creed, still on her lips. She ran her tongue along her lower lip and tasted him there. She certainly didn't want to wipe her mouth on her sleeve as she had once upon a time.

Cricket smiled. How the mighty had fallen. She had wanted Creed to kiss her. And it had felt so good! Look what she'd been missing all these years—what she would still be missing if it weren't for Creed. At the moment, she was feeling decidedly benevolent toward the Ranger. In fact, she was feeling downright grateful. Yes, that's what she felt. That must be why she was so willing to be touched. Of course that didn't explain her desire to touch the Ranger in return. There must be some other reason for that.

If she listened to Amy there was a perfectly logical explanation for what she was feeling toward Jarrett Creed.

"No, that can't be it. It's just not possible."

Cricket guffawed, a loud hooting sound, accompanied by a slap on her knee. "I don't believe it!"

But it explained a lot of otherwise unexplainable things.

Cricket's hoots got louder, turning into deep belly laughs. She doubled over with laughter and realized as she did so that thanks to Creed she was laughing today instead of moaning. She laughed until tears streamed down her face. And this was *so funny* she didn't know if she'd ever be able to stop laughing.

She was in love with Jarrett Creed.

CHAPTER 17

Cᴿɪᴄᴋᴇᴛ ᴡᴏɴᴅᴇʀᴇᴅ ᴡʜʏ Creed was being so mysterious about where he was taking her. After all, he'd made it perfectly clear they weren't going to be more than five minutes from the plantation house because he was concerned about the Comanches whether she was or not. He grasped her hand firmly and tugged her along behind him. They'd postponed her dancing lesson twice in the past week because of emergencies at the gin site. Here it was the day of the party and she'd yet to take the first toe-tapping step. Creed had promised her she'd learn how to dance this afternoon, but seemed bent on taking her for a wild goose chase first.

When Cricket saw the dense foliage through which Creed proposed to lead her, it looked impenetrable. So when he shoved aside a tree limb as though to enter the stygian gloom, she ground to a halt. She'd wanted privacy for their dancing lesson, but this was ridiculous.

"Creed, wait."

"Come on, Brava. It's only a little farther."

"There won't be room to move in there."

Creed turned to her and smiled. "There's room. Trust me."

It was a sign of how things had changed between them that she did exactly that. For the first few yards it appeared she'd made a mistake. Suddenly the undergrowth magically disappeared and she found herself in the middle of a kelly-green glade that framed a glistening pond, the kind with dragonflies skimming the surface, bullfrogs squatting on lily pads like kings on thrones, and lizards scurrying from stone to stone along the edge. Bluebonnets had sprung up in the surrounding grass, providing a pleasing purplish-blue blanket patterned with yellow butterflies, upon which a doe and her fawn reposed. The doe raised her head, but didn't bolt. Rather, she licked the fawn, as though confident no harm could come to them here.

"Aaaah. It's so . . . so . . ."

There was no way she could explain to Creed with words the serenity she felt in this beautiful place, but Cricket turned, and their eyes met, and she knew words weren't necessary. He understood.

"How did you find this place?"

"When I first came to Lion's Dare after living among the Comanches Tom set me to clearing away the brush to keep me busy. I saw a stag caught by its antlers in the branches of a low tree, and when I freed it I noticed a path nearby in the undergrowth. It led here. After I found this place I convinced Tom it wasn't worth it to clear away all the brush in this hollow for such a tiny, marshy plot of land."

"You never told him this was here?"

"No one knows about this place except me . . . and now you."

"Oh, Creed." Cricket spread her arms wide and whirled in a circle. Her skirt floated around her, curling and flipping to give an occasional glimpse of her shoes and even her stockings. She whirled faster and faster in delightful abandon, her skirt flying higher, her voice rising in peals of laughter at the effort it took to keep from falling down from dizziness. She twirled until she was breathless, and when she finally stopped she found herself somehow standing directly in front of Creed. She curtsied impishly before him, almost losing her balance the way things were still whirling in her head, and then held her arms out to him.

"Shall we dance?"

He smiled at her and answered, "My pleasure."

Cricket was unprepared for Creed's firm hand at her waist, even less prepared for the hand that clasped her own so surely. She kept her eyes focused on his chest and swallowed uncertainly. "What now?"

She hadn't realized she'd whispered until Creed answered in an equally soft, husky voice, "Follow me."

"There's no music."

"Sure there is," he said. "Listen."

What Cricket heard wasn't music, exactly, but it was melodic. The low, steady buzz of insects. The croak of a bullfrog. The plunk of a fish as it jumped in the pond. The clarion caw of an angry bluejay. And under it all, the dulcet harmony of leaves rustling in the gentle wind.

Cricket followed as Creed began to move in rhythm to nature's serenade. As the pace of their dance increased, Creed's hand tightened at her waist, drawing her close to his muscular length.

"Mine," he murmured in her ear. "You're mine."

Cricket knew his claim was only temporary, and that when his work was done he'd send her home. Caution suggested she ought not to lay herself open to the heartache she'd feel when he left her, as she knew he would. But she'd ceased to care what she ought or ought not to do. There was only Creed, and the need to be a part of him, and to make him a part of herself. She molded her body to his, became one with him.

Creed stopped dancing abruptly and took her face in his hands. He tipped her head up so they were only inches apart and let his blazing eyes speak for him.

You belong to me.

Somewhere in the back of her mind a voice warned that through such possession came male dominion. So she fought an inner battle against acknowledging the depth of his claim. She felt herself losing the battle, yet did not wish to retreat from his gentle assault. She stood stock-still as Creed reached behind her back and took her long auburn braid in his large hands. Before she was aware what he intended, he'd removed her green ribbon and begun unraveling the thick, heavy braid.

His eyes warmed her, his voice gentled her to his touch. "I've wanted to do this since the moment I saw you."

He gently threaded his fingers through her waist-length hair, gradually releasing it from its constraining fetters as he'd released her from the ties that had bound her to Rip's dream. The breeze picked up the silky strands and carried them in flowing freedom behind her and around her, while the sun reflected off their burnished copper glory. At last he thrust his hands through her rich russet mane and tilted her head back to draw her lips up to his. He let the tension build, keeping his mouth a breath away from hers so their essences mingled until they became as one.

"You're a beautiful, desirable woman, Brava."

"So I've been told."

Their lips were so close Cricket could feel the beginning of Creed's smile. She curved her lips so they would fit his and lifted herself onto her toes so she could reach his mouth.

At the first touch of Cricket's tongue on his lips Creed's whole body trembled. She withdrew her tongue slightly and savored the taste of him before she went back for more. Her tongue mimed Creed's actions when he'd kissed her in the past, teasing along his lower lip and then slipping inside, raking his teeth and the roof of his mouth. She could feel his need hard against her belly, could feel his heart bursting with excitement under the hand she had pressed to his chest. His tortured breathing told of the battle for control that raged within him.

Suddenly Creed took over and Cricket found herself being kissed by a man starving for the taste of her. His tongue invaded her mouth and claimed it as his own with an erotic promise of how he would claim the rest of her. His sinewy arms clasped her to him, and his hands cupped her buttocks as he drove himself against her. Just as suddenly he took her shoulders in his hands and thrust her away from him.

"Wh-what . . .?" Cricket was gasping for breath, afraid she'd been rejected and unsure why, when Creed's deft fingers released the first button at the throat of her dress. Cricket's hand reached up and covered his.

She searched his eyes and discovered uncertainty—and an agony of need.

"I'll do it," she said.

Creed's hands dropped to his sides in tight fists. His eyes were hot on her as she slowly raised her hands to the shell buttons. As each button was released the green linen fell away in a V from skin as golden as honey. Her breasts were swollen and crested beyond the confines of her chemise. Cricket ached, and didn't know why. She tried to swallow, but her mouth was dry.

Whatever shallow bonds of civilized constraint had bound Creed, broke. His hands reached through the seductive V and roughly forced the linen off her shoulders, binding her arms to her sides as his mouth clamped onto one of the budding tips that had taunted him through her chemise.

The feel of Creed's mouth and tongue suckling her through the wet cotton was so pleasurable Cricket had to bite her lip to keep from crying out. She couldn't stop the reflexive arch of her body that gave him the access to her he sought. Creed's mouth moved to her other breast, and this time she didn't suppress her moan of delight. She fought the linen that bound her, seeking the touch of Creed's silky hair, wanting to imprison him in her grasp and bind him as close to her as she was to him.

Creed's hold tightened to subdue her until he realized she was struggling toward him, not away from him. His head came up and he rasped, "I have to have you. Now."

His pupils were dilated, his golden eyes hooded, his gaze almost feral. It was as though she'd unleashed a hungry wolf and waited to be devoured by it. She wanted to provide the sustenance Creed sought, but she was suddenly, mindlessly afraid. Her body began shivering uncontrollably, and she couldn't seem to stop it.

Before Cricket loomed another female hurdle, this one

considerably higher than all the rest. Cricket was so certain she wouldn't be able to get over it that she didn't even want to try. She'd failed at every wifely task Amy had set, and she couldn't bear to fail at this as well. What if she couldn't give Creed what he asked from her? Her feminine confidence had been too freshly sown, the shoots were still too tender to support her. She couldn't take the chance that Creed would test her and find her wanting, not even for the heaven on earth he seemed to be promising.

She took a deep, steadying breath, and said in a shaky voice, "No, Creed. Stop."

At first Cricket didn't think Creed had heard her because his hold tightened rather than loosened. Then he shoved her away to look at her and she saw the untamed passion in his eyes. She pleaded silently for understanding, but the ruthless man who stared back at her had every intention of taking what he wanted. She quailed before his fierce gaze, until the old Cricket, Rip's brat, reasserted herself. She, by God, had no intention of giving anything to Jarrett Creed!

"I said no!"

Cricket's violent refusal abruptly halted Creed's ardor. He could see her breasts rising and falling in agitation, while her whole body stiffened. The sudden fear he'd seen in her eyes had been quickly replaced by stubborn determination. If her fear had remained longer, he might have sought out the reason for it. But in seconds, and for no plain reason he could see, the willing woman was gone and he held in his arms his untameable *brava*. Of course, that only made her even more desirable to him, increasing both his frustration and his ire.

"You're my *wife!* You don't tell me no!"

"I'm your wife in name only. I'm your wife until you decide you don't want me anymore. I'm your wife because you didn't know what else to do to keep me from interfering with your plans," she spat. "If you force me to do this now, I'll kill you for it."

He could see she meant it. Creed's astonishment was exceeded only by his fury. He closed his eyes, struggling for control. When he achieved it he realized he'd been ready to take her by force. He almost bellowed in rage at the thought of it. He loved her! How could he have come so close to taking her against her will? But she hadn't been unwilling until . . . until she'd remembered the truth about their relationship . . . which he'd somehow conveniently forgotten. He opened his mouth to tell her how his feelings had changed, but quickly shut it again. Only a fool would tell a woman he loved her when the woman so clearly didn't return the feeling. He let go of his hold on her and turned away.

"Button yourself back up," he snapped. "Unless you want to continue where we left off."

The disgust in Creed's voice was almost enough to make Cricket cry. Oh, how she wanted to cry! For someone who never cried she'd spent an awful lot of time in tears lately. But then, lately she'd felt a lot less in control of her life than she ever had before. For instance, how could she tell Creed she loved him and wanted him, when she was afraid she wasn't woman enough to be a wife to him.

When Creed turned back she blinked quickly to hide the tears that threatened to spill.

"Do you think you'll be able to manage your duty dance tonight?" he asked curtly.

"Yes." Her voice was no more than a strained whisper.

"Then we're finished here. We'd better get back to the house. I'm sure Amy could use your help to get ready for the party and I've got work to do." He walked away, not looking back to see if she followed.

Cricket took one last glance around the secluded glade before she bent to delve into the underbrush. Everything was as beautiful as when she'd first seen it, but somehow the magic had fled the place.

Cricket knew Creed was avoiding her when he sent Belle to the bedroom to ask for his wool frock coat, embroidered waistcoat, tucked linen shirt, and kerseymere trousers. He also sent the message he was going to dress downstairs so Amy would have time to help her with her hair. Cricket wasn't fooled. She knew the real reason he was staying away was that he couldn't stand to be near her after she'd acted like such a ... *lily-livered coward* ... in the glade. She cringed at the memory of how she'd shivered like a scared rabbit in Creed's arms. Somehow she kept her composure while she collected the formal clothes and gave them to Belle, adding the neckcloth Creed had forgotten to ask for when he'd made up his list.

Amy's excitement made it difficult for Cricket to concentrate on her self-pity. The young woman was determined to act the Fairy Godmother to Cricket's Cinderella. Meanwhile, Cricket had never felt so much like an ugly stepsister.

"Look at you, Cricket!" Amy exclaimed as she scrubbed Cricket's back in the tub. "You have the most beautiful skin."

"It's brown. From too much sun."

"Nonsense. It's like golden velvet. Jarrett's a lucky man!"

Amy wrapped Cricket in a large white towel and sat her down in front of the dressing table in her bedroom. "Anything I add to this face will be icing on the cake," Amy insisted. "But I've always liked icing myself."

"In my case you'll have to take the bitter with the sweet."

Amy laughed. "You have the most marvelous sense of humor, Cricket ... and the most mysterious eyes."

"They're plain gray. Like a barn cat."

"Oh, no! A man could lose himself in those eyes. And see how they change color when you're angry? From light gray to a much darker, more smoky color ... definitely mysterious," Amy said with a laugh.

Cricket snorted.

"Hold still now while I add some rouge to your lips."

"Ur asting ur ime," Cricket said through stiff lips.

"If polishing an apple to make it pretty before you eat it is wasting time, then perhaps I am," Amy agreed cheerfully. "But, oh, Cricket, how delicious you look! Jarrett will gobble you down in one bite."

"He's going to be put off when he finds the worm inside," Cricket muttered.

Amy hauled Cricket out of the chair and handed her a sheer chemise and matching pantalettes.

Cricket's eyebrows arched in amazement.

Amy blushed. "Tom gave these to me. I . . . I've never quite had the nerve to wear them. But Tom says no woman wearing such filmy underclothes can fail to feel like an enchantress. Won't you wear them, Cricket?"

Cricket gulped.

"Please?"

"All right, Amy. I'll wear them. Hand them over."

When Cricket was dressed (barely), Amy pulled her over to the bed where Belle had laid out the beautiful gown she'd altered for Cricket. "This emerald gown will be perfect with your auburn hair. Oh, my goodness. I guess I better do your hair first. Come back over here and sit down again."

Cricket trudged back to the dressing table and sat down. "I can do it, Amy. I'll braid it like—"

"You'll do no such thing! I've been planning all week what to do with your hair. Now you sit back and let me work. We haven't much time."

Amy chattered on vivaciously, tugging and pulling and mussing and arranging Cricket's hair. Of course Cricket knew her hair was too long for the fashionable sausage curls Amy wore, but there was no convincing Amy of that. She was determined Cricket should wear her hair in the most current style. Amy parted the unmanageable mess down the center, and drew it back on either side, decorating it with ribbons. Then she went to work with the curling iron. The result was a riot of copper curls framing Cricket's face, sliding across her bare shoulders and trailing halfway down her back.

"It isn't exactly what I set out to do, but considering what I had to work with, I'm more than satisfied," Amy announced at last.

Cricket was impressed. She looked almost . . . pretty.

"Now, let's get you dressed," Amy urged.

Cricket crossed to pick up the gown, but Amy caught her before she could slip it over her head.

"You've forgotten your corset, Cricket."

"I haven't forgotten anything. I'm not wearing a corset."

Amy stomped her foot. "This isn't a matter of choice,

Cricket. A lady *always* wears a corset! Besides, that tissue silk dress won't fit unless you're tied tightly into a corset."

"Amy, I—"

"Put *it* on!"

Cricket sighed as she picked the corset up off the bed and circled it round her. Amy quickly pulled the laces snug.

"That's enough," Cricket said.

"Oh, no. Breathe out and I'll pull tight once more."

"I can't breathe out anymore."

"Oh. Well, let me tie these laces off."

Cricket tried to bend to pick up the emerald silk dress and couldn't. She turned to Amy and put her fists on her hips. "This is ridiculous."

"It is, is it?" Amy grabbed Cricket's elbow and pulled her over to the full-length oval mirror in the corner. "Look at that woman, Cricket. Isn't she a picture? Tiny waist, lush, full breasts, womanly hips."

Cricket had trouble accepting the description Amy gave of her, but as she stared into the mirror she grudgingly admitted that it fit. Thanks to the corset her waist looked inches smaller. Or perhaps it was the way her bosom was shoved up and out at the top. . . . Where had the brat in buckskins gone?

"Now," Amy said, all business again, "let's add a few petticoats, and then slip your dress on."

In moments Amy had Cricket laced into the emerald gown. The long-sleeved gown framed her shoulders, but left them bare. It fit snugly through the bodice, ending in a V just below her waist and falling in gathered folds to the floor. As she gazed at herself in Amy's mirror Cricket was surprised to see a pretty . . . no, a beautiful . . . young woman looking back at her. Why, a woman like that could seduce Jarrett Creed with both hands tied behind her back!

"Oh, Cricket. You're so lovely! Such a lady!"

"Yes, I am, aren't I," Cricket agreed with a delighted laugh. She turned from admiring herself in the mirror to embrace Amy. "Oh, Amy, thank you. Thank you for everything."

"Just remember what you've learned, and use it to enjoy

yourself tonight," she said. "That'll be payment enough. If you're ever in a pinch, look at me and follow my lead. Don't worry about anything because you're going to do fine. Jarrett will be so proud he'll be strutting like a peacock before the evening's through. You wait and see!"

Cricket still couldn't believe she was the woman in the mirror, who could easily sweep Jarrett Creed off his feet and into bed. That woman could not doubt her femininity. That woman could not fail to satisfy her man. She had never been as beautiful as she was tonight. She took a deep breath as she came to a decision. Tonight she would find out what it meant to be Creed's woman.

She was more nervous than she was willing to admit. Her palms were wet and her knees were knocking. But any doubts she had about her success fled when she saw Creed's expression as he stood waiting for her at the foot of the stairs. His eyes adored every inch of her, then came to rest on her lips, making Cricket ache to have him kiss her. Her lips parted in invitation, and she heard Creed's hissing intake of breath.

Creed hardly recognized the woman in the emerald silk gown, her lips invitingly rouged, her smoky gray eyes exotic with kohl, her hair cascading around her like a copper nimbus. There was an aura of femininity surrounding Cricket he'd never noticed before. He almost took her in his arms and carried her back up the stairs to bed, but managed to catch himself before he did such a recklessly impulsive thing. After all, the beautiful woman who stood before him had already rejected his advances once today.

Creed's jaw tightened in irritation. He'd intended to dance with his *brava* once and leave her to the country gentlemen, but he could see he was going to have to revise his plan. If he left this innocent beauty in the clutches of those lecherous bumpkins, who knew what could happen! He determined without further ado to spend the balance of the evening with his lovely wife at his side.

As they greeted their guests, Cricket's fingertips rested on Creed's arm with enough pressure to make him constantly aware of her. Each time he leaned down to speak to her and tell her a little about the guests they were greeting, a flowery perfume assailed his nostrils. Soon he found his head bent more than it was upright, because he was trying to identify all the places she'd dabbed that alluring scent. He'd noticed it was strongest at her temple, and at the base of her throat behind her left ear. He knew she'd put some on her wrist, too, because he'd smelled it through her glove when he'd taken her hand to lead her down the stairs. He wondered where else she'd put it. Between her breasts? Behind her knees? Perhaps a drop in the navel? He wanted all these people gone so he could find out.

Cricket felt a sense of triumph at Creed's attentiveness. She was totally unaware of the sensation she was causing amongst the other men. The gentlemen planters of the upper Brazos were entranced with the new Mrs. Creed. More than one bewailed the fact she was already taken, but almost all planned to indulge in the privilege of holding her for the length of a dance.

The fiddlers finished tuning at about the same time the last guest arrived. Tom stepped to the center of the parlor, from which all the furniture had been removed to make an area in which to dance, and announced, "My friends, I've asked you here tonight to celebrate the marriage of my brother, Jarrett, to Creighton Stewart. The servants are passing among you now with glasses of champagne all the way from France by way of New Orleans. Please help yourselves."

Creed saw Wilmer Peatman eyeballing Cricket like she was a new racehorse he'd consider buying. He possessively slid his arm around her waist to make it clear he'd tolerate no trespassing. When the champagne came around he took a glass in his other hand.

Cricket also took a glass of champagne, since it seemed to be expected. She looked to Creed to make sure he had no objection, but he wasn't paying any attention to her. He appeared to be glaring at some man across the room. Cricket followed his gaze and found a tall, heavy-framed gentleman boldly staring at her. Cricket tried to remember if Amy had ever told her what she was supposed to do in such a situation. Nothing came to mind, and she couldn't very well search out Amy to ask, so she did what came naturally. She smiled and stared right back.

Wilmer Peatman had never received quite so much encouragement from a pretty woman when her husband was standing right next to her. Maybe that explained Jarrett's scowl. It wasn't Wilmer's fault if Jarrett's wife liked variety. He sure wasn't going to deny her the pleasure of sampling him! He'd wait a while and give her a chance to catch him alone. Then he'd taste those ruby-red lips, and stick his hands in all that long, curly hair.

Cricket knew she'd done the right thing when the tall man winked at her and headed for the refreshment table. This wasn't going to be so difficult as she'd feared. Everything was going to be fine, just as Amy had predicted.

Creed saw Wilmer's wink and turned quickly to see if Cricket had done anything to precipitate it, but her attention was on the glass of champagne in her hand.

"Now that you all have a libation, I propose a toast to the newlywedded couple," Tom said, his arm around his wife's shoulder, his glass held high with the other hand. "To Jarrett and Creighton, may they live long, love well, and raise lots of healthy little Creeds in the great Republic of Texas."

Shouts of "Bottoms up!" along with the clink of glasses signaled that the party had begun. The fiddlers bowed into their first tune, a slow one, and Creed turned to take Cricket's glass and set it on the tray of a passing servant so they could dance.

"The first dance will be led by the bride and groom," Tom said. There were cheers and huzzahs from the collected company that melted to a general buzz as the ladies and gentlemen remarked on the beauty of the bride and the handsomeness of the groom.

"Shall we?" Creed asked, holding his hands out to Cricket.

Buoyed by Creed's expansive smile, Cricket stepped confidently into his embrace. She saw his surprise when he realized her waist was corsetted.

"That was Amy's idea," she whispered.

"You don't have to explain, Cricket. I know about women's underclothes," he whispered back.

She tried not to think about how he knew so much.

Creed laughed gently at Cricket's worried frown as he grasped her other hand in his and they began to dance.

There was something magic about being in Creed's arms. The glow in his eyes was warm. More than warm, it was welcoming. Cricket couldn't keep her eyes off his lips. She imagined those lips on her flesh, touching and caressing. She closed her eyes and tilted her head back as though to allow Creed's mouth access to her throat.

Cricket was brought from her reverie when Creed tightened his grasp on her waist, bringing her hard against the full length of his body. His lips came to rest against her temple and his nose buried itself in her hair as he murmured harshly, "Ah, Brava, you are a woman worthy of the name. How you tempt me with this fond display. But we know the truth, don't we? You want no man . . . least of all me."

Cricket jerked her head back to contradict Creed and came face to face with the fierce, almost overwhelming blaze of passion in his eyes. He wanted her. He wanted her as a man wants a woman. But the sardonic curl of his lips held her silent. He'd found her wanting once, and expected to do so again. She parted her lips seductively, and watched his eyes blaze. She brushed the tips of her breasts against his chest, and watched the pulse race at his temple. She gloried in her ability to arouse him. He would not find her wanting tonight.

They were still staring into one another's eyes when the music ended. Tom tapped Creed on the shoulder and said, "I believe this dance is mine, little brother." Creed reluctantly released Cricket and she moved into Tom's arms. Creed stepped away, but his watchful eyes stayed on her.

The dancing went on and on, with Cricket gathered into one man's arms after another. She had never known how enjoyable such an evening could be. She was feeling especially good because she'd used the right utensils with every course during the midnight supper, and hadn't had to think twice about it. After supper, she had such a good time talking with the ladies she never even missed having a cigar with the gentlemen. Not only that, but, as far as she knew, she hadn't committed a single faux pas all evening.

Creed had left her side for a moment to talk with Tom when a voice said, "You look like you could use a breath of fresh air."

When Cricket turned, she recognized the dashingly dressed gentleman beside her as Wilmer Peatman, the man who'd winked at her earlier. Since then they'd danced together once, and he'd been impeccably polite. His offer sounded like exactly what she needed to cool off before the dancing began again.

"A breath of fresh air sounds like a great idea," she agreed with a smile. "Let me tell Creed—"

"Jarrett's talking with Tom and some other gentlemen in the parlor. We'll probably be back inside before he even notices you're gone," Wilmer said with a smile.

Cricket hesitated only a moment before she agreed, "You're probably right. Let's go."

Cricket was glad they'd come outside when she saw how beautiful the stars were in the vast Texas sky. A slight breeze rustled through the spring growth of leaves on the pin oak in the side yard. She scooped her hair up off her neck with both hands so the cooling zephyr could reach her damp skin.

Wilmer didn't think he'd ever seen anything quite so lovely as Jarrett Creed's wife with that mass of hair in her hands and her head thrown back and aimed at the moon.

Cricket shivered as the cool wind did its work.

"Cold?" Wilmer asked. "Here, let me put my arm around you to warm you up."

Before Cricket could tell him not to bother, a hard Tennessee voice cut through the moonlit night.

"Get your hands off my wife!"

Wilmer Peatman was no idiot. His arm came off Cricket's shoulder faster than a lizard gave up its tail to a hawk. "Your wife took a chill. I was only going to help warm her up a little."

"Like hell you were, Peatman. I know exactly what you were doing."

Cricket tried to control her growing temper. Creed had grabbed her arm and yanked her over next to him as though she were helpless. She could have taken care of Wilmer Peatman herself. Besides, Creed was making something out of nothing.

"Creed, I think you're making a—"

"Shut up, Brava," Creed warned. "I'll handle this."

Wilmer's neck hairs stood on end in fright. *Good Jesus Lord preserve me,* he thought.

"I can handle this myself," she argued back. She turned to Wilmer and said, in the way Amy had taught her, "I'd like to thank you, Mr. Peatman, for the walk in the night air."

Wilmer began to feel a renewed sense of rightousness. After all, it wasn't *his* fault the woman was a hussy.

"That's all right, Mrs. Creed. The pleasure was all—"

Creed's fist landed in Wilmer's mouth, cutting off the rest of his sentence, sending the man flat on his back in the grass at Cricket's feet.

Cricket whirled on Creed, her legs spread wide, her fists on her hips. "You woodenheaded ninnyhammer! What the hell did you do that for? He was just being nice to me!"

"You're no longer acting the lady, I see," Creed mocked.

"You're no longer acting the gentleman," she spat back.

Wilmer Peatman sat on the ground in astonished silence. *Dear God in heaven what had he stumbled into?* He rose carefully, backing away as he dusted off his new plaid wool trousers. "If you two will excuse me, I think I'll join the ladies and gentlemen in the parlor."

Neither of them noticed him leave.

"If anyone's going to put his hands on you, it's going to be me!"

With that, Creed gathered Cricket in his arms and headed away from the house.

"Put me down!"

"Soon enough, Brava. Soon enough."

CHAPTER 18

CREED TOOK HER to the glen and laid her down on a velvet bed of bluebonnets. He'd desired Cricket from the first moment he'd set eyes on her, and he'd more than once imagined making love to her in this forest bower, with Orion standing watch over them and the night sounds setting the tempo for their dance of love. Cricket's eyes would be jewels set in an opalescent frame, her fiery hair a torch in the moonlight. Her hands would stretch out above her head as they had in her father's barn, leaving her totally vulnerable to his touch. The reality of it was somewhat different, however.

Cricket's eyes flashed with angry fire, and the wind created a minor tornado with her auburn curls, completely masking her face except for the moments when it revealed the lower lip which stuck out in a mulish pout. Her hands were stretched out above her head all right, but only because he held them there while the rest of his body pinned her to the ground.

When Creed had settled his hips between hers with his upper body supported by his arms, Cricket quipped sarcastically, "I suppose this behavior is fitting to a lady?"

"It is if the gentleman with her is her husband." Creed

nearly added, "who loves her," but fortunately caught himself in time. If he spoke words of love to Cricket right now she was likely to spit them back in his face.

Cricket was upset because this wasn't the way she'd planned Creed's seduction at all. As long as she'd made up her mind to find out what "it" was all about, the least he could have done was to cooperate and let her seduce him the way she'd imagined it would happen—when they were both alone in the feather bed later tonight, with a single candle giving a golden glow to their naked skin.

"Creed, if we don't show back up at Amy's party soon, someone's going to come hunting for us."

"They'll never find us here."

"You'll ruin Amy's dress."

"I'll buy her another one."

"I have on a corset."

"I'll take it off."

Creed used his nose to shove aside Cricket's windblown hair, and covered her mouth before she had a chance to say anything more. Despite any reservations she might have had about the circumstances of their encounter, Cricket threw herself wholeheartedly into the kiss, and they were soon lost in a canyon of passion from which there rose only the echoed song of their pleasure. When Cricket showed no signs of resisting his desires, Creed released his hold on her wrists so his hands would be free to pleasure her. Unfortunately, when he tried caressing his wife through the tissue silk dress, the corset hindered him. Frustrated, he broke the torrid kiss and ordered, "Sit up."

When Cricket was too dazed to respond, Creed stood and pulled her to her feet. He yanked off his frock coat and had the buttons of his waistcoat undone and the satin garment torn off before Cricket had gotten her balance. He held her upright while he reached around behind her to undo the laces on the dress. He tugged it forward and it slid down off her shoulders and past her hips to a silk puddle at her feet. Then he turned her around so he could work on the corset.

"Damn laces are knotted," he muttered.

"Let me try," Cricket said. She reached behind her, but her callused fingers didn't do any better than Creed's.

Creed reached down to his boot, and then remembered he'd removed his knife for the dance. "I don't even have a knife with me to cut the damn thing off!"

Cricket smiled. She reached down inside her shoe and pulled out a small folding knife. "Will this do?"

"I knew there was a reason I loved you," Creed said as he kissed her quickly and took the knife. With a wolfish grin on his face he slit the corset laces from bottom to top.

The admission of love had slipped by without Creed taking notice, but Cricket hadn't missed it. However, since he'd said it in such a flippant manner, neither did she grant it much credence. He wanted her, and she wanted him. That was enough for the moment, without dragging love in to cloud the issue. Instead of remarking on it, she said, "Amy will have a fit when she sees what you did to her corset."

"Amy should have known better than to truss you up in that thing."

With the corset and her muslin petticoats gone Cricket stood dressed in the sheer chemise and pantalettes. "It was your idea to make a lady out of me."

"A woman," Creed corrected. "It was my hope to make a woman out of you." He reached out and cupped her breasts, enjoying the puckered nipples visible through the chemise.

Cricket trembled. "And have you succeeded?"

Creed acknowledged the tartness in Cricket's question by softening his voice when he answered, "I don't know. Have I?" Creed let his thumbs caress the tips of Cricket's breasts. "You tell me. Do you feel like a woman now, Brava?"

Cricket brought her hands to rest on Creed's chest and let her fingertips survey the strength beneath the pleated linen shirt. She released the buttons, one at a time, until his chest was revealed to her gaze. Hesitantly she replied, "I feel great pleasure from your touch. I feel the need to touch you, and to make you a part of myself. Does that make me a woman, Creed?" She turned her face up to him, her eyes plaintively searching his for a response.

Creed didn't answer with words. Instead he dipped his head and hungrily settled his mouth over hers. At the same time he lowered them both to their knees, facing one another. He nudged Cricket's thighs apart, and his hand slipped down to cup the pulsing heat of her femininity.

Cricket gasped at the intimate capture. The feelings rushing through her were nothing like she'd imagined they'd be. She was aware of her whole body melting toward Creed. She arched into his hand, her hands flying to his shoulders to keep her in touch with the only reality she knew—Creed. Only Creed.

Creed reveled in his possession of her, let his tongue incite her, his hands excite her. When he'd brought her to a frenzy of need in his arms he paused to slow his ardor, lest he take her too quickly. It was Cricket's first time, and he sought to be gentle with her. With great care, he laid her down and covered her body with his own, letting her feel the weight of him wanting her.

Creed could feel her quivering beneath him like a wild animal, could feel his own body quivering with need of her. He looked deep into her dark, smoky eyes and said huskily, "You're woman enough for me, Brava."

Cricket smiled at him, and when he smiled back she laughed with joy. Together they fumbled over buttons and laces and pants and shoes until both she and Creed were naked as Adam and Eve in the garden of Eden.

Creed tried to slow her down, but Cricket raced toward the culmination of her need for him. She urged him to touch, she urged him to taste, she touched and tasted with abandon, until she made him forget she was untried, that he'd lied when he'd proclaimed they were truly husband and wife. When he should have been gentle, and careful and slow, he thrust with all the frenzied excitement of the moment.

And he hurt Cricket.

Cricket couldn't believe the pain. The pain only came the first time, Sloan had said. The pain only came when you were a virgin. The pain could only mean one thing. Creed had lied to her. It left her stunned.

He knew he'd hurt her from the stunned look on her face. He knew he'd hurt her from the way her body cringed from his. He knew he'd hurt her from the way she fought him to stop.

"Don't fight me, Brava," he rasped. "It's done now. You're mine. You'll always be mine."

Suddenly Cricket knew that if she succumbed to him now she would never be free. So like a wild thing that fights the gentle hands that will ultimately tame it, she resisted him. She writhed and struggled, bucking her hips against the man who'd joined his body to hers. But her attempts to escape Creed only brought him more quickly to that point where he was no longer man, but animal, responding to the dictates of his barbarian nature and its unassailable command to procreate the species.

When he finally emerged from the red well of pleasure into which he'd descended, Creed's first sane thoughts were regret and remorse. He was still lying half on top of Cricket, but she'd covered the offended portion of her body with her hand, as though she were ashamed.

Cricket felt drained . . . wrung out . . . betrayed. She was sticky with semen and her own blood, both of them damning proof that Creed had at last claimed her for his wife.

"You lied to me."

"Cricket, I—"

"I was a virgin, Creed," she cried. "And now you've made me your wife . . . against my will."

"Who's lying now, Brava," Creed whispered.

Cricket felt the flush rise in her cheeks. She'd wanted him. Until she'd discovered the lie, she'd wanted him deep inside her, making her full, ending the emptiness she felt when he wasn't near.

Creed's throat was thick with pain, and with guilt. He rose and reached out to touch her where he'd hurt her. When she flinched he removed his hand. Could he speak words of love now? Would she believe them? Was there a way to explain to her how he felt? "I lied for a good reason, Brava. But I—"

"There are no explanations good enough to excuse this!"

she interrupted harshly. Then the untried girl was back in the voice of the woman, "Oh, Creed, you hurt me."

Creed's throat closed as he gathered her up into his arms and held her in his lap, ignoring her feeble attempts to stop him. He could see the effort it took her to fight him. He'd have let her go free, except he knew they'd both suffer if they didn't talk about what had happened between them. He dearly regretted his lack of control, but it was too late to worry about that now. He would make amends in the only way he knew.

"Whatever went before is over and done with, Brava. It's the past. You're my wife now, and it's my duty as your husband to take care of you. I won't hurt you again. I can promise you that. The next time you'll feel only pleasure."

Duty. No word of love. Cricket's stomach tightened into a knot. Her chest ached. The blood pounded at her temples. This pain was much worse than the pain of consummation, because that had been so brief, and this didn't feel like it was ever going to go away. She had no experience with romantic love, but it was much overrated, she thought bitterly, if it made you feel this bad. She wasn't about to become one of Creed's *duties!*

"You won't ever hurt me again because you won't touch me again," she said.

Creed was amazed at the vehemence of her statement, and that made him all the more firm in his response. "Yes, Brava, I will. When you've had time to heal, we'll—"

"NO!"

The stark fear in Cricket's eyes brought another lump to Creed's throat, but he knew he had to be strong for both of them. "We'll talk about this later, when you're feeling better."

"I won't change my mind, Creed."

"I won't change mine, either," he said, and then regretted it because he'd only caused her eyes to smolder so he felt a quickening in his loins. God, if they didn't get dressed soon he was likely to take his wife again and pain be damned!

Creed picked Cricket up and, cradling her in his arms,

walked waist deep into the pond. Cricket shivered as he gradually lowered her feet and legs until she was standing in the cool water. He reached down beneath the surface of the pool and rinsed away all signs that he'd claimed her as his woman. He brought a cupped hand of water to her shoulder, and let it stream across her breasts, sore where he'd suckled like a newborn babe. His wet fingertips brushed away the streak of a tear on her cheek, then soothed the raw skin where his day's growth of beard had scratched her cheeks and chin. He pulled Cricket into his arms, and they stood silently in the moonlight, letting the water eddy around them, taking the pain away.

"I'm sorry, Brava."

Cricket didn't know how to deal with this gentle Creed. He took away her defenses and left her vulnerable to him. But she didn't forgive him.

"Saying you're sorry doesn't change anything, Creed."

Creed hadn't expected Cricket to forget what he'd done, but he'd hoped she'd understand. He carried her from the pond and used his soft linen shirt to dry her.

"Do you need any help getting dressed?"

"No, I—" But the soreness between her legs was making it hard for Cricket to get into her pantalettes.

"Lean against me."

Cricket leaned back against Creed and he held her upright as she awkwardly stepped into the thin cotton garment. As soon as she could, however, she moved away from him. And she didn't thank him.

When she was completely dressed, Cricket looked down at the wrinkled satin in dismay. "I can't go back to the house like this. Everyone will know. . . ."

She was right, of course, Creed thought, as he gazed at her, but not only because of the wrinkled satin. Her eyes were luminous, her lips swollen with passion. His hands had raked her hair a dozen, dozen times and her auburn curls were decorated with bits of bluebonnet and grass.

"Then let's stay here tonight," he suggested. "It'll be warm enough if we sleep close to each other." When she frowned and opened her mouth to object he added sardonically, "And the bluebonnets are a good deal softer than the floor of the bedroom."

Cricket didn't want to be close to Creed because, despite everything, her body still clamored for his. If he found out how much in his thrall she was, she'd lose herself to him forever. She couldn't let that happen.

"All right. I'll stay here with you," she said. "But don't touch me."

"No deal, Brava. You're my wife. I'll touch you whenever I please! And it pleases me to sleep with you tonight."

"You don't own me!"

"You're mine!"

They stood across from one another, eyes blazing, fists clenched. Cricket was torn between pleasure that he demanded to be near her and fury that he thought he could command her to obey his will.

As suddenly as he'd bristled, Creed relaxed his body. "All right, Brava. We'll compromise."

Cricket's eyes narrowed, watching for a trick.

"How about if I sleep here because it's what I want to do, and you sleep here because it's what you want to do. We'll be sleeping close not because it brings either of us pleasure, but because otherwise we'll be cold. Will that satisfy your stubborn streak of independence?"

Cricket hated to admit how much sense Creed was making, but said, "That suits me fine."

Creed heaved a silent sigh of relief, and lay down among the bluebonnets. "Coming to bed anytime soon?"

Cricket heaved an equally silent sigh of disgust, and lay down next to Creed. She held herself stiff when his arm circled round her waist, but allowed him to pull her close so they could share the warmth of their bodies. She had no choice now, but as soon as the sun was up and the party guests had gone, she was going to put some distance between herself and Jarrett Creed.

Some time during the night Cricket's body forgot how angry she was with Creed. When she woke she was stuck to him like a fly to honey.

Creed grinned. "Good morning."

Cricket grimaced. "What's so good about it?"

"Sun's shining. Birds are singing. The beautiful woman in my arms is my wife. All in all it looks like it could turn out to be a mighty fine day."

"Let me go, Creed."

"Or it might not." Reluctantly, he released her. "What are your plans today?"

"I thought I'd take a ride around the plantation." Cricket dared him to object, and when he didn't, she rose, biting her lip at the soreness between her legs when she stood.

Creed didn't want to play the protective, possessive husband. It reminded him too much of puppets and strings. But Cricket should have known the Comanches weren't a danger he could afford to ignore. There was no way he'd let her ride the bounds of Lion's Dare alone. It was too dangerous. He had more to lose now than ever before. He'd given a part of himself to her last night he hadn't thought to ever give again. He had no intentions of losing this wife to fire, flood, famine, or Comanches. Perhaps if he were tactful enough in forbidding her to ride alone, he could avoid a full-blown feud.

"Why not wait a little later and I'll go with you," he said.

"I want to go now."

"Be reasonable, Brava. You're in no condition to sit a horse."

Cricket blushed. He was right about that, but she'd manage somehow. She had to get away. "I'm going!"

Creed could see he was going to have to come up with another plan. "Let's go get some breakfast, then, if your mind's made up."

Cricket was surprised at Creed's capitulation, but realized that unless he intended to hogtie her, he didn't have much choice. Creed suddenly seemed in an awful hurry, and Cricket followed him from the enchanted place at almost a run.

Creed was anxious to leave because he'd found Cricket even more irresistible this morning than he had last night. He'd woken hard as a rock at dawn, and his condition hadn't improved since then. Under the circumstances the only solution he could see was to remove himself from Cricket's company.

Fortunately, Amy and Tom's overnight guests had left, and Creed and Cricket found the couple alone at the dining room table. Tom said nothing about their absence the night before, but as he picked a wilted bluebonnet from Cricket's hair he gave her one of those knowing looks she was coming to recognize so well.

Amy tried not to look as distressed at the condition of Cricket's dress as she felt, because it was apparent the dress had served its original purpose well. "You were a success last night," she said. "There wasn't a woman at the party who wouldn't have killed to look as beautiful as you did, Cricket. And you were a perfect lady. Perfect."

Cricket and Creed exchanged a look that said otherwise, but didn't interrupt Amy's effusive praise. They helped themselves to food from the sideboard and sat at the table to eat. Neither of them had much of an appetite.

Creed was busy worrying how he could keep Cricket safe.

Cricket was busy worrying whether she'd have Creed's baby now.

"I've been trying to convince Cricket she should stay close to the house today," Creed said.

"Oh? Where are you planning to go, Cricket?" Amy asked.

"I thought I'd take a ride."

"Could I come along?"

"I don't know," Tom said. "With the Comanches—"

"Oh, Tom, you worry too much. We'd stay close to the house, and you know the Indians aren't going to ride right up to us with the field hands all around. We wouldn't go far, would we, Cricket?"

"Sure she'd stay close," Creed said, meeting Cricket's obstinate stare with one of his own.

Cricket didn't say anything. They'd already decided everything without letting her get a word in edgewise. She hadn't asked for company, but she was going to get it, like it or not. She'd ride exactly where she pleased. If Amy wanted to join her, fine. If not, that was fine, too. She was going to make her own decisions. And that was that.

But once she and Amy were out riding together, Cricket discovered it wasn't as easy as she'd thought it would be to send Amy home and take off by herself.

"I want to be by myself for a little while, Amy," she announced.

"You can't go off by yourself, Cricket. It's too dangerous."

"I've brought my Pattersons and I have a rifle and a knife, and I know how to use them all. I've been taking care of myself for a long time, Amy. There's no reason for you to worry."

"But I will worry. Please don't go off by yourself. You promised Creed—"

"I didn't promise Creed anything," Cricket hissed. "Creed has himself convinced he can order me to do anything and I'll obey. He's wrong. I won't be broken to the bit like some docile mare. Go home, Amy. The house is just over that rise. I want to be alone."

Cricket turned Valor and kicked him into a gallop. She was sure Amy wouldn't follow her. She didn't need anyone caring about her. She just wanted to be left alone.

"Cricket! Wait for me! Cricket!"

Cricket ignored Amy's cries, riding away as fast as Valor could carry her. She closed her eyes and hid her face in the stallion's white mane, letting him take her where he would. Valor passed the northern border of Lion's Dare and kept on running.

Amy followed, falling farther and farther behind, but determined not to let Cricket out of her sight. She was scared, even more so when she saw where Cricket's mad race was leading them. Surely when she caught up with Cricket she could convince her to turn around and go home.

It wasn't until Valor had leapt several obstacles that Cricket opened her eyes. Once her gaze adjusted to the sun's glare, Cricket realized the land they traveled now was uncleared wilderness. She pulled Valor to a halt and glanced around her. Far behind her a cloud of dust rose.

"Oh, Amy!" Cricket muttered. "Why couldn't you go home?"

Then Cricket realized the cloud of dust she saw behind her was too large for one rider. Of course, there was a chance Amy had met up with some friends. *Not out here in this wilderness!* a frightened voice inside her screamed. Cricket's stomach clenched and her throat burned with the copper taste of fear. She pulled one of her Pattersons from the saddle holster and checked to make sure it was loaded, then returned it and did the same with the other. She checked her rifle and looked around for cover, but there was none. The closest oak was almost a half-mile away in the wrong direction. She wanted to run toward Lion's Dare, not away from it. Besides, she'd never get there in time for it to do her any good.

If only she'd listened to Creed! Oh, dear God, what had happened to Amy? She was alone and unarmed! Cricket forced herself not to think about it. She had to concentrate on staying alive herself if she hoped to be any help at all to Amy.

Cricket's worst fears were realized as the cloud of dust drew nearer. In the midst of the Comanches on their painted ponies she saw a bright splash of color. It looked like the same sky blue as the calico short gown Amy had worn that morning with the pair of Tom's trousers she'd cut down to her size. Cricket prayed she was wrong, but knew deep down inside she wasn't mistaken. Her suspicion was confirmed when she saw Amy's long blond hair lash out in the wind. The only thing she found the least bit encouraging was the fact the Comanches had taken Amy prisoner. At least they hadn't killed and scalped her on the spot.

For a while it appeared the Indians hadn't seen her. She remained still in the hope her dull buckskins and her pinto stallion would blend into the landscape. When the Indians turned in her direction, she knew that remaining undetected was a lost hope.

Only in the face of the twenty-odd Comanches riding toward her did Cricket see the true folly of her boasts to

Creed that she could take care of herself. Perhaps if she were close to the plantation house her weapons would have delayed the Comanches long enough for her to ride for help. However, even if she killed a great many Indians—and she planned to try—she had ridden so far from Lion's Dare she was bound to be caught in the end.

It never occurred to Cricket to give up—to kill herself to escape her fate. With her steady optimism, her belief in herself and the benevolence of the Creator, Cricket denied the reality of her circumstances. She couldn't be captured by Comanches. They wouldn't harm her. She'd save herself, or Creed would come to the rescue. This simply couldn't be happening.

As soon as the Comanches came into range, Cricket took careful aim with her Kentucky rifle and saw an Indian fall from his racing pony when she shot. They were coming much too fast for her to take the time to reload. She dropped the rifle and pulled the two Pattersons from the saddle holsters, forcing herself to wait until the Comanches were close enough to be sure she didn't miss.

Cricket saw a bullet hit one brave in the chest. She was dispassionate, she thought, about his death. Comanches were cruel, inhuman animals. As she watched the young man clutch his wound in agony, she aimed at another. Her hands were amazingly steady, but she still missed the next shot—and the next. Cricket almost cried in frustration. She was a crack shot. How could she be missing? The next bullet found its mark, but by then the Indians were within range for their bows and arrows to be put into action.

When the first arrow whizzed past her head Cricket knew she could no longer stay where she was. She turned Valor and ran, but the stallion was tired, and the Comanches gained on her. Cricket spent the last bullets in her Pattersons by firing over her shoulder. It kept the Comanches at bay, but didn't diminish their number. The Colt Patterson had to be broken into three parts to be reloaded, and while Cricket was desperate enough to try such a feat at a full gallop, she wasn't successful. She dropped the butt of one gun when

Valor jumped a cactus, and never had a chance to break the other apart because by then the Comanches had surrounded her.

The Indians closed the circle of horses around her until she sat atop the heaving stallion, her back proud and straight, her teeth bared, her knife in her clenched fist. She hadn't stopped to think why the Indians didn't kill her with their bows and arrows or great, long lances when they had the chance. The reason became clear when she saw who'd captured her.

"Do with the yellow-haired one as you will," Tall Bear said. "The Woman of the Wolf belongs to me."

CHAPTER 19

CRICKET WAS FULLY PREPARED to fight to the death. However, when the Comanches held a knife to Amy's throat and gestured to the one in Cricket's fist, she saw how very naive she'd been when she'd bragged to Creed that she could defend herself. She had no choice but to surrender. It was a particularly ignominious defeat for Cricket because she could see Amy expected her to resist capture, or die trying. But Cricket couldn't take the risk that the Comanches would kill Tom's wife, and she wouldn't help to make Seth a motherless child, even if it was what Amy clearly wanted at the moment.

Cricket's hands were laced cruelly tight to her saddle horn and her feet were tied uncomfortably under Valor's belly. The band of Indians rode straight for *Comanchería*, never stopping for more than a short rest to water the horses or to attend to the call of nature. She wouldn't have believed their endurance if she hadn't seen it with her own eyes. When the horses were too tired to carry the Comanches, they paced along beside them. They ate pemmican on horseback, and drank water sparingly from gourds they'd brought along. Cricket was never allowed near Amy, though she could see her friend was exhausted and terrified.

Dried blood had crusted on the edges of Amy's swollen mouth where she'd been hit, and there was a large blue bruise on her beautiful cheekbone. The fair skin she'd always protected with a bonnet was sunburned, as were her shoulders, where the sleeves had been torn from her short gown. Her yellow hair had been freed from its neat bun, and whipped around her in the wild Texas wind. The Indians rode by and touched the golden crown at will, cuffing Amy when she cringed away from them.

As long as they were still traveling Cricket could hope they'd be rescued. But as the terrain became increasingly unfamiliar, and the rolling plains became rolling hills, Cricket's hope gave way to despair with disturbing frequency. She clutched the memory of her encounter with the Mexican bandits, where Creed had saved her in the nick of time. The Ranger couldn't be far behind. He and Tom would rescue them. Nothing bad would happen. It just couldn't. It was her fault Amy was here. It was her fault Amy had been hurt, and she'd bear the responsibility if anything worse happened.

At sunset on the second day the Indians crossed a river Cricket guessed was the Colorado, then followed along its banks until they reached a fragrant grove of cedars. There, with the setting of the orange-red sun, they stopped their long, grueling flight. She and Amy were forced to gather wood for a campfire, and then to carry water from the river. Cricket tried to talk to Amy, but was slapped for her efforts. They communicated with their eyes, but the horror each foresaw for the other was too painful to contemplate.

Cricket's heart was in her throat. She searched frantically through the deepening darkness for shadows that moved. Nothing beyond the Indians' campfire could be as frightening as what awaited her and Amy in its cheery light. The Indians talked and laughed among themselves as they cooked several rabbits and ate them. The very fact they were so relaxed brought a knot to Cricket's stomach. They no longer feared pursuit. They could enjoy tormenting their captives at their leisure.

Cricket and Amy had been bound hand and foot with

rawhide ropes while the Indians enjoyed their repast, but at least they hadn't been gagged. It was the first time they'd been allowed to remain close enough to converse, and Cricket took advantage of the opportunity to find out how Amy had survived the endless trek across the wilderness.

"Amy," Cricket whispered, "are you all right?"

Amy's blue eyes were vacant when she turned them toward Cricket. Both of them were aware of their probable fate. Amy had already accepted it.

"I'll never be all right again," Amy said.

"Don't say that!" Cricket hissed. "Tom and Creed will——"

"They'll never find us, Cricket. How long do you think it took before Tom and Jarrett realized we were missing? How much longer before they could find our trail? The Comanches never stopped once. Even if they do find us . . . it'll be too late."

"It's not too late until we're dead!"

Amy met Cricket's eyes and her lips turned up in a sad smile. "Do you remember the sunrise this morning, Cricket? It was mostly pink, with some orange along the horizon. I watched it because I kept thinking *this will be the last sunrise I will ever see*. And . . ." Amy glanced significantly at the circle of Indians. "I was right." As Cricket's expression became horrorstruck Amy added, "I don't blame you, Cricket. I want you to know that. I knew the risk I was taking when I followed you. I'm only sorry for Tom and Seth."

Amy didn't say "and the baby," but when her eyes lowered to her slightly mounded abdomen Cricket heard the words anyway.

Cricket was furious with Amy. "How can you just give up like this? How can you be so resigned to dying? You have a husband and a son. They need you!"

"Cricket, do you know what's in store for us when these savages have finished filling their bellies?"

Cricket swallowed hard. "Yes."

"Do you think Creed will have you back when the Comanches are done with you?"

Cricket opened her mouth to reply but Amy interrupted,

"I love Tom, Cricket. He's my life. I don't think I could live if he ever turned away from me. I hope the Comanches kill me."

"Don't say that, Amy! Tom loves you. He'd never give you up no matter what the Comanches do to you."

Amy pondered Cricket's argument seriously before she asked, "Do you really think so, Cricket?"

Cricket didn't think even Tom really knew his feelings on the subject, but Amy's wistful question had brought the first spark of hope to her worried eyes, and Cricket wasn't about to put it out. "I know so," she said with conviction. "Just stay alive, Amy. That's what counts now. Stay alive as long as you can. They'll come and get us. I know they will."

When the Indian Cricket knew as Tall Bear rose and came toward them, along with several of the other braves, Cricket had to admit, at last, that Tom and Creed were not going to come in time to prevent the atrocities planned for them on this cool, early summer evening.

It irked Tall Bear to see that the journey hadn't broken the spirit of the Woman of the Wolf. That same feral gleam which he'd seen when they'd captured her—and which he'd observed in Wolf's eyes on more than one occasion—shone from her eyes. The Yellow-Haired Woman was another story altogether. She crouched in a fearful ball and stared at his feet, rather than confronting him.

Tall Bear had spent the whole trip into *Comanchería* contemplating how best to have his revenge on Wolf. It was not enough to simply kill his woman. He could rape her, of course, and then burn off her nose and ears, but even that would not be enough to make up for the theft of Summer Wind. He wanted this too-proud woman cowering at his feet when Wolf came to fetch her—and he had no doubt Wolf would come—perhaps even as soon as the rising of the next sun. He'd set an extra watch in the darkness to be safe, but he'd make sure tonight that Wolf came too late to help his woman.

He eyed the Yellow-Haired Woman thoughtfully. Perhaps if the Woman of the Wolf saw the fate in store for her she would fear it more. Yes, she would scream for mercy before he was through with her. But Tall Bear would be merciless. Since he'd lost Summer Wind, he had no heart to be moved by the pitiful wails of a dying woman.

"Bring me the Yellow-Haired Woman. We will leave a message to show the White-eyes in San Antonio what happens when we do *not* come in peace, so they will know the difference next time."

Cricket had a second's regret that she'd given Amy hope, because when the Comanches hauled her to her feet she emitted a heartbreaking scream and began biting and thrashing, which seemed to please the Indians, who subdued her with little effort. Cricket's voice caught in her throat when she was grabbed and yanked toward the campfire, or she might have screamed herself, so frightened was she.

"I want the Woman of the Wolf to watch. Do not let her look away," Tall Bear said.

Cricket couldn't understand Tall Bear's orders, but it soon became clear she'd be forced to witness Amy's terror and pain at the hands of the Comanches.

When Amy continued screaming the Indians stuffed a dirty piece of rawhide into her mouth. Her hands and legs were freed and her clothes were ripped from her body. Once she was naked, two Indians held her shoulders to the ground, while two spread-eagled her legs. Then the first Comanche mounted her and thrust his manroot deep inside where only Tom had been before.

The two braves who held Amy's shoulders neglected their duties in their enjoyment of her rape. Cricket watched in awe as Amy wrenched herself free and clawed the face of the Comanche who violated her. The Indians brutally ended her brave resistance by putting a Comanche war lance through her shoulder, pinning her to the ground.

Cricket screeched out her rage and horror, and had her mouth gagged as a result with a strip of rawhide. Tears streamed down her face. She was almost grateful to the Indian who'd speared Amy, because she'd fainted, and was not witness to the next five braves who used her so pitilessly. Cricket tried to turn her face away, but the two Indians on either side of her held it viselike so she could look nowhere else. When she squeezed her eyes closed one of them held a knife to her throat and pressed until she could feel the warm blood oozing beneath its cold point.

It would have been easy to let him kill her, but Cricket loved life and couldn't give it up so easily. She opened her eyes again, but they were sightless. She simply refused to see what was happening on the ground before her. Nevertheless, she experienced Amy's agony. The grunts of the Indians, and the slap of their skin against Amy's as they raped her, could not be shut out.

She knew when Amy regained consciousness because the abused woman's garbled groans came in rhythm with the thrusts that tore at her insides, and the bursts of laughter from the Comanches when one or another was particularly exuberant at his task. Still more Indians took turns torturing their captive while pleasuring themselves, until the odors of blood and sweat blended with the musk of sexually sated males. Cricket was never going to forget that smell. She felt the gorge rising in her throat, and concentrated on holding it back, knowing that if she vomited now she'd choke to death beneath the gag.

Cricket couldn't have imagined the next hour in her worst nightmares. Nearly every Indian in the camp, including the two who held her captive, took their turn at Amy's torn flesh. Amy had long since ceased to make any sounds at all, and the disgruntled Indians voiced their displeasure at her lack of response.

Cricket's body quivered with tension. Her chest ached and her belly spasmed as though she'd been the one assaulted. She had no more tears left to cry. She was empty, barren, hollow . . . but she wasn't dead . . . and Amy was. Cricket didn't know how she was so sure Amy was dead, except no woman could have survived such an onslaught, especially not one as fragile, as delicate, as Amy Creed. Guilt and remorse tightened Cricket's throat until it hurt when she swallowed.

If only she'd heeded Creed's warnings! If only she'd listened when Amy wanted to turn back! If only she'd shot

Amy when she had the chance, or let the Indians slit her throat! Cricket retreated to a world inside herself where she turned back the calendar and relived the past days' events. She didn't argue with Creed. She didn't go for a ride with Amy. She and Amy weren't captured by Comanches and Amy wasn't repeatedly raped.

An Indian rose from Amy's body and adjusted his loin-cloth. Suddenly, he sank to his knees, clutching his groin, as a bloodcurdling war whoop came out of nowhere and gunshots exploded around them. The two Comanches holding Cricket simply fell away from her, dead with bulletholes between their eyes, as Jarrett and Tom Creed came galloping pell-mell through the camp, killing Comanches like rats in a barn. Cricket saw it all as part of her dream, where she changed the way things happened. This, of course, was the rescue, where Tom and Creed came in the nick of time.

Tall Bear cursed Wolf. How had he found them so soon? The Comanche war chief was nowhere near his weapons, and there was no chance he could reach the Woman of the Wolf to kill her now. It was better to make good his escape and save his revenge for another day. As he slipped into the shadows he saw that Wolf had dismounted and was scalping the dead and the dying. He must be truly crazy with grief and anger. Wolf did not usually take scalps.

Tall Bear smiled maliciously, and shouted from his hiding place, "You may have your woman back for now, Wolf. But look well at the Yellow-Haired Woman, and remember. For that will be your woman the next time."

"Come and fight me, you woman killer!" Creed bellowed in Comanche as he brandished a bloody scalp.

"Another day, Wolf," Tall Bear shouted back. "When you have no woman left to mourn your death."

Creed's urge to follow his enemy was strong, but he wouldn't leave Cricket now that he'd found her. He clenched the grisly object in his hand, furious at his impo-tence. It was the utter quiet of the camp that drew Creed's attention back to it. The cedar brake was littered with the mutilated bodies of dead Comanches. Cricket was alive, but she was still standing frozen exactly where she'd been when he and Tom had attacked. Creed's berserk rage left him as suddenly as it had come. He shuddered when he recognized what he held in his hand, and threw the scalp to the ground near the Comanche he'd taken it from. He crossed to Cricket, feeling a surge of guilty relief that she hadn't suffered Amy's fate.

As Creed soon discovered, Cricket hadn't escaped totally unscathed. She looked at him, but she didn't see him. Yet there was an awful knowledge in her eyes. She was shivering and her skin was cold to the touch.

"I'm here, Brava," Creed said as he took her by the shoulders with his bloodied hands and drew her into his embrace. "I'm here."

At the touch of Creed's hot, sweaty flesh against hers, Cricket finally believed he was real. "You came." She grabbed him then like a drowning person grabs a lifeline, almost strangling him, so tightly did she clench his neck. She pressed her body to his, holding him, absorbing the warmth and life of him, praying she could somehow forget what she'd seen and smelled and heard, but knowing she never would.

Tom kneeled by the broken body of his wife, but couldn't bear to touch her. Her beautiful blonde hair fanned out in the dirt around a face that showed the ravages of what she'd suffered. Her lush eyelashes lay feathered on sunburned cheeks. Her lips and nose were swollen and crusted with dried blood. Except for the lance in her shoulder, the Comanches had left Amy's upper body untouched. Her skin was as white and smooth as he'd remembered it, her breasts full and round, the nipples pink as primroses. Her abdomen still mounded with their unborn babe. But her thighs . . . her thighs were bloody and bruised and he could see and smell the signs of passage of many, many other men.

Tom fought what he was feeling because it made him ashamed. Surely he would have been able to take Amy back after this. Surely what had happened to her was no fault of hers. But the words of his father came back to him, and he knew now what Simon had been feeling when he'd rejected Mary. Rage . . . and pain . . . and disgust. God help him! What would he have done if she'd lived?

Neither man was conscious of the time he spent alone with the woman he loved. Neither man was conscious of the tears that streaked his face. It was a noisy fight between scavengers prowling the edge of the camp for Comanche carrion that finally forced them from their lethargy.

Creed went to his horse to retrieve a blanket to cover Amy, while Cricket approached Tom. She'd never comforted a grieving person before, and she wasn't sure how it should be done. She had to make him understand how sorry she was for everything that had happened. Tentatively, she laid a hand on Tom's shoulder.

Tom whirled on her with hate in his eyes and hurt in his heart. "Stay away from me! It should be you lying there instead of my Amy!" His face contorted and he jeered, "But I guess the Comanches didn't want to waste their time fucking just half a woman like you."

Cricket gasped at Tom's words, which wounded her to the quick. She had no idea why the Comanches hadn't raped her as well as Amy, but the thought they hadn't considered her woman enough to do so had never even crossed her mind.

"You got your ride around Lion's Dare," he shouted. "Are you satisfied? You killed my wife and our child as sure as if you'd stuck a knife in her gut yourself."

Tom was incoherent with rage and pain by the time Creed arrived at his side with the blanket. Cricket backed up when Tom struggled to his feet as though to attack her, and Creed stepped quickly between the two of them. "Stop it, Tom! You don't know what you're saying!"

"Get her away from me and my wife!" Tom snarled.

Creed could see there was no reasoning with his brother. He threw the blanket at him and said with steel in his voice, "Take care of your wife, Tom."

When the weight of the wool blanket hit Tom's hands, it snapped the thread of anger inside him, leaving only the terrible grief. He stared, shocked, at the gray blanket that would shroud his dead wife, and then he turned away from Cricket and Creed and knelt again beside Amy. Tom reached over to pull the lance from her shoulder as gently as he could—which was crazy, he knew, because she couldn't feel anything now.

When the lance came free, rich, red blood spurted from the wound. And Amy groaned.

Tom threw the lance from him as though it were Satan's staff and had conjured the dead to life. He stared in disbelief as Amy's eyelashes fluttered and her delicately veined eyelids opened to reveal pain-glazed blue eyes.

"Tom?"

"Oh, my God." Tom felt a rush of thankfulness so strong it brought tears to his eyes and he choked on a joyous laugh that threatened to bubble up from deep within him. That fierce gladness was followed so rapidly by horror at what he'd have to accept if he took Amy back into his embrace that the smile he would've smiled was crushed beneath lips clamped tight to keep them from curling in disgust.

Cricket rushed to Amy's side. "Amy, you're alive!"

Creed stood stunned where he was. It wasn't possible. After all she'd endured, Tom's wife should be dead.

"It hurts, Cricket," Amy whispered. "But I stayed alive."

"Yes, you did," Cricket choked out. "You're going to be all right, now. Don't worry, Amy. We'll take care of you. Everything will be fine."

"The baby?"

"Don't worry about the baby right now. Let's get you home where you can rest and get well."

"Tom?"

Amy got no answer from Tom. With great effort, she turned her head so she could better see her husband's face. It was shuttered, and she couldn't tell what he was thinking. She lifted her hand, surprised when it moved, and reached out to trace a tear on his stubbled cheek.

"Tom?"

Tom jumped as though burned when he felt Amy's fingers on his skin. She was alive! But lost to him all the same! She was soiled with the kind of dirt that wasn't ever going to wash off, just as his mother had been. He'd never be able to hold her in his arms without remembering that her legs had been spread for an entire band of filthy Comanches.

But this was Amy, his lovely Amy. Oh, God he loved this woman. What could he do? What should he do? He reached out to touch her hand on his cheek. It was cold. So cold. He tried to meet her eyes, but his gaze slipped to her mouth, which trembled. He took her hand in his and laid it down next to her body very gently. He covered her with the blanket, ordering Cricket tersely, "Hold that tight over the wound." Then he stood and walked away.

Creed quickly caught up with him. "Where the hell do you think you're going!" Creed hissed in a whisper Amy couldn't hear.

Tom didn't turn around. "I . . . I have to get something from my saddlebag."

Creed grabbed Tom's shoulder and yanked him around. "Amy needs you. Tell me what you want. I'll get it."

Tom paled and the skin tightened along his jaw, but he didn't speak.

"All these years I thought you were different," Creed accused, his quiet voice barely under control. "You're no better than Simon!"

"I . . . I'll be right back." Tom jerked out of Creed's grasp and kept walking.

Cricket was aghast. How could Tom leave Amy's side when she needed his reassurance so much? Her eyes sped to Creed, only to find his face as bleak as Tom's, and then to Amy, who looked back at Cricket with betrayed hurt.

"You said he wouldn't care . . ."

Amy turned her face away and then cried out in anguish as she grabbed her distended belly.

Cricket stared with horror at the blood that began to pool beneath Amy. "She's losing the baby. Tom, Creed, help me! She's losing the baby."

Creed hesitated another moment before he turned from Tom and strode back to Amy's side.

Tom stood by his horse, trying to decide whether to stay or go. He wanted to run from everything he'd seen here . . . but that meant running away from the one person he loved more than his own life. He loved Amy. That hadn't changed, had it? Then why wasn't this decision easier? Oh, God! What should he do?

Tom's shoulders sagged as he admitted there was no escape in running. His life would be hell without Amy; it could be no less a hell to face what had happened. He didn't know what else to do except pretend nothing had changed between them—and hope the pretense became a reality. Tom choked back his disgust and swallowed his guilt as he slowly turned and walked back to his wife.

Cricket watched as Tom worked skillfully to keep Amy alive. He stopped the bleeding from her wounded shoulder and bound it. But there wasn't much Tom could do about the baby except wrap Amy in the wool blanket and keep her warm while her body rejected the child, just as a part of him had rejected its mother.

"I want to die," Amy begged. "Please leave me here and let me die."

"You don't know what you're saying, Amy," Cricket soothed. "You'll get well and what happened here will be forgotten in time."

Cricket watched as Amy tried to catch Tom's eye to see if what she'd said was true. But no matter how long Amy stared at him, Tom avoided her gaze. Tom cared for his wife with efficiency, rather than tenderness, and although he carried Amy in his arms all the way back to Lion's Dare, Tom kept his body stiff, touching her only when and where it was necessary. And he didn't kiss her . . . not even once.

The trip to Tom's plantation took almost a week. Fortunately, Amy was delirious most of that time, and living in a world of innocence that was gone forever.

Every time Cricket thought Amy might die, Tom or Creed found a way to bring down the fever, or stop the bleeding, or counter the infection, and contrary to her often-voiced wishes, Amy survived.

The constant tension between Amy and Tom transmitted itself to Cricket and Creed. Cricket wasn't sure exactly what had gone wrong. Creed never said a word to blame her for what had happened to Amy, nor did he condemn her for the rift the incident had caused between him and Tom. In fact, he said very little to her at all. He treated her politely, but like a stranger. And she didn't know how to break through the barrier he'd erected between them.

They hadn't spoken about Tom's harsh words to her in the cedar brake, but neither had Creed touched her as a woman. Cricket's heart was like lead inside her—heavy and cold. Perhaps what Tom had said was true. Maybe she was only half a woman.

Creed saw the pain and dread in Cricket's expressive gray eyes. He wanted to take her in his arms and hold her, to make love with her, to comfort her and be comforted. But he didn't dare for fear it would spark the memory of what she'd seen happen to Amy. Cricket had been distant with him, stiffening every time he came near. He didn't know what else to do except give her time, and so he kept his distance from her.

Word of Amy and Cricket's kidnapping spread from Tom's slaves to the slaves of his neighbors, so that soon after they arrived back at the house planters and their wives descended on Tom's doorstep like vultures to see for themselves whether the stories they'd heard about Amy's "disgrace" were true. Cricket took the same pleasure in scattering them as she would have the ugly black birds.

"The only *disgrace* around here is the way you cabbageheaded harpies have imposed on Amy and Tom's hospitality at a time of great bereavement," she snapped. "Now if you don't fly out of here in a hurry, I'll get a gun and see to you myself!"

Cricket stayed constantly by Amy's bedside, so she was there when Tom came to see his wife. He came at regular times in between his duties on the plantation, but stayed only long enough to exchange a few words with Amy. Neither seemed to know what to say to the other. It was what they couldn't say that tore at Cricket's heart. The easy touching, the loving looks, the laughter between them, were all gone.

It was another week of constant care before they were sure Amy wasn't going to die from her injuries.

"She'll be all right now, won't she?" Cricket asked when Creed pronounced Amy's fever gone for good.

"We'll have to wait and see if her spirit will cooperate and let her body do its healing work." He sighed, obviously discouraged. "I don't know, Cricket. I think maybe it's going to take something neither you nor I can give her to make Amy want to get well."

"She has to get better! I won't let her die!"

Creed met Cricket's blazing eyes with a sympathetic look. She lowered her gaze. Creed didn't blame her, but she knew everything that had happened was her fault. It lay unspoken between them that although Tom had been to see Amy every day, he obviously hadn't been able to reconcile his feelings about what had been done to her by the Comanches. Nor had Creed been able to forgive Tom for his attitude toward Amy—so reminiscent of Simon's rejection of Mary. Their suppers were somber affairs, each of them caught up in his own thoughts.

Then the day came when Creed announced they would have to leave Lion's Dare. "We can't stay here much longer, Brava. We're already late for our rendezvous with Commodore Moore. We've done everything we can. Amy's fate no longer rests on whether we stay or go."

"Just a little longer, Creed," Cricket begged. "A few more days, please."

Creed shook his head.

Cricket reached out and grasped his arms. "Please."

It was the first time Cricket had touched him or asked anything of him since the incident at the Comanche camp. He didn't believe it would change anything if they stayed, but he couldn't deny her. "Two days. That's all. Then we'll have to leave."

Cricket threw herself wholeheartedly into assuring Amy's recovery. She talked to her and fluffed her pillows and changed her chambray wrapper. Amy remained cocooned in a world of her own. Cricket brought Seth in to visit, and let the child's laughter fill the room. Amy simply closed her eyes and willed herself to sleep. Despite Cricket's efforts, Amy's condition worsened.

"Amy, you have to eat," Cricket coaxed. She held a spoonful of steaming broth under Amy's nose, hoping the aroma would tempt her. It was no use. The sallow-faced, bitter-eyed woman who lay sprawled listlessly in the center of the huge feather bed was nothing like the loving beauty who'd greeted her the first day she'd arrived. Even the sight of Seth hadn't roused Amy as Cricket had hoped it would. Amy had given up. If she wouldn't eat, it was only a matter of time before she'd have her wish and leave a widowed husband and a motherless child.

Cricket was fed up with Amy for wanting to die, furious with Creed for setting a deadline for their departure, and she'd had a bellyfull of Tom, who could with a look and a word of love bring his wife back from the brink of death. All too soon the time Creed had allotted her was up, and Cricket decided she had no alternative except to confront Tom and make him see reason. But Cricket was equally sure Tom wouldn't want to listen to what she had to say. He was likely to simply walk away from her when she started talking . . . unless she could convince Creed to help her.

Cricket cornered Creed in the parlor before supper. He was stretched out in a chair with a brandy in his hand, staring into space. She hadn't much time to enlist his aid before Tom came downstairs to join them. Cricket walked up to Creed and stood spread-legged next to him with her fisted hands on her buckskin-clad hips.

"She won't eat."

"I didn't think she would," he replied quietly.

"She wants to die."

Creed looked up at Cricket, and she could see the pain in his eyes. "Should I be surprised?"

"We have to do something."

"I've already told you there's nothing you or I can do to help Amy now."

Creed had answered exactly as she'd expected. She took a deep breath and said, "But Tom could help, couldn't he?"

Creed swore loudly and acidly. It was all the assurance Cricket needed that he agreed with her assessment of the situation.

"I've thought so, too. I only wondered how he could be made to see that Amy's still the same woman he married."

Creed's bitterness about past wrongs harshened his speech. "He isn't going to change his mind, Brava. I ought to know. He's as narrowminded on this subject as my father was, and Lord knows he never saw the light. You'll be wasting your breath."

"I have to try, Creed. All I ask is that you keep Tom in the room long enough to listen to me. Will you do that?" Cricket could hear Tom's bootsteps on the stairs. "Please, Creed. Will you make him stay here and listen to me?"

Creed struggled with her request. He didn't want to talk about this with Tom. He didn't want to be reminded that the brother he'd worshipped had feet of clay. He didn't want any part of this. But Cricket, who never needed anybody, needed him now. She might never ask again. He had to be there for her. And so he agreed to endure the hurt for her sake.

"All right, Brava."

He'd spoken so quietly Cricket barely heard him. She released the lungful of air she'd been holding and then took another deep breath as she pivoted to confront Tom.

CHAPTER 20

CRICKET TRIED TO catch Tom's attention when he entered the parlor, but he ignored her. He crossed to the liquor cabinet and helped himself to a whiskey, then nodded absently to Creed and sat bent over like an old man in the chair that faced the cold, ash-blackened fireplace. His head hung down between his slumped shoulders and his elbows rested on his spread knees, the whiskey glass balanced in his hands between them.

Cricket self-consciously tugged down her buckskin shirt and walked over to stand across from Tom. Her plan had to work! She glanced over her shoulder to find that Creed had risen from his chair and followed her. He stood behind her, ready to back her up.

"Tom, I want to talk to you."

For a long time Tom said nothing. Finally he looked up at her and replied, "We have nothing to say to one another. I want you to stay the hell out of my life."

Cricket cringed inwardly at the harshness of Tom's voice, but steadied herself and said, "Amy's upstairs dying while you sit there pretending nothing's wrong. Why did you work so hard to keep her alive if you were just going to treat her like something dirty you were too good to touch anymo—"

Tom lunged from the rawhide chair, sending his whiskey glass crashing into the stone fireplace with one hand, while the other whipped around to slap Cricket. Creed caught Tom's hand before it struck home, his grip like steel. Disillusionment, disappointment, and anger sparked between the two brothers as their eyes clashed above Cricket's head.

Tom jerked free and let the momentum carry him completely around and away to the window that overlooked the towering oak in the side yard. He grabbed his head with both hands, massaging the constant headache that never left him, trying to manage some semblance of self-control. At last he turned to face Cricket, "Haven't you done enough? Get away from me. Leave me alone."

Cricket could see Tom was suffering. His face was stubbled with two weeks' growth of beard and his eyes were red-rimmed and sunken within dark circles of exhaustion. He might pretend he was unaware of the battle for life being waged upstairs, but she had to believe that wasn't the case.

"What the Comanches did to Amy was—"

"I won't listen to this," Tom said, lurching toward the door.

Creed placed himself in Tom's path. "You're not leaving until Cricket's done talking."

Tom stared at his brother's stony face, his eyes bleak, his will broken. He sighed raggedly and turned back to Cricket. "Say what you have to say, then, and be done."

Cricket didn't know where to start, and struggled for words that could make Tom take back the wife he'd shut out of his life.

"What the Comanches did to Amy left a wound, like the lance in her shoulder, that can heal with care." As Tom's lips flattened bitterly Cricket added, "Not that what happened won't leave a scar on your lives. But people can live with scars, Tom, even ugly ones. It's when the wound stays raw that it festers and you die. Amy loves you and she needs you."

"Do you think I don't love her and need her, too?" Tom's anguish was palpable. "I can't forget! I can't get it out of my mind! I see her lying there bloody and bruised and . . ." Tears stung his eyes and his chin quivered. "So many . . ."

"You haven't needed words to tell her she's been sullied in your eyes beyond redemption. It's not her wounds that are killing Amy. She'd rather die than live without your love, although Lord knows it hasn't been very constant! She needs a reason to keep on living. She needs to know the two of you will have a life together with a chance at happiness. And there's nothing stopping you from having it but your own blind selfishness!"

"Selfishness? How dare you—"

"You're only thinking about how you feel. What will the neighbors think? How will you be able to endure having a wife who's been raped by Comanches? What about how Amy feels? It wasn't even her fault!"

"No, but we know whose fault it was, don't we!"

Cricket blanched. "I can't change what happened. But I know how Amy feels and—"

"How can you possibly know how my wife feels? You had to be taught how to be a woman! How would you know what a woman feels when she's robbed of her dignity like my Amy? Maybe she wants to die because she can't live with the shame of what happened. You can't understand feelings like that because you're no more a woman than—"

"Shut up, Tom." Creed's voice threatened as well as cautioned.

A silence descended around them, no one willing to make the next move, to take the next step, until Cricket looked meaningfully at Creed and then back to Tom and said, "I know how it feels to be betrayed by someone I trusted."

Cricket's words tightened like an unseen hand on Tom's throat, choking him with the truth. It was his own cowardice that kept him from telling Amy how much he loved and needed her. He knew her shame was only as great as he let it be, and his fear was the only thing that kept them apart. But Cricket was wrong. Even if he found the courage now to go to Amy, he couldn't believe she would ever forgive him for turning his back on her when she needed him most. Because of Cricket his love had been tested . . . and found wanting.

"You half-bitch from hell! Why don't you go back where you came from? You've ruined enough lives trying to be something you're not, don't you think?"

The last word wasn't out of Tom's mouth before Creed's fist landed on his jaw. The punch knocked Tom off his feet. Creed didn't wait for his brother to get up, but threw himself on top of him. Tom wrapped his arms around Creed and rolled him over until the two of them were no more than a tangled heap of pummeling arms and thrashing legs on the floor.

"Stop it, both of you!"

The sound of Amy's sharp, quavery voice shocked the other three people in the room. Both Tom and Creed froze where they were, but their breathing shattered the tense silence with its stormy gusts.

"I'm ashamed of you two. That's no way for brothers to behave." Amy held herself upright by sheer determination. Step by careful barefoot step she walked farther into the room. Perspiration covered her face, while her body shivered with cold. The lance wound had broken open and blood seeped through the bandage on her shoulder, creating a huge red stain on her chambray gown. Her eyes were glassy, and she had an otherworldly air about her. Her voice when she spoke again was soft and lightly admonishing.

"I could hear you yelling at Cricket, Tom. I couldn't let you blame her for—"

Amy's eyes rolled up and she crumpled before three sets of horrified eyes. She hadn't hit the floor before Tom's arms went around her. He eased her into his lap as he settled on the rug. Once he touched her, something melted inside him and he poured out his anguish and his fears.

"Amy, Amy, please, sweetheart, don't die. I love you, Amy. Please forgive me. Please be all right."

Everything had ceased to exist except the woman in his arms, the woman he loved. When Amy's eyelashes fluttered open, the cautious, fearful look in her eyes wrenched a groan from deep inside him.

"I love you, Tom."

Taking care with her shoulder, he tucked her head under his chin and rocked her back and forth. "Everything's going to be all right. You're safe with me now. I'll be here for you, Amy. I'm sorry, Amy. I'm so sorry. Please don't leave me, sweetheart. Don't ever leave me. I can't live without you. My life's nothing without you."

Cricket's throat was tight with tears of happiness. Without warning, her belly rolled and heaved and she hurried from the room because she was going to be sick. She raced outside, and under the pin oak where Creed had first made her understand she was a woman, with a woman's needs and desires, she gagged and choked and spilled the contents of her stomach.

Tom's accusations had pounded her like bunched fists, leaving her battered and broken. His punishing words had struck at her fragile shell of womanhood with deadly accuracy, shattering it so it fell away in great hunks, leaving behind. . . . What was she? Cricket was very much afraid that what remained was the same freak who'd attended Amber Kuykendall's ninth birthday party.

It hurt to look honestly at herself. She'd never be a lady like Amy. The sooner she faced that fact, the better for everyone involved. But was she also a failure as a woman? That conclusion was painful to face, yet Cricket knew she must. It would be better if things could simply go back to the way they'd been before Jarrett Creed had come into her life. Then there had been no choices to make, and she'd known exactly who she was, and what she was. Now nothing was clear anymore. She straightened up and wiped her mouth with her sleeve. One thing was for sure. She would no longer try to be what she was not.

Creed had followed Cricket outside, but paused when she turned from him to be sick. He stood ready to help, but the hand Cricket stuck out to keep him away made her wishes plain.

"Are you all right, Brava?"

"Why wouldn't I be? Isn't it about time we got started for Galveston?"

Creed didn't like the brightness of Cricket's eyes, or the flat, uncompromising line of her lips. "You don't look well to me, Brava."

"I'm fine!" she snapped. "Now are we going to Galveston to meet Commodore Moore, or are you ready to send me home to Rip?"

Creed's stomach dropped when he realized Cricket must have taken Tom's vituperative words to heart. "What Tom said—"

Cricket's shrill voice interrupted him. "I don't want to talk about Tom or Amy anymore. I think enough's been said. I'm going to saddle Valor. If I'm not mistaken, my welcome here has worn rather thin." She turned on her heel and walked away from Creed toward the stable.

When Creed reached the parlor he found Tom still on the floor with Amy asleep in his arms. Tom looked up from his wife when he felt a presence in the room. His cheeks flushed, but he swallowed hard and said, "I owe you and Cricket an apology."

Creed ran his fingers through his hair in frustration. "It's a little late for that. I don't think Cricket's planning to hang around long enough to hear any contrite words you have to spout. She's saddling Valor now."

"I'm sorry, Jarrett. For everything."

It was an apology for more than what he'd said to Cricket, and Creed knew it, but the chance for whatever help Tom could have given to rescue their mother was long past. Creed found he was no better at forgiving than Tom had been. "It's too late, Tom. Sorry won't help now." He pivoted and headed out the door.

"Jarrett—"

Creed paused, but didn't turn around.

"Can I tell Amy that you and Cricket will be back to visit us when your business is finished?"

Creed sighed and hung his head. "I don't know, Tom," he said finally. "I don't know. We'll see."

Cricket found the view of Galveston harbor from the deck of the 600-ton Texas Navy sloop-of-war *Austin* breathtaking, for the other six ships of the navy authorized by the Texas Congress in 1837 were docked there as well. The ocean-going steam side-wheeler *Zavala;* the 170-ton schooners *San Jacinto, San Antonio,* and *San Bernard;* and the 400-ton brigs *Wharton* and *Archer* made an impressive picture of naval power.

Yet even the magnificent ships couldn't keep Cricket's mind from straying to the awful things Tom had said to her. *Half-bitch. Half a woman. Not a woman at all.* Dear God, she'd let herself care . . . and the names hurt.

"Those ships will ensure the Mexican government never invades Texas by way of her gulf coast."

Cricket started at the sound of the quiet, authoritative voice and turned to look down into the face of Commodore Edwin Ward Moore. The commander of the Texas fleet was two inches shorter than she was and didn't look much older than she did. His skin was fair for a seaman, an indication he'd spent more time in his cabin plotting strategy and courses than he had on deck. He had ordinary brown hair and nondescript features, except for his bright blue eyes, which sparkled when he smiled, as he did now.

"Welcome aboard the *Austin,* Mrs. Creed. I'm sorry I didn't have a chance to greet you sooner, but I've been busy making preparations to set sail tomorrow morning. You seem to have survived your first sailor's supper very well."

"I enjoyed meeting the captains of the other ships, and the food was as good as the company," Cricket said sincerely.

It had surprised her when the captains of the Texas fleet accepted her buckskin attire at the supper table in stride, since they'd all been dressed formally in tailored blue naval uniforms trimmed with gold epaulets and shiny brass buttons. Had she been dressed in silk they couldn't have been more polite and considerate. She hadn't been aware of Creed's warning stare which had dictated that anything less would not be tolerated.

The talk at the table had all been of the man who stood beside her now. The captains of the *San Antonio* and *San*

Bernard had spoken glowingly of Moore's exceptional seamanship, which he'd refined as a lieutenant in the United States Navy. Moore, they'd said, ruled by sheer dint of his personality. It was apparent he was well-liked by his subordinates, and the full measure of their respect for his leadership was evidenced by the toast offered by John Lothrop, captain of the *Zavala:*

> Float on Navy, whilst a foe
> To Texas breathes in Mexico;
> Till every tyrant on her shore
> Shall tremble at the name of Moore.

Much to Creed's chagrin and the captains' delight, Cricket had heartily joined in drinking a cup of grog to Moore's success.

Now that she'd met him, Cricket found herself willing to believe that the stories she'd heard at supper about Moore being a small man with a big heart were true.

"It was thoughtful of you to make your cabin available to us."

"It was my pleasure, although I apologize the accommodations aren't more suitable."

"The cots are fine, Commodore." She wondered what he'd think if he knew she'd often spent the night on a bed of straw in the barn . . . and once on a bed of bluebonnets beneath the Texas sky.

Cricket had been dreading this first night on board ship because it would force her into the kind of close contact with Creed they'd somehow managed to avoid the entire trip from Lion's Dare to Galveston. Creed hadn't touched her since the night they'd consummated their marriage. She'd made up her mind under the pin oak not to let Creed touch her again as a woman. But the moment had never come when it was actually necessary to tell him so. It appeared their bedtime confrontation wasn't far off.

"It's beautiful this evening, isn't it?" Moore said, interrupting her thoughts. "There's something about the sea at sundown, with the spars making shadows on the water, and the gulls soaring overhead for one last dive at the fish, that I find relaxing."

"It's not as quiet as I expected it to be," Cricket said. "The harbor's so noisy."

The commodore laughed. "I guess it depends on what you're used to."

"I hope it didn't cause any problems for us to be so late arriving."

"Not at all. Of course, Mr. Summers threatened dire consequences if we left without you," Moore said with a chuckle, "and his letter from President Lamar requesting passage to New Orleans for a Texas Ranger on government business was difficult to ignore. But I must admit I'm anxious to set sail. The sooner we pick up that load of Colt repeating rifles in New Orleans, the sooner we can begin our voyage to Campeche to bedevil the Mexicans. By the way, I take it Mr. Summers found your husband earlier this evening and delivered his message?"

"Luke Summers is on board this ship?"

"I sent him below to my cabin when he arrived while my lieutenant searched out your husband. When I saw you here I naturally assumed he'd found him with you and—"

"If you'll excuse me, Commodore, I'd like to speak with Luke before he leaves."

"Certainly, I'll escort you to your cabin."

It surprised Cricket how easily all the polite conventions had rolled from her tongue. It appeared Amy's deportment lessons were going to stand her in good stead. Unfortunately, she'd also learned other lessons which Amy hadn't intended. Cricket had learned from Amy's loving relationship with Tom that the rewards of caring were great; but she'd concluded in the aftermath of Amy's rape that the risks of caring were even greater. She had shared Amy's pain as though it were her own, and Tom's accusations had burned an indelible brand in her mind. It was far safer not to care, far safer not to love.

When they arrived at his cabin door, the commodore nodded and said, "Good night, Mrs. Creed. I'll see you in the morning when we set sail."

"I wouldn't miss it, Commodore."

Cricket didn't bother to knock, she simply opened the door and walked in. Creed was standing spread-legged next to the table where Luke was seated. Luke stopped talking abruptly when she entered and stood up to greet her.

"You're looking well, Cricket. Marriage must agree with you."

Cricket shot a look at Creed to see if he might have said something to Luke about the tensions between them, but at his slight shrug she realized the young Ranger was only being polite. She refused, however, to be distracted by formalities. She marched up to Luke and, placing her fists on her hips, got right to the point. "Have you satisfied yourselves that Sloan is not working with Antonio Guerrero?"

Clearly discomfited by Cricket's blunt question, Luke's eyes slid to Creed for guidance. When he nodded grimly, Luke sighed and admitted, "Yes."

Cricket whipped around to face Creed. "Then I can go home."

"It isn't quite that simple, Brava. Sloan isn't out of hot water yet. Tell her the rest, Luke."

"On several occasions Sloan has unwittingly delivered messages to the rebels that Antonio had hidden in her saddlebags," Luke said. "Our man inside the camp has been present and seen how it works."

"I can't believe it!" Cricket said. "If only I could talk to her. . . ."

Luke put a comforting hand on Cricket's shoulder. "That's exactly what you can't do. The key word here is 'unwittingly.' Sloan doesn't know she's being used, and since she's apparently in love with Antonio, there's no doubt she'd warn him if she got wind of what we're up to and thought he was in danger. If she were to help him escape—no matter what the reason—we'd have to arrest her for conspiring with the enemy."

Creed tried to ignore the jealousy that curled in his stomach when Luke put his hand on Cricket's shoulder, and he fought the urge to yank Luke away and take his place.

He'd been relieved when it had turned out Sloan wasn't working with the rebels, and then upset when he'd realized he might have to send Cricket home. Sloan's tentative situation had given him the excuse he needed to keep Cricket at his side until they could work out their differences. He loved her. He had no intentions of letting her go.

"So what happens now?" Cricket asked.

"It seems President Lamar wants to make an example of Guerrero." Creed's lips thinned to an unpleasant line when he added, "And he wants the American chargé to be there when he does."

"When he does what?"

"Hangs Guerrero."

Cricket paled. "And Sloan?"

Luke reached across the table and took Cricket's trembling hand in his own.

Creed's fists tightened again and he clenched his teeth when Cricket looked anxiously up into Luke's face as the young man reassured her, "Nothing's going to happen to Sloan. She's just a woman who's been used as a pawn by her lover."

"But if I talked to her—"

"Luke will keep an eye on Sloan," Creed snapped, then tempered his voice to keep his irritation with Luke out of it when he said, "You're coming with me to New Orleans. You can help me talk Beaufort LeFevre into coming to Texas with me."

"What makes you think I'd be any help?" Cricket snapped, reacting to the irritation she perceived in Creed. She could find no reason for it except that he was still stuck with her. It was just as well he wanted nothing to do with her—especially since she'd decided trying to be a woman was something she wanted no part of anymore.

"LeFevre's a bit of a free spirit himself. You two ought to get along fine. President Lamar is convinced that if the American chargé sees the towns we've built and the land we've settled in the four years since San Jacinto, he'll realize how advantageous it would be for the United States to have a few trade agreements with Texas. Publicly hanging Guerrero is Lamar's way of proving to the chargé that Texas is a sovereign nation that can handle any threats from Mexico."

"When do you think you'll be back with LeFevre?" Luke asked.

"According to Commodore Moore, the trip to New Orleans can take anywhere from four days to two weeks. With luck we can convince the chargé to travel back to Texas with us on the *Austin*. If so, we'll arrive at Three Oaks a little over a month from now."

"We're taking the chargé back to Three Oaks?" Cricket asked, startled.

Creed smiled wryly. "When Rip found out the American chargé was coming to Texas he volunteered to put him up at Three Oaks. With the state of the Texas treasury what it is, President Lamar was only too happy to accept his offer."

"I'll be looking for you in a month or so, then," Luke said. "Meanwhile, we'll be watching Guerrero. He rarely does his own dirty work, but things seem to be building toward some kind of major military operation. If that's the case, he'll be meeting with the Mexicans. When he does, we'll be waiting for him."

"Do what you have to. I'll be back as quickly as I can."

"Oh, by the way, Cricket, Rip sent a message to you."

"He did?" Cricket was surprised, but pleased Rip had thought of her at all after the way she'd spoiled his plans to marry her to Cruz Guerrero.

Without blinking an eye Luke responded, "He said to tell you not to worry about anything. He'll handle the situation when you get home."

Cricket shook her head incredulously. Leave it to Rip to call her marriage to Creed a "situation."

"Is that all?" Creed asked sharply.

"Yes, sir," Luke replied with the deference due to his commanding officer. "So long, Cricket." Luke leaned over and kissed her on the cheek as though it were the most natural thing in the world.

It never occurred to Cricket how unusual it was for her to have allowed Luke to touch her so casually during the past conversation, and she turned her cheek up for his kiss goodbye without thinking. It was just—Luke was different. She didn't try to explain it, she simply accepted it.

But Creed didn't understand or accept it. When Luke left the cabin he whirled on Cricket.

"You've been keeping me at arm's length for three weeks. What's Luke Summers got that I haven't?"

Cricket was stunned by Creed's outburst, and even more so by the fact he'd suited word to deed and she found herself jerked out of her chair and enfolded in his embrace before she could do more than stutter, "W-w-what?"

"I told you once before, Brava, if anyone's going to put his hands on you, it's going to be me. I've kept my distance because—"

Creed stopped abruptly because he wasn't sure how to explain exactly why he'd stayed away from Cricket. At first he'd stayed away because she tensed whenever he came near. He'd thought perhaps what she'd seen happen to Amy had frightened her, or maybe even disgusted her. Then he'd feared she must be remembering how he'd hurt her that first time. . . .No, he refused to believe she was afraid of him.

"—because of what happened with Amy," he finished. As soon as he spoke Amy's name Cricket stiffened in his arms. So, he thought, he was right in his conjecture. But she was his wife, and he wouldn't allow her to hide behind her fears indefinitely. "It's past time you started acting like my wife."

"I tried it your way, Creed," Cricket spat. "I tried being a woman and look what happened. I think it would be best for both of us if you admitted I'm not what you thought I was and left me alone."

Creed couldn't hide his surprise and didn't try. "You didn't believe that babble Tom was spouting about your not being a real woman, did you?"

Cricket remained silent, but her face flushed.

"Yes, I see you did. He was hurt, Brava, and lashing out at the nearest target. He didn't mean what he said."

"He was right!"

"He was wrong. You're more woman than most women ever dream of being." Creed's arms tightened around Cricket, pressing her breasts into his chest and cradling her belly

between his thighs, letting her feel his arousal. "See what you do to me?"

Cricket could feel exactly what she was doing to him. In fact, from the state of her puckered nipples against his chest, he was having the same effect on her. For the barest second she allowed herself to wonder what would happen if . . . Then her sense of self-preservation came to the rescue. She placed her palms on Creed's chest and shoved with her not-inconsiderable strength. Creed merely tightened his hold.

"It won't work, Brava. In a contest of strength I'm always going to win, and I've learned too many of your tricks for them to work anymore. Face it. Accept it. You're my woman, and nothing anybody says can change that."

Cricket jerked her head up to argue, but found her lips captured by Creed's. He held her firmly against him with one iron-thewed arm while his other hand came up to cup her head and hold it steady. Under his punishing mouth, her lips parted so his tongue could thrust its way inside. His thigh came up between her legs to keep her off-balance, lodging against her mound of venus and then subtly moving, abrading, the delightful friction bringing a groan of protest from Cricket.

"No," she begged when Creed released her mouth, his lips tracing a passionate path across her cheeks and throat to the racing pulse beneath her ear.

"Yes, Brava," he rasped as he lifted his head to peruse her troubled face, his hooded eyes bright with need. "Most definitely, yes."

CHAPTER **21**

W HEN CREED'S LIPS came down to cover Cricket's in a dominating kiss, an image of Amy being raped flashed before her eyes. The thought of Creed taking her as the Comanches had taken Amy made her stiffen in terror. As though reading her thoughts, he instantly released her and sought to allay her fears.

"Don't be afraid. I won't hurt you, Brava."

Cricket could feel the terror dissipating as his lips came back to cherish hers in a tender lover's caress.

"We can go as slowly as you want."

His strong hands gently roamed her body, soothing, exciting, then soothing again. He rocked her hips into his, giving her time to accept the way they would soon join together.

"We'll be a man and a woman giving themselves to one another. You'll feel only pleasure."

"And enjoy myself . . . immensely?"

She watched Creed's lips curve in a fond smile. "Yes."

He reached down and lifted her into his arms, carrying her the short distance to the captain's bed. There he laid her down before him. Slowly, carefully, with infinite patience, he kissed the last of her fears away. His lips teased hers, then traced a tingling path down her throat. His hands stroked her through her buckskins, preparing her for a more intimate embrace. He slowly undressed her, as though her body were a precious gift, to be enjoyed as much in the anticipation as in the actual receipt.

His caresses removed the hateful images from her mind, and she discovered there was no resemblence whatsoever between Creed's loving possession and what Amy had endured. Gradually, he increased the tempo and intensity of his touches, until finally she needed something. . . .

"Creed . . ."

He looked into her eyes, then took her palm and placed it against his broad, muscular chest, holding it there for a moment before he took his hand away. "Touch me, Brava. I need for you to touch me as much as you need to touch."

She reached out for him in wonder, her fingers skimming the warm flesh, appraising it. Her own ardor increased a hundredfold as she perceived the greatness of Creed's need, which he held in abeyance till she should say the word that would join them.

But she wasn't ready to release him from her thrall. Her hand reached below his waist to touch what she had only seen. He was hot and hard, and she wanted him deep inside her. She gloried in the desire she saw in his hooded eyes as her hand caressed him.

And then his hand found her, his thumb teasing her until she was gasping with pleasure. His lips found her breasts and then moved down to her belly and beyond.

"Creed . . ." she breathed.

"I know, Brava, I know," he rasped.

And he did know exactly how to bring her to a plane of excitement, of possession so beautiful it made her cry out to him.

"Come to me! Now, Creed! Now!"

He seated himself deep inside her, filling her, making her his.

"You're mine. Now and always."

"No!"

"Yes, Brava. Most definitely, yes."

And then Cricket had no rational thought left with which to deny him. There was only incredible, wonderful sensation, as Creed proved she was his woman.

Half asleep, Cricket heard the drum-and-fife reveille followed by the striking of eight bells and the piping of the boatswain and his mates that signified the day had begun. The sun had not yet risen. She waited, cozy in her cot, for the cry of "All hands!" followed by "Up all hammocks!" The routine was familiar after the four days she'd spent on board the *Austin*.

The morning they'd left Galveston port she'd escaped Creed's possessive embrace and joined the sailors on deck, and so she could see them now in her mind's eye. They'd straggle up from the berth deck, each one with a hammock slung over his shoulder that was rolled and lashed and ready to be stowed on the hammock rail by the quarter-master.

According to Commodore Moore, the dialogue which preceded the order to strike the bell eight was an ancient ritual also used by the United States Navy, and by the British Navy before that. The quarter-master touched his hat to the midshipman and said, "Eight bells, sir." The midshipman reported the message to the officer of the deck in the ward room and was ordered by the officer of the deck, "Report it to the commodore, sir." Commodore Moore then commanded the officer of the deck: "Make it so, sir, and pipe to breakfast," at which point the officer of the deck "made it so" by ordering the quarter-master to strike the bell eight.

"Grog!"

Cricket smiled. Before breakfast every sailor drank his tod, a tin cup of grog served from a grog-tub at the larboard gangway. On the second day out she'd snuck into line and surprised the master's mate, Thomas Riley, when she arrived at the grog-tub. The sailors in line behind her, and those who lounged nearby, waited to see how Riley would handle the situation.

Riley was clearly perplexed. On the one hand, he knew a woman had no business drinking grog. On the other, Cricket had proved by climbing the rigging with the captain of the tops her first day at sea that she was no ordinary woman.

Jenks, the purser's steward, stood with his ladle poised to fill a cup, awaiting Riley's order. He'd seen Cricket scramble like a monkey in the rigging. He thought perhaps she'd bitten off more this time than she could chew. The grog was strong stuff. But, by a mermaid's tail, she'd earned the right yesterday to be served her tod! From the rueful look on Riley's face, it appeared he'd come to the same conclusion.

"Serve the seaman, Jenks," Riley ordered.

Cricket's face lit with a pleased grin and she lifted the cup and emptied it all at once. It was different from the whiskey she was used to, but no stronger. When she was done, she turned the tin cup upside down, and when a drop of grog fell into the palm of her hand she rubbed it into her hair, as she'd seen the sailors do.

At that moment Cricket won the heart of every seaman on the *Austin*. She was one of them. Over the next two days they taught her every sailor's skill they knew. There had never been any question of disrespect to a lady. Cricket was no lady. She made that clear by the buckskins she wore, by the sailor's oaths she gleefully blasphemed, and by the capable way she mastered every seaman's job she tried.

She further proved her mettle when she broke up the fisticuffs between Timothy Owen and Alexander Trigg on the berth deck. She tripped up Timothy and then threw Alexander over her shoulder in an intricate move that had the watching sailors roaring with laughter. Timothy and Alexander smiled sheepishly and chose to shake hands rather than deal with a wrathful Cricket.

In the background, broodingly watchful, stood Cricket's husband. The seamen could see the relationship between Cricket and Creed was fraught with tension. Sparks flew when their eyes met. It was also clear that while Creed clearly didn't condone his wife's actions, neither was he willing—or perhaps able—to control them. When they hung up their hammocks and retired for the night every sailor on board the *Austin* imagined what was going on in the captain's cabin.

What would it be like to have a woman like Cricket in your bed? Though no man would admit it, the thought was as frightening as it was exciting. It would take a hell of a man to handle a wildcat like Cricket. Sometimes in the morning her mouth was so kiss-swollen it made a man ache, and her eyes had that dreamy, unfocused look of a well-loved woman that choked a man with envy. Then the picture came to mind of Timothy and Alexander sitting whipped on the floor of the berth deck. Jarrett Creed must be one hell of a man.

Cricket turned enough in her cot to see the outline of Creed's shape in the predawn dark. He slept on his side with one knee drawn up, and his cheek resting on his arm. She'd tried everything to convince him over the past four days she was no fit woman for a wife. During the day she rejected the role with a vengeance. At night he allowed her no doubt of it. Worst of all was the knowledge that when he took her in his arms she didn't want to fight him. By the time he thrust deep within her, claiming her body, she'd already given him her soul.

Cricket shifted on the cot to accommodate the melting heat which had built between her legs. She'd woken wet and ready—from a dream of Creed's lovemaking. She closed her eyes and ground her teeth. Lately she was always ready. She would catch Creed's eye on deck and her breasts reacted as though his tongue were licking the tips. Her belly would tighten at the thought of his mouth at the juncture between her thighs. She'd nearly fallen from the rigging once as a result of one of those potent stares.

Creed also had been awakened by the sounds of the sailors' ritual, but kept his eyes closed. His body hurt from wanting Cricket. He was tempted to cross the distance between their cots, but knew she would fight him if he did. She always fought him at first. It would have been easy to let her initial, token resistence sway him from his goal, but he was determined to prove to her she was all the woman he ever wanted or needed. And he'd found it to be the truth. When he touched her she turned to fire in his arms, blazing with anger that became fiery passion, and finally a bed of white-hot coals that took him to levels of pleasure he'd thought beyond mere mortal beings.

He would have welcomed the tussle with Cricket this morning, except they were due to reach New Orleans and he needed all his energy for the argument he knew was coming when he met Angelique LeFevre again. How many years had it been since the last time he'd seen her? Almost five, he thought grimly. They hadn't parted on the best of terms. Actually, she'd cursed his soul when he left. She'd wanted him and he'd turned her down—but not because he hadn't desired her. That witch knew how to touch a man so he found himself aroused despite his best intentions. He heard Cricket moving restlessly in her cot and casually turned so he could watch her from slitted eyes.

"I know you're awake." Cricket bunched her fists under the covers, wishing she'd kept her mouth shut.

Creed's lips turned up at the corners, acknowledging her statement before he let his eyes blink open.

"Good morning, Brava."

Cricket sat up and swung her feet over the edge of the cot. "Why can't I stay on the *Austin* while you go talk with Beaufort LeFevre?"

"I've already explained that to you."

"And I told you Angelique LeFevre is welcome to you," she retorted.

Creed's eyes went stone cold. "Be careful what you wish for, Brava."

Cricket's chin jutted forward and her lower lip pouted like a spoiled child's. Before she could argue further there was a knock at the door and a youthful voice announced, "We've sighted New Orleans, sir. Commodore Moore wishes to know if you and Mrs. Creed would like to meet him on deck."

"Please tell the commodore thanks and we'll join him shortly," Creed replied.

"Yes, sir."

Creed rose languidly from his cot and stretched, his hands almost touching the ceiling. Cricket found herself watching him despite her better judgment. He was long, and lean, and naked. Her eyes dropped to the line of black hair that arrowed down from his waist to that particularly male part of him. To her dismay an amazing and instantaneous transformation occurred. She dropped her eyes and flushed when she heard Creed chuckle.

"Perhaps you'd rather stay here in the cabin," he murmured, his voice husky.

Cricket jumped out of bed and grabbed her buckskin shirt and trousers, yanking them on. She was out the door in minutes and headed up the stairs for the spar deck without Creed. As soon as the breeze hit her face she knew they were near land. She could smell it. Magnolias. And offal. She climbed the rigging to get a better look.

In the distance she could see the harbor, teeming with sailing ships and steamers. She could imagine the noise and bustle, probably double what she'd heard in Galveston harbor. She looked again and tripled the sound in her mind. Deafening. Cacophony. She closed her eyes and listened to the crash of waves against the hull and the snap and pop of the *Austin's* sails in the brisk wind. Quiet. Harmony.

When Creed came on deck he knew where to find Cricket. She'd spent most of the trip floating above them all. He fought the fear that haunted him every time she took one of her dangerous rides in the rigging. He looked up into the cloud of sails and found her leaning out as far as she could over the ocean, her unbraided hair blowing freely in the wind, the fringe on her buckskins whipping to and fro. Her eyes were closed. Her chin was tilted up and her nostrils flared to bring her the scents from land. Her lips were curved in a joyful smile. He felt desire so strong it made him tremble.

"A beautiful sight."

Creed wasn't sure whether Commodore Moore referred to Cricket or the port of New Orleans. Both were equally breathtaking. "Yes, beautiful."

"We should reach the harbor within the hour. Will someone be meeting you?"

"I'm not sure," Creed said. "I sent word overland when I knew I'd be making the journey, but I don't know whether the American chargé received it."

"No matter. There'll be a carriage at my disposal. You're welcome to use it."

"Thank you."

"It's been a pleasure having you and your wife on board," Moore said. "Cricket is—" The commodore searched for a courteous way to describe the unusual woman who'd captivated his officers and crew and astonished him with her uninhibited behavior. "—a natural-born sailor," he finished.

Creed smiled wryly. "Tactfully spoken, Commodore."

Moore grinned. "She's one hell of a woman, man. How'd you find her?"

"She found me." Creed's smile broadened in remembrance. "Stark naked in a pond."

Moore whistled in appreciation, then gazed up at Cricket. He wondered how she'd fare with the belles in New Orleans. He was saddened to think they'd scorn her, but he didn't hold out much hope they'd treat her otherwise. "Will you be staying with Beaufort LeFevre and his daughter?"

"Yes."

"Do they know about Cricket?"

There was more than one level to Moore's question, but the answer was the same no matter what he was asking.

"No."

Moore pursed his lips and made a steeple of his hands, a habit Creed had observed whenever the commodore had something serious to say.

"I'm probably interfering where I'm not wanted," Moore said, "but have you thought about letting Cricket wait for you aboard the *Austin.*"

Creed swore under his breath before curtly replying, "She's coming with me."

The commodore steepled his hands again. His eyes shifted up to the admirable woman who'd carved a niche in a heart which had previously belonged only to the sea. "I'd hate to see—"

"Damn it, Moore!" Creed drew rein on his temper and repeated firmly, "My wife will stay with me."

The commodore knew when to back away. He changed the course of the conversation as deftly as he changed the course of his ship. "How long before you'll be ready to return to Galveston with the chargé?"

"How long will your business take?" Creed countered.

"No more than a week."

"If LeFevre's coming back with me, we'll be ready to leave then."

"I'll send word to the chargé's home in the French quarter when we're ready to sail."

"Fine."

The two men stood at the ship's rail, each lost in his own thoughts, unaware they converged on the same woman.

"A mistress of the sea," Moore murmured, his gaze on Cricket, who arched out over the water like the graceful carved maiden on a ship's bow.

"*My* mistress," Creed replied tersely.

Moore chuckled. "Perhaps."

Creed snorted. "If you weren't such a gentleman—"

"—we wouldn't be standing here so amicably right now. I trust you'll be as cautious of your wife in New Orleans, sir."

Creed's eyes narrowed on the commodore. "You can bet on it, Commodore."

Moore grinned. "I shall."

Angelique LeFevre held a perfumed handkerchief to her nose, but it wasn't doing much good. New Orleans harbor stank as bad as the pigs she'd slopped when she was a country preacher's kid. Fortunately, her father's gift with words had propelled him beyond the pulpit of his church and into Louisiana politics in time for her to be educated in one of the best eastern schools. Nowadays the closest Angelique LeFevre ever came to a pig was eating a slice of the honey-sweetened, clove-laced ham her father's kitchen slaves baked for Easter dinner.

Angelique clamped the handkerchief down tighter over her nose and breathed through her mouth. In her other hand she carried a parasol which provided shade but did little to relieve the humidity causing perspiration to gather in her armpits and run down in ticklish streams between her breasts and shoulder blades.

She was beginning to think she should have stayed in the carriage. On her way to the edge of the wharf she'd stepped into a pile of refuse and the hem of her silk gown was soiled with . . . well, God only knew what it was. If the *Austin* didn't dock soon, she mused, she wasn't going to smell any better than the weasely drunkard who'd been leering at her for the past ten minutes. Stubbornly, she remained where she was. She planned to greet Jarrett Creed with a kiss so passionate he'd be sorry he hadn't made her his wife when he'd had the chance.

She'd been outraged when Creed had left her in Boston five years ago, spouting some nonsense about having a Comanche wife. It was the most imaginative excuse she'd ever heard for breaking an engagement. Of course they hadn't actually been engaged, but she'd known it was only a matter of time before he put a ring on her finger. She'd waited a long time for this second chance to become Mrs. Jarrett Creed.

The years in the interim hadn't been empty. She'd always been a hungry woman, and it would have been folly to think she could have lived without the sexual sustenance other men provided. But there was only one man she truly desired. The Boston bitches might have polished off her rough edges, but Angelique LeFevre, the digger-poor preacher's daughter, knew how to fight for what she wanted. When Jarrett Creed left New Orleans for Texas, she intended to be his wife.

As the *Austin* berthed and the lines were made secure, Angelique scanned the decks for Jarrett. She found him standing next to a short man in a gold-trimmed blue uniform, who was constantly being consulted by other officers. She removed the handkerchief from her nose and, ignoring the offensive smells that surrounded her, forced a cheerful welcoming smile to her face. She waved her handkerchief just vigorously enough to catch Jarrett's attention.

When she was certain he'd seen her she posed prettily and waited for him to come ashore.

Cricket saw the blond woman dressed in lavender silk wave at someone on the *Austin*. She followed the direction of the woman's sparkling eyes and ended up on Creed and the commodore. With a sinking feeling Cricket admitted the woman on the dock was probably Angelique LeFevre. Did she have to be so very beautiful? For a reason she wouldn't have cared to acknowledge, Cricket decided that when Creed left the *Austin* she would be at his side.

Moore had seen the frankly sensual look the American chargé's daughter had given Jarrett Creed. "It appears you may have some quick explaining to do."

"It looks that way." Creed glanced over his shoulder at Cricket. Maybe it would be best if he disembarked before she did, so he could talk with Angelique privately for a moment. He didn't think she was going to be pleased to find him married. When he'd sent his message to the chargé he'd been an unmarried man and had asked about seeing Angelique. Her appearance at the dock could only mean she'd received his message and interpreted it exactly as he'd meant it.

Cricket couldn't believe her eyes when she saw Creed striding down the gangplank without her. She gasped when the beautiful blond woman threw her arms around Creed's neck and passionately kissed him. It was the kind of intimate greeting long-lost lovers share. Creed did nothing to stop her. In fact, he lifted her completely into his arms so their two bodies became one.

Cricket was unaware that the sailor next to her bristled in outrage. Nor did she notice that the entire crew of the *Austin* had gone silent. The eyes of every seaman on board shot from the embracing couple to Cricket. Her face paled, but her back stiffened noticeably.

Creed had been surprised by Angelique's sudden action. She hadn't even taken the time to say hello. When he tried to free himself from the unexpectedly explosive kiss, she dug her fingernails into his scalp, and at the same time bit down hard on his lip. Had he really enjoyed this five years ago? It only disgusted him now. The only way he could avoid being clawed and devoured was to draw her closer into his arms and completely off her feet. He hoped Cricket wasn't watching.

At last Creed untangled himself. He whipped his head around to search the deck of the *Austin* for Cricket, only to discover her standing right next to him. She'd neatly braided her hair and put a leather band around her brow to keep it in place. Her cheeks were pink, and her eyes were the darkest gray they'd ever been. She'd never looked more beautiful to him.

He'd thought he would be glad if she weren't angry. It was more distressing than he could have imagined to discover no emotion at all on Cricket's face. Didn't she care that another woman had kissed him? He sure would've raised Cain if she'd kissed another man!

"Are you going to introduce me?" Cricket asked.

"Of course."

Creed sounded angry to Cricket. She was the one who should be angry. However, she wasn't allowing herself to feel anything at all because when she did what surfaced was garden-green jealousy. It was a new emotion for Cricket—and one she decided she didn't like—because it meant she cared more for Creed than she had any right to care under the circumstances.

"Angelique LeFevre, this is my wi—"

"My purse!"

The weasely drunk skulking nearby had snatched Angelique's silk reticule and started to run past Cricket. She reacted as she always had, on instinct, putting Rip's lessons to use without thinking of the impression she'd make on the chargé's daughter. She reached out a hand and caught the thief by the arm, jerking it in a circular motion. It was essentially the same throw she'd used on Creed, but at the speed the thief was moving he turned a complete somersault before landing in a heap on the garbage-littered ground.

Cheers rang out from the *Austin.* Cricket turned and bowed like a gentleman, then grinned back at the dozens of friendly faces beaming down at her. The thief saw his chance and, abandoning the purloined purse, made good his escape.

Creed reached down and retrieved the reticule. It looked a little the worse for wear, but he handed it to Angelique anyway.

Angelique pointed a dainty, white-gloved finger at Cricket. "Who is that?"

Creed fought a grin and lost.

"Angelique LeFevre, I'd like to introduce my wife, Creighton Creed."

CHAPTER 22

Aɴɢᴇʟɪᴏ̨ᴜᴇ ᴄʀɪᴛɪᴄᴀʟʟʏ ᴇʏᴇᴅ herself in her handheld mirror. What she saw was not a beautiful woman. Individually her features were each a bit too large or too small or oddly shaped. Together they made her stunning. Add to that her education, her proper Boston manners, and her insatiable sexual appetite, and she was the perfect wife. She didn't understand how Jarrett Creed could have ended up married to a woman like Cricket—not only married to her, but maybe even a little infatuated as well.

Cricket! What kind of nickname was that for a wife? Her clothes and her manners were equally strange. Cricket didn't fit any traditional feminine mold, that was for sure. Which was why Angelique now found herself stuffed into the surgeon's stateroom on the *Austin* headed for the Texas coast. If Jarrett Creed had been married to anybody else she might have given up and gone on to greener pastures. But because Cricket was what she was, Angelique believed she would eventually get Jarrett back. No husband could be expected to put up with Cricket's antics for very long.

Cricket's behavior at the formal dinner Angelique and her father had hosted the evening before they'd left New Orleans gave ample proof of Angelique's point.

It wasn't that Cricket hadn't looked lovely. She had. She'd worn a silk dress in a green and red and gray tartan plaid that hugged a waist so tiny a man's hands could easily span it. Her breasts were, contrarily, large enough to barely fit a man's hands. Her shoulders begged a man's hands to curve around the tawny flesh, and the curls in her lustrous auburn hair summoned a man's hands to tangle in them. In fact, whatever part of Cricket you chose to look upon seemed made for a *man's hands.* If Jarrett hadn't stood guard at Cricket's side before they sat down for supper, Angelique shuddered to think how many of the statesmen and bankers and merchants at the party would have been tempted to actually touch.

Nor could Angelique fault Cricket's manners at the table. She observed all the amenities and unerringly chose the correct utensil and laid it down at the proper time. It was during the dessert course, when Jarrett had leaned over to whisper something private in Cricket's ear, that things seemed to go so deliciously awry.

Cricket's response to Jarrett's unknown remark had been loud and succinct.

Jarrett's warning "Bra-va" was ignored, and there poured from Cricket's lightly rouged mouth such a stream of bitter epithets that even Angelique, who'd made a study of such terms from the Bible, had trouble understanding some of them. To say that the gentlemen at the table were shocked would have been to underestimate the effect of Cricket's tirade.

Angelique had quickly suggested that everyone retire to the parlor for cigars and brandy. If there had been any additional women other than she and Cricket at the dinner, the ladies would have retired to a separate room and left the gentlemen to themselves. As it was, Jarrett never let go of Cricket's hand and Angelique wasn't about to be the only one excluded. Little did she know the show was only beginning. Cricket had—

A knock on the door interrupted Angelique's thoughts. When she answered, one of the commodore's several dapper young lieutenants stood there.

"Dinner will be served shortly, Miss LeFevre. Will you need an escort?"

"Why, yes. Thank you, Lieutenant. I appreciate your thoughtfulness." She gave the young man a glance that promised everything and watched him catch his breath. Teasing was one of the things Angelique did best.

The young man cleared his throat. "Shall we go?"

Angelique smiled radiantly and placed her gloved hand on the gold-braided sleeve he held out to her. She looked forward to her first dinner on board the *Austin*. Jarrett would certainly be there with his wife. She doubted whether Cricket could manage to make as big a fool of herself this evening as she had in the parlor of the chargé's home in New Orleans.

But she could always hope.

Cricket critically eyed herself in her hand-held mirror. What she saw was not a beautiful woman. It was a freak. Despite her vow to give up on being a woman, her awakened femininity had taken root too firmly to be ripped completely out. She was like a hardy desert succulent whose stems had all been chopped off. To the naked eye, the desert flower appeared dead. But underneath the warm earth an elaborate system of roots remained, ready to grow when nurtured with the tiniest bit of rainwater.

So it was with Cricket. To outward appearances she was once again Rip's spoiled brat. On the inside, Creed's wife waited unseen for the opportunity to blossom and grow. It was anyone's guess which of the two personalities would finally hold sway. In any event, thanks to her jealousy of Angelique LeFevre, Cricket was forced to see everything now from both points of view.

Rip's brat had already forgotten the American chargé's formal dinner party.

Creed's wife cringed at the memory.

She'd been delighted at first when Creed leaned over during dessert to whisper in her ear. She'd quickly become incensed, however, when he'd compared her manners to those of the chargé's daughter, even if he had done so favorably. She couldn't explain the irrational jealousy that had possessed her at the mention of the blond-headed woman. But had she really shot a dangling bauble off the chargé's lead crystal chandelier with one of his dueling pistols on a dare? And debated the respective tastes of Cuban and American tobacco while she smoked her favorite Havana cigar? And cussed out a congressman when he vilified the Texan heroes who'd fought at the battle of the Alamo?

Rip's brat had dressed in plain, brown buckskins for dinner this evening.

Creed's wife worried that Angelique in pretty pastels would be more attractive to Creed than she.

Rip's brat liked Creed and respected him.

Creed's wife wanted her husband's love and feared that the only way she would ever have it was if she stopped being Rip's brat.

And that was the crux of the problem. Cricket was fairly certain she could never stop being Rip's brat. Which was to say, she was fairly certain she would never have Creed's love. He tolerated Rip's brat by day—and he desired his wife by night. Cricket had never despaired more over something she felt she could do nothing about. And she hadn't realized how much she'd come to care about Creed until now that she had a very real fear of losing him to another woman.

Creed came up behind Cricket, but he didn't touch her as he yearned to. Ever since Angelique had kissed him, Cricket had kept him at arm's length. She looked so very sad. He wondered if she was remembering all they'd been through together so far. These past weeks had been some of the best, and worst, times of his life. Even though it had been the plan to return her to her father, now that the time to do so was nearly upon him, he found himself unwilling to let her go.

It had finally dawned on him when he'd met Angelique again that he was never going to find another woman to compare with Cricket. She was gutsy, and opinionated, and willing to fight for what she believed. She was exactly the kind of woman the growing Republic of Texas needed—one who could thrive in a land still wild and free and untamed. She was the kind of woman he needed. He only hoped it wasn't too late to make her understand how much he appreciated her.

"It's time to go, Brava."

Cricket dreaded the coming meal, and it showed on her face. "After what happened last night are you sure I'll be welcome again at the same table with the chargé and his daughter?"

Creed grinned. "The commodore doesn't have a single chandelier on board."

Cricket fought not to smile. "But I know the chargé brought him a whole box of Havana cigars."

"Don't worry. You'll do fine."

She hoped so. Another night like the last one and she'd be handing Creed to Angelique on a silver platter. *Creed's wife* made up her mind that tonight she'd be a model of proper behavior—and keep *Rip's brat* firmly under control. By God, she wasn't giving Creed up without a fight! She smiled up at Creed and said confidently, "I'm ready."

The halls were too narrow for them to walk side by side, so he sent her out the door ahead of him. They strolled in companionable silence to the ward room, where a table large enough to accommodate twelve had been set up. Commodore Moore had invited several of his senior officers to join them, including his secretary and the ship's surgeon.

Cricket's heart sank like a stone when she saw Angelique LeFevre. The chargé's daughter was dressed in a pink layered gown. Every time she nodded, her perfect blond sausage curls bounced. Beside the tall young naval officers she looked like a beautiful porcelain doll. Never in her life had Cricket felt as tall or as uncomfortable in buckskins as she did right now. How had she ever thought she could compete with this woman for Creed's attention? Even now he was staring at the petite young woman.

When the commodore arrived he urged, "Let's be seated." Commodore Moore sat at the head of the table with Angelique to his right and Cricket to his left. The chargé sat next to Cricket while Creed was seated next to Angelique.

Cricket liked Beaufort LeFevre. He enjoyed arguing and he made a worthy adversary. His eyes were black and serious—some might even have said wise if they'd listened to him for any length of time—but he had a chipped front tooth that gave him a foolish appearance when he grinned, so he rarely smiled, even at his own witticisms. His solemn mien made him seem a less tolerant man than Cricket knew him to be . . . otherwise, she'd never have been allowed the freedom in his home to express her feelings in such an unorthodox manner.

During the course of the long dinner, Cricket listened to several controversial topics of conversation without commenting, thinking that if she said nothing, she could say nothing wrong. Only on the most innocuous of subjects did she speak, and then she was careful to agree with Creed. She was patting herself on the back for her success when LeFevre asked, "So tell me, how do most Texans feel about annexation?"

Creed and Cricket both answered at the same time.

"They're for it."

"They're against it."

Right then, Cricket knew she should have kept her mouth shut. She'd wanted to be the docile, obedient wife for Creed, but this was an issue on which she couldn't stay silent. She saw the frown that furrowed Creed's brow. *Creed's wife* was glad he didn't suggest she hold her peace, because *Rip's brat* wouldn't have agreed even if he'd asked. However, the instant Cricket opened her mouth to speak, Creed cut her off.

"What my wife and I meant to say," Creed inserted smoothly, "is that some Texans are for annexation and some are against it. Almost all the Anglos in Texas were once citizens of the United States. Many of them want to belong again to the mother country. However, right now the Texas Congress and President Lamar are against annexation."

"That's pretty apparent," LeFevre said with a flourishing wave of his hand. "We Americans have been watching Mirabeau Lamar's negotiations with various foreign powers for recognition of Texas as a sovereign nation. He hasn't done half bad—France last year, and maybe England this year—if your president can convince Lord Palmerston that Texas won't always be a Negro slave territory and that the United States won't soon be gobbling Texas up."

"We'll never allow Texas to be gobbled up by the United States," Cricket vowed fervently. "We're going to be the greatest, the biggest, the grandest Republic on earth. Our borders will extend east to the United States, south to the Rio Grande, and west all the way to California!"

Creed closed his eyes and prayed for patience. It was true that under international law Texas could claim any land not a U.S. territory that it could win and hold. But such ideas were far-reaching and unsettling to some citizens of a Republic that had barely secured itself from the threat of Mexican sovereignty, and who felt a strong allegiance to the United States.

"How do you feel about annexation, Commodore?" LeFevre asked.

"I'm not sure the Republic would be better off as a part of the United States, sir. Texas is well on the way to proving herself a strong sovereign nation. Now that we have a navy to blockade Mexican commerce and to defend our shores, Mexico will have no choice but to concede that the southern border of Texas extends all the way to the Rio Grande."

"You don't even have a bank in Texas," LeFevre argued. "Or an army to defend yourselves, or—"

"It's only a matter of time," Cricket interrupted. "Texas has stores and schools and churches—"

"But no preachers," Angelique interjected.

"What?"

"There are no preachers for your churches, or at least that's the reason Jarrett gave me for the fact your wedding vows have never been spoken in a church. I believe he said you have a common-law marriage."

Cricket's glance shot to Creed, whose eyes betrayed he had indeed told Angelique that much about the facts surrounding their marriage. How could he!

Creed now knew why Angelique had pried so deeply the past evening into the details of his marriage to Cricket. He'd only wanted to be sure Angelique understood that the marriage was legal under Texas law, so she wouldn't think there was any chance he was free to come to her. Looking at the stunned faces around the table, he realized her revelation was going to have some unwanted repercussions.

Creed took a deep breath and said in an amazingly calm voice, "In Texas a man and woman often begin living together as husband and wife and then have their marriage vows solemnized when the preacher comes to call."

"I could have married you at sea on the trip to New Orleans if you'd only said something," the commodore admonished.

LeFevre's concerned voice asked, "So you've never had your wedding vows to each other confirmed before a man of God?"

Creed swallowed hard. "No. We haven't." He could see what was coming. Anger rose in him. His lips thinned and the muscles along his cheek jumped as his jaw tightened. He'd wanted to make Cricket his wife, but not this way. Now she'd never believe he wanted her for herself. She would think he'd married her because he'd been cornered by circumstance. Damn it, he loved her! Couldn't she see that?

Cricket closed her eyes to escape Creed's intense gaze and clenched her fists in her lap. *Rip's brat* had done it again. Creed would never forgive her for this.

"I'd be pleased to officiate at your wedding," LeFevre volunteered.

The commodore steepled his hands before him on the table. "And I'd be proud to assist."

LeFevre stared pointedly at Creed. "When shall it be?"

"What better time than the present?" Creed replied with no trace of the cynicism he felt.

Cricket glanced up at Creed, aghast. Did he expect her to attend her own wedding dressed in buckskins? From the disparaging look on his face, he did. It was clear he believed the coming ceremony to be a mockery. He'd already said once he'd divorce her when it was convenient to do so. The vows he was forced to speak tonight weren't going to change that. But, oh, how she wished things were different!

By the time a midshipman arrived with a Bible, the table had been completely dismantled and removed from the ward room. A sailor had appeared with a harmonica to provide music, and the chargé and the commodore had taken their places at the center of the room with Creed and Cricket standing side by side before them.

Angelique could have chewed through nails, she was so enraged. She'd only intended to embarrass Cricket, and to show how low she stood in Creed's estimation if he'd never bothered to really marry her. She'd had no idea Creed would allow himself to be coerced into matrimony like this. If she had anything to say about it, this was going to be one of the shortest marriages in the history of marriage. And the next time Creed got backed into a corner, she intended to be the blushing bride!

The brief ceremony seemed endless to Cricket, whose eyes never left her feet until Creed took her hand in his to place a ring upon her finger. Then she glanced from the ring to Creed's face. He didn't look any happier than she felt. Somewhere over the passage of time she'd come to love this man. She wanted to be a good wife to him. She just didn't know how.

Creed was determined to make Cricket happy. Right now she looked about as miserable as he felt. Somehow he'd make her understand he loved her as she was. He'd act the way he supposed a good husband should act. He wanted to do the right thing. He just wasn't sure what that was.

Cricket knew her fate was sealed when Beaufort LeFevre announced, "I now pronounce you man and wife. You may kiss the bride."

Creed put his hands on Cricket's shoulders and turned her to face him. His fingertips brushed her chin, tipping it up slightly, and his mouth came down to meet hers in the lightest of kisses. It was over before Cricket realized it had happened.

"This calls for a celebration," the commodore said with a grin on his face. "Grog for all hands," he ordered, "in recognition of my first wedding as commodore of the Texas fleet."

A sailor with a fiddle joined the one with the harmonica and gay music filled the ward room. A cheer was heard from the berth deck when the announcement came that a ration of grog would be served. Creed shook hands with LeFevre and Commodore Moore. The several young lieutenants took advantage of the opportunity to kiss the bride. When Angelique LeFevre offered snide congratulations, Cricket couldn't stand the farce any longer and fled the room.

Creed saw Cricket's desperate escape. He had to find her and talk with her alone. He turned quickly to the gentlemen who'd performed the ceremony. "If you'll excuse me . . ." he said with a confidential wink. Creed left the ward room with the sound of friendly laughter following him out the door.

He searched first on the spar deck. Despite the danger, he half expected to find her in the rigging. Then he checked the berth deck and the steerage. He went lower into the bowels of the ship to the magazine, the spirit room, and the purser's stores. No Cricket. Then he came back up to investigate the bread locker on the starboard side of the steerage. All he found there was thousands of pounds of sea biscuit. She could be hidden anywhere. She could even have jumped overboard.

Creed raced to the spar deck and peered out over the dark gulf waters. He couldn't believe Cricket was desperate enough to end her life, but it was plain he wasn't going to find her until she wanted to be found. Discouraged, anxious, he returned to the captain's cabin to wait. And there he discovered his wife.

Cricket's first inclination when she'd reached the captain's cabin was to bar the door against Creed. She'd quickly realized that to keep Creed out was to send him right back to Angelique's arms. He hadn't wanted to marry her, but he was her husband now in the eyes of God and man. She had the opportunity to show him how much she loved him, and she intended to make good use of it.

She had taken off her buckskins and put on the only feminine night dress she had, a plain chambray gown. She'd quickly released her braid and let her hair, still wavy from the heavy plait, spill over her shoulders and down her back. She'd turned down the covers and perched on the edge of the cot, one bare foot atop the other on the wooden floor. Creed was welcome in her bed, and she wanted him to know it.

When Creed came through the door Cricket raised her eyes to greet him, and his loins tightened at the promise of passion in the smoky gray orbs.

"I looked everywhere for you."

"I've been here, waiting for you to come to me."

It was an invitation no husband could deny. Her willing gaze reassured him that tonight there would be none of the initial restraint that had marred their loving in the past. Creed took the few steps that brought him to his wife. He seized her hands and bid her stand up before him. Under his steady perusal her nipples peaked beneath the chambray wrapper. He brought his hands to either side of her face and tenderly stroked the soft skin with his callused thumbs. He splayed the fingers of one hand through her hair, grasping a handful of the silky stuff while his other hand encircled her throat.

Then his lips took the kiss he'd foregone at the end of the wedding ceremony. His tongue boldly searched her mouth, claiming the territory as his own. He gently sucked her lower lip into his mouth and nipped at it, then allowed her the freedom to possess him as he'd possessed her. Cricket gave herself wholeheartedly to her husband, and took from him what she wanted and needed.

She put her hands on Creed's chest, and felt the strength beneath his linen shirt. She broke the kiss between them, undressing him slowly, carefully, tantalizingly, unable to endure the cloth barriers between them but prolonging the moment when he would be unclothed to her gaze. She slipped off his frock coat and shirt, and then his trousers and drawers until he stood before her resplendently naked, his manhood full and ready. Cricket stepped back to look at what she had—a magnificent man, a tender man, a stubborn man—a man with a very pleased grin on his face.

She grinned back at him.

"You look very satisfied with yourself," Creed said.

"That's because I am." Cricket put her lips to one of Creed's nipples and smiled against his salty skin when his whole body tensed in response.

Creed had opened his mouth to tell her of his love when her lips drifted downward. When her tongue came out to lave the sensitive skin of his belly he had to hold his breath to keep from groaning aloud. His hands grabbed her at the waist, intending to stop the delicious assault, but before he could move her away, her mouth tasted its way even further down his body.

"Bra-va . . ."

Then it was too late to stop her. He grasped her hair in his hands and held her where she was, his feet wide apart, his head thrown back, nostrils flared, eyes closed, mouth gaping wide in an agony of ecstasy, while he surrendered himself to her love.

Cricket loved the taste of him, loved the soft-hard feel of him, loved the power of bringing him such intense pleasure. At last, she kissed her way back up his body, until her tongue found the pulse behind his ear. She nipped his neck and buried her nose in the slick wetness of his hot skin.

Creed held her tight against him, fitted them together like staves of a barrel, waiting for some measure of control to return. He kissed her ear, dipping his tongue inside. He kissed her throat, finding the pulse that raced unchecked. He kissed her temple, her cheek, her chin, her closed eyes, her nose. He found her mouth and ravaged it, tasting himself there.

Creed laid Cricket down on the captain's bed and followed to lie next to her. He began a thorough search for all the spots on her body that were sensitive to his fingers and his tongue.

He found one beneath her arm.

Cricket quivered.

Another on her hip.

Her hands grasped his shoulders and enjoyed the feel of the corded muscle there.

The pads of her fingers, and the spaces between.

Sweet lord, how good that felt!

Her breasts.

He suckled like a babe and she wished to succor him like this always.

The small of her back.

She stretched her arms above her head and arched, making a deeper dish for him to drink from.

Her buttocks.

He made her laugh with his nips, and then choke on that laughter as his love bites released a flood of passion.

The hipbones that protruded beyond her concave belly.

His tongue was rough like a cat's, and wet, and she wished he would go lower with it.

Her thighs.

She could feel his silk hair on one thigh, and his warm tongue on the other.

The heat and the heart of her.

She wantonly spread her legs so he could rest his head between them and taste, and suck, and lick and . . . oh, God . . . oh, God. . . .

Cricket's pleasure pleasured Creed. He couldn't get enough of her. He gave her only a moment's respite before he seated himself deep inside her, possessing her, being possessed by her, making them one.

Cricket wrapped her legs around him and clutched his shoulders with her hands, holding him tight, fearing the closeness would not last, fearing that when all was said and done he would drop her off at her father's door and return to the beautiful Angelique.

Creed forced himself to be still; a moment from now it would be too late to stop. He wanted to speak the words. He wanted Cricket to know how he felt.

"Look at me, Brava," Creed rasped.

Cricket's glazed eyes focused on the angled face so close to her own.

"This ceremony was forced on both of us tonight. But you should know Angelique means—"

Cricket stopped his words with her hand. She couldn't bear to hear him say Angelique meant more to him than she did. "You don't have to say any more." It was better to live with the illusion of love than to face stark reality. He belonged to her tonight. And she intended to fight and keep on fighting for his love. She burrowed against Creed, holding him tight.

Creed brushed the hair away from her forehead, glad that she understood his love without the need to have the words spoken aloud. He kissed her lips, and found there the promise that she returned his love. They spoke through their passion. Creed's powerful thrusts were met by the strength of the woman beneath him. The sense of desperation that seized them both lent ferocity to their lovemaking. It was a tumultuous coupling, a merging of bodies and spirits that left them exhilarated and exhausted.

Cricket lay beneath Creed, his breath coming in heaving bellows that forced the air in and out of her gasping lungs in time with his. He had desired her. She knew he had. Surely he could not leave her now at her father's door. But he hadn't said he loved her. Nor had she said she loved him. But they had the rest of their lives to say the words. Didn't they?

CHAPTER 23

CRICKET KNEW SHE was home when she heard Rogue's ululating cry of welcome.

"My God! It's a pack of wolves!"

Cricket followed Angelique's pointing finger to the three young wolves running on a parallel course with them. She whistled and the wolves changed direction, heading directly for the two riders who flanked the open carriage carrying Angelique LeFevre and her father.

"They're coming this way. Somebody do something!"

Cricket exchanged a conspiratorial grin with Creed over the top of Angelique's head. "What did you have in mind?" she asked.

"Shoot them! Kill them!" By now Angelique was hysterical and had practically climbed into her father's lap. The chargé, true diplomat that he was, geared his behavior to that of Cricket and Creed. Seeing they weren't particularly alarmed, he remained outwardly calm, hiding his agitation.

"All right," Cricket said, warming up to the game. "Here goes." She pulled a Patterson from her saddle holster and began shooting high above the wolves' heads.

The three wolves split apart, Rascal and Ruffian breaking off to the right and left, while Rogue came straight ahead. In fact, Rogue appeared to be coming faster now than he had before Cricket had blasted away with her gun.

Angelique clung to her father but turned to Creed, the whites of her eyes huge, and begged, "Save me!"

Creed flashed an admonitory glance at Cricket. Teasing Angelique was one thing. Scaring her half to death was another.

"Angelique, there's nothing to be—"

"Look at that!"

The chargé had interrupted Creed to point with disbelief at Cricket. She'd spurred her mount away from the carriage toward the center wolf, and now dismounted directly in the vulpine creature's path.

Angelique's wide-eyed fear had become wide-eyed wonder. Was Cricket about to get herself killed? How absolutely marvelous!

The chargé pulled the carriage to an abrupt halt, watching aghast as the three wolves converged on the defenseless girl. "Do something, man!" he shouted at Creed.

"Cricket is—"

Then there was no more time for words. The three wolves were all over Cricket. The chargé turned his face away, hearing the wolves' ferocious growls and Cricket's shrieks, and unable to bear the sight of the poor girl being torn to shreds by the wolves' sharp fangs.

Angelique, however, wasn't about to miss her moment of glory. Her eyes stayed on Cricket, who disappeared beneath the mound of gray fur—and bounced back up again with a grin on her face. Cricket ruffled the fur on the largest wolf's neck, petted the ears of another, and scratched the chin of the third. She was *playing* with the wolves! Angelique blinked her eyes once to make sure she wasn't mistaken.

"The wolves are *licking* her!"

The chargé whirled to confirm his daughter's discovery and then laughed out loud with relief.

Angelique turned to Creed, her eyes narrowing to an unflattering squint and her lips flattening in anger.

"I tried to tell you there was no danger," he placated. "The wolves are Cricket's pets. She raised them from pups."

The chargé laughed again to release the last of his nervous tension. "You had me worried there for a moment," he admitted. "You know, this really is an uncivilized place if a girl makes pets of wolves. It looks like you and I will have to learn to expect the unexpected in Texas," he said to his daughter.

Creed didn't deny the chargé's observation. Those who lived in Texas met the ruthless demands of the wilderness and did what they had to do to survive. To be always on the cutting edge of danger made life a precious thing, always to be lived to the fullest. Life promised plenty of misery, so you took your joy where you could find it. It was hard to blame Cricket for the harmless trick she'd played on Angelique. He'd seen a lot worse. Frontier fun was often as hazardous as frontier life.

Hazardous. That word brought to mind Creed's coming meeting with Rip Stewart, which he expected to be anything but fun. He'd been thinking during the whole ride from Galveston to Three Oaks how best to approach Rip. He hadn't found any answers.

Cricket had barely sent the wolves on their way when they had another visitor. "Luke!"

The young man greeted Cricket with a grin. "Nice to see you again, Cricket."

"You, too," Cricket said.

"Hello, Creed. Glad you're back. Your timing couldn't be better. It's about to get real busy around here."

Creed could tell Luke wanted to elaborate, but not in the chargé's presence.

"I expect you're Beaufort LeFevre," Luke said, extending his hand to the chargé. "Luke Summers."

"Good to meet you, Mr. Summers. This is my daughter, Angelique."

"Ma'am." Luke touched the brim of his hat to acknowledge Angelique. He could see she was one of those women who found her worth in a man's compliments, and his assessing look quickly labeled her an easy woman. He smiled knowingly. Luke never refused a woman's gift, freely given.

Angelique thought Luke Summers might as well have touched her down between her legs, the way she felt beneath his smoldering gaze. She hadn't expected to find this Texas character appealing, and the fact she had irked her. She allowed herself to be rude in retaliation, ignoring the man as though he didn't exist.

Such cutting behavior might have worked in Boston and New Orleans, but it was soon clear the rules were different in Texas. Luke spurred his horse up close to the carriage and murmured for Angelique's ears only, "Give a holler when you're ready, Angel, honey. I'll be there."

Angelique opened her mouth to snap a biting response, but the man's husky voice had sent chills down to the very bottom of her spine and by the time she recovered he was speaking to her father.

"If you'll excuse us, Mr. LeFevre, I need to speak privately with Creed for a moment," Luke said.

"Certainly."

The two Rangers rode ahead of the carriage some distance, speaking in low voices that made Cricket certain they were discussing Sloan and the rebels. She had no intentions of being excluded any longer. She kneed her horse and brought him abreast of the Rangers.

"You might as well tell me what's going on. Otherwise I'll ask Sloan and find out from her," she said.

"This is none of your business, Brava," Creed warned.

"Why not tell her what's going on," Luke said. "If she knows Sloan's not going to be in any danger maybe she'll stay out of the way."

Creed snorted. "I doubt it."

Cricket rolled her eyes.

"All right, but hear me well, Brava. If you get Sloan involved in what we have planned, she's liable to wind up getting hurt or killed. Do you understand what I'm saying?"

Cricket nodded.

"Antonio Guerrero is meeting tomorrow morning with several Mexican military officers. Our spies have found out they'll have documents with them that outline plans to invade San Antonio with a Mexican army. As soon as we're sure everyone is present, we'll spring our trap. According to our spies, Antonio has agreed to meet Sloan *after* the meeting, so she's not expected to be anywhere near the revolutionaries camp when we make our move. And I want it to stay that way."

"Yes, sir!" Cricket snapped off a reckless military salute.

"Dammit, Brava, I mean it."

Cricket turned her face away from Creed. She wasn't going to interfere. She wanted this all over with as much as he did. But what if she couldn't convince him to stay with her when his business was done? If she wasn't going to be Creed's wife anymore did that mean she could go back to being just Rip's brat? Somehow, Cricket didn't think so.

Creed knew what he'd promised Cricket: The end of the rebel threat meant the end of their relationship as well. He'd racked his brain for a way to make things come out differently, but she'd never said she loved him, and if she wanted to be free of him he'd have to let her go. The hell he would! He fought the anger and frustration that rose within him. He'd be in no shape to deal with Rip Stewart if he didn't keep his wits about him now.

Luke rode with them the rest of the way to the plantation house. When he saw Rip waiting on the front porch he grinned and said, "Uh-oh. Think I'll leave you here. Good luck." Then he was gone.

Cricket had imagined this reunion a hundred ways. The one she liked best was Rip standing on the front porch with his arms open wide to welcome her back. Well, Cricket thought wryly as she dismounted, she had half her wish.

Rip stood on the front porch with his hands bunched on his hips. "Go to your room, Cricket," he ordered.

Not even a hello. Not even an "I missed you." If her father was going to ignore the fact she was Creed's wife, then so was she. Rip's brat let him have it with both barrels.

"Like *hell* I will!"

"Like hell you *will!*"

They faced off as though the interim had never happened. This was normal. This was comfortable. This was safe.

"Do as your father says, Brava."

Rip and Cricket both turned on the Ranger in astonishment. Creed looked only at Cricket. He said quietly, but firmly, "Go to your room, Brava."

Cricket had expected Creed to rid himself of her, but not like this. She'd defied her father out of habit, but if this was Creed's way of telling her their relationship was over, there was no reason to deny Rip's request. In fact, the privacy of her own room began to look quite appealing. She only hoped she could contain her grief until she reached that safe haven.

"All right, I'll go," she said at last, all signs of fight gone.

Rip frowned. Cricket had shouted down his order, then obeyed that—that—kidnapping sonofabitch without so much as a peep. He watched Cricket, head held high, enter the front door and close it softly behind her. This wasn't like his Cricket at all. Something was very wrong. He whirled on Creed.

"What have you done to her?"

"I made her my wife," he answered simply. "I need to leave Cricket in a safe place while I take care of some dangerous business. Is she welcome to stay here?"

"Of course!"

Creed stepped aside so Rip could see the white-haired man and the pretty young woman who'd accompanied the Ranger to Three Oaks. Creed made the introductions that confirmed they were, as Rip had suspected, the American chargé d'affaires to Texas and his daughter.

"I have to leave you now," Creed said to LeFevre, "but you're in good hands." Creed turned back to Rip. "I'll return when my business is finished. We'll talk then." Without another word, he stalked away to his horse, mounted, and rode away.

Rip didn't know when he'd ever been dismissed quite so completely by someone he'd as soon have shot as given the time of day. That penniless bastard had kidnapped his youngest daughter right from under his unsuspecting nose and ruined his carefully laid plans to have Cricket marry one of the richest men in Texas. Juan Carlos Guerrero had withdrawn his son's offer of marriage the instant he'd learned Cricket had run away with the Ranger.

But he had only himself to blame for Creed's presence at Three Oaks. He'd been the one to ask Jack Hays for a Ranger to help curb the theft of his horses by the Comanches. He hadn't seen hide nor hair of a Comanche in months! It was unfortunate Creed had returned to Three Oaks with Beaufort LeFevre and his daughter in tow. Otherwise Rip could have shot the Ranger on sight and been done with it.

However, to be truthful, it was probably a good thing he hadn't gone off half-cocked, because from the look of things Cricket was a bit enamored of the fellow. At least, he didn't know what else to make of her blind obedience to the Ranger. He shook his head disgustedly, then turned back to the diplomat whom he'd agreed to escort to a meeting with President Mirabeau Lamar.

"Come on in," he invited. "You might as well freshen up before supper."

Cricket's worst fears had been realized when Creed dumped her at her father's front door. She went to her room, lay on her bed and closed her eyes, trying not to think, trying not to feel. She ignored Bay's pleas through the closed door to be allowed to come in and talk with her. She didn't know how long she'd been alone in her room when there was another knock at the door, but the shadowy darkness suggested the day was nearly gone.

"Cricket? It's me, Sloan. Can I come in?"

"Go away."

The door opened and Sloan came in, closing it behind her. "I missed you, Cricket."

"Humph." Cricket sat up in the center of the bed. "Looks like you and Bay are the only ones who did."

Sloan stopped long enough to pull her boots off, then joined Cricket on the bed, sitting Indian fashion across from her. "You missed supper."

"I wasn't hungry."

"So. How's married life?"

"Damn, Sloan! You don't tiptoe around the pansies, do you?"

Sloan laughed. "I never did. I want to know, Cricket, really. Imagine you married. I never thought I'd see the day!" Sloan didn't say aloud what else she was thinking. *I'm so jealous!*

The two sisters looked each other over for changes that might have occurred while they'd been separated.

"You don't look any different," Sloan said at last. "Marriage must agree with you."

"You've picked up a little weight, Sloan," Cricket countered. "Right here." She poked Sloan in the belly. "That used to be flat. Been eating too many sugared *buñuelos?*"

Sloan laughed nervously. She placed a hand on her gently rounded abdomen. "I guess I must have. . . ." Sloan had needed someone to talk to, and with her favorite sister gone she'd kept her secret locked up inside her. Because Cricket had eloped with a man she loved, Sloan felt sure if she spoke the truth, her sister would understand. "No, actually I'm—"

"But you're wrong about marriage agreeing with me," Cricket interrupted. "I'm glad to be out of it."

"Out of it?"

Cricket took a deep breath. "It was never a real marriage, Sloan, not from the very beginning."

"What? You never . . ."

Cricket blushed. "We did that, all right."

"Then you never said the vows?"

"We did that, too."

Sloan sighed, exasperated. "Then, I don't understand what you mean, that it wasn't a real marriage."

"We only got married because . . ." Cricket realized she was headed for shaky ground. If she explained to Sloan why Creed had wanted her away from Three Oaks she would likely end up telling Sloan about the Rangers' planned sneak attack on the rebels. Then she remembered the other reason she'd gone with Creed.

"Did you know Rip had planned a marriage between me and Cruz Guerrero?"

Sloan whistled. "So *that's* why Rip went so crazy when he

got the message from Creed that you'd eloped. The thought of Juan Carlos's empire slipping through his hands must have been awful. So you ran away with Creed to escape the marriage to Cruz Guerrero."

"Yes."

"And you don't love Creed and you want out of your marriage to him."

"I . . ." Cricket couldn't lie to her sister. For as long as she could remember she'd shared everything with Sloan, no matter how personal. There might be raging anger, cutting criticism, or hysterical laughter when the secret was first revealed, but in the end there was always acceptance and love. So she admitted, "I do love Creed. I don't want out of the marriage . . . he does."

Sloan felt the pain of Cricket's admission. "Are you sure?"

Cricket pulled her braid around to chew on the end of it. "About my feelings? Or his?"

"Let's start with yours."

"Can you tell me what love is, Sloan? I'd give a lot to know for sure that what I feel is the real thing."

Sloan hesitated before she answered. "I know what I feel for Tonio. I can share that with you if you think it will help."

The room was silent.

"I'm becoming something of an expert on the subject." Sloan paused and took a deep breath before adding, "I'm going to have Tonio's child."

"Oh, no! That's impossible!"

Sloan grinned. "I assure you it's not impossible."

"I mean, it's terrible." All Cricket could see in her mind's eye was Antonio Guerrero hanging at the end of a rope held by Jarrett Creed.

The grin left Sloan's face, and she replied heatedly, "Not to me. I love Tonio, and I want this baby very much."

Cricket could see her sister had misinterpreted what she'd said. "You don't understand, Sloan," she wailed. She'd practically promised Creed she wouldn't speak of what he'd told her, but if she didn't say something Sloan's baby would be fatherless before it was born. What should she do?

"No, *you* don't understand," Sloan snapped. "You asked me what love is. Well, I'll tell you what it is. It's caring so much about someone else you'd give your life for him. It's putting his happiness before yours, yet finding your own happiness in the pleasure you give to him. It's caring and helping as much as needing and wanting. I love Tonio and he loves me!"

"If he loves you, why aren't you married and living together?"

Sloan paled. "I told you there are reasons. . . ."

"The only reason is he doesn't love you at all! He's just using you to carry messages to his rebel camp!" Cricket slapped her hands over her mouth as soon as she'd made the awful condemnation, but it was too late.

Sloan frowned and slowly shook her head. "Wha—what?"

Cricket lunged off the bed and crossed to the window. What did she know? Maybe Antonio did love her sister. But how could the Spaniard love Sloan and still involve her in his lawless activities?

"What rebel camp are you talking about?" Sloan asked, swinging her feet off the bed to stand at its edge.

Cricket said nothing.

Sloan crossed to Cricket and grabbed her shoulder, forcing her to turn around. "What camp, Cricket? Tell me."

"Antonio leads a band of Mexican revolutionaries, Sloan. He's working with the Mexican government."

"How do you know all this? . . . of course . . . Creed. But you're both wrong. Tonio would never do such a thing."

Cricket's mouth came open to contradict Sloan, but no words came out. It was obvious Sloan had been used terribly by the Spaniard. He hadn't even told her who, and what, he was. Cricket blanched, already enduring the pain she knew Sloan would feel when the cold, hard evidence forced her to accept the fact that the father of her child was a rebel and a traitor.

Sloan was very good at reading Cricket's face. "What else do you know, Cricket? Is Tonio in danger?"

Cricket said nothing.

"He is. He's in danger." Sloan headed for the door. "I have to go to him."

Cricket raced after Sloan. "No, Sloan! Wait! You can't help him now." She caught Sloan by the sleeve of her shirt at the door and wouldn't release her. When the shirt ripped, Sloan turned on Cricket, her eyes wild with fear and threatened by tears.

Cricket had never seen her eldest sister cry, and the thought that Sloan was going to break down any second frightened her. Sloan was invincible.

"Please," Sloan begged. "You have to tell me what you know, Cricket. I have to help Tonio."

Cricket stared helplessly at Sloan. Creed's warning rang in her ears. Sloan was liable to be hurt or killed if she interfered.

Cricket said nothing.

"For me."

It was Sloan she was thinking of when she held her tongue. Cricket said nothing.

"For my baby. My baby needs a father, Cricket. Please."

Cricket thought of Seth. She thought of Amy Creed's unborn baby. She thought of Tom. Men, impulsive, inexplicable creatures that they were, made mistakes. Antonio deserved a chance to explain his actions to Sloan.

"We'll have to hurry," Cricket said. "The Rangers are planning to ambush the rebel camp early tomorrow morning."

CHAPTER 24

I'M GLAD YOU could meet with me earlier than we originally planned, *Capitán* Silvio. I'm sorry *Coronel* Reyes could not come tonight as well," Antonio said without rising from his seat. "Please sit down and join me." He gestured the Mexican officer to the only other chair at the narrow wooden table in the otherwise unfurnished adobe hut. There were large open windows on three sides of the room and the battered door gaped wide, held only by a single leather hinge, but since there was no breeze, the June heat was oppressive. The candle on the table flickered as Antonio fanned himself with the invasion plans he intended to outline for the Mexican captain.

Captain Silvio tested one of the rickety chairs, and then carefully sat down. "The *coronel* ordered me to come see what business you thought so urgent it could not wait until tomorrow morning, Señor Guerrero."

Antonio pursed his lips in disgust. He'd rather have presented his plan directly to the colonel, but the Mexican officer had dismissed Antonio's request for his immediate presence. Antonio didn't bother to hide his irritation from the captain when he spoke. "One of my men, Alejandro Sanchez, intercepted a secret dispatch of *Los Diablos*

Tejanos. The Rangers will be here in force tomorrow morning at dawn. It therefore seemed wiser to have our meeting tonight."

The captain's face darkened ominously. "If you were really wise, Señor Guerrero, you would not have called me here at all. What if *Los Diablos Tejanos* move their plans ahead? We'll be caught here like—"

"Por favor, mi capitán, do not concern yourself. We shall be safe enough for the time being. Alejandro is a good man, and he says the spy in our midst will trouble us no more. By morning you will be long gone with these plans"—Antonio stopped fanning himself long enough to hold up the papers in his hand—"and I will have the extreme pleasure of making fools of *Los Diablos Tejanos."* Antonio caught a movement from the corner of his eye and shouted out the window, "Oscar, bring us something to drink."

"Sí, Señor Guerrero."

Antonio turned his head the other direction and shouted out the front door, "Clemencio, come in here."

Clemencio got only so far as the threshold before shots rang out all around them. The Mexican fell through the doorway face first, a huge hole yawning where the center of his back was supposed to be. At the same time, Alejandro and Oscar came flying in through opposite windows, seeking safety inside the thick adobe walls.

Captain Silvio dove under the table, crossing himself. He'd fought all of his battles on paper, and wasn't prepared for the deafening report of the Rangers' rifles, nor the sight of a man's pink and purple insides spilling out upon the floor. *"Madre de Dios!* We are lost!"

"Idiota!" Antonio swiped the candle off the table, so the room was dark except for what moonlight seeped in through the windows. He shoved a musket across the dirt floor to the uniformed officer. "Start acting like a soldier. Defend yourself."

A strong Tennessee voice shattered the quiet that had descended after the initial barrage of gunfire. "You're surrounded by Texas Rangers. Throw down your weapons and come out with your hands above your heads."

338

"Alejandro, how is this possible?" Antonio hissed to the bandido, who was curled up under a window without any weapon at all. "I thought you killed the Ranger spy."

"So did I," Alejandro muttered. "So did I."

"We are dead men," Oscar wailed. "We must surrender."

"I agree," Captain Silvio said.

"And be hanged?" Antonio said with a sneer. "I prefer to die like a man."

"I would not mind dying like a man," Alejandro barked, "but I do not even have a weapon to defend myself."

"Take the musket from the *capitán,* then. He is apparently not going to use it."

Alejandro crawled across the floor on his belly and retrieved the weapon from the whimpering soldier.

"I do not want to die."

"Shut up, *Capitán* Silvio," Antonio snapped. "I need to think."

An occasional gunshot, followed by a yell or utter silence, gave witness to the fact the Rangers were making short work of the bandidos who'd been waiting outside the adobe house for further orders from Antonio.

"They will kill them all and we will be next," Alejandro said. "We have to give ourselves up." He figured he had a much better chance of escaping alive from a Texan jail than he did from this adobe hut.

"No!" Antonio's skin drew tight across his face. He would never give up. He knew the fate that awaited him if he did—and there was no one who'd fight to keep him from the gallows. Thanks to his brother, Cruz, he couldn't count on the support of his wealthy family to protect him.

Cruz hadn't been satisfied to leave his investigation solely to the *Diablo Tejano,* and had sent his own man to infiltrate the rebel operation. When he'd discovered Antonio was heading the rebel contingent he'd threatened to go to Juan Carlos unless Antonio ceased his revolutionary activities.

Antonio had thought the threat a bluff and so had disregarded it. He'd been galled when his father approached him and demanded he cease "this nonsense." Juan Carlos had threatened to disown him and warned he'd do nothing to help Antonio if the Rangers discovered his involvement with the rebels.

But he'd seen that neither his father nor his brother would go so far as to betray him to the Rangers, and so he'd promised obedience and then thumbed his nose at them— at their weakness—and continued as before, using the Stewart woman as a cover for his activities.

She'd been a gullible bitch, so in love with him that she refused to see how he used her, and now there was the bastard she carried to worry about. He'd cross that bridge when he came to it. First he had to find a way to fight free of the Rangers.

"Los Diablos Tejanos" will show no mercy," Antonio said. "We have no choice except to fight. If we surrender, we will all hang."

"You will hang, Antonio," Alejandro said quietly. "I have done nothing worth hanging for."

Antonio eyed the bandido warily. Alejandro was a survivor. He'd bear close watching. "You will stay right where you are, Alejandro. I am giving the orders here. And I say—"

The sound of galloping horses drew Antonio's attention out the window. The horses drummed to a stop not far from the adobe house and a woman's voice yelled, "Stop shooting! Don't shoot!"

Creed's voice was sharp with fear and anger. "Dammit, is that you, Brava? Get out of the line of fire!"

The India Company Brown Bess musket jerked against Alejandro's shoulder when he pulled the trigger. The sound reverberated in the confines of the small room, making him temporarily deaf. Gunpowder choked his lungs. Smoke kept him from seeing the condition of his victim.

A spate of Ranger gunfire erupted in response to the shot from within the adobe hut.

"Hold your fire!" the Tennessee voice roared. "Hold your fire!"

The captain's shrieks escaped through the open window. *"Madre de Dios!* Murderer! Murderer!"

A slap was heard, and then a man sobbing pitifully, and finally a voice in Spanish, "We wish to surrender. We are throwing our weapons out to you."

Two muskets came out through the open door, followed by three men with their hands above their heads. In the darkness Creed couldn't tell whether Antonio Guerrero was one of them or not.

"Tonio!" Sloan's shrill voice pierced the night air. She broke from Cricket's hold and raced toward the front of the adobe hut.

Creed moved quickly to intercept her and reached the three men about the same time as Sloan and Cricket did.

Sloan quickly searched the three faces—two unshaven ruffians and a soldier in Mexican uniform. She refused to admit Cricket's accusation bore any merit. Tonio couldn't be a spy for the Mexicans. He wouldn't have used her for such purposes. Sloan whirled on Creed. "Where is he? What have you done to him?"

Creed grabbed Sloan's shoulders in an attempt to stem her rising hysteria. "He was inside the hut, but—"

Sloan tried to jerk herself from Creed's arms, but he tightened his hands to keep her from escaping.

"—if he's still in there, Sloan, he's dead." Creed finished.

"Noooooo."

"Take care of these three men," Creed ordered the closest Ranger. "Luke, check and find out whether Guerrero's inside."

Luke disappeared inside the hut for only a moment before he returned to Creed. "He's done for. The plans we've been looking for were next to his body." He eyed the two bandidos who stood with the Mexican officer. "He was shot at close range," he added.

"Creed!" Cricket's warning came barely in time for Creed to catch Sloan as she fainted. He lifted her limp form into his arms and headed toward the horses. "You take care of things here, Luke. I'm going to take Sloan and Cricket home. And Luke . . ." Creed turned back to the young Ranger.

"Yes?"

"Have someone who speaks Spanish take Guerrero's body home to his family. Tell his father I'll come and explain what happened here."

"Be sure to tell his *padre* he was murdered!" Captain Silvio glared at Alejandro, who shifted his gaze casually to Creed.

"He did not wish to surrender," Alejandro said with a shrug. "I merely saved *Los Diablos Tejanos* the trouble of hanging him. I should be thanked."

Creed shook his head, disgusted by the Mexican's traitorous behavior, and by the fact he was unable to deny the truth of his words. By the time Creed reached the horses, Sloan had regained consciousness.

"Put me down."

"You're still a little weak. I—"

"Put me down."

The Ranger answered Sloan's growing agitation by releasing her. When she was steady on her feet he stepped back from her.

"You killed him!" she accused.

Creed removed his hat and ran a hand through his hair. "No, Sloan. He was killed by his own man."

Sloan looked shocked. It was easier to be angry when she had a target upon whom to vent her rage. "Why did you come here in the first place? Tonio wasn't doing anything wrong."

"I don't enjoy being the one to tell you this, Sloan. Antonio Guerrero was a traitor. He worked for and with the Mexican government. He used you to deliver messages to this camp—messages full of information to help Mexico invade Texas." Sloan continued shaking her head in denial as Creed added, "Antonio was surrounded but didn't want to surrender, so his own man shot him and then surrendered himself. I'm sorry."

Sloan's face, pale in the moonlight, got even whiter. She turned to Cricket. "Tonio lied to me, Cricket."

Cricket choked out, "I'm so sorry, Sloan. So sorry." She, of all people, knew what Sloan was feeling now.

"Let me take you home, Sloan," the Ranger said.

"I want to see Tonio," she countered. "I have to see his face once more."

"I've had his body sent home to his family," Creed said, trying to deter Sloan from her goal.

"I'll go there, then."

Creed met Cricket's eyes, asking if she could help convince her sister to change her mind.

"Think of the ba . . . think of your health, Sloan. You need to rest. You don't want to take any chances now."

Sloan's pain-filled eyes met Cricket's. Her determination wavered for a moment, then firmed again. "I want to see him one more time."

"All right, all right," Cricket soothed. "We'll go home and get some sleep tonight and start for the Guerrero hacienda at first light."

Creed opened his mouth to object to Cricket's suggestion but closed it when she frowned at him behind Sloan's back. Maybe Cricket had the right idea. Perhaps when Sloan had time to think the matter over she'd be more reasonable.

However, Sloan was no more reasonable at dawn than she'd been the night before. Cricket refused to let her sister travel alone in her distraught state, so Creed accompanied both women on the long ride to the Guerrero hacienda.

They rode through the hacienda's fortress gates close to the noon hour, but there were none of the preparations underway that suggested the midday meal would be served any time soon.

"It looks deserted," Cricket said, fighting an unaccountable shiver.

Sloan said nothing, simply rode up to the house and dismounted. She left her mount ground-tied and crossed the porch to the front door, knocking loudly upon it. No one answered, so she knocked again, louder this time.

Cricket and Creed had dismounted and joined Sloan by the time a mestizo servant finally opened the door.

"We are not receiving visitors," the old man said. "We are in mourning for the death of the *patrón*'s younger son."

"I want to see Tonio," Sloan said.

From the old man's reaction Sloan might have asked to see the devil. "But *gringa,* you cannot—"

"I want to see Tonio!"

The old man started to close the door and Creed put out a muscular arm to stop him.

"Please tell Señor Guerrero that Jarrett Creed is here to see him." Creed pushed the door the rest of the way open and the three visitors stepped inside the hacienda. It was cool, and dark, and smelled of a priest's incense. The sounds of mourning came to them from the back of the house.

"Please wait here, señor," the servant said.

It was a much-aged Juan Carlos who greeted them, his son Cruz by his side.

"You are not welcome here, *gringo,*" Juan Carlos said.

"Why have you come?" Cruz asked the question of Creed, but his gaze was focused on Sloan, taking in her large, liquid eyes and her somber mouth.

"I want to see Tonio," Sloan said.

"I wished to explain the circumstances of Antonio's death and to offer my condolences," Creed said.

Juan Carlos ignored the young woman and turned to the Ranger. "Neither your explanations nor your condolences can bring back my son." Juan Carlos was suffering greatly over Antonio's death because he blamed himself for not keeping a closer eye on his firebrand son.

"I wanted you to know Antonio wasn't killed by a Ranger," Creed said. "One of his own men killed him because he refused to surrender."

Juan Carlos fought a moan of anguish. Despite what he'd told Antonio, he'd have fought with every weapon he had to keep his son from being hanged by the Rangers. Antonio simply had not known him well enough to understand that. And to be told now that one of Antonio's own men had shot his younger son, to know Antonio had died such a senseless death, was a hard burden to bear.

"I want to see Tonio," Sloan repeated.

Juan Carlos turned to the lovely young woman dressed in planters' clothes who'd spoken. "My wife has asked to be alone with Tonio. I am sorry, but I must refuse your request to see him."

"But I have to see him!"

Juan Carlos was unmoved. "The answer is no."

Denied by the father, Sloan turned her eyes to the son. "Please, if you have any mercy in your soul, help me. I must see Tonio!"

Cruz hated his brother in that instant for the pain he'd brought to the beautiful woman who stood before him. It was obvious she'd loved Tonio. It was more than his deceptive brother deserved. Cruz couldn't bear to see the woman suffer further.

"I will speak to my mother, and see if she will allow you a few moments with Tonio," Cruz said. He had no business feeling so much emotion at the relief in the woman's eyes. Those huge, sad brown eyes. He'd been lost since the first moment he'd looked into them at the *fandango* celebration. He shook his head to break the spell. She'd been his brother's woman. His brother's *puta!* Cruz rejected the label *whore* as soon as he'd given it to the young woman. Should she be condemned because she'd loved the wrong man? No more so than a man who lusted after the wrong woman, he thought bitterly. He'd make sure Sloan Stewart said her last goodbyes to Tonio, and then stayed far, far away from the Guerrero hacienda.

Juan Carlos left with Cruz, and the voices of the mother and the son raised in argument could be heard from the back of the house. Moments later, Cruz returned, his face flushed, his eyes sparking with anger. "Come with me," he ordered Sloan. When Cricket and Creed started to follow he said, "She must come alone."

Cricket started to protest, but Creed silenced her. "We'll wait here."

"We will not be long," Cruz promised.

His hand rested lightly on Sloan's elbow, directing her to the room at the rear of the house where Tonio's body had been laid out in his finest clothing. The darkened salon was filled with candles and the smell of incense was suffocating.

Lucia Esmeralda Sandoval de Guerrero stood regally

beside her younger son's body. Her eyes were red-rimmed and she clutched a wrinkled handkerchief in her hand, but otherwise she showed no outward signs of her loss. She didn't acknowledge Sloan's presence.

Sloan looked down upon the young man who'd been her lover and who was the sire of her child. His face retained much of the beauty it had possessed in life. She reached out a hand to touch his cheek. It was cold, the skin clammy to the touch. She bent down and kissed his lips, but none of the warmth of life remained. She shuddered as she conceded the finality of his death and the magnitude of the deception for which he could never be brought to task. She'd loved this man beyond her own life, and he'd used her as a messenger for his rebel games.

Cruz watched amazed as the various emotions traveled the sharp angles of the young woman's face. Sorrow was there, and love also—which he coveted to his everlasting shame. But there was something else as well which he struggled to identify.

How great had Tonio's deceit been? Had the woman known how little he really cared for her? Cruz thought perhaps the knowledge of his brother's dishonesty had only just come to her, for at last he recognized in her expression the disillusionment of one who has finally accepted an unpleasant truth. Her face hardened with anger—untapped rage which pared away her fresh youthfulness and replaced it with ragged lines of bitter experience.

Sloan discovered she could shed no tears. She felt certain if she could only cry, the huge knot in her breast would go away, but the tears didn't come, and she didn't force them. She was afraid they might wash away the hate that was all she could feel now, and which was all that kept her from falling apart in the wake of Tonio's betrayal. She turned to Tonio's mother and cleared her throat to speak.

"In the winter I will have Tonio's child."

Cruz saw the flicker of satisfaction in his mother's eyes, followed by a gleam of anticipation.

"Were you secretly married to my son?" Lucia asked.

Sloan's chin quivered. Cruz agonized with her for the

answer he knew she must make. It came out on a bare breath of air. "No."

"Ah." There was a wealth of condemnation in the word. "Do you wish me to take the bastard child off your hands, Señorita Stewart?"

Cruz watched Sloan waver in indecision before she turned without speaking further and left the room.

"So, Mamá," Cruz said softly. "You have not completely lost your favorite. His son or daughter lives." Cruz felt a tightening in his gut. His brother had kept his hold on the brown-eyed woman even beyond death. He swore under his breath and left the room.

When Cruz arrived once more at the front of the house, only Creed remained.

"I wanted to thank you for what you did for Sloan," Creed said.

"Tonio used her badly," Cruz replied, then regretted his flare of honesty with the Ranger who was at least partly responsible for his brother's death. As long as he'd gone so far, however, he went a step farther. "You will take care of her?"

Creed masked his surprise at the Spaniard's outspoken concern for Sloan. "Of course. As much as she'll let me do, I'll do."

Cruz smiled ruefully. "It is true, then, what they say about the Stewart women?"

Creed returned an equally rueful smile. "In spades."

"Then I extend both my congratulations and my condolences on your marriage to Creighton Stewart."

"Thank you. I accept them both."

The two men shook hands, but by then the smiles had disappeared.

"*Adios, señor.* I hope when next we meet it is under more pleasant circumstances."

"Don't worry about Sloan," Creed said with more understanding than Cruz could willingly accept. "I'll make sure she's taken care of."

"Of course I am concerned for her," he replied stiffly. "She was my brother's woman."

Creed cocked his head at the remark that suggested there was nothing personal behind Cruz's request, but he didn't probe where the wound was still so obviously raw. All he said was, "Of course."

Creed joined the two women on horseback, and they promptly left the confines of the eerily silent adobe fortress. Sloan brooded the whole distance to Three Oaks, but neither Cricket nor Creed noticed, because they were each too busy pondering their own disastrous love life.

Cricket was trying to work up the courage to ask Creed to take her with him when he left Three Oaks.

Creed was busy thinking of reasons why he never needed to leave.

It was on both their minds that the time was not far off when they'd have to either speak their minds and resolve their differences—or lose each other.

Rip was waiting for them when they got back.

"Come into my office this minute, Sloan," he snapped. "I've spent the past hour trying to explain to Beaufort LeFevre how my daughter, *my daughter,* was the innocent dupe of a ring of Mexican revolutionaries. And I didn't like it one bit!"

"Nobody asked you to apologize for my actions," Sloan replied. "And I'm certainly not going to apologize for what I've done, either." Instead of going through the open door to Rip's office, Sloan turned and headed for the stairs instead. She hadn't gotten beyond the first step before Rip grabbed her arm and spun her around.

"Don't walk away from me when I'm speaking to you."

Rip's thundering voice brought Bay and Angelique to the head of the stairs, and the American chargé to the door of the parlor. Cricket and Creed stood uncertainly in the hall near the front door as Rip began unbuckling his belt.

Sloan didn't move.

Cricket feared for her sister. It had been years since Rip had taken a belt to Sloan. Cricket vividly remembered that last momentous occasion. Sloan had defied Rip over some minor incident and he'd pulled off his belt in much the same manner as he had today. But Sloan had remained unmoved by Rip's show of force, standing stoically silent under the strap. It had seemed almost a test as he waited for her to break, to cry like a woman, to admit she was wrong and beg him to stop. But Sloan was as stubborn as her sire. She hadn't broken, and finally Rip had given up.

Sloan's bruises had remained for weeks . . . but from that day Rip had treated his eldest daughter as an equal. He'd never again tried to intimidate her into doing his bidding. A new, very special respect had grown between them that Cricket had envied.

That's why this sudden threat of force was so frightening. Cricket knew that Sloan wouldn't beg for mercy . . . and that Rip wouldn't offer it. If it had only been the two of them she might have let them fight it out. But now there was the baby to consider. If Sloan wouldn't think of herself *and* the child, then Cricket would have to do it for her.

Aware of Rip's growing audience, Creed relaxed slightly, certain the man wouldn't dare discipline his daughter under the circumstances. When he saw Rip fold his belt in half and grasp the leather firmly in his hand, he realized he was wrong.

"Are you defying me, Sloan?"

Beaufort LeFevre couldn't believe Rip Stewart actually intended to beat his lovely daughter with the thick leather belt in his hand. In all his tactful life he'd never interfered where he didn't belong. But Beaufort found his old rules didn't work very well in Texas, and he was nothing if not adaptable, so he spoke up.

"Rip, surely there must be—"

"Keep your nose where it belongs, Beaufort."

"LeFevre is right, Rip," Creed said from behind the big man. "There are other ways to handle this."

Rip turned on Creed and the two men faced off like wolves fighting for leadership of the pack. The hair bristled on their necks, their muscles tensed for action, and their teeth bared in grimaces of determination.

Cricket was so close to Creed she could feel the killing instinct rise in him. She knew Rip blamed the Ranger for ruining his plans to marry her off to Cruz Guerrero, and this argument with Sloan was as good an excuse as any for the two men to come to blows. But she had no intention of watching the two men she loved most in the world do their best to kill each other bare-handed.

"Give me one good reason why I shouldn't beat Sloan for her disobedience," Rip demanded of Creed.

Creed opened his mouth to reply, but before he could speak Cricket blurted, "Because she's pregnant!"

Five stunned faces focused on Sloan, who flushed a deep, dark red.

"Holy Mary, Mother of God," Rip said. "Is that true, Sloan?"

Sloan nodded.

"And who is the father of this miraculous child?" he demanded.

Sloan lifted her chin. "Antonio Guerrero."

Stunned, Rip exclaimed, "He's dead!"

"Yes, he is." Sloan kept her head high, although her eyes were feverishly bright.

"Yes. He is, isn't he," Rip repeated. His eyes narrowed thoughtfully, and then he snapped his belt against his thigh with excitement. "By God, I've got Juan Carlos by the balls this time. You'll marry the other son. You'll marry Cruz and legitimize this Guerrero bastard!"

Sloan flew back down the stairs and stood toe to toe with Rip, belt and all, her hands balled into fists at her still-narrow waist, her brown eyes flashing.

"By God, I'll do no such thing! If you even suggest such a marriage to the Guerreros I'll disappear and you'll lose your firstborn heir to Three Oaks. Do I make myself clear!"

Sloan didn't budge an inch until Rip cleared his throat and said, "It was only a thought."

"Think again!"

"I'll enjoy having a grandson," Rip said more quietly.

"Or a granddaughter," Sloan snapped back.

Rip placed his hands firmly on Sloan's shoulders, lest his touch be misconstrued as the caress he wouldn't, or couldn't give. "Yes. Most certainly a granddaughter like you."

The onlookers relaxed visibly at the tentative peace that had come so suddenly between the two combatants.

"Whew! If this incident is any sample of Texan fighting spirit I wonder that you haven't thought of moving the Republic's borders east, as well as north, south, and west," LeFevre remarked.

Rip turned to the chargé with a grin. "Come have a drink and a cigar with me, Beaufort. I'm going to be a grandfather." Rip was still trying to make up his mind whether to include Creed in the invitation when they heard several loud shrieks outside.

"What's that?" Beaufort asked with a laugh. "More Texans having an argument?"

"Hell, no!" Rip replied, racing for the rifle over the mantel. "That's a goddamned Comanche war cry!"

CHAPTER 25

"THE HOUSE IS ON FIRE!" Bay shouted when she saw thick smoke cascading in white waves from one of the upstairs bedroom doors.

A flaming arrow came in through the parlor window and Beaufort LeFevre raced over to yank it from the opposite wall and stomp it out. That arrow was quickly followed by four more, one of which almost hit the chargé. From the side windows they could see the barn was already engulfed in flames. The Comanches circled the house on horseback, dodging, feinting, rarely giving enough of a target to shoot at.

Creed did a quick check and discovered not only were the roof shingles on fire, but several places on the outside of the house had begun to burn as well. "We're going to have to leave the house," he said tersely to Rip. "Soon."

"Leave the house?" Angelique cried, her dress billowing as she raced down the stairs. "Those savages will kill us if we go out there!"

"The fire will do their job for them if we don't get out of here!" Cricket barked from Creed's side.

Rip's eyes narrowed. He'd planned for this. There was a secret underground passageway from the root cellar of the house to a spot not far from the river. Some of them would have to stay in the house to keep the Comanches distracted while the rest escaped by that route.

"Is there anyone else in the house besides us?" Rip asked.

"There was no one upstairs besides myself and Angelique," Bay supplied.

Sloan had efficiently searched the downstairs and come up with several more weapons and ammunition, which she passed out among those present. "I didn't find anyone," she said. "The house slaves must have been outside in the kitchen when the attack started."

"I can't use this," Angelique protested when Sloan handed her a Patterson.

"You don't know how?" Sloan questioned.

"I can shoot a dueling pistol, but this—"

"Take it," Sloan said curtly. "All you have to do is cock it and pull the trigger five times. If the Comanches get too close, you may decide you have a use for it."

"What can I do to help?" LeFevre asked Rip.

"There's an underground passage from the house to the river. You'll be safe there. My daughters will show you and Angelique the way. When you get to the river, stay hidden until the danger is past."

"What about you?" LeFevre asked.

Rip turned to Creed. "The Ranger and I will stay here and keep the Comanches entertained." Creed nodded his acceptance of Rip's command.

"I'm staying, too," Sloan said.

Rip looked at her, then nodded.

"Bay and I will make sure the chargé and his daughter are safe. Take care of yourselves," Cricket said to all those who would remain.

She stopped before Creed. She might never have another chance to tell him what she felt. One of them, or both, might be killed. Cricket sought desperately to stop time in the middle of the Comanche attack. Forgetting the whoops and shrieks of the Comanches, Angelique's whimpers of fear, the chargé's words of comfort, Rip's crisp orders, and her sisters' efficient obedience to them, she put her hands lightly on Creed's arms, looked up into his face, and spoke three parting words.

"I love you."

Creed pulled his wife into his embrace, crushing her with his strength. He twined her braid around his hand and arched her head back so he could look into her eyes. He spoke for her ears alone. "I've been waiting to hear those words for a long time, Brava."

"But Angelique—"

"What's Angelique got to do with us?"

"But you love—"

"I love you. You're my wife. I want you with me always." He gave her a hard kiss and then released her. "Except I think maybe you'd better leave me for a little while right now," he said wryly. "We'll talk when this is all over. Get going."

Cricket watched him over her shoulder, stunned by what she'd just learned. She followed the others to the root cellar. Creed loved her! Now all she could do was pray they both managed to survive long enough to live happily ever after.

Tall Bear had planned his moment of revenge carefully. His braves had set fire to the house, knowing the White-eyes would be forced to flee. The wonderful thing was Tall Bear knew where their escape route would end. For during his forays to scout this attack he'd discovered the opening in the ground near the river. He intended to be waiting when the Woman of the Wolf emerged.

As Tall Bear watched from his hiding place his quarry appeared, followed by another woman with hair the color of the sun, and an older man—Tall Bear imagined the full head of white hair hanging from his war shield—and then a woman with hair so bright a red he smiled at the thought of her value in trade. He wanted the Woman of the Wolf alive. As for the other women, if he could take them captive, he would, but it didn't really matter to him.

He waited for more White-eyes to appear, but when none

did he concluded they must have stayed longer in the burning house. That was good. His braves would keep them occupied as he'd instructed. Tall Bear frowned when he saw that all four of those who'd emerged from the tunnel carried weapons. He decided he would kill the man first. Once he had the Woman of the Wolf in his arms he would do as he'd done once before, and threaten the life of his captive if the other women did not throw down their guns.

Tall Bear kicked his pony into a full gallop. As he intended, his war shriek and the arrow striking the old man in the chest distracted the three women long enough for him to sweep the Woman of the Wolf into his arms.

Cricket knew who'd captured her, knew her fate if he took her alive. She would have shot herself if she could have gotten her gun up in time, but Tall Bear had anticipated her move and the blunt edge of his battle-ax came down hard on her gun hand and stunned her so she lost the Patterson.

"Bay!" Cricket shouted. "Shoot! Shoot!"

Bay's face whitened. "I can't! I'll hit you, Cricket!"

"Shoot!"

The Comanche tapped Cricket's temple with the heavy wooden handle of his battle-ax, knocking her unconscious. He danced his pony around the two women, taunting them, showing his disdain, all the while using Cricket as a shield and making plain his intention to kill her if the two women didn't put down their weapons.

Both women were protected from the Comanche's arrows behind a rotting cypress log near the exit from the tunnel. Angelique lay prostrate over her father's form, but her gun was still in her hand. Bay grabbed her by the shoulders of her bloodied silk dress and shook her. "Angelique! Are you a good shot? Can you kill that Comanche without hurting Cricket?"

Angelique roused from her stupor and focused on the Comanche who'd killed her father. "You want me to shoot him?"

"Yes!" Bay swallowed hard. "If you can't hit him, then you have to kill Cricket." Bay was certain it was only a matter of time before more Comanches arrived to help this one. She prayed she wouldn't have to shoot Cricket herself. But she'd see to it that what had to be done was done.

Angelique looked from Bay to Cricket, and as the situation became clear, she began to laugh hysterically. "If you only knew . . . how much I wanted . . . to be rid . . . but now I don't . . . have to do . . . anything. . . ."

Tall Bear frowned at the hysterically laughing yellow-haired woman. Perhaps she'd been touched by the spirits. That was bad medicine. He would leave the Laughing Woman behind, but the other woman, the red-headed one, was valuable, and he was determined to have her if he could manage it.

Bay was a quivery mass of jelly inside, but for Cricket she had to be strong. She wasn't a good shot, and she knew it. She still didn't know whether the hysterical Angelique could be any help, but she had to find out. Bay slapped Angelique as hard as she could, cutting off the insane laughter as quickly as it had begun. Angelique's eyes widened in disbelief as her hand flew to her smarting cheek.

"I'm sorry I had to do that," Bay said. Before she lost her courage she added, "I'm a fair shot, Angelique, but if you're better than that I expect you to use your gun on that Comanche." The hateful look on Angelique's face made Bay edge back slightly but she stubbornly persisted, "Do you understand what I'm saying?"

"I understand. You want me to shoot at the Comanche who's holding Cricket. If I can't kill him, I'm to kill her."

Bay closed her eyes and nodded quickly.

"All right." Angelique got up on her knees and laid the barrel of her gun on the log to steady it, squinting at her target.

Angelique had her gun aimed at Cricket's heart when she heard a low, menacing growl that made the hairs on her neck stand on end. Angelique's eyes sought the source of the sound, focusing in horror on a large wolf, fangs viciously bared, crouched not ten feet from her, ready to spring. Without a second's thought she turned the gun on the beast.

"No! Angelique!"

Angelique fired as Rogue leapt at her. The wounded wolf went for the woman's unprotected throat. Angelique threw up an arm, and Rogue sank his fangs into the tender flesh as he bowled her over.

Angelique screamed and kept on screaming.

There was no time for Bay to try to halt the wolf's ferocious attack, and there was only one way she could think to end it quickly enough to avoid Angelique's death. She didn't allow herself to consider she might miss. She simply aimed and fired.

Bay shot Rogue twice before the wolf released its grisly hold on the chargé's daughter. As soon as Rogue fell, Bay threw her gun aside and rushed to render aid to Angelique. The woman was in shock, her flesh torn open, her forearm crushed by the wolf's powerful jaws. Her face bled where Rogue's teeth had raked it.

At almost the same moment Rogue had attacked, Rascal and Ruffian had appeared on either side of Tall Bear, frightening his pony so it reared. The appearance of three of Wolf's namesakes was too much for the superstitious Comanche, who dumped his burden unceremoniously in the path of the two fierce wolves who chased his nervous pony. To have Wolf find his woman torn to pieces by the beasts would be revenge enough for him. He'd done what he came to do, and it was time to leave.

Tall Bear didn't plan to leave empty-handed. He kicked his pony away from the wolves and converged on the red-headed woman who crouched behind the cypress log. He grabbed a handful of her long hair and yanked her away from the Laughing Woman. As soon as she was in the open he grabbed her arm and pulled her across his pony's withers on her stomach. He had no time to waste on the red-headed woman's struggles, so he used his battle-ax again and silenced her.

He knew the Laughing Woman's screams and the gunfire must have alerted those in the house that all was not well. He turned and saw that the two wolves growled and slavered over the body of the Woman of the Wolf. It was done. Tall Bear turned his pony and galloped away to collect his band and make good their escape.

When Creed heard the female screams followed by distant gunfire he yelled at Rip, "They're in trouble! Let's get out of here!"

Rip led the way through the tunnel. When they emerged at the river they half expected to find the Comanches waiting for them, but it was ominously quiet. Around them lay the bloodied bodies of Angelique and Beaufort LeFevre, the dead wolf, and not far away, Cricket, with Rascal and Ruffian standing sentinel over her inert body. Though they searched and shouted out her name, Bay was nowhere to be found.

Rip reached Cricket's body before Creed, and gathered her into his arms. "She's alive."

"I'll take her."

Rip made note of Creed's fighting stance, his feral glare, but refused to relinquish his burden.

"She's my daughter."

"She's my wife."

Rip still made no move to surrender his favorite daughter to her husband. The muscles bunched in Creed's jaw as he fought to control his temper. Then Cricket spoke.

"I want to go to Creed."

Startled, Rip looked down at Cricket. She could barely keep her eyes open, but she met Rip's inquiring gaze with determination. Her face was pale except where bright red blood streamed from her temple. Her eyes drifted closed again but she repeated in a whisper, "I want Creed."

Rip had raised Cricket to be totally self-sufficient, yet to look to him for advice and succor. He'd somehow never expected her to seek solace from another man. It was painful to accept the fact she'd transferred to Jarrett Creed the trust that had previously been given only to him. However, because he'd raised her to know her own mind, he accepted her decision.

Creed held out his arms and Rip gently eased Cricket into

them. For a moment both men held her together. Their eyes met and a silent understanding passed between them. She belonged to both of them—and to neither of them. Cricket was what she was—a frontier woman, fiery-tempered and bold, demanding all that the vast new Republic had to offer her—and both of them would do everything in their power to see that she got it.

Once the exchange had been made, Creed held Cricket close. He brought her face up and pressed his cheek to hers, feeling the rightness of it. He smelled the familiar fragrance of her hair. He held the weight of her in his arms and swore she'd never be far from him again.

Rip watched the tender way Creed held Cricket, certain the Ranger would now be stepping into his shoes and taking care of her, until he heard Cricket speak.

"You can put me down now. I can stand on my own two feet."

To Rip's surprise, Creed smiled ruefully, then complied. "Sure, Brava . . . your own two feet."

But Rip noticed Creed slipped an arm around Cricket's shoulders to support her and she accepted his assistance.

"They're both still alive!"

Sloan's exclamation brought them all on the run to see to the two injured visitors. Rip bent down on one knee next to Sloan as she explained what she'd discovered.

"LeFevre is barely alive, but if we could stop the bleeding he might make it," she said. "Angelique's injuries are not as serious, but she's also losing a lot of blood."

The shadow of a man appeared so suddenly at Rip's shoulder that Sloan almost shot him. "Luke! What are you doing here?"

"I was out riding and saw the smoke. I came running, but by the time I got back here the Comanches were long gone—and so were you."

Luke fought to hide his trembling relief at finding them all alive, which would have seemed extraordinary under the circumstances. He'd been worrying for days over whether to tell Rip Stewart who he really was, and during the short ride from the house to this hidden passage he'd had time to work up a pretty good fear that he'd be too late, that Rip would be dead and he'd never have the chance to say, *"I'm your son."* But the old man had survived. He should have known. Now he could sit on his secret until the time was right for his revelation . . . if it ever was.

He turned to Rip and said in a perfectly normal tone of voice, "I'm glad to see you're all okay. I found one of your Negroes at the house, a man named August, who told me you'd be here if you were alive."

"Is anyone else hurt?" Rip asked.

"One field hand is dead, and a few are wounded. Your house is burnt to the ground, and so's the barn, but the bachelors' quarters are still standing."

"What about the gin?" Sloan asked.

"It's still there as far as I know."

Sloan breathed a sigh of relief. It was mere weeks before the field slaves would begin picking cotton—not time enough to build a new gin.

"We'll live in the bachelors' quarters until I can get another house built," Rip said. The big man picked up the chargé and cradled him gently in his arms as though he were a child. "We'd better get these two taken care of. I'll carry Beaufort. You take his daughter, Luke."

Luke looked down at Angelique's mangled arm and the bloody grooves that would leave thin scars on her cheeks. *Don't worry, Angel, honey,* he thought. *I'll make sure you know you're still a beautiful woman, marks or no.*

"What about Bay?" Sloan asked, voicing the subject everyone had been so carefully avoiding.

At the sound of Bay's name Cricket roused and she searched the faces around her to find her sister. "Bay? Isn't she here?"

"Shh. Don't fret, Brava. We'll find her," Creed soothed.

Cricket only got more frantic. "If she's not here then Tall Bear has her! We have to rescue her. Creed, you can't let him do to her what he did to Amy. . . ."

Rip had keyed on one aspect of Cricket's ranting. "You *know* the Indian who kidnapped Bay?" he asked Creed in a voice that was more dangerous for its calmness.

"I know him. We go back a long way. I'll find your daughter and settle with Tall Bear as soon as I'm sure Cricket's okay." As Creed turned away toward the guest house, Cricket suddenly saw the body of her wolf.

"Rogue!" Cricket knelt by the wolf's bullet-torn body. His open eyes were glazed, and his pink tongue lay in the dirt. She slowly leaned down to listen to his great heart . . . but it had stopped. She rested her cheek against his shoulder. It was so soft. She thought of all the times she'd fallen asleep with his warm body beneath her head . . . of all the times he'd played with her . . . of all the times they'd howled out their anger against a cruel world together.

Cricket choked back a sob. She should have returned him to the wild a long time ago. Rip had warned her something like this might happen. He'd told her she had no business trying to cage a wolf with love. But she'd ignored him. Now Rogue was dead. She could feel the pain swelling in her chest, and her throat had that awful constricted feeling . . . almost like being hanged by God's hand.

Creed knelt beside her. "Come away, Brava. You can't help him now."

"It's my fault," she whispered. "Rip warned me I couldn't tame a wild animal. But I wouldn't listen. I never thought . . . I was sure I . . ."

Creed brushed the tears from Cricket's cheeks with his thumbs.

"It looks like he attacked Angelique and Bay shot him," Sloan said. She kept her gun out and ready, despite Luke's assurances the Indians were long gone.

"But why? Why would he attack Angelique?" Cricket choked out.

Creed put a consoling hand on Cricket's shoulder. "We'll have to ask her that."

As Creed and Cricket stood, she turned her face into his shirt, and his arms enfolded her. She leaned against him and found his strength, and the particular smell she identified with him, comforting. She wanted to hear Angelique's explanation of Rogue's attack. Perhaps the wolf's death had not been in vain. Even so, she vowed to return Rascal and

Ruffian to the wilds of *Comanchería* when she and Creed went in search of Bay.

The sight of the charred and blackened ruins of the house sobered them all. It was hard to carve a human niche in the Texas wilderness. Now it looked as though the house had never been there. Only the three giant oaks remained, scarred in places by the fire. But defeat was not a word in the pioneers' vocabulary. They would rebuild, reclaiming the land. They had learned enough about the vagaries of frontier life to be grateful none of them would be planted under the rich Texas soil.

The tiny bachelors' quarters away from the main house had only one bed, and Rip and Luke put both the chargé and his daughter on it. Cricket had revived enough to argue with Creed that she was fine in the ladderback chair in the corner of the room. He took the cloth and water offered to him by one of the Negroes who'd come to help and cleaned her wound himself. He felt better when he saw the cut on her temple was small.

"How does it feel?"

"I have a slight headache, but I'm not dizzy at all."

"That's good," Creed said. "Sit and rest for a while." When she started to object Creed added, "It'll make *me* feel better."

Angelique's moan of pain brought everyone, including Cricket, to her bedside. "Take it easy. You're okay, Angel, honey," Luke said, taking her good hand in his. "Angel, can you tell us what happened to Bay?" Luke asked.

Angelique moaned again. "My arm. My arm."

"Your arm's going to be fine, Angel, honey."

"I hate this godforsaken land! I want to go home!"

"Sure honey, soon as you're well I'll take you home. Right now can you tell us about Bay?"

Angelique opened her eyes to an audience that included practically the entire Stewart family—including Cricket. "What are you doing here?" she asked, stunned. "The Comanche had you on his horse . . . you weren't going to be any more competition for me. . . ." Angelique stopped and glanced guiltily at Creed. "Not that I'd stay in this awful land full of savages for *anyone* now, let—"

Luke interrupted her, bringing her back to the subject at hand. "Angel, honey, tell us what happened."

"Bay said I should shoot the Indian, or if I couldn't kill him . . . then I should shoot Cricket. And I would have—in fact I already had my gun aimed—"

"Except the wolf attacked you," Sloan finished.

"Yes, so I shot the wolf instead."

Creed shuddered at how close he'd come to losing his wife.

"But I only wounded it," she continued. "I guess Bay must have killed it, because there were two shots and I don't remember anything after that."

Cricket closed her eyes and swallowed over the huge lump in her throat. Rogue had given his life to save her.

"We have a few more pieces to the puzzle," Luke said. "I guess it's pretty clear Tall Bear must have taken Bay with him. Who's going after him?"

"Tall Bear is my problem," Creed announced.

"And Bay is mine," Rip countered.

"You need to be here to mend diplomatic fences when the chargé recovers," Creed pointed out. "Besides, I know this Indian. I know how he thinks. I'll have a better chance of catching him than you will."

"I want Bay back," Rip said. "I don't care what she's been through. I want her back."

"If she can be found, I'll find her," Creed vowed. "And I'll make sure Tall Bear never troubles you again." He turned to Cricket. "Are you ready to go?"

"She's in no shape to travel," Rip said sternly. "She'll be here when you get back."

"Brava?"

Creed had left the choice up to her. She could go with her husband or stay with her father. The choice had already been made. Cricket turned to Rip. "I'm going with him. Don't try to stop me, because it won't do any good."

Rip sighed. He had to get used to the idea of Cricket

choosing the Ranger over him. It wasn't a comfortable feeling, but he figured he'd better start learning to live with it. "What're you waiting for? Hurry up before you lose the light."

Cricket threw her arms around Rip's neck and hugged him tight. "I love you," she whispered in his ear. "I'll find Bay. I promise."

Rip gently pushed her away. "Just take care of yourself."

Creed grasped the hand Cricket held out to him and tugged her along behind him out the door of the tiny bachelors' quarters. As soon as they were out of sight of those inside he brought her into his arms and claimed her mouth in a devastating kiss.

"What was that for?" Cricket asked breathlessly when he finally released her.

"For being you. For not being like any other woman I've ever known." He claimed her mouth again before he said, "You know what's ahead of us?"

"I do."

"We'd better go, then," he rasped. "Before I decide I can't wait any longer to have what's finally, truly mine."

CHAPTER 26

CRICKET WIPED THE sweat from her brow with her sleeve and felt the fatigue in the muscles of her arm when she did. It was hot, and getting hotter. Cricket had always loved the endless, clear blue Texas skies. Now she wished for a cloud or two to block the scorching rays of the sun. She was so tired it took all her effort to stay in the saddle. They'd crossed the borders of Lion's Dare a day past, but hadn't even considered stopping. The memory of Tall Bear's cruelty to Amy had brought tears to Cricket's eyes, but they hadn't fallen. She didn't allow herself to waste the energy. She needed all she had to keep the pace Creed had set. She knew as well as he that until the Comanches were certain there was no further pursuit, Bay was safe. It was up to her and Creed to keep the Indians moving until they caught up with them and rescued her sister.

It was different, Cricket had discovered, to be a hunter of men. An animal might use stealth to elude a pursuer, but it paled beside the cunning the Comanches had exhibited, keeping them in constant jeopardy of losing the trail. She and Creed had started out no more than an hour behind the Indians. Yet the Comanches had covered their tracks in ways Cricket hadn't been aware of when she'd been a captive. Several times they'd had to double back to find them. Even now, the hilly terrain showed no sign of their quarry. But they knew the Indians were headed north toward *Comanchería,* and even if they couldn't see the hoofprint or crushed grass or overturned rock that told them which direction to go, they doggedly continued riding, knowing that sooner or later they would.

And then there was the worry. Having been Tall Bear's captive herself, Cricket didn't need to use her imagination to know what Bay must be suffering. She need only search her memory to discover the terror of helplessness she'd felt when anticipating her fate, and Bay wasn't used to the hard riding or other tribulations that were sure to be visited upon her. It was ironic that the most gentle of the sisters should be the one the Comanches had kidnapped this time.

"Aw, hell!"

Cricket yanked her mount to a stop to keep from running into Creed's horse. "What's the matter?"

Creed stepped down from the saddle and paced ahead a few steps. He walked in a semicircle ahead of them before returning to his mount. "They're splitting up."

Cricket's heart began to beat faster. "So? We'll follow . . ." Cricket frowned.

"Ah, you do see the problem. There's only one shod horse in the bunch, but is Bay riding it? If she were a smaller woman it would be easier to tell. I don't know, Brava. Tall Bear is clever. He might put a Comanche on that shod horse thinking we'll be sure to follow it . . . and when we do we lose Bay."

"Do you know which of the ponies Tall Bear is riding?"

"Yes, I recognize it from the last time I tracked you. The right front hoof has a crack in it. See?" Creed showed her the tiny triangular mark in the dirt at the corner of one of the hoofprints.

Cricket walked her horse forward to check the prints around it. "The shod horse is going the same direction as Tall Bear."

"Yes, it is."

"I think we should keep following Tall Bear."

Creed walked over to stand at Cricket's knee. He took her hand in his and looked up into her bleak eyes. "It could be a trick, Brava. He could have sent Bay off on one of the Indian ponies."

"If she's not with him, then at least we'll know he won't be alive to torment her." Cricket knew Tall Bear was a dead man if—when Creed caught up with him. She refused to think of the end of their quest in less than positive terms.

Creed left her side to remount his horse. "Let's go."

Cricket didn't bother to ask if they could rest. The Comanches wouldn't rest, so neither could they. From what she could see there were two riders with Tall Bear, one of them on the shod horse and one on an Indian pony. The Indians traveled single file, with Tall Bear in front and the shod horse in the middle, giving further credence to the guess it was Bay who rode the animal.

The grueling march continued through the heat of the day. It wasn't enough that they simply keep pace with the Comanches; Creed pushed even harder so they could catch up to them. The farther into *Comanchería* they rode, the more dangerous it became. For now they might very well become the hunted themselves.

Creed felt restless. Uneasy. It was dusk—not his favorite time of the day because there were too many shadows. His eyes searched the horizon, then dropped to the ground ahead. The dirt was packed hard, leaving very little trail to follow, but there was no sign at all of the shod horse. Why hadn't he noticed it sooner? Why was only the shod horse missing? Tall Bear wouldn't have sent Bay off by herself, and Creed hadn't seen evidence that anyone had met them and taken her away—which wasn't to say that it hadn't happened. He hadn't been watching for a rendezvous. The signs might still be there if he backtracked to find them, but then they'd be even further behind Tall Bear—and Creed was sure they were so close. . . .

Creed checked over his shoulder and discovered Cricket asleep in the saddle. Lord knew they both needed the rest. He wasn't sorry he'd brought her along. She hadn't held him up, and had been a help in fact, sharing the burden of tracking. And when they found Bay she was likely to need her sister's support.

The tingle at the base of his neck warned Creed someone was nearby. His muscles tensed, but he gave no indication he was aware of the intruder. "Wake up, Brava."

The words were calm and quiet, but they brought Cricket instantly awake. "What's wrong?" she asked, equally calm but alert.

"I'm not sure. I think there's someone following us. The shod horse dropped out of the pack a ways back. Maybe Tall Bear's planned an ambush. Be ready to run."

The next few minutes were tense ones. Cricket listened for any sounds that might reveal the presence of another human being, but there were none.

"Hu! Haints!

Cricket watched Creed stiffen at the first Comanche cry, and relax completely at the second. Then she saw why. Long Quiet stepped out from between two hills onto the trail in front of them, the reins of his pony in his hand.

"Well, *friend,*" Creed said with a chuckle of relief, "you certainly gave me a few bad moments back there. What are you doing here?"

"I met Buffalo Waters, one of the braves who rode in the raid led by Tall Bear. He said Tall Bear had stolen a girl with violet eyes and hair the color of copper from the home of the Woman of the Wolf. I came to see whether he might want to trade for her."

Creed eyed his friend askance. Long Quiet wasn't telling him everything. The Indian had long since adopted the Comanche way of life as his own, and his choice was clear in any conflict between the white man and the red. Creed was confused by Long Quiet's words. What, exactly, did Long Quiet intend to do with the girl if Tall Bear agreed to the trade?

"What's your interest in Bayleigh Stewart?"

In his mind's eye, Long Quiet saw the flash of violet eyes, the demure smile, the shy blush of a tall young maiden at her first cotillion, where the gentlemen were all older men from a nearby school in Boston. He answered only, "I thought only to do my brother a kindness. Have you no need of me?"

Cricket slanted Creed an annoyed grimace. Why was he questioning Long Quiet? They could use all the help they could get to find Bay, and Long Quiet didn't look anywhere near as exhausted as Cricket felt. "Of course we'd welcome your help."

"I'll ride ahead and see if Tall Bear is willing to make a trade for Bay. That will be easier than trying to fight him for her," Long Quiet said.

"I'm not sure she's still with him," Creed replied.

Long Quiet waited for Creed to elaborate.

"Tall Bear's band split up some time this morning. We've been following three horses, or at least we were until about a half-hour ago. One of the horses, the one we thought Bay might be riding, isn't with Tall Bear anymore."

Creed saw the flare of irritation in Long Quiet's eyes, quickly hidden, and wondered again about the half-breed's interest in Bay Stewart.

"There's only one way to find out the truth. Follow me, but stay back out of sight." Long Quiet mounted his pony and was gone as suddenly and quietly as he'd appeared.

Cricket pulled her horse abreast of Creed's and reached out her hand to him. He grasped it and their fingers intertwined. "Do you think he'll be able to get Bay away from Tall Bear?"

"If Tall Bear still has her, I've no doubt Long Quiet will be as persuasive as necessary to get what he wants." Creed didn't voice aloud his uncertainty about Long Quiet's motives. What did the hardbitten half-breed want with the gentle white woman?

Creed had only an instant's warning, but it was enough to avoid the death Tall Bear had planned for him. The Indian's weight knocked Creed from the saddle, and because she was holding his hand, Cricket came tumbling off her horse as well, but Tall Bear's knife landed in the fleshy part of Creed's upstretched arm, instead of his heart.

The two men rolled on the ground in a tangle of arms and legs, so Cricket couldn't tell one from the other to get a clear shot at Tall Bear. When Creed at last managed to roll clear, Cricket would have killed the Comanche except Creed barked, "No, Brava. Tall Bear and I have a lifetime of differences to settle. This is between the two of us."

"Tabeboh! I will kill you, and then I will take your woman as my slave. I will burn off her nose and her ears so no man will desire her. I will beat her each morning, and offer her to any braves who wish a woman for their pleasure."

"I am not dead yet, Tall Bear," Creed answered in Comanche. "But come greet the Wolf and I will introduce you to Our Sure Enough Father."

Cricket watched Creed shed the thin veneer of civilization and become once more the consummate Comanche warrior. He stripped away the rest of his torn shirt, leaving himself dressed in buckskin trousers and knee-high moccasins. His scarred chest was shiny and slick with sweat. Blood dripped unattended from his slashed arm and was soaked up by the parched ground beneath him. The wind whipped his black hair back from the sharp angles of his proud face.

Across from Creed, Tall Bear crouched in readiness, naked except for a buckskin breechclout and moccasins. His skin was darker than Creed's, a burnt sienna that blended with the earth. His shiny black hair was braided with fur and decorated with feathers that floated out gently behind him. He wasn't as tall as Creed, but his body was equally muscled, lean, and wiry, while his black eyes were intent, deadly.

Cricket's nostrils flared when they caught the musky scents of the two men who sought to kill one another. The hills had gone silent to witness yet another combat to determine the bravest and the best. As it had been for centuries for both man and beast, so it was now. She would be the prize of the victor, yet neither man was aware of her any longer. She would let them fight their noble battle without interference. Then, if Tall Bear still lived, she would kill him.

Tall Bear made the first slicing attack, catching Creed off guard and cutting through the skin of the four fingers holding his knife. "Shall I leave you with as many fingers as you left me, Wolf?" Tall Bear fanned a hand missing the third and fourth fingers, which Creed had cut off in their last encounter. *"Hu!* I think I shall take a few more."

The waning sun cast tall shadows that distracted Cricket's attention and kept her eyes focused on the eerie black lines rather than the two men who warily circled one another. Yet, as in the past, the fact she didn't watch the two men didn't keep her from experiencing the life-and-death conflict being waged before her.

She shivered at the guttural Comanche taunts exchanged between the two men, the swish of air as a knife blade descended, the grunt of pain as the blade found its mark. Her fist clenched around her gun as she remembered more than she cared to of Amy's horrible rape, knowing Tall Bear surely had an even worse fate planned for her should he win. She felt hate for the Comanche twisting inside her, and fought the nausea as her stomach churned with anxiety for Creed.

The blood seeping from his knuckles where Tall Bear had cut him made the knife slippery in Creed's right hand. He wished he'd practiced more with his left. Not that his left hand was in much better shape, since the slashing wound in his arm troubled him more than he cared to admit. Creed had never felt so little like an invulnerable *Diablo Tejano* as he did right now, when it counted most to be strong. Yet, so long as Tall Bear lived, Cricket was in danger. That knowledge revitalized Creed, and gave him the strength to attack.

Creed circled the Comanche brave, waiting for his moment. Suddenly, Tall Bear lunged at him and the two men grappled and fell to the ground, rolling and twisting through the rocky terrain. Then they were on their feet again, the bear and the wolf, with different strengths and weaknesses, yet evenly matched. They slashed, they cut, they tripped, they recovered, they feinted and parried, until both were bathed in dripping ribbons of red.

Exhaustion became their common enemy. Their chests became heaving bellows. Their mouths hung open to drag in the air to stay alive. Their eyes remained narrowed and wary. Neither man was winning. Nor was either man losing.

It appeared the battle might rage until they fought it on their knees.

It was Cricket, mesmerized by the shadows on the ground, who first recognized the buff-and-gray threat that lay around them all. The diamondbacks had been disturbed by that first violent free-for-all, and now several of them had slithered out from beneath the tumbled rocks looking for another refuge. Cricket couldn't warn Creed without distracting him, giving the slight advantage to Tall Bear that was all he'd need to finish the deed he'd well begun. It was amazing none of the rattlers had coiled to strike, but Cricket feared it was only a matter of time before one of the crawling creatures felt itself threatened and did so.

Suddenly, Tall Bear tripped Creed, who lost his weapon as he fell. Tall Bear leapt on top of his adversary, one forearm at Creed's neck holding him down, his opposite arm raised for the kill, held poised there by no more than Creed's awkward, bloody grasp on his wrist. At that precise moment Tall Bear became aware of a low, rushing sound as two rattlers inflated their bodies with air and coiled in a deadly S, their rattles raucous. The Comanche froze. If he struck Creed with his knife, he would likely be struck himself by the rattlers' fangs. Then he saw it was not just two snakes, but six or seven that slithered around them.

Creed became aware of their precarious situation at the same instant. A feral smile came to his face. The two men's eyes met, but neither so much as twitched a muscle. Fate had intervened to put them at each other's mercy. If either man moved, the snakes would strike. One eight-foot rattler's bite might not prove fatal, or even two, but more than that surely would.

Cricket tried to remember everything she'd ever heard about rattlesnakes. Supposedly they were defensive creatures, never attacking unless provoked. Even now there was no hysterical striking by the threatened snakes, merely careful watching with their glittering black eyes while their forked tongues slipped in and out, back and forth. Even as she watched two of the snakes glided for cover, back to their disturbed hiding places. That left only five snakes, two coiled to strike and three at the edge of the tumbled rocks, but all of them were close enough to see, or feel the vibrations, if either man moved.

Cricket fought against the urge to scream that was building at the back of her throat. She held her breath until she could no longer ignore the pain of her bursting lungs. The air finally came out in a rushing hiss not unlike that of the inflating snakes, easily audible in the tense quiet that had fallen on them all.

Tall Bear held Creed in his cruel grip, ready to deliver the death blow, yet unable to do so for fear of being killed himself by the diamondbacks, and Cricket was helpless to do anything. She could surely eliminate at least one coiled snake with her Patterson, but the other coiled snake would probably strike when she fired. Not only that, but her movement was likely to alarm the other three diamondbacks, which were closer to her than to Tall Bear and Creed. Cricket came to the same unpleasant conclusion as the two combatants. There was nothing any of them could do except wait the snakes out.

Both Tall Bear and Wolf had been trained in their Comanche youth to remain motionless for hours, if necessary. Both hoped it would not be necessary now. The heat brought perspiration to both men's brows, and the trickles of sweat were the more irritating because they couldn't be attended. Creed became conscious of an itch on his thigh caused by a small stone underneath him, and tensed his muscles trying to relieve it. Tall Bear grunted when Creed's slight movement brought up the head of one of the coiled snakes for a closer look. Creed wondered whether it was safe to blink. He waited as long as he could, and when he did his answer came in the agitated buzz of the rattlers. Tall Bear's eyes warned him to be careful, and Creed had to fight the ironic smile that threatened to curve his lips.

Creed had never thought he'd be grateful to a pair of rattlesnakes, but he owed his life to the two on either side of him. He put his mind to work thinking how he could take advantage of the chance they'd given him to save himself, for Creed knew that the moment it was safe to move Tall

Bear's strike would be as swift and deadly as that of the diamondbacks.

The strident hell went on, and on. While they waited, the light waned. After what seemed like an eternity the angry buzzing became a monotonous *chick-chick—chick-chick—chick-chick,* and finally slowed to a *chick—chick—chick.* And then, at last, ceased to sound at all.

Cricket could feel the tension building between the two men as first one, and then the other of the snakes uncoiled and began their slow progress toward the rock bed from which they'd been so unceremoniously rousted.

As the last of the snakes disappeared within a nearby crevice Creed's grip, sticky from half-dried blood, tightened on Tall Bear's wrist, anticipating the Comanche's death thrust. But the wait had taken its toll on Creed. His muscles were stiff, and he ached from the dozens of cuts on his body. Although his knuckles had stopped bleeding, he'd lost a great deal of blood from the gash in his arm. As the Comanche's knife descended inexorably toward Creed's heart he realized he hadn't the strength anymore to stop it. Desperate, he resorted to one of the wrestling maneuvers Cricket had employed so effectively against him.

Creed scissored his legs around Tall Bear and, using a foot for leverage, twisted with all his might, catching the Comanche off-guard. Their momentum rolled them over precariously close to the rock ledges into which the diamondbacks had disappeared. The Indian broke free of Creed and scrambled away from the snakes' den, leaving his enemy at the mercy of the rattlers. Creed came off the ground like a bolt of lightning, throwing himself on the fleeing Comanche, tumbling them both to the ground again.

Cricket's heart was in her throat and showed no signs of heading back where it belonged. She hadn't breathed while the two men skirted the edge of the rattlers' den, and only had a chance to gasp before Creed threw himself on Tall Bear's back. Now the two enemies thrashed on the ground, each angling the other toward the rocks—and the rattlers.

The end of the battle came so suddenly it startled them all. One second Creed and Tall Bear had struggled upright in a tight clinch. The next Tall Bear tripped and fell away from Creed, knife in hand, arms flailing. As he landed, a section of the rocky ledge broke away, revealing dozens of rattlesnakes. Before the Comanche could move, or even cry out, he was bitten repeatedly by the morass of diamondbacks. The snakes struck quickly, their fangs sinking deep and leaving potent poison. The Comanche's eyes glazed with pain as the venom paralyzed him. He made a silent plea before his eyes closed that was answered when Creed took Cricket's Patterson from her limp hand and shot Tall Bear in the heart.

"Suvate. It is finished," Creed said.

Before the booming echo of the shot had stopped resounding, Creed and Cricket had left the place. They found their horses and mounted them, riding in the direction Long Quiet had gone. Neither of them spoke. There was nothing they could say. It was a horrible death. But when they caught up with Long Quiet and heard what he'd discovered about Bay's whereabouts, Cricket wished the cruel Comanche alive again so he could endure that hellish demise once more.

"He sold her."

"When? How? To whom?" Creed questioned Long Quiet. "We followed Tall Bear the whole time. There was never a chance—"

"She was on the shod horse. Remember when the tracks disappeared? A chief of one of the northern bands was returning to *Comanchería* with a herd of Spanish horses he'd stolen on a raid into Mexico. He took one look at Bay and had to have her. He offered every horse he had for the Woman with Violet Eyes."

"Every horse?"

Tight-lipped, Long Quiet nodded.

Creed's shoulders slumped and he closed his eyes. He'd seen the tracks from the unshod ponies, but ignored them, thinking them mustangs. If only he'd . . . regrets weren't going to help now. If the Comanche chief had been willing to pay an entire herd of horses to possess Bay, he probably wasn't going to give her up without a fight. However, having spent so much, he was likely to treat his expensive property with care. It was a pretty safe guess Bay wouldn't suffer the deforming cruelties so commonly inflicted on white captives.

Cricket was stunned. She'd been sure that once Tall Bear was dead they'd soon have Bay safe and sound. The news Long Quiet had brought meant their journey had to begin all over again. "Do you know where to find her?" she asked Long Quiet.

"I know where to look. There are many chiefs to the north, but only one will have such a woman. I'll find her."

"And bring her back?"

Long Quiet pursed his lips at Cricket's anxious question. He wouldn't lie to her. "It's possible that by the time I find her she won't want to come back."

Cricket gasped.

"The Comanche I questioned said the chief who bought Bay was a powerful warrior with many scalps."

"And very rich," Creed added, "if he could afford to give so many horses for one woman."

"Your sister may be a Comanche woman for many suns and moons before—"

Cricket cut Long Quiet off impatiently. "You have to bring her back. If you don't promise to do that I'll—"

"We can't go after Bay," Creed interrupted. "We'd be caught and killed before we got another hundred miles into *Comanchería,* and Long Quiet will be headed even farther north than that. We tried, Cricket. We did the best we could. We have to trust Long Quiet to do the rest. It's unfair to ask promises from him that he may not be able to keep."

Tears gathered in Cricket's eyes. "But Bay—"

"Will probably be cherished by the Comanche who bought and paid for her. You have to believe that, Cricket."

"What will Rip say if we come home without her?"

"He'll have to understand . . . and accept what can't be changed," Creed said with finality.

"We can't just leave her out there." Cricket gestured toward the wilderness the Republic of Texas had claimed, but had not conquered. "She's so gentle, so fragile, she'll never survive. . . ." Cricket looked quickly at Creed, trying to read his expression. Had it also occurred to Creed that this ordeal might kill Bay? Was that why he didn't want her to go after her sister, because she wouldn't find her alive?

Creed quickly disavowed Cricket of that notion. "Bay's stronger than you think, Brava. She'll likely have that Comanche chief eating out of her hand in no time." His words didn't lighten Cricket's burden of worry, so Creed kneed his horse closer to her so he could take her hand in his. "We have to trust Long Quiet, Brava. If Bay can be found, he'll find her. If she can be brought back to us, he'll bring her back."

Cricket squeezed Creed's hand and then turned to the half-breed. She took a deep breath and said, "When you find Bay, and I know you will, tell her we love her and want her home. Then you do whatever will make her happy . . . whether it means leaving her where she is, or bringing her back to Three Oaks . . . or something in between."

Long Quiet didn't speak right away. Cricket's words had pleased him, because they showed that she'd recognized the possibility Bay would never belong to the white world again. He'd find the chief who'd taken Bay and he'd bargain for her. If he were not successful . . . there were ways and ways to take a woman from a man. But he was ahead of himself. First he must find the Woman with Violet Eyes.

He said only, "I will do as you ask." Then he turned his pony and rode away.

CHAPTER 27

"D̲O̲ ̲Y̲O̲U̲ ̲T̲H̲I̲N̲K̲ I'll ever see Bay again?"

"Yes, I do." When Cricket rewarded Creed's positive response with a grateful smile, he turned her into his embrace. He wrapped the blanket more snugly around her and hugged her more tightly to him, thanking all the spirits he knew—and having lived among the Comanches that was quite a few—that he hadn't lost her to his enemy. They were lying together near the pond in Creed's secret glade, where the bluebonnets had bloomed earlier in the spring. Now the purplish-blue flowers were gone, replaced by summer blossoms whose fragrance perfumed the night air.

They'd ridden as hard away from *Comanchería* as they'd ridden into it, arriving at Lion's Dare so late they'd chosen to sleep in the glade rather than wake Tom and Amy. Now the dawn of a new day had come, and Creed blessed the privacy that gave them a chance to say things that had remained unsaid for far too long.

Creed ran the bandage-wrapped knuckles of his hand down Cricket's baby-soft cheek. "It's time to talk, Brava."

Cricket turned her face into Creed's palm, which opened to receive it, and angled her chin up so she could meet his tawny gold eyes. "I love you, Creed. What more is there to say?"

Creed grinned. "You do have a way with words." He kissed her, intending only to taste the full red mouth that had tantalized him since he'd woken. But Cricket's tongue reached out to slip between his teeth and the banked fires of desire quickly raged out of control. It was Creed who, with the last vestiges of his sanity, pulled his eager mouth from Cricket's to rasp, "I mean it, Brava. We have to *talk.*"

Cricket giggled, reaching a hand down below Creed's waist and tracing the length of the hard bulge she found there. "I thought we were talking. I understood perfectly everything you just said."

Creed grabbed Cricket's hand and brought it to his mouth to kiss her palm. She immediately replaced the hand Creed had removed with her other hand, again stroking him. He grabbed that hand as well. "All right, Brava," Creed said through gritted teeth, "since you're in a hurry I'll make this fast. I love you. I think I always have, since the first time you threw me on my . . . since the first time we met. I meant my wedding vows when I said them, but if you'd like, I'll say them again."

Creed paused long enough for Cricket to answer.

"That won't be necessary," she said.

He kissed her quickly to acknowledge her trust in him, and then pulled himself back lest he forget the rest of what he had to say. "I want us to build a life together here in Texas. I want our children to grow as this great land grows. I want . . ."

Cricket's dazzling smile brought a lump of emotion to Creed's throat that cut him off.

"I want the same things, Creed," she whispered. "I want you. . . ."

"Brava, I—"

"Jaaaaaaarreeett! Are you in there?"

Creed closed his eyes and ruefully shook his head. They'd left their horses at the entrance to his "secret" bower, and Tom had obviously found them.

"Cricket and I are in here, Tom. We'll be out in a minute,"

Creed shouted back. "We'll finish this later," Creed said to Cricket. He let his hands roam one last, lingering time over Cricket's breasts and belly, groaning as he gave her a quick, hard kiss. Then he stood, pulling her up after him. He embraced her again, dipping his nose into the silky hair at her nape. His lips found her salty skin and his tongue slipped out to savor it. When Cricket trembled and moaned, he ground his hardened shaft against her, giving them both a teasing taste of what awaited them. "I'll never make it until tonight."

Cricket arched into Creed, her softness cradled by his hardness, her breasts peaked against his chest, her fingers threaded through his hair, her mouth a breath away. "I'll meet you here after supper," she promised with a sultry smile, "and we can finish our . . . conversation." She tore herself from Creed's arms and, grabbing the blanket that had shielded them from the morning dew, fled toward the narrow opening that led from their private paradise.

Creed followed more slowly, giving his body a chance to recover from its heightened state of arousal. She was a minx, all right, Creed thought with a grin. And like a child offered candy for dessert, he knew he'd spend the rest of the day looking forward to the moment supper was done.

"What's inside that tangle of weeds?" Tom questioned when they both stood before him.

Cricket and Creed exchanged surreptitious glances before Creed said, "Nothing much. Just a safe place to sleep. We got here late last night. We didn't want to disturb you."

"You should have come to the house," Tom chided. "Amy and I would have . . ." Tom paused when Creed cocked a brow at the mention of Amy's name. The awkwardness of their last meeting rose to both men's minds. It was Tom who now bridged the gap that had risen between the two brothers. "Amy's fine. Come," he said, grabbing the reins of their horses and leaving no choice except for them to follow him. "Come to the house and see for yourselves."

Tom called out to Amy as they neared the house. By the time Cricket and Creed reached the porch she was waiting there for them. Tom hadn't lied. Before them stood the same smiling, vivacious woman who'd first greeted Cricket what seemed like ages ago.

"It's so good to see you, Cricket, Jarrett," Amy said as she hugged each of them in turn. "How was Galveston? Did you like sailing on the high seas? What was New Orleans like? I want to hear all about it."

Amy's effervescence was catching, and soon they were all laughing and talking. Their mood sobered when Cricket told how Sloan had lost the father of her child when the Rangers attacked the Mexican rebels' camp.

"Does Sloan plan to keep the baby?" Amy asked.

"Of course! Why wouldn't she? Rip's already planning how he'll spoil his first grandchild," Cricket said with a grin. The grin disappeared, however, as she went on to describe the Comanche attack that had followed, how Three Oaks had burned to the ground and Beaufort LeFevre and his daughter had been wounded and Rogue had been killed.

At that point Creed interrupted Cricket to say, "I think maybe my trip to New Orleans was wasted. I doubt whether Beaufort LeFevre will be in much of a mood to discuss trade agreements with President Lamar after everything that's happened to him and Angelique. Lamar will be disappointed about that, but perhaps it'll turn out for the best. If LeFevre makes enough critical remarks to Washington congressmen about the savages in Texas, Lamar won't have to worry about anyone pressing the annexation issue for a while."

"Is the rest of your family safe, Cricket?" Amy questioned.

Cricket hesitated only a moment before she related the story of Bay's disappearance. Creed picked up the tale at their close brush with the nest of rattlesnakes that had proved the end of his enemy, Tall Bear. He finished with an account of their meeting with Long Quiet and the half-breed's promise to continue the search for Bay north into *Comanchería*.

Amy's face had gone white at the news of Bay's fate, but Tom's arm went around her shoulder to support her, and Cricket quickly changed the subject to relate her more outrageous adventures on the *Austin,* including the fact that she and Creed had finally been married in a ceremony led by both a preacher *and* a ship's captain.

"Not leaving any room for error, are you, brother?" Tom said, slapping Creed on the back.

"None at all," Creed replied, his arm encircling Cricket's waist possessively.

Cricket basked in the glow of Creed's love for a moment before she quipped teasingly, "Actually, Beaufort LeFevre was never ordained as a minister and the *Austin* wasn't at sea, so the commodore's authority—"

Creed's mouth covered Cricket's, his tongue driving deep inside to lay claim to her in God's eyes, and the eyes of anyone else who damn well cared to look. Cricket returned the kiss with all the ferver she felt for the man she planned to spend a lifetime loving.

In the silence caused by Creed's stunning kiss, Amy realized how long they'd all been standing. When the couple finally broke apart she said, "I feel awful having kept you standing on the threshold like this, but it's so beautiful out here this morning I hate to go inside. Why don't you sit here on the porch and I'll bring some coffee out for all of us."

"I'll help," Cricket offered. She withdrew from Creed's arms and disappeared inside with Amy before he had a chance to object.

Tom and Creed stood on the porch looking at one another for an awkward moment before Tom said, "Sit down, Jarrett. I need to talk with you about something important." Tom gestured Creed to the wide porch swing and took a seat in one of the two wooden rockers across from it. "I've come to a decision, Jarrett, that hasn't been easy for me."

Tom paused, but Creed said nothing, his face devoid of expression. Tom's hands clenched and unclenched several times before he said, "I'm leaving Lion's Dare. I'm taking Amy back to Tennessee."

"You can't be serious! You love this place!"

"I love Amy more."

Tom's avowal touched Creed to the quick. This was not the same judgmental man who'd shut his wife out of his life.

FRONTIER WOMAN

The two men sat in silence until Creed said, "I'm sure you've thought this out very carefully."

Tom sighed. "I have. Amy's made a remarkable recovery. To look at her you'd never suspect she's been through such a terrible . . . you'd never suspect. Except none of our neighbors have to *suspect*. They *know* what happened to Amy. Whenever they visit, whenever anyone comes to call, the truth of what happened to Amy is in their eyes. Every time she sees one of them she remembers, and she hurts all over again. I won't let them hurt her anymore."

"In time your neighbors—"

"No, Jarrett. None of them is ever going to forget, and neither are we if we stay here. My mind's made up. We're leaving . . . and that's why I wanted to talk with you. Lion's Dare has always been half yours. How would you like to buy me out?"

Creed flushed. "You know I don't have that kind of money, Tom."

"I know. That's why I have a suggestion to make." Tom took a deep breath and said, "Amy and I won't need much to start, so I'd be satisfied with a quarter of the cash you earn from the cotton crop each year until you pay me what my half of Lion's Dare is worth."

Tom's offer was more than fair—it was generous. Creed should have jumped at it. But he didn't. He'd be happy to stay at Lion's Dare, to grow cotton and raise fine horses and healthy children, but that picture of the future was nothing if Cricket wasn't part of it. "I'll consider it Tom. I've thought about having a place of my own. If Cricket is willing—"

"If I'm willing to what?" Cricket interrupted, coming through the front door with a tray of biscuits stuffed with sausage. She set the tray on the small table near the rockers, and picking up one biscuit each for herself and Creed, gave his to him and joined him on the porch swing.

Amy had followed Cricket with four cups of coffee, which she handed out. As she sat down in the rocker next to Tom, Creed said, "Tom's made me an interesting offer."

"Which is?"

Creed watched Cricket's face as he asked, "How would you like to become mistress of a fine cotton plantation?"

Cricket eyed Creed warily. "Which plantation?"

"Lion's Dare. Tom's offered to sell his half to me on most reasonable terms."

Cricket gaze shot to Amy and Tom in time to see them join hands and look into each other's eyes. From the smile on both their faces, it was clear they'd discussed Tom's proposal and were agreed upon making it.

"Where will you be going?" Cricket asked Amy.

"Tom and I are heading for Tennessee."

"Back east?"

Amy laughed. "It's not as though we're going all the way to New York, Cricket. Tennessee isn't all that far east."

But, thought Cricket, it was plenty far east of the Texas frontier. Tom and Amy were retreating to the safety Tennessee's comparative civilization offered. There would be no more surprise Indian attacks, no need to fight the isolation of rainy springs when the mud brought travel on dirt roads to a standstill, no need to be wary of bandidos or the threat of Mexican invasion. They could live and work without having to constantly fight the hostile elements that made up the warp and weft of the growing scarf of land known as Texas.

Cricket turned to Creed. "What did you tell Tom?"

Creed set down his coffee cup and the rest of his biscuit on the small table nearby. "I told him I'd like it very much, and if you're willing . . ." He held his breath waiting, hoping she'd say she wanted to stay with him on Lion's Dare, wishing her to say she'd spend her life helping him settle the land.

"I'm half tempted to say I'm not willing, because I know how pleased this will make Rip," Cricket said with a teasing laugh. "He considers you a penniless Ranger, and becoming a respectable gentleman planter is going to make you so acceptable a husband he's liable to gloat. But I'm not about to cut off my own nose to spite Rip." Cricket set down her coffee cup. "Oh yes, Creed, I'm willing."

Creed's arms encircled Cricket and he pulled her close for a fierce hug. He lifted his head and said to Tom, "You heard my wife. We accept your offer."

Tom and Amy both rose and walked arm in arm the few steps necessary so Tom and Creed could shake hands. "This means a lot to us, Jarrett," Tom said. "It'll be a new beginning for us as well."

"I feel like we ought to celebrate," Amy said.

"Sounds like a good idea to me, too," Cricket said. "What did you have in mind?"

"How about a swim?"

"A swim?" three voices responded in chorus.

Amy hesitated at the astonished looks that surrounded her. "Well, it's been very warm these past few days, and the river is so cool I thought . . ."

"You're right," said Tom.

"A swim it is," agreed Creed.

"Let's go!" Cricket urged, prodding Amy from the porch. "What're you waiting for, an invitation?" Cricket grabbed Creed's hand and the two of them raced for the river with Tom and Amy close behind. They were all laughing, hot and breathy from the run by the time they got there. Amy insisted that she and Cricket retreat behind the bushes to strip down.

Amy unbuttoned her dress and pulled it down off her shoulders, unmindful of the horrible scar left by the Comanche lance. Cricket gasped when she caught sight of it.

Amy's head snapped up and she caught Cricket's horrified stare before Cricket had a chance to control her features. Amy's fingertips came up to touch the awful, puckered skin around the wound, which had completely healed during the months that had passed since the Comanches' attack on her.

"It's ugly, isn't it?" she said.

"Oh, Amy, I . . ."

"Please don't pity me, Cricket. I couldn't stand that from you, too."

Amy reached out for Cricket's hand and brought it up to touch the scar. "It's healed. I'm healed. I'm not saying I'll ever be able to forget what happened. Or that Tom . . . Tom loves me, Cricket. You can't imagine how gentle he's been. It wasn't easy the first time—"

"Amy, you don't—"

"Let me say it, Cricket."

Cricket bit her lip to hold in the rush of words that ached to come out.

"It hurt the first time. I was frightened. I thought I'd never be able to love Tom that way again. But I can, Cricket. I can. And it's the most wonderful thing you can imagine to know there's nothing . . . *nothing* . . . that could ever tear us away from each other again."

"Hey, are you two women coming out here sometime today?" Tom shouted.

Amy smiled at Tom's impatience, her eyes shining with love as she gazed out at him. "Come on, Cricket. Let's go celebrate."

Even though her throat ached with unshed tears, Cricket squeezed Amy's hands and smiled back. "All right, Amy."

Once Amy had stripped down to her chemise and pantalettes she raced past Tom and Jarrett into the river, yelling, "Last one in peels potatoes for dinner."

Tom splashed in after her in just his trousers, with Cricket and Creed close behind, similarly clothed in what turned out to be, once they were all wet, completely immodest attire.

They played tag, they played blind man's bluff, they splashed and shouted and swam like carefree children.

"This was a wonderful idea," Creed murmured to Cricket.

Cricket gasped as his hidden hands skillfully caressed the juncture of her thighs through the thin covering of her pantalettes.

"You said it, Jarrett," Tom added, his hands similarly occupied with his own wife. "Only I'm so worn out from this swim I think I'm going to need a quick nap before we eat."

"I'm feeling a little poorly myself," Creed agreed. "What

do you say, ladies? Shall we give up this watery playground?"

Amy and Cricket exchanged lambent-eyed looks and burst out laughing.

"If you two don't hurry up and get us out of this water we're going to resort to desperate measures, right, Amy?" Cricket said.

"Desperate, desperate measures," Amy agreed. Her hands slipped from Tom's shoulders to his chest and disappeared under the surface of the river.

Tom gasped. "Swim," he ordered his wife, his eyes hot with desire, "before we both end up drowning." Amy basked in his sensuous gaze for another moment before she swam for the river bank. Once up the muddy bank, Amy headed into the bushes to retrieve her clothes, followed closely by Tom.

When Cricket started to follow after them Creed grabbed her hand and pulled her in the opposite direction. "You may find yourself getting a different kind of education from Tom and Amy if you go in there. Come with me."

Cricket followed Creed, knowing where he was leading her. "I thought we were going to come back here this evening after supper," she said as they pushed their way through the undergrowth that led to their forest glade.

"I can't wait," Creed replied, not slowing his pace. "I'm hungry now."

Creed's words sent a shiver of anticipation down Cricket's spine. The sun was high in the sky, yet the circle of leafy trees surrounding the glade kept it cool. Creed took Cricket's hand and led her to a grassy spot in the shade of a pin oak. He stripped himself and then took his time removing Cricket's sodden underclothes. By the time he was done Cricket was trembling. When they were both naked he laid her down upon the cool grass and followed after her.

"Let's see," Creed said. "Where were we when we left off this morning . . .?"

Cricket came up on her elbow and leaned over to press her lips to Creed's. "I love you, Creed." Her tongue came out to trace his mouth from edge to edge. Creed opened his mouth and Cricket's tongue slipped inside for a quick foray.

"Ummm," Creed murmured. He sucked on her tongue, keeping it inside his mouth when she would have retreated, and then his velvet tongue sought out her mouth with a tenderness that belied his need to possess her. They were both breathing hard by the time Creed broke the kiss and fell back upon the grass, pulling Cricket into his arms. Her head lay on his shoulder and her hand rested on his heaving chest. Their legs were entwined, Cricket's foot casually caressing Creed's calf.

"Will you be happy as the mistress of Lion's Dare, Brava? Really happy?"

"So long as you're with me I can be happy anywhere, Creed." Cricket dipped her head and found one of Creed's nipples with her lips.

Creed's hand slipped down to cover Cricket's breast and he rolled the nipple between his thumb and forefinger. "You won't mind acting the hostess for our neighbors?"

Cricket brought her mouth up to Creed's throat, seeking the pulse there. She nipped at his shoulder and was rewarded with a sensuous shudder. "Not at all, as long as I can do it in buckskins."

Creed's lips curved into a smile as they surveyed Cricket's face, lingering on her temple, her high cheekbones, her nose, and finally her chin. "You promise not to blacken any eyes or flip anybody in the dirt?"

Cricket's fingertips caressed the length of the scar that began at Creed's left nipple and angled across his belly all the way to his hipbone, where she scraped his skin gently with her fingernail before starting back the other direction again. "Of course I won't . . . unless I think it's necessary."

Creed's eyes were hooded, heavy, his body hardened with his need. He turned so the two of them were aligned one to the other. "I knew I could count on you to be reasonable, Brava."

They held each other without speaking for a moment, simply enjoying the marvelous fit of flesh to flesh. At last

Creed tilted his hips and his shaft rubbed against Cricket where she could appreciate it most. He buried his nose in her fragrant hair and his lips began a sojourn down her throat toward her breasts. His tongue circled the tips, then laved them as though he were licking up honey before he took up his journey again. When his lips reached her belly Cricket asked breathlessly, "Are you done talking now?"

"Mmmmm." Creed's tongue dipped into Cricket's navel.

"Does that mean yes?"

"Mmmmm." He stroked her belly with his cat-rough tongue.

Cricket gasped and thrust her hands in his silky hair. "Because I have one last thing to say."

"Mmmmm?" Creed's hands grasped Cricket's buttocks and he tilted her hips upward, angling her so his lips and tongue could reach that most feminine part of her.

Cricket groaned, a sound wrenched from deep inside her, and feverishly arched her body up to meet Creed's mouth. "I wanted . . . to . . . say . . . ahhh. . . ."

In all the times she and Creed had made love, Cricket had never felt such intense pleasure. Perhaps it was the knowledge that he loved her, perhaps it was the fact she'd fought against submitting to her body's needs for so long . . . whatever had caused it, Cricket found herself on a joyous plane of euphoria beyond anything she'd imagined possible . . . and Creed wasn't letting her come down. He kept her there, on the brink of something . . . something incredible.

Her nails raked Creed's shoulders, her hands grasped the muscles of his back and tugged at his hair. He had to *do* something. She was dying. She couldn't stand the pleasure anymore.

"Creeeeed!"

Creed felt a surge of masculine satisfaction. "Soon, Brava, soon," he promised. Cricket was almost there. He could help her find what she needed. He covered her body with his, mating his shaft with the sleek wetness of her. His lips found hers and his tongue plundered her mouth, frenzied, voracious, as desperate for her as she for him. His hands captured her breasts, kneading them, pinching the tips, heightening sensations that were already aflame.

Cricket welcomed Creed's manhood inside her. He filled her until she could take no more of him, and then he reached down and arched her hips in his hands so he could thrust even deeper. She couldn't get enough of him. She grasped his buttocks and demanded, "More . . . more . . . don't stop. . . ."

Cricket's words incensed Creed, sending him beyond the last restraining bonds of rationality. And then they were both flying together as he released his seed and she arched up to accept it, both of them crying out with the joy and wonder of it.

It was a long time before either had recovered enough to be aware of the other. At last they turned, and surveyed what their love had wrought.

He looks so pleased.

She looks so happy.

Their hands reached out to touch one another, tentative, gentle, concerned at what they found.

I scratched him.

I bruised her.

Their eyes dropped, in awe of the fierceness of what had passed between them—a passion as rough and wild as the land they both loved.

Will it always be like this?

Will it always be like this?

"I didn't mean to hurt you, Brava."

"You didn't hurt me. I didn't mean to scratch you."

Creed became aware for the first time of the scratches on his back. "I didn't even notice." He hadn't, and realized she probably hadn't noticed the bruises either—although she would tomorrow.

"We'll both have to be more careful," Cricket said with a grin.

"Whatever you say, Brava." Creed chuckled. "Now, what was it you had to say that couldn't wait?"

"Oh, that." Cricket chewed on her lower lip.

"Well?"

"I made a promise."

Creed cocked his head. "To whom?"

"To Rip."

Creed sat up, his body tensing. This was *not* going to be good news. "A promise to Rip," he repeated, to be sure he'd heard her right.

Cricket sat up, too, her body tensing in response to Creed's obvious anxiety. "Yes."

"Come on, Brava. Spit it out. What did you promise Rip?"

"That I'd keep looking for Bay until I found her."

Creed sighed. "You know that's not possible, Brava."

"I promised, Creed."

Creed saw the determination in Cricket's jutting jaw and knew he wasn't going to change her mind by arguing. He reached out to pull her into his lap. "All right, Brava. We'll wait to hear from Long Quiet. If he doesn't find her, I promise you we'll try again."

Cricket sighed contentedly, and relaxed in Creed's arms. "Did I tell you that I love you?"

"No."

Cricket grinned. "I did, too!"

"I never get tired of hearing it. Say it again."

"I love you, Creed."

Creed's head bent down until his lips nearly touched Cricket's. "I love you, Brava. I always will." He kissed her gently and added, "You're all the woman a man could ask for"—Creed grinned and gently cupped her full breasts in his palms—"and as much as I can handle."

Cricket's laughter was cut off when Creed's lips came down to possess hers.

AUTHOR'S NOTE

Retaliation by the Comanches for the Council House massacre finally came during the time of the Comanche Moon in August, 1840. A band of between 400 and 1,000 warriors, led by Buffalo Hump, raided the town of Victoria on August 6. They left driving nearly 2,000 horses ahead of them. The Texas militia followed, but was kept busy burying dead bodies. One corpse was found with the soles of his feet sliced off. He'd been forced to march for miles on the tender skin before the Indians scalped him. The Indians burned out homes and killed Texans with impunity all along their trail of revenge.

On August 8 the Comanches raided and destroyed the town of Linville on Lavaca Bay. Linville townsfolk escaped on boats into the bay. The triumphant Comanches headed home with mules loaded down with booty, many prisoners, and between 2,000 and 3,000 horses.

The Texans, naturally, now cried for Comanche blood. On August 11, Texans led by men experienced in Indian fighting attacked the Comanches at Plum Creek. Eighty Indians died compared to only one Texan. Much booty was recovered and split among the victorious Texans. After the Battle of Plum Creek the Comanches never again attacked a town or raided along the coast. They contented themselves with the hit-and-run tactics that were to be so devastating to life and property in Texas for years to come.

As for the Texas Navy and Commodore Edwin Moore, both were destined for hard times. After Sam Houston was elected president of Texas in September, 1841, he sought peace and recognition of Texas as a sovereign nation with General Santa Anna at the same time as he sought annexation with the United States. Houston wanted the Texas Navy to leave Mexico alone. On January 16, 1843, in secret session, the Texas Congress voted to disband the Texas Navy and to sell all its ships, which at the time were in New Orleans.

When that plan failed, President Houston published a proclamation dated March 23, 1843, declaring Commodore Moore and his fleet pirates, and asking any friendly nation to intercept and hold them. On May 16 the *Austin* and the *Wharton* engaged Mexican ships off Yucatán and caused many Mexican casualties. This was the last operation of the Texas Navy.

On July 14 Commodore Moore returned to Galveston, having heard on June 1 of Houston's piracy charge. He tried to surrender but received a hero's welcome instead. Houston didn't dare try him as a pirate, but dismissed Moore with a dishonorable discharge. Moore insisted on a trial and in August, 1844, was tried on twenty-two counts of neglect of duty, misapplication of funds, disobedience of orders, contempt and defiance of laws, treason, and murder. He was cleared of all but four charges pertaining to disobedience of orders. Houston was furious. The Texas Congress reinstated Moore by joint resolution, only to have Houston's successor, Texas President Anson Moore, veto the resolution.

The Texas Navy ships were put in dry dock until they became part of the United States Navy when Texas became a state in February, 1846. Only the *Austin,* the *Wharton,* the *Archer,* and the *San Bernard* remained, and only the *Austin* was accepted for service by the United States. Within two years she was broken up as being unworthy of repairs.

Dear Reader,

I hope that for a few hours you've enjoyed sharing vicariously with me the thrilling adventures of frontier life, and that you'll find equal pleasure in reading Bayleigh's story in *COMANCHE WOMAN*, coming soon from Pocket Books.

I'd appreciate hearing your comments and suggestions about *FRONTIER WOMAN*. If you have questions that need answering, please send a self-addressed stamped envelope to P.O. Box 53-0334, Miami Shores, Florida 33153-0334, so that I can respond.

Joan Johnston
August 1988